Daimons

A Novel

Nina Fitzpatrick

"Daimons are not demons . . ." So begins this magical, utterly beguiling new novel by Nina Fitzpatrick, author of *Fables of the Irish Intelligentsia*. Uggala is a rainswept, unwelcoming rock off the west Irish coast. It's charmingly insular and backwards inhabitants are known mainly for once either rescuing or slaughtering the shipwrecked Spaniards of the Armada — depending on whom you talk to. On to this rocky beach is cast Ethna O'Keefe, the island's prodigal daughter, pregnant, without prospects, but oddly undefeated. In *Daimons*, Nina FitzPatrick weaves a lushly patterned tapestry that combines the mythic Irish tropes of triumph and sorrow with the magical realism of a Borges or Márquez.

A lush tapestry of mysticism, pre-destination and hope, brought to life through a hauntingly beautiful sense of place and vividly drawn characters, *Daimons* is a deeply satisfying novel.

NINA FITZPATRICK is the nom de plume of Nina Witoszek, a Polish-born writer now living in Oslo, Norway, and the late Patrick Sheeran, of Galway, Ireland. *Daimons* is their third, and final, jointly written work, after *Fables of the Irish Intelligentsia* and *The Loves of Faustyna*.

DAIMONS

Nina FitzPatrick

Justin, Charles & Co. Publishers

BOSTON

FIRST EDITION 2003

This is work of fiction. All characters and events portrayed
in this work are either fictitious or are used fictitiously.

Library of Congress Cataloging-in-Publication Data

T.K.

Published in the United States by
Justin, Charles & Co., Publishers,
20 Park Plaza, Boston, Massachusetts 02116
www.justincharles.com

Distributed by National Book Network, Lanham, Maryland
www.nbnbooks.com

Printed in the United States of America

10 9 8 7 6 5 4 3 2 1

To my other half, PAT SHEERAN,
with whom all the thinking
and writing was done

I

RETURN

Through some connection, without opening your eyes
You've seen in your mother's womb, as you see in your dream
How birds dart in the air; how Adam is the earth

From which he sprang to sing it
How Moses came to rid Egypt of its plagues
How a fragile vessel contains sweet wine

So the eyes receive what's invisible
and a mixture of one hazy substance with the other
is the great secret of love.

— Jelaluddin Rumi

The Daimon of Ethna

🐌 Daimons are not demons. Demons are nefarious creatures that skulk and rage in the dark. Daimons are radiant beings that impart a pattern to people, animals, plants, and places.

Daimon-spotting is a lost art. As we darken and densify with every passing century, only the adolescent grace of a birch tree or the quietude of a ledgy pool intimate the presence of a nymph or a naiad. Most of the time, and for nearly all of us, the carapace over our subtle eye shuts them out.

Our own daimon, though closer to us than our left hand, is even less palpable. Up to around the age of six or so we know precisely why we have come into this world and what we have to do. Then — pstryk! — all is forgotten. And so the world is a jumble of men and women who have failed to find their destiny. They are like hungry rivers that never reach the sea.

Which is why Ethna was pondering the brighter aspects of suicide. She would be spared the shame of stepping ashore on Uggala and everybody gawking at her big belly. She wouldn't have to face into being a single mother on an island where mothers of any kind were as scarce as cuckoos. She wouldn't have to confront the moral fury of Colm and Concepta. And she'd be spared the daunting task of finding out who she was and where she was heading. It would be over and done with and she wouldn't need to die anymore.

She hunched over the rails of *The Morning Star* contemplating her defeat and the approaching island. She felt that chronic anguish, that gap in the midriff, that bedevils those who have failed to find their daimon. Not that any of the five or so other passengers on the trawler would have noticed a gap. Her belly bulged with six-month-old twins. Me and Thresheen.

Just at this moment the design of Ethna's life, her destiny, was completely obscure to her. Her days seemed a random accumulation of things and events with no connecting tissue. What had the slobbery Atlantic sliding under her to do with the sharp-edged symmetry of the marching cypresses she had sketched only the other day? Or the protuberance in her body with her real self, limber and unencumbered and eager to coquette and conquer?

Her hand gripping the wet rail remembered the exuberance of the curves it had traced in charcoal: that cornice, that cupola, that bend of amber shoulder. What line could she draw now between the luminous forms in her sketch pad and the lumbering, insolent island ahead, where even God was blue with the cold?

She would have to surrender her Tuscan eyes.

She was sick of the pendular sway of the sea and of her own indecision.

Yes. No.

Yes. She would be humble and face up to her failure.

No. She would not. She would yield to the ocean's appetite for her. Its slavering maw drew and repelled her.

Suicide note, draft one. Dear Mammy and Daddy. I'm sorry for putting you through all this. But all of a sudden everything fell to pieces for me in Florence and I can't go on. Please give my sketches and books to Danny Ruane. Your loving daughter, et cetera.

There was a maddening buzzing sound coming from somewhere. Was she the only one to hear it? Nausea rose in her and spilled over. She imagined a hot viscous treacle that poured down her sides, scalding and streaking as it went. Half in earnest, she glanced down to see if her inner throes had stained her dress. She stumbled heavily.

"You're OK?"

The last thing she wanted was help from a priest. She caught a glimpse of jeans under a brown Franciscan habit as he lifted her from the jumble of lobster pots and the coils of loose rope on deck.

"A few deep breaths perhaps?"

Ethna looked at him and smiled wryly. Now she knew what monks wore under their habits. He looked back with uncomprehending eyes, unaware of the contempt she felt for men of his calling. He had the smooth sulky face of a Renaissance courtier: square jaw, obstinate lips, iridescent eyes. Surely his chestnut hair was too long for a priest? Pollaiuolo's David, somebody like that. There was a Goliath's head bleeding at his feet.

"What's the joke?" he asked.

"Oh, nothing. Thanks."

Beside the wheelhouse there was a pile of bags and boxes that had a clerical look about them. And a leafy exotic plant in a tub tied up in black plastic bags.

Where was the damned buzzing coming from?

Suicide note, draft two. Dear Mother and Father. I know you won't understand this. It has just struck me that my death is actually quite normal. Look at it like this. Once upon a time young men left the island to take on the world. As priests or policemen mostly. Lots of them failed and felt the island's contempt. Especially the spoilt priests. It's an old story now. But remember Johnny Doherty and how they treated him when he came back from Maynooth? Women didn't have to go through the same thing because their destiny was collective, like the destiny of plants. Or animals. But now we're all in the same boat. When we don't make it we become spoilt actresses, spoilt teachers, spoilt lawyers. I can't go back to being a plant or an animal. The best I can do is to regard myself as a necessary casualty, one of the inevitable ninety percent that fail. Please leave my sketches and books with Danny Ruane, who will know what I'm on about. Your loving daughter, et cetera.

"Are you sure you're OK?" The Franciscan pretended not to notice her belly.

"I could do with the Last Sacrament."

"That's what I'm here for." He smiled. "You'll be my first sick call. Are you from the island?"

"I've been away for a very long time."

He looked ahead at the looming gray mass on the horizon.

"It's very beautiful," he said conventionally.

"It's dreadful," said Ethna.

"Oh."

Suicide note, draft three. Dear Danny. I should have written this to my parents but I can't get down to it. You know what a pair of complete gobshites they are.

"Uggala," said the priest, drawing out the vowels. He relished the name that sounded like a seagull regurgitating a bony fish up its craw. "I've the next four years to find out about it."

Ethna looked up. He was lighting a cigarette.

Uggala will break you, she thought pitilessly. Even if you have aquamarine eyes. It'll drive you stark staring raving mad like half your predecessors.

"I can tell you exactly what you'll find out," she said. "It's a place that can't teach its people how to breathe, eat, drink, walk, or . . ."

She paused. She didn't know how he would take it.

"Love?" he asked, looking at her with strained gentleness.

Fuck, Ethna thought. Drink, walk, or fuck properly.

She nodded curtly and looked down.

Uggala.

She shrank from the sight of the familiar cliffs and rocky shores under perpetually bloated, premenstrual skies.

The Daimon of Uggala

❧ The island of Uggala pretzels from the sea with hard tangy edges and a soft boggy center. You had to be born in such a place — preferably at a time when children still played cowboys and indians — to relish its intimate geography and to avoid sinking to your elbows in quag.

Biafra O'Dee, in his more inspired sessions in Balor's Bar, liked to stress that there was a similarity between the island and the cosmos. The universe too is shaped like a pretzel, with looping strands interspersed with black holes.

The memory of Uggala is likewise uneven and dependent on the terrain. The rocky parts hold clear, definite recollections of things from megalithic tombs to nineteenth-century coast guard cottages. In the center, however, all is vague and diffuse, a shadowy dementia that now and then throws up a torn, leather brown corpse or a battered copper kettle.

The place that remembers most is the ruin of the Cromwellian castle from which felons were once dragged out and staked on the strand at low tide in sight of their fellow Papishes. Even on bright sunny days people instinctively shun the tower and its dark, piss-sour interior brooding.

Apart from the crumbling castle, there are a few other places with clear-cut but unhappy memories: the Stone of the Spaniards, where something still yearns to be appeased; the stern Parochial House, built to a rural fantasy of Georgian grandeur and solidity; Colm O'Keefe's pub; and the twice-burnt-down community center.

At the time of Ethna's return there were only two spots with unsullied memories on Uggala. One was a low hill with a clump of Scots firs spiking the summit and a clover meadow stretched beneath. This was Danny Ruane's Thinking Place.

The other was concealed behind a scrub of brambles and thorns to the east of the island, just off a green path that connected the two main settlements. It was called the Danes' Fort, though it was neither a fort nor Danish. In times gone by men coming home late at night had heard airy music there and seen dancing lights on the path before them. Such apparitions were held to augur good fortune: a quarter-ticket win in the Sweepstake, the uncontested will of a dead uncle in Boston, or first prize in the Spot-the-Ball competition in the *Sunday Independent.*

Once upon a time there were four seasons on Uggala and a full complement of people to work the fields and the sea. By the time of Ethna's return there were only two: a long lethargic winter, stretching from September to the middle of June, and a frantic summer, when the tourists came and the population increased tenfold, the toilets overflowed, and all the bachelors hoped to get laid, if only by an inquisitive anthropologist.

Those who visited in summer were prey to different sorts of illusions. Some were driven by the romantic urge to find their very own Gaeltacht at the edge of the world and were half pleased to discover that the island was actually English speaking. Others again were seduced by ads in the holiday supplements of the Sunday *Times*: the Isle of Uggala, warm mythical home of one-eyed Balor, where the spirit of timeless, deep Ireland lives on.

One such ad was framed in O'Keefe's pub with "My Arse" scrawled on the margin.

For three months everybody woke up and had a job to do and a story to tell. For the rest of the year Uggala sank in on itself, like a creature unable to generate its own body heat, immobilized by bitter winds and sea spray. Anybody who had any cravings or desires that required speedy satisfaction left the island. Only the dreamless and the patient remained. They were like the wingless butterflies on the windswept Keregeen Islands; incapable of flight, they were in no danger of being blown away.

Only Danny Ruane and Biafra O'Dee were levitating caterpillars.

In the summer of 1988, when our mother was writing suicide notes in her head aboard *The Morning Star*, Biafra O'Dee discovered that the island's inert condition would last for only seven more years. In 1994 Uggala would become one of the most fashionable places in Europe. As usual, Tom O'Reilly dismissed Biafra's prophecy as so much reactionary bullshit and pointed to at least five other predictions that had failed to materialize.

"Listen here, fuckface!" shouted Biafra. "I've cast the island's horoscope on the basis of three different birthdays, OK? The Fomorian settlement after the Second Battle of Moytura, the death of Saint Coleman, and the arrival of the first Garda sergeant after Independence. And all dates concur that 1994 will be the year when Uggala will reveal its destiny. It's going to happen! It will be the place where everybody who's anybody — Mick Jagger, Meryl Streep, and that shagger Mickey Rourke — will want to be seen. And every last troglodyte — even you, fuckface — will have an orgasm!"

The Daimon of Father Francis

The priest who helped Ethna to her feet and who had aquamarine eyes was Father Francis.

He discovered his daimon early on in life when he lay dying of meningitis and the angels came for him. They perched on the posts of his iron bedstead, from which they were occasionally driven by the doctor or the district nurse. Francis wasn't in the least afraid of dying and wondered why everybody was holding him back. He wanted more than anything to leave his body, which was like a pincushion from injections. He longed to dwell forever in that state of ecstasy that engulfed him whenever the angels fluttered down the Jacob's ladder of the bed end.

He was never to be so happy again.

When his mother's ministrations and his father's pilgrimage to Lough Derg (God only knew what the man promised on his behalf) eventually pulled him through, Francis realized that his real life was at an end. From now on everything would be posthumous.

As his mother sterilized the needle for the last time over a Bunsen burner, she said: You've been saved for some great evil or for some great good.

From the ominous way she said it, he feared for a long time that it must be some great evil. So he kept a low profile and examined his every word and impulse for the seeds of wickedness. He read as much as he could about Hitler and Stalin and compared their lives with his own. In the end he became indifferent to the lures of the world. As a young man he felt no compulsion to smoke or to curse or to touch a girl's breast. He was uninterested in his own striking beauty though aware, in a pitying way, of the effect it had on women and men. The callousness that others sometimes saw in him, his envy rather than compassion for the grievously ill and dying, came from his secret certainty about the bliss they savored despite all appearances. Now, at thirty, he was easy about being moribund.

The Archbishop had spotted this unnatural detachment in him when recruiting Order men to fill the gaps in failing parishes. Maybe the island that was the terror of the diocesan clergy. Maybe it would shake him up a bit?

"So what's the joke?" Father Francis asked Ethna as he helped her to her feet. He was disturbed at the sight of her tiny girlish body carrying such a huge weight. It didn't seem fair.

"Oh, nothing. Thanks," said Ethna.

She dressed in defiance of her condition in an elegant black and white jacket over a flowing cream dress. Her long mahogany plait gave her an endearing Pre-Raphaelite look. Her face was drawn, but her eyes were large and dangerous.

Father Francis had pretended not to notice her pregnancy in order to chat away normally. It was the way he dealt with dwarfs and hunchbacks and homosexuals. His posthumous existence allowed him to cherish numerous evasions. He liked to fancy, for example, that menstruating women secreted a clear blue liquid as in the ads for panty pads on American TV.

"Do you really have to go to Uggala?" asked Ethna.

"Any other suggestions?"

"Mozambique, the White Man's Grave, Antarctica, Alcatraz . . ."

He shrugged his shoulders. "I don't have much in the way of choice."

"That makes two of us then."

They smiled briefly at one another and turned in unison to look at the island coming up ahead.

The crooked arm of the Famine-built quay clutched possessively a half dozen fishing boats and currachs. There was a whiff of the infrahuman smell of diesel and rotting shellfish. Father Francis glanced at his watch. It was 1:00 P.M.

An alarm clock rang.

The Daimon of Danny Ruane

↬ The alarm clock sat on the mantelpiece of Danny Ruane's kitchen. It had a Mickey Mouse face with tremulous blue eyes that shook up and down as it rang out the hour.

There were two other clocks on the mantelpiece. One red

and chunky and set for nine o'clock, the other grim and metallic showing twelve. All three had labels underneath: Austin, Tokyo, Copenhagen.

"Danny Ruane, you're a fucking genius!" Danny complimented himself as he slammed down the alarm on the Mickey Mouse clock.

Sharik raised his left ear and barked his assent.

The beehive he had just assembled stood on the kitchen table. He loved its clean lines and the smell of freshly planed wood. For a moment he imagined the insides dripping with golden honey, and he could taste it on his tongue.

He would rub it in circles into Clare's navel.

He picked up the phone on its long extension cord and, circling the table, dialed a lengthy number.

This was the best moment. Clare was still asleep in her loft, her clothes scattered over the floor and yesterday's *Austin Tribune* crushed beside her on the pillow. He relished the instant like a child about to dip his finger in a pool where a somnolent trout hangs motionless near the bottom.

"Rise and shine, Clare!"

"Hi, Danny! I thought you'd never call."

"You sound a bit wired."

"I haven't slept a wink."

So he was wrong. She was sitting up in bed in her powder blue T-shirt, smoking French cigarettes and drinking cold coffee.

"So how's your book coming along? Have you finished the chapter on the Etruscans?"

She was softening him up for something.

"Out with it, Clare. There's something else on your mind."

"I need your advice, Danny."

"Uhm."

"I got this new job, right? It's, well, it's dancing."

"And it ain't ballet?"

"It's kinda more individual."

"Topless?"

"And bottomless . . . to a degree."

Wrong again. She didn't need his advice. She wanted his absolution.

"Jesus!"

"Look, I really feel bad about this. But at the same time I get this incredible elation and sense of power when I'm doing it."

"Go on."

"All those guys worshiping at my feet! And they can't ever touch me."

To touch without being touched! To sway shamelessly in a soft light as if before a mirror. But a mirror that glows and breathes faster and faster with every exposure, that gawps and throbs as you rise outrageously up through yourself. And then the magical moment when you have gathered enough energy and desire from the mirror to leave your body and to tower masterfully over those who are mere flesh and desire. Yes! Yes!

"Are you still there, Danny?"

Danny was momentarily embarrassed by the phone in his hand, as if he had been caught exposing himself.

"It's some career move. From a librarian to a stripper in three weeks flat!"

"But what do you think?"

"I don't know. It's a borderline case. It's sex and not sex, dancing and not dancing, lust and not lust. I suppose it keeps you fit?"

Clare snorted. "Danny, please, you know how shy and vulnerable I am."

"Ha ha ha."

"Thanks a bunch. Would you rather I teach yoga to Peruvian drug dealers? Or ambush middle-aged housewives with perfume sprays in Macy's? Have you any idea how much I earn?"

Danny was about to ease himself down on the mat beside the Peruvian drug dealers but straightened up. She would be earning, let's see . . .

"More than the price of twelve lobsters a night?" he teased. "You're so primitive!"

Danny glanced through the window. *The Morning Star* followed by a scarf of gulls was breasting its way into the harbor.

"I've got to go, Clare. The trawler's come with my bees."

"But what about my —"

"We'll sort things out when you come over in August, OK? Have I told you that we're going to have a new priest on the island? A Franciscan. Maybe he'll straighten you out?"

"A fran what?"

"Take care and God bless."

Whenever Danny was on the phone to one of his girls, he was also on another line to his dead mother. With her it was a purely one-way conversation. She abused him for his failure to go to Mass on Sundays and his willingness to entertain, even for a second, the likes of Clare, who was clearly nothing but a common slut and a pervert. She was shaking her head and muttering with icy compassion: "Her eyes are too close together. Haven't you noticed?"

She judged people like greyhounds and could spot deviancy at a hundred yards. She hadn't been a mental nurse in Manchester for nothing.

Unlike himself and his mother, Danny and his daimon got on well together. He listened to her promptings, and he could sit all evening by the fire communing happily with her while Sharik bit at the fleas in his tail. That was when the best ideas came to him for his big book on the Book of Creation. He loved that moment in the process of composition when he didn't actually have to do anything, when the hazy and impersonal outline of a chapter drifted in the air free from the weight of words and syntax.

Often in his intense reveries Danny imagined that others

felt what he felt and saw what he saw. At times, of course, they did. Those few who are intimate with their daimons can mesmerize the daimonless ones and bring them along with them, at least for a little while. That's why the inhabitants of Uggala were alternately in a state of falling under Danny's sway and fighting him off. They watched with expectant horror as he introduced innovation after innovation. One summer it was grafting damsons, another it was windsurfing. This year it was bees. For Danny it was enough to hear a program on the BBC World Service about quail netting in the Sudan or read a book on water divining and, Mother of Sweet Jesus! he had to have a shot at it himself.

Soon even his mortal enemies, like Colm O'Keefe, would be windsurfing or taking ginseng or — who knew? — investing in bees. There was one thing the islanders could not and would not emulate: Danny's un-Irish attitude to women. According to O'Keefe, nailing the bastard on that score was only a question of time.

The Daimon of Thresheen

⤳ Although Thresheen was smaller than me she occupied the catbird seat in Ethna's womb.

We were twins, and yet we differed on the question of our birth. I wanted to break out into the world as soon as possible, even though it would mean crossing the River of Forgetfulness and beginning all over again from scratch. Thresheen loved the luxury of prenatal omniscience and the serenity of Otherwheres. She bossed me and had an answer for everything. She had delighted in Tuscany and loved the nutty warm smell of the olive oil that Ethna rubbed on herself. As we lay in the Italian sun we had talked about being famous. Thresheen was going to be a prima ballerina and would have painful ordeals with her tendons and lovers. When she would be interviewed, she would always made a point of attributing her beauty to Ethna and her chattiness to me.

The Daimon of Ethna

Our troubles began one March evening in Florence when Ethna decided to introduce us to our biological father.

Every Friday for five months she and Armand had mated in a tiny studio he rented in Via Roma near the Duomo. He mounted her on a big four-poster bed under a pair of golden swooping amorettos amid the clamor of motorinos and cathedral bells. They met at 6:00 and made love till 6:35. Between 6:35 and 6:50 they showered and then went out for dinner to Cibreo. They were home by 10:00 and scandalized the amorettos a second time until 10:35, when Armand turned off the light and went to sleep. He had everything timed to a T because he had to catch the 7:00 A.M. flight to Paris to spend the weekend with his wife and two sons.

Thresheen, no more than myself, had little more enthusiasm for this Armand than I did.

"To hell with the genes." She scowled. "The man gives me the creeps."

"Come on," I protested. "He is our father."

"There is nothing between him, Ethna, and us. He's of no more consequence than a dandelion seed blown across a field. It'll all end badly."

I peeped into the future just a wench bit, and it drove me back like a gust of icy wind.

We hated the smirk on Ethna's lovely face that said: Look at me! A raw country girl from Uggala flooring the most powerful art mogul in Florence! She melted inside when Armand whispered: "In repose you resemble a Donatello Madonna." She broke out in crass gooseflesh when he knelt between her Botticelli haunches. "Ah, my little Irish Primavera!"

"A woman is most a woman," he would say, "in the small of her back and the silkiness of her inner thighs. These are her secret, sacred places."

Balderdash! snorted Thresheen.

Armand loved to take off Ethna's clothes, but he loved even more to dress her up in flamboyant robes that brought out her Quattrocento looks. At first Ethna lit up with pride and pleasure at the revelation of her own special beauty. No Irishman would ever come within an ass's roar of Armand's refined appreciation of her. Linking his arm at openings, exhibitions, receptions, she felt blessed and humbled in the presence of such panache and eloquence.

On the day of our introduction, Ethna arrived in Via Roma wearing a pair of old tennis shoes. Armand ignored the cheek tilted for a kiss. Without a word he pointed at her shabby footwear. She laughed and shrugged her shoulders. But he kept pointing at her runners like a master reprimanding his spaniel for shitting in the wrong place. He was inarticulate with rage.

"I have something to tell you," she said, trying to overcome the trivial horror of her lapse.

"How could you? I want you to go home and change now!"

And he slammed the door in her face.

That's how in thirty seconds flat our mother-to-be slipped from being a statue to being a mere mortal in scruffy footwear.

Over cappuccino in Piazza Santa Croce she reflected on what had happened. It dawned on her that in the suede brown eyes of Armand she had never existed as Ethna. She was but a grace from this or that painting, a vestal from this or that monument. For a moment she thought that maybe she should drop him, buy herself a gross phallic ice cream, wear any kind of fucking shoes that took her fancy, and have an abortion.

She went as far as to treat herself to a banana split doused with syrup and fresh cream. True, without Armand she was genuine Ethna. But then she was nobody. She preferred to be somebody, even if it wasn't herself.

So she went home like a good little girl and changed her shoes.

Later that evening she arrived in Armand's apartment wearing his favorite violet and purple skirt and bodice and a pair of blue stilettos. But instead of falling into his arms, she unbuttoned her imperial tunic and announced the recent arrivals in her womb.

Armand hopped from one leg to the other and opened his mouth several times. Thresheen nudged me and said: "He doesn't know whether to wet himself or preach a sermon!"

He preached a sermon, then he consulted his watch and left.

Ethna stood at the window and gazed at the last of the tourists leaving the Duomo. They were shaking off their disappointment. The cathedral was like a great pomegranate fruit: alluring on the outside but stony and sterile within.

Her mind went back to some of those long labored meals in Armand's favorite restaurants, where he made a point of displaying his vegetarian virility. He would extol the virtues of tofu, a soy curd that could, in the right hands, be turned into practically anything. It could be cut into slices, marinated in garlic or in fresh grated ginger. It could become minced meat, shepherd's pie, burger, or savory loaf. It was nothing on its own — tasteless, shapeless, and colorless. It acquired identity only when it borrowed form and savoir from something else.

There was no point in deceiving herself any longer. She was a Tofu Woman. She was spiced with Armand's opinions, ornamented with his dressings, and shaped by his lustful hand. She was smoked tofu, aromatic tofu, dried tofu, or deep-fried tofu. Just as he wished.

Still standing in the window and gazing at the Duomo, Ethna finished unbuttoning her purple tunic. She dropped it on the floor without a second look. Then she slid off her addled violet skirt with the golden sickle moons on the hem. After a moment's hesitation she took off her silk vest and lacy bra. She kicked off her blue stilettos and peeled off her stockings. The puffy white satin of her knickers was the last bit of Armand's fantasy to land on the floor. The Nina Ricci she would wash off at home.

She looked at the sprawled ornate remnants of her former tofu self and grimaced. She was Ethna again, naked as the day she was born. She wrapped herself in her coat (that, at least, she had bought herself in Brown Thomas in Dublin) and, barefooted and high-headed, she descended to the street.

The Daimon of Thresheen

❧ Thresheen had an explanation for everything.

"Some women," she said, "become obsessed by the man they lose. The rarer kind become obsessed with their own stupidity in having had anything to do with the man they lose. Look at our mother!"

All of April and May, Ethna sat at home and reproached herself for succumbing to Armand's charm between 6:00 and 6:35, his money and power between 7:00 and 10:00, and the cosmopolitan nonchalance with which he grabbed her bottom between 10:00 and 10:35. She shook her head, sobbed, and cursed her pigheadedness.

I felt for her.

But Thresheen grew angry and fundamentalist. "Stupid girl!" she said with her back to me. "She doesn't have a clue about the French. It's enough to look at their sauces and scents, wigs, perfumes, and lovers! All designed to avoid suffering and ugliness. At the first hint of pain a Frenchman takes to his heels. I noticed it the last time I was in Bordeaux."

"Bordeaux! When were you in Bordeaux?"

"Eighteen seventy-five. Don't even remind me."

We must have been giving Ethna a hard time, because she fainted twice at the café where she worked to put herself through art school. The first time she smashed a tray load of glasses. The second she spilled risotto con porcini over a captain of carabinieri and was sacked on the spot.

When we got back to the apartment, Ethna's bags were on the street, and on the balcony above, Signora Bertini was working herself into a passion about the decline of moral values among the Inglesi.

Ethna had never been in the gutter before and didn't know how she should behave. The railway station seemed the obvious place to go with her packed bags, so she went there. The destination board clacked desultorily: Naples, Palermo, Bologna, Milan. Ethna felt an overwhelming desire to be at the horse show in Dublin. In one of her bags there was sure to be — if Signora Bertini hadn't stolen it — a straw hat that had been bought with an eye to Ladies' Day.

Her hat fantasy was the last time before our birth when Ethna rose above her destitution. She wasn't going to Naples or Bologna or to the horse show in Dublin. She was going to Uggala.

We both knew that for our mother returning to Uggala was not going home but going into exile. Ethna had never really inhabited the island. She was born an outsider. And now she was being rebanished to the place of her first estrangement.

Already on the boat Thresheen's mood darkened as she glanced back and forth in time. I could sense her reluctance to be born. "Maybe not this time," she said. "Maybe I'll pass." She would go silent for long periods and not answer my questions.

I thought of us as two climbers roped together on a glacier. My task was to keep her awake and alert while I led her inch by inch through the blizzard. I talked to Thresheen about our fame, and she would wake up and make an effort for a while.

But then she would slip back again, discouraged by a bitter wind from the future.

Thresheen was afraid of the trials and tribulations we both saw so clearly ahead. I was afraid to lose touch with my daimon.

I badly wanted my sister to stay around, so I kept nagging her on.

"We'll see. We'll hang that door tomorrow," she would say and go back to sleep.

The Daimon of Ethna

☙ Many of the Italian cities Ethna had explored so avidly had triumphal arches that proclaimed their grandeur to the world. Little places like Uggala ought to have defeat arches, she thought. Under them, the failed and beaten could crawl back to their ignoble origins with nothing to show for their journeyings but nervous tics and cheap suitcases.

How blatantly they stared at her as she stumbled down the via dolorosa of the gangplank, a rucksack on her back and two miserable carryalls clutched in her hands.

Seven years' absence had made no difference to the quay and not much to the scatter of people who came traipsing down to meet the ferry. Mercifully it was just after one o'clock, and most were laying into their dinners and listening to the news on the radio.

Here was Tom O'Reilly with an expansive Jesus, is it yourself, Ethna? that faded on his lips as soon as he looked closer.

Here was the priest's housekeeper, Mrs. O'Halloran, down to meet the curate, more stooped and gray than before and not paying any attention to anybody but the new priest, who was as welcome as the flowers in May even though it was June.

And Sean Mannion, wallowing in the same rubber boots and baggy gray gansy. He glared at her, moved his jaws, and whispered something salacious to his brother, Seamus, who couldn't have agreed more.

And good old Holy Paddy hail-marying his way backwards down the quay and miraculously navigating between lobster pots and bollards and bags of cement.

Her father's face was smooth and expressionless as a freshly unwrapped caramel. But she knew that under its crust mantled a dark laval rage. All eyes were on the two of them, wondering how Colm O'Keefe and his brazen daughter would destroy one another.

"Give me them yokes and get up on the tractor," Colm said curtly.

"I'd rather walk if you don't mind."

"Suit yourself."

An inappropriate shaft of sunlight warmed the quay as Ethna refused him the satisfaction of taking her rucksack. People who were well established, who had made it, didn't carry rucksacks. She would bear it as an emblem of her failure, as Santa Rufina bore the instruments of her torture.

She trudged up the road to the village, yes, no, yes, no, her soul salty with unshed tears. She stopped several times to fight her nausea. She couldn't tell if it was caused by the journey over or by her humiliation.

A familiar figure in a long black coat came cycling towards her. The long blue scarf was familiar too, as was the highly choreographed way in which he dismounted as soon as he drew level with her. He hopped off the pedals while the bike was still moving and ran along with it, his hand on the saddle. Finally he tossed the contraption against a telegraph pole and rushed to embrace her.

"Ethna! I'll be damned!"

Her heart was racing while he held her. That hadn't changed either.

"You could have let me know you were coming. Seven years and look at you!"

"Yeah. Look at me."

Her voice broke. She couldn't hold back the tears any longer.

Danny took off her rucksack and held her close. She could smell the old familiar smell of turf smoke on his greatcoat mixed with the tang of the lemon cologne with which he always dowsed himself before meeting the boat. Just in case.

For the length of the embrace her own cloudiness and confusion were no longer painful. They even felt pleasant.

"Danny, I made a total balls of everything."

"Of course you did! But what matter. Now you're home."

The Daimon of Father Francis

❧ Father Francis had always longed to encounter the wise old man of fable on some hillside or by the fire in a smoky cottage. The wise old man who would tell him the story or astonish him with the aphorism that he needed to hear and that would enable him to rise from the grave of himself.

For an excited moment, as the boat approached Uggala, the adolescent longing stirred in him again. Surely beyond the boggy hill that loomed over the harbor dwelt a man that had so steeped himself in silence, so clarified his perceptions, that he would look up with a glittering eye and speak the needful word.

But as soon as he jumped ashore and saw the reverential, expectant faces on the quay, the priest realized with dismay that for these people he was the wise old man who carried the holy word in a pyx in his inside pocket. To cover his dejection he returned to the boat to collect his plant.

The Skipper leaned out of the wheelhouse. "Are you going to grow bananas on the island, Father?"

"It's a fig tree."

"So it's figs then."

As he turned away from the Skipper's sly gibe, he tripped over a straw skep.

"Careful!"

A tall, sturdy man in a black coat grinned disarmingly. Father Francis had the disquieting feeling that he had seen him before someplace, that the roguish blue eyes, red bushy hair, even the blue scarf were elements from a long lost encounter.

He was wrong. He was remembering the future rather than the past.

"Welcome to Uggala, Father," said Danny Ruane and lifted the skep gingerly as if he were a bomb disposal expert.

They faced one another, Father Francis cradling his plant, Danny dangling the skep.

"What's the plant, if you don't mind me asking?"

"It's a fig tree. Isn't it a bit exposed for your bees on the island?"

"Well, the monks kept them here in the old days."

Father Francis nodded and struggled ashore with his ungainly plant.

"You know what?" Danny shouted after him. "I'll give you a pound of honey if you give me a pound of figs!"

Father Francis looked around him, not so much to see as to think. There was a seventh-century Christian graveyard with a ruined oratory somewhere on the island. Suppose there had been twelve priests per century in the parish. Let's see: twelve by twelve makes one hundred and forty-four, round it up to one hundred and fifty. He was the one hundred and fiftieth priest, give or take a dozen, to minister on Uggala. And they talk about the antiquities of Oxford and Padua and their living traditions!

"Welcome to Uggala, Father."

The voice held equal measures of challenge and deference. A small man with wispy white hair thrust his hand into Father Francis's. He had a bundle of fresh newspapers under his other arm.

"Tom O'Reilly. You're a brave man to come here, Father."

Father Francis couldn't determine his age. He had a pink baby face and wore a striped collarless grandfather shirt.

"I see you like your newspaper."

"I'd read four of them a day if I could get my hands on them. Do you think the Poles are going to rise against the Russians? I hear the CIA are putting a lot of money into that quarter."

Father Francis had no privileged information from the Vatican. He could sense a hunger in the baby-faced man for news from the outside. For a moment he felt guilty that his own world of monastic discipline seemed even more shrunken than that of the islanders.

"You're very well informed."

"If the Poles move when the Pope returns to Krakow — and that's what I'd do myself — there'll be all hell to pay. Am I right, Danny?"

Danny drew abreast of them with the skep balanced on the carrier of his bicycle.

"You've been advising the Pope and NATO again, Tom! Jesus, if you're not careful Brzezinski will get jealous."

The sea smashed itself against the blunt granite blocks of the quay. A seagull stood on the shingle shouting endless obscenities. But nothing could jar on the strange hopeful psalm that had begun to sound in Father Francis's head.

Perhaps it was something in the brief exchanges between Danny and Tom that induced him to lift the lid of his coffin half an inch. He had just been given a glimpse of a Dadaist map of Europe, where the island of Uggala and the city of Krakow lay cheek by jowl and England, France, and Germany were terra incognita.

Or perhaps it was that Danny had smiled at him with such a piquant mixture of irony and warmth?

Or maybe, as Biafra O'Dee was to insist, Father Francis had stepped ashore at the right minute, right hour, on the right day of the right month of the right year. It was the fifth of June 1988. If on that day he were to strangle the Archbishop of Tuam and fry his entrails in methylated spirits, he could not but come up smelling of violets.

The Daimon of Tom O'Reilly

❧ Tom O'Reilly could still remember the time when there were children on the island and the one-teacher national school was alive with hopscotch and hula hoops. He passed by it every day because he was courting Alice O'Malley, who had come down from Dublin inspired by the example of Edel Quinn's mission to Africa. Locked in him was the image of her standing before her class, shaking her dark curls, and swaying the pleated lampshade of a dress she had copied from Natalie Wood in *Rebel Without a Cause*.

He could still get an erection remembering that lampshade and the opalescent bulb that glowed beneath it.

As he peeped through the school window and worshiped her, it came to him that together they would make the revolution.

The idea of revolution occurred to him shortly after he got a job as a storeman in the new French fish-processing factory. There he discovered the reality of worker oppression and capitalist exploitation. His soul swelled with delight at the injustice.

A handy little blue-backed edition of James Connolly's *Labour in Ireland* supplied him with the requisite vocabulary. He wrote a manifesto to the small farmers, fishermen, and wage slaves of Uggala and showed it to Alice.

Alice corrected the grammar with a disapproving hand, but she loyally hung the manifesto beside the Dedication of the Family to the Sacred Heart in the alcove where nobody would see it. Her secret dream as head of the local presidium of the Legion of Mary was to have every last man, woman, and child on the island march behind the banner of Our Lady, Queen of the Legion.

All her life she was astonished at her love for Tom, who marched in the phalanx of Satan. She admonished him and prayed to Saint Alphonsus Liguori for him. Tom, in turn, read her Lenin's *What Is to Be Done?* Their attempts at mutual conversion were gentle and uncoercive because they dreaded to lose one another. On the subtle daimonic plane they were so much one and the same person that none of these grosser differences mattered.

Tom accompanied her to Mass every Sunday and to the annual acies of the Legion just so she wouldn't be too much on her own. He passed the time fantasizing about lampshades and opaque bulbs. The lampshades grew shorter as he grew older.

Alice corrected the letters he wrote to *The Irish Times* where he quoted himself from various unpublished articles and manifestos. He had grown used to not being famous since everybody on the island read the *Irish Press*.

Tom and Alice were both embarrassed about their affection. The rule on Uggala was that men and women hated one another as they hated themselves. In the past, husband and wife got together to reproduce, and thereafter they lived in silent hostility and suspicion.

Danny Ruane was the only sexual dissident to hang on. Which is why Tom always defended him when others tried to intern him in the petty gulags of their spite.

Years passed. Tom and Alice's only son, Rory, drowned, the fish plant closed, the national school became a goat shed, Tom went on the dole. But nothing altered his inexplicable love for Alice. It flourished all the more as she came down with depression and refused to get out of her bed. She was confused and cried for Rory, even though at the time it happened she hardly shed a tear: it was God's holy will. Then one morning, as Tom brought her breakfast in bed, he remembered a story.

"Listen, Alice," he said in a soft voice. "There's this hospital for sick children in Moscow. In one of the wards the youngsters wouldn't walk unless they had something to hold on to. So the nurses stretched a rope across the room. Sure enough, the children trooped across from one end to the other. Over the weeks they made the rope thinner and thinner until at last it was only a piece of string. It didn't make a damn bit of difference. The children walked across as gaily as ever.

"And then this nurse had an idea. She cut the string up and gave a piece to everybody. So the kids just picked up a bit of string and walked wherever they pleased. What do you think of that?"

Alice listened intently and said nothing more than Fancy that now! But the next morning she was up and about feeding the ducks and geese and watering the geraniums. Round her hand she had wound a length of blue knitting wool. From then on she took it off only when she went to bed.

When Tom told Danny what had happened, Danny's first thought was that the whole island needed a magic end of string to get it moving. But what could it be?

The Daimon of Alice

❧ There was a time when Alice was bothered by the question of whether she should have a purpose in life or just drift along. But very quickly she realized that she should simply let the purpose have her. She felt she was being lived by something greater than herself, something that knew better than she did where she was headed. That something was God.

Her everyday life was stitched together by wandering pains, which she accepted as part of God's holy plan for her. As far back as she could recall there was something the matter with her joints or her head or her back or her lower bodily strata. Ever since her first excruciating period she knew the meaning of the liturgical vale of tears and prayed daily for deliverance from it. She became a pathologist of her own body, scrutinizing every change and variation in skin and bone, listening for the soft implosions of gut gas, dissecting the texture and consistency of earwax.

She had a brief respite from pains and aches after Tom married her. He had a cheerful, chimney sweeper's view of her anatomy and saw his marital task as keeping Alice's flue clean with regular blasts from his willy-nilly.

While Tom worked away at her cavities, Alice herself sat like a bird in a tall tree oblivious to the source of her joy. Her body was weightless and painless and ready for flight. Love was such a new and disembodying experience that it took her some months to rediscover her old aching self.

When she got pregnant she found herself back in her ambient torture chamber, and her organs resumed their rebellion against her. Tom said that she had grown so attached to her afflictions that if she woke up one morning without a throbbing leg or a stuffed nose he would fear that there was something seriously wrong with her. But she would gladly have opened herself down the middle like a waistcoat, ripped out all the offending clots and lumps, and zipped herself up again with a There now, that's that.

After Rory's death she redoubled her prayers. Everybody in Uggala knew that she was an Olympic class athlete of prayer. In making her petitions she struck just the right balance between gratitude, humility, and pushing apologetically for her own requests. Others harassed heaven shamelessly or prayed in a merciless hail of scruples. It was all very well to say "Thy will be done." But to mean it and at the same time not to give up on one's own needs was a high art. A good prayer shot straight across space to the Divine and hit its target, unlike other wants and wishes that had to go roundabout. So people in trouble came to Alice and asked her to intercede for them.

She became a spiritual broker between Uggala and the Almighty.

Tom was secretly disturbed by her success in lessening the pain and suffering of the islanders. Deluded as she was, she seemed to achieve much more than he did, though he was equipped with the right philosophy.

The Daimon of Ethna

🐦 Silence has many textures. There is the silence of the womb strobed with aquatic murmurings and happy heaves, where I snuggled up against Thresheen. There is the teeth-grinding silence of Uggala after everybody has gone to bed and the electric generators have been shut off. There is the silence of mere getting through the night with no luxuriating in the arms of another and no voyaging into secret places.

The silence of our grandparents' house was sour and stagnant as sauerkraut. When we walked into the kitchen, me and Thresheen bobbing away in Ethna's tummy, Concepta went on washing the dishes. I could feel her rancor. It had the smell and taste of zinc.

Ethna took off her rucksack and said, I'm back, Mum.

Concepta rattled the knives and forks as much as to say: I wish you were dead.

Ethna did the only thing she could do to resist the homicidal silence. She went to the sideboard and filled the kettle with water as if she had left only yesterday instead of seven years ago. She paused occasionally in the hope of a human word from her mother.

Nothing.

So she opened the fridge and rummaged around for something to eat. We shrank in her womb from the fetor of stale cheese and rotting lettuce.

Ethna sat at the table, ate bread and jam, and drank tea.

Concepta mopped the floor, pushing the scum of her indignation closer and closer to Ethna's feet.

"Where do you keep the sugar now?" asked Ethna.

Concepta drew herself up to the full length of her misery. "Sugar! Do you think you can come back here just like that and ask for sugar?"

Concepta immediately regretted that she had lowered herself to say anything to her hussy of a daughter, who was no daughter of hers anyway. She had disowned her a long time ago.

"Why don't you sit down and talk to me?" said Ethna quietly. But we knew how worked up she was inside.

Concepta stopped her mopping once again.

"You'd better get one thing straight. I'll have no bastards in this house. You can take your bag and baggage and leave here as soon as you finish your tea."

"I have nowhere to go."

"You should have thought of that seven years ago."

We felt the ice and fire of Concepta's loathing and her fear of her own loathing. I saw her in a square in Wittenberg among a crowd of spectators that cheered a flaming pyre and the billowing black smoke that streaked the mullions with human fat. Thresheen saw her in a slave market in Zanzibar.

It will take her another eight years to wear out her bitterness and to slip from under the blanket of depression that settled on her after Ethna's birth. Impossible as it seems, she will one day think of Ethna as her dear daughter and will carry her sketches in her handbag to look at when she draws up the account of her own life.

Hard as we could we tried to broadcast this image of the weary, reconciled Concepta to the heart of Ethna, but she was too absorbed in the present. And Concepta was still a good Christian, full of hatred for her daughter's turpitude.

Colm O'Keefe burst in with Ethna's bags.

"You can leave her things at the door," said Concepta. "She's on her way out."

Colm glanced from one to the other and said, "She's not going anywhere."

"I'm not having her here."

"You'll have what I tell you to have."

My mother's heart was pounding, and I could taste an almondy bitterness in her blood.

"It's me or her," said Concepta. "You can take your pick."

"I'd be glad to be rid of the pair of you."

Concepta and Colm underestimated Ethna. While they spat gobs of venom at one another across the kitchen, she took her sketch pad from her rucksack and began to draw.

Her hand flew over the page, imaging their bristlings and shriekings. ("If you raise a hand to me I'll call the Guards!") Rapidly she sketched two scald crows with stiletto beaks stabbing at the taut mound of her belly, with me and Thresheen curled up inside. Dribbles of blood fell into a knobbly chalice underneath. Above, the eye of God, in an equilateral triangle, gazed impassively on.

By the time Ethna had finished, they had began to flitter one another's families. Colm hinted at a dark crime committed by Concepta's mother about which he would say no more for the present. Concepta retaliated by going over again the rake of suicides, idiots, and alcoholics in O'Keefe's family. And then she pointed at Ethna and her shame. "There's an O'Keefe if ever I saw one."

They both looked at our mother. She sat at the kitchen table and held up her drawing without a word.

I've learned the scene by heart: Ethna at the end of her tether with exhaustion and despair, the cartoon of me and Thresheen being pecked alive, Colm and Concepta pausing for a moment to decipher the symbols.

Concepta was basically a socialist realist. She saw nothing in the drawing but further evidence of her daughter's instability and depravity.

Colm was more given to allegory and superstition. He

swallowed hard. "Go upstairs to your room," he said to Ethna. "I'll bring your stuff."

He carried up her bags and later a hot-water bottle and a mug of warm, syrupy carrageen.

Ethna lay on her old bed and put the finishing touches to her icon. In the space of a sheet of matte paper, in the balance of proportions and the hatchings of light and shade, she drew close to her daimon.

I keep her drawing as a talisman over my desk and muse at the clever way Ethna managed the situation. Had her parents thrown her out, she always said, she would have done away with herself.

When Colm came downstairs, Concepta was busy kneading dough for an apple tart. It was her specialty. She shook flour on the breadboard and pressed out with the rolling pin what was left of her anguish into the smooth yielding pastry.

"She's staying," said Colm. "She'll earn her keep in the bar."

"That's right. Put her on exhibition."

"She'll work in the kitchen."

Concepta cut little hearts out of the dough with a metal mold. She felt relieved. At times like this she hated O'Keefe and all the seed, breed, and generations of O'Keefes. But she needed him to save her from the fear which her own extremism roused in her.

Ten years later, when he is dead and gone, she will recall him with the greatest affection, commencing each fond reminiscence with "Poor Daddy!"

The Daimon of Colm O'Keefe

∿ The Daimon of Colm O'Keefe was huddled on a rock in the Holmenkollen Forest above Oslo Fjord in Norway. She waited and waited for him to make a move in her direction, but he remained attached to his sluggish misery off the West

Coast of Ireland. Twice he became aware of her summons and twice he passed it up.

On the first occasion he caught sight of a calendar with a photograph of a snowy valley surprised by the flare of the aurora borealis. On the instant he felt an intense longing to taste the icy air and to trudge through the fresh falls of snow. But an hour later he shrugged off the impulse as a vague half memory of childhood Christmas cards and the magic of watching out for Santa Claus to cross over the sound to Uggala.

On the second occasion the allure of the Northlands took the shape of a woman called Signe. She came one August, swam topless in the ocean, and spent hours in the pub, badgering old men to teach her how to dance "The Walls of Limerick" and "The Corncrakes Lament."

Colm besotted with her to the point of panic. He had never been in love, so that the flurry of feelings she stirred in him was like the combination of terror and exhilaration he felt when jumping sixty feet from the top of Balor's Rock into the sea.

When Signe left he felt so bereft that he booked a flight to Oslo the same weekend. He even equipped himself with a heroic anorak, a hunting knife, and a Norwegian-English phrase book. He never got further than Oslo airport. As soon as he disembarked the plane and began walking towards Passport Control, a paralyzing sense of his own foolishness and lostness overwhelmed him. What in Christ name was he doing at the North Pole?

He booked himself first-class return on the same plane and arrived drunk and happy in Dublin five hours later.

He never allowed himself to think that it was faintheartedness. For him his triumphant return remained a moment of deep insight: he was a solid man on a solid island. There his ancestors were buried and there he would be buried with them. He professed his devotion to Uggala so many times and to so many people that he became the island man incarnate.

The more he feared a meeting with his destiny, the more passionately he praised the superiority and purity of Uggala over a rotten world. If his father had been sneered at as a gombeen-man, Colm's local patriotism was like an amulet against criticism. To attack Colm O'Keefe was to attack what was best and most virile in the West of Ireland. And so the purity of his vision allowed him to fleece his neighbors at every hand's turn.

Though brutally handsome, he was unsure of himself and approached women like one might approach wild mushrooms, never knowing which one was poisonous, which one edible. His mother had died shortly after his birth, and he was brought up by loveless men, first his father and later an uncle who sent him to the diocesan seminary.

He married Concepta for the same reason as Sir Edmund Hillary climbed Mount Everest: because she was there. Everybody said she was a fine thing. So she must be. Once he had climbed her and planted his flag on the summit, he espaliered back down and left her to her own devices. Her initial efforts to win him back confused him. Why did he have to understand her or talk to her for Christ sake? Wasn't it enough to feed her and fuck her?

Like that of many a daimonless man, Colm's energy was invested in various phobias. He detested Tom O'Reilly for his Marxist analysis of Fianna Fáil. It was simply antinational. And he didn't even bother to ignore Mad Arse O'Dee. But the pole star of his enmity was Danny Ruane. When Colm drove his tractor over stoned fields, he mauled and massacred, strangled and quartered that pox-ridden pimp from Portmarnock. When he practiced on his fiddle (as every decent Irishman), the more he thought about Danny and his piss-poor tin whistle and spoons, the more fluent and masterful became his control of the bow. When he drank with his cronies in his own pub, he was at his most brilliant once the conversation turned to Danny.

What Colm hated most about Danny was the way he puked out ideas: there seemed to be no end to his projects, improvements, and innovations. Already when they were boys beachcombing for messages in bottles during the summer holidays, Colm was an open receptacle into which Danny would fling everything from misquotations from Thomas Aquinas to stories of the Royal Flying Corps. They flew in formation together on offensive patrols over Uggala in their Sopwith Camels. The Germans put up Fokker D.VIIs and Albatrosses against them with Spandau guns under their center sections. Danny was Captain James Bigglesworth, D.S.O., D.F.C., and Colm covered his tail as Algeron Montgomery of No. 266 Squadron, R.F.C. "By Jove, Algy!" shouted Biggles as he flung the Camel into a half roll, guns stuttering vicious staccato bursts — *rat-tat-tat-tat, rat-ta-ta-tat!* The bogs of Uggala were littered with the remains of black-crossed enemy planes.

Even though he was seven years younger, Danny always knew what to do, where to go, what was crap and what was A-1.

Colm never forgot one afternoon when he tried to impress Danny with adult talk he had picked up in the pub about the atom bomb and the Yellow Peril. Danny only looked at him with pity and announced with conviction: "Forget about the bomb and the Chinks. The real threat in the future is from women. You'll see, they'll take over everything and men won't be needed anymore."

Such pronouncements both puzzled and dazzled Colm, and he used them as his own the minute Danny left for Dublin.

When Danny came to live permanently on Uggala, Colm froze with apprehension. He had already established a court on the island made up of men who were less able and less witty than himself. He saw Ruane as a usurper who had come to steal his island from him.

The worst of it was that there was no respite from Danny, even when Colm closed the door of his own house behind him and sat in his own kitchen. Not five minutes passed before little Ethna would sit Danny's phantom at the table and exult in his latest exploits and discoveries. Had they heard that Danny was going to build a windmill so that he wouldn't be dependent on the ESB when it came? In fact he was going to sell electricity back to the ESB! Danny explained everything to her: why water was wet and what the wind was doing when it wasn't blowing. He even drew diagrams so that she could —

"Enough!" Colm flung down the *Irish Press*. "Can't a man have his dinner without having to hear about that half-witted poltroon?"

That was why, for all his huffing and puffing at the time, Colm was secretly relieved at Ethna's running away from home at sixteen years of age. At last he was free to hate Ruane in peace.

The Daimon of Father Francis

❧ While Colm O'Keefe pondered the fateful crows drawn by Ethna, Father Francis was being shown around his new home by Mrs. O'Halloran. The first thing he noticed was the smell of stone, a limy astringency that reminded him of cellars and dungeons. Perhaps that was how the secular clergy smelled?

The Parochial House was the finest house on the island, two stories high with a slate roof and a lopsided Georgian entrance. In the previous century it had belonged to the absentee landlord's agent, but after Independence it had been taken over by the other imperium.

Distractedly, Mrs. O'Halloran led Father Francis from room to room, drawing his attention to a fine fireplace here, a piano there, a coffee machine, a dishwasher (the only one so far on the island).

The walls of the sitting room were lined with photos of happy young men on their ordination days clustered around the presiding Bishop.

"I hope you'll be comfortable here, Father," said Mrs. O'Halloran without conviction. "The place takes a bit of getting used to."

"I'll be fine," said Francis and approached the armchair in front of the fireplace. As he was about to sit down, he heard the housekeeper's involuntary cry.

"Don't!"

"What is it, Mrs. O'Halloran?"

She was flustered and didn't know how to tell him. "That's the Dead Priest's Chair."

"So?"

"Father Mahony, no, I'm wrong, it was the one before him, Father Skerrett, died in that chair and there's a cold spot ever since." She spread her hands. "You can feel it with your fingertips. Will you have a cup of tea? Sure what am I saying; it's only a cold spot."

The cat was out of the bag. The Parochial House was haunted. It was so haunted than nobody on Uggala called it the Parochial House anymore; they called it the Quare Place. A generation of mothers had threatened unmanageable sons with locking them up there for the night. It had even become a minor tourist attraction, and more than once the resident curate had been scared by nosy visitors peering in the windows or emerging unexpectedly from behind the laurel bushes.

Even though Mrs. O'Halloran was the priest's housekeeper, she never went to the Quare Place on her own. Her fears were exacerbated by her absentmindedness. She could never remember where she left anything. If she found a teapot in one of the beds or a full ashtray in the fridge, she couldn't be sure if it was her own doing or Father Skerrett up to his antics again.

She hoped and prayed it was Father Skerrett.

When Mrs. O'Halloran's fussing was over and she had toddled off home, Father Francis sat in the Dead Priest's Chair and dragged on a cigarette. He sat for an hour without a thought in his head. Towards evening the fireplace lit up with a warm gold effulgence. He turned to look at the window and into the blind face of the sun.

It brought anxiety rather than solace. Such elative moments in the weather he associated with his father's smile, fleeting and fragile and ready to give way in an instant to frowns and fretfulness. It made him long for the sun of the South, which rose serenely in the morning, held its buoyancy all day long, and sank down, round and pleased with itself, in the evening.

He didn't feel like reading the daily office. Instead he ventured out to see the sun on one of its rare appearances over Uggala.

The whole village had come out to see the sun. The single straggling street looked cheerful, and as people passed him by they said, "Lovely evening, Father," or "Great weather we're having at the end of all" or "Uggala plus sunshine is heaven itself!"

Father Francis took the path along the coast, pausing only to gather bunches of sea pinks and marvel at their waxy sweet smell. The strange littoral plants excited him: perhaps he should compose a flora of Uggala with the names in Latin, Irish, and English?

Flora Uggalensis? He rebuked himself. It sounded far too much like the project of a Protestant parson who had no congregation and no scruple about wasting his time on secular pursuits.

He rebuked himself again: that was sectarian.

He would have gone on rebuking his rebukes had he not been distracted by the sound of cursing.

From round a low cropped hillock to his left, a grotesque figure emerged in boilersuit, hat and veil, and huge gloves. Behind the samurai, like a vengeful cloud, billowed a swarm of angry bees.

"Fuck off, will ye!"

Danny Ruane raced like a madman and waved his arms.

"Fuck off, ye shower of shites!"

He made straight for the sea. He stopped for a split second on a ledge over the tide as if waiting for a last-minute reprieve. The heavens were silent. So with a running jump and a "Fuck the lot of ye!" he plummeted into the sea.

The swarm hung in the air for a moment and then swung back inland.

Father Francis ran to the ledge. Beneath him Danny thrashed about in a little cove trying to retrieve his bee-keeper's hat.

"Are you all right down there?"

Danny glanced up, surprised and gratified. "Yeah. You can't trust the little bastards."

"Can I give you a hand?"

Another man would have been embarrassed to find himself in Danny's predicament — lolling half-inflated in a boilersuit, furious bees in his hair, and his straw hat preceding him with every wavelet to the shore.

But not Danny. He had a sense of his own island life as a series of adventures accruing into a legend. When he'd arrived on Uggala it was still crowded with stories, and he was determined to make room for his own among them. So dramatic encounters and spectacular failures were all grist to his mill.

Caught up as he was in his own abstruse studies, it never occurred to him that the heroic world of parish fable was dying around him. Seven years on, Uggala will be an island of virtual stories. Who, with a remote control in his hand, will get a kick out of Danny Ruane being chased by his own bees into the Atlantic? Or believe that one summer night Father Francis saw the apparition of a dead schoolgirl who talked haltingly of the pain of love?

My Daimon

❧ It might seem that it was cramped and claustrophobic in Ethna's womb. Not a bit of it: I never felt such glorious breadths and depths. The reason is simple: the more love the more space. So naturally enough Thresheen was reluctant to be contracted into a country with fifty-two grouchy people per square kilometer.

As Thresheen's anxiety grew, I too became restless. But my worry was different: how to remain in touch with my Daimon after crossing the River of Forgetfulness.

I thought up various schemes to remind myself of my vocation. First it was a word that I repeated to imprint it on my memory: Dreamkeeper. So morning noon and night I murmured "Dreamkeeper" over and over again, sinking it deeper and deeper into my being so that at least a trace fossil of the word would remain when I crossed the River.

So insistent was my mantra that one night our mother sat up suddenly in bed, said, "Dreamkeeper who?" — and went back to sleep.

"A word is not enough to span from Here to There," said Thresheen.

So I thought up a system of correspondences to awaken the word: a smell, a sound, a color, a feeling in my chest.

The smell is the delicate balmy fragrance of just-crushed lady's bedstraw. Dreamkeeper.

The color is the papery silver-white of birch bark. Dreamkeeper.

The sound is the *crex crex* of a corncrake in June. Dream-keeper.

The feeling in my chest is the trepidation of a scrupulous schoolboy about to receive the Eucharist.

What I hadn't foreseen was that the world into which I was about to enter would be like the reverse side of a tapestry: a jumble of threads and knots without rhyme or reason. On my side there was pattern and clarity and precision: a red roof on a white house in a green field. Turn over and there's nothing but confusion, ungainly lumps and zigzag lines going everywhere and nowhere.

The scent of lady's bedstraw, the call of the corncrake, the chipped enamel of birch trees would stir only a vague unease and a sense of incompletion.

The trepidation in my chest would become the only link with my destiny.

I feel it before each blank page.

The Daimon of Ethna

୬ While Father Francis was ruminating on the wildflowers of Uggala, Ethna paced the floor of her bedroom. She was repelled at every step by the florid pink and brown tea roses of the carpet her father had bought from one of the Tinker McDonaghs. She couldn't inhabit herself, still less the room. In the past when such vacancy and homelessness attacked her, she had waited for her anger to flare up and give her direction and purpose. But now strong feelings of any kind — fury, hatred, lust — were beyond her. So she paced back and forth in a stupor on the outrageous tea roses. Were the ocean to rear up and batter Uggala senseless she would be grateful to the ocean. Were all the small farmers and fishermen her father had defrauded to surround the house with pitchforks, fish knives, and billhooks she would open the door wide to

them. Were her mother to call out: Come down here, you un-
grateful slut, and wash the floor for me! she would have
found her latitude and longitude in the universe.

"This prison cell pacing is driving me nuts," said Thresheen.
"Why don't you do something to stop her?"

We were both frightened by Ethna's complete disengagement from us. Another five minutes and the self-absorbed
misery of our mother would settle like a toxic fungus on our
brains. It would break out in rancor and fuck-the-lot-of-you
malice in our teens.

"Stop!" I shouted. "Look out the window!"

But Ethna went on with her tormented five steps to the
north, five steps to the south and the vain clanking of the
wheels and pulleys in her skull.

"Stop!" I pleaded again. "Just get out of this room!"

"You'll kill the three of us!" said Thresheen.

Our combined agitation brought Ethna to a halt. She sat
down on the bed, and the sunlight that taunted Father Francis poured over her face. She drank it in as if it were a subtle,
translucent honey. The pucker in her brow faded away.

Thresheen grunted with relief and went back to sleep. I
stayed on guard.

We went to the window and gaped out. Ethna saw a glis-
tening higgledy-piggledy street full of paranoid people who
gossiped about her defilement. I saw a set of probable futures.

In one Ethna decides to take a walk by the sea. She follows
a willie wagtail that dithers from rock to rock ahead of her.
Mesmerized by his chrome yellow belly and his quivering
tail, she forgets about pain and time. Heedless of where she's
going, she slips on a wet stone and falls heavily.

Holy Paddy on his backwards way home from church
shouts: Mother of Jesus, what am I to do now?

After a helicopter ride to the mainland, Thresheen is
ejected into the world against her will. She cries disconso-
lately for seventy-two hours, to the point where the nurses

want to strangle her. No breast, no milk, no cooing or patting on the back will ever assuage the crime of her birth. And I see myself, the quiet one, gasping for breath and groping after Thresheen.

In the second probable future I watch Ethna stealing towards Danny's cottage just as he and Father Francis are listening and talking to one another as they will never listen and talk again. It is that tensile moment between people before the grime and dust of familiarity settles on their relation and consigns it to the ordinary and the everyday. Ethna joins them, and what she says will haunt Father Francis for the rest of the summer.

In a third future I see Ethna rushing to catch the last boat to the mainland. I shudder and blank out. I cannot look on what happens next.

Ethna began to pack up her things in the carryall. But then (had my panic reached her?) she stopped her packing as if hit by despondency. She put on a jacket and stumbled down the stairs.

At the gate she paused again. She could still go back. The last boat wasn't leaving for another hour.

She went towards the shore, taking deep breaths, savoring the salty rottenness of the sea. The stone that would precipitate us into the world lay only yards away. I adopted the crouched position and waited for the crash. Thresheen was better off asleep.

But Ethna stopped again, blew back the hair from her forehead, and stiffened. She stood rooted to the ground like Lot's wife until the sun sidled down into the sea and *The Morning Star* blew three long blasts on her whistle to hurry on the last laggard tourists of the day.

There are a variety of ways to descend into desolation. Some people drift hither and thither slowly like autumn leaves, only half aware that they are lifeless and at the beck and call of the winds. Others plummet like frostbitten apples, bruising their flesh against every passing branch and knocking themselves senseless as they hit the ground. Others again are like chestnuts for whom a fall is a revelation. At the moment of impact the spiked shell breaks open and ejects a new shimmering kidney brown self.

Ethna belonged to the second, contused category. Were her mother to see her now, all frozen inside and unable to move, she would gloat: A typical O'Keefe if ever I saw one. All nerves and no gumption!

The Daimon of Holy Paddy

☙ If Ethna had followed the wagtail and stumbled on the stone, our life would have been in the hands of Holy Paddy. Everybody knew all there was to know about Holy Paddy. You saw him on Sundays and Holy Days of Obligation walking backwards to church. He shuffled slowly, glancing ever so often over his shoulder to see where he was going.

Everybody knew he was walking backwards because he was doing penance for his days of drinking and screwing in Manchester. Screwing of course wasn't generally mentioned, but everybody knew just the same.

He'd push open the heavy front door of the church with his back, turn on his heels, and hobble straight up to the altar rails. That was the only stretch of God's earth that he walked normally. He genuflected with both knees before the Divine Presence and then slid himself along the front pew right to the very end, where the radiator was. There he crinkled up his eyes, stuttered his Hail Marys, and stank.

He prayed the rosary steadily the whole way through Mass. A patient God had to listen with one ear to the priest expounding the need to pray for the conversion of Russia and with the other to the mutter mutter mutter of Holy Paddy.

The priest didn't mind the inattention either. He understood that Holy Paddy in his halo of stench and dirt embodied the final ambition of all Christians.

Once after Mass, when the sacristan glanced out the window and said, "Will ye have a look at that galoot reversing all the way home?" Father Skerrett replied, "Maybe he's the only one of us that knows where he's going?"

Ever since then the islanders savored Father Skerrett's remark as a piece of profound wisdom and repeated it to strangers with a sagacious nod of the head.

Holy Paddy's house was a derelict mud-walled cottage that had once been painted a poisonous blue. Inside there was a kitchen and bedroom that rarely saw the light of day. Ragged curtains were nailed directly to the wall, and the embrasures of the windows were choked with rapacious geraniums that had come as slips from Alice. They were fed irregularly with dregs and slops of tea and powder soup.

In the bedroom there was an iron bedstead that would eventually become the gate to Seamus Mannion's lower field. The bed was a place of terror. At night Holy Paddy dreamt, not of his screwing days in Manchester but of burning villages and the gaping red-black holes of cut throats.

A pale blue ewer preened itself in its enamel basin on a stand in the corner. The only other piece of furniture was a rickety wardrobe with a moldy mirror. Holy Paddy's coffin suit hung inside, the pockets stuffed with camphor balls.

The fireplace in the kitchen opened an empty black jaw. Above it hung an old pendulum clock that had once imprisoned the pupils of the national school. Winding it every evening when he returned from doing the Stations of the Cross gave Holy Paddy his only real pleasure in life. Then he would sit down in front of the dead fireplace, staring patiently at the infinitesimal forward jerks of time.

I once saw him like that, watching and watching the ineluctable approach of death, and the sight made my blood curdle.

Nobody knew anything about Holy Paddy.

The Daimon of Danny Ruane

꙳ When *The Morning Star* blew its whistle three times, waking Ethna out of her stupor, Francis and Danny were seated in Danny's living room drinking tea and talking about sex.

More precisely, Danny talked and the priest listened. Though he had heard many tremulous confessions and considered himself well briefed on the subject, sex was the last thing that Father Francis expected to talk about on Uggala.

He had followed Danny to his cottage in the hope of making some real pastoral contact with a parishioner. They would chat about bees. Or about the village. Or at a pinch, gossip about Francis's predecessors. Perhaps then he would lead the conversation on to more spiritual concerns. Instead he found himself asking about the clocks on Danny's mantelpiece.

"The time of each clock is the time of a woman," said Danny and grinned. "Clare, Yoshiko, and Liselotte. It's not the kind of thing I imagine you'd be much interested in."

"Whyever not?"

Danny cast a quick testing glance at the priest.

"There aren't all that many women on the island. I mean female women. Not the bog-oak, leached-out creatures you get on Uggala."

Father Francis nodded.

"You know men are supposed to think about sex once every ten minutes or so."

"Well well."

"When I think of my women I like to imagine the time of day in their world. Where they are, what they're up to, what they're wearing. Well, just now in Austin, Clare is hardly wearing anything. She won't be getting up for another hour or two."

"And who's seven o'clock?"

"Yoshiko. Right now it's seven in Tokyo. I'd say she's in the middle of a rehearsal. You'd like Yoshiko."

"Why so?"

"You're both at least five hundred years old!"

"Go on." Francis smiled.

"It's nine in the evening in Copenhagen. Liselotte in her white coat is still wandering through the laboratory like a Bride of Frankenstein. I'm Frankenstein."

"Three girls!"

Father Francis wanted to have a normal conversation and to ask intelligent questions but was at a loss. The only questions that came to mind were the old formulaic ones from the confessional: Did you engage in immodest acts together? How many times?

"Do you ever go to visit them?" he asked.

"No. But I phone them every week at seven o'clock in the morning their time. It starts the week off on the right foot for all of us."

Father Francis nodded again. His efforts in pursuit of the social apostolate had more than once brought him into contact with the acceptable forms of lunacy.

"And what do you talk about?"

"What happened to them, what happened to me, the atom bomb, Northern Ireland, the Russians, contact lenses, the Gaia hypothesis . . . Have you ever listened to a beautiful woman talk intensely on some topic she feels passionate about? It could be anything from DDT to tarot cards. Forgive me, Father, but a man could get an erection just listening to a woman like that!"

Father Francis had never got an erection while listening to a beautiful woman. Or a man for that matter. It dawned on him, not for the first time, that he was born to indifference the way cuckoos are born to neglect their young. So he swallowed his tea and said humbly, "Could you tell me about it?"

Danny was only too eager. Except for Biafra O'Dee, he had never confided in anybody on the island. He jumped out of his armchair and went into the bedroom to reemerge with an old Jacob's biscuit tin stuffed with photographs.

"Take Liselotte!" He pulled out a crinkled photo of a moody girl with dark blond curls.

The Daimon of Ethna

✒ "Take Liselotte!"

Ethna felt the shock of the name running through her as she stood in the porch unseen by the two men. She was accursed. After seven years of disengagement from Danny, of being sure she had outgrown him, at times forgetting about his very existence, she found herself spying on him once again.

She watched the two men as they bent over the photo of Liselotte. She could tell what they saw. They saw a Valkyrie in blue jeans with the remorseless gaze of someone who had never been hurt or rejected. She saw the woman she had once tried to be.

Her larval fifteen-year-old self had been possessed by Liselotte. Bits of Liselotte clung to her even now — her habit of blowing her hair off her forehead, her self-effacing smile at the end of a sentence, an occasional balletic perching on the toes and a slow swaying of her hips, especially if she was wearing a pleated skirt.

Stealthily, Ethna moved back to the garden. She searched out her old seat on the swing that hung from a branch of the only sycamore tree on the island. Every time she plunged forward she was enveloped in a fragrant mist of honeysuckle, so she timed her breathing to the upward stroke of the swing.

Her memory of Liselotte's first appearance on Uggala had composed itself into a David Lean sequence. Bare pewter gray crags, an immense silver sky, and crossing left to right, a slim girl in khaki shorts carrying a red plastic bucket. And Danny's eyes under a peaked cloth cap lighting up and following the apparition to where the sea broke in a blizzard of spray.

Were the camera to pull back further it would find a teenage Ethna, her father, Colm, and Danny, fitting together the bits and pieces of a cloudbuster.

Danny had always been determined to do something big. He thought the biggest thing would be to change the weather on Uggala. It had been pouring nonstop for months, and the rain was coming out of everybody's ears. So Danny got a book by Wilhelm Reich on how to build a weather-changing machine and persuaded Colm to invest in the frame and metal pipes.

There was no point whatever in going for mediocre ambitions on an island like this.

Though at first skeptical about the technical side of the contraption, Ethna was enchanted by the idea. In her mind's eye she had already planted palm trees on the embankment of the Danes' Fort. She luxuriated in the warm sands of the coral beach under an impossible kitschy blue sky. So after the strange girl passed across the horizon and Danny muttered something about having to lift his lobster pots, Ethna felt nauseous with despair.

It was not the kind of despair that was content to retreat to a dark room and brood. It had to know the facts, to torment itself with them, and to drink the very last dregs of degrading truth.

Danny was so intent on his prey that he never as much as glanced over his shoulder. He put on a spurt as he neared the cliff overlooking Moinin Bay. His body went slack. Nobody there. He turned and headed back for the Yellow Strand, his long black coat and blue scarf appearing and disappearing behind the crags. In his excitement he knocked the stones off the tops of walls and never paused to replace them.

Ethna was breathless. Would anybody ever run as heedlessly after her?

She had kept closer to the cliff edge than Danny and saw the tent first. It was tiny and had a few T-shirts strung out to dry on the guy ropes. Far out, on a sandbar, stood the blond girl. She was absorbed in watching the incoming tide. No, she was calling out in a singsong voice to a seal who poked his black head out of the waves.

Ethna saw the danger at once. The sandbar was islanded by inrushing currents, which could turn treacherous in a matter of minutes. Some said Tom's boy had drowned there, caught in a turbulent vortex of water and sand. Ethna felt a surge of malicious joy.

"Come out of that!" she heard Danny shouting. "Come out!"

The girl turned and waved her acquiescence.

That image would plague Ethna for years: Liselotte, her hair blown forward across her face, wading thigh-deep through the channel, like a sea nymph, like a siren, like a Lorelei, towards Danny.

From the moment Liselotte turned and glanced upwards at Danny, Ethna's sole purpose in life became to know in devastating detail what was going on between them. She lay in ambush behind stone walls and under Danny's window. She lurked in the long grass of Danny's Thinking Place and ran ahead of them like a hare. She went to the mainland and bought herself a pair of binoculars with the money for her fifteenth birthday. All to see in close-up what gestures, smiles, and glances ensnared Danny.

There were many torments to treasure over the next fortnight.

Liselotte, in Danny's shirt, which is miles too big for her, curls up in front of the fire with a mug of tea clasped in her hands. Danny stands in a snowstorm of feathers and down, in one hand a plucked goose, the big white Toulouse he killed especially for her. She reaches out, and her hand closes over the weightless white fluff of his infatuation as it drifts past her.

"Is there children on the island?"

"Are there children on the island? I'm afraid we ran out of children a long time ago. No, I'm wrong. There's a girl called Ethna."

Danny leads Liselotte over the fields to his Thinking Place. The larks thrill in the air above them. He is as puffed up as an Aborigine escorting a white woman to the tribal initiation grounds. She looks around. There's nothing there. But she's kind and listens and nods attentively as he explains the magical significance of bush and stone. But then the biologist in her takes over. She hunkers down and examines the herbage.

"I know why you like this place," she exclaims. "It's a living pharmacy!"

This is our place, festers Ethna, sprawled on a patch of clover. It was our secret.

Liselotte flings around the Latin words for plants and flowers. She gives things their proper names. Danny repeats them, marveling. It becomes the White Woman's Place.

Danny and Liselotte dash through the rusty heart of Uggala in pursuit of a green-veined white. Liselotte chases the butterfly. Danny chases Liselotte. Ethna chases Danny. If Danny catches Liselotte he will . . .

Ethna won't allow it. All her suppurating jealousy is leveled like a laser at Liselotte from behind a turf bank. Liselotte screams out as she falls, her foot caught in a snare.

Ethna feels ugly and full of power.

Hours later the black magic boomerangs and turns against her. Ethna must watch Liselotte lying on Danny's bed with her leg propped up. She must watch Danny playing doctor.

He brings Liselotte a mug of chamomile tea. Peremptorily he puts his hand on her forehead to check her temperature. Liselotte keeps his hand there with her hand. Her pain is gone, she says. Danny has healing hands, just like her grandmother from Jutland.

Ethna has to watch, to bear Danny's hands traveling over Liselotte's willing body. The lobster pot on which she balances gives way with a crash. She runs into the night. Has he seen her?

He stands in the open window and leans out.

"Who is it?" he says softly. "Ethna, are you there?"

The Daimon of Ethna

❧ "Ethna, are you there?"

The creaking of the swing as the iron rings bit their way into the sycamore bough brought Danny to the door. Ethna looked like a plump pigeon rocking herself back and forth under a sky of milky stars.

The last time the swing had creaked like that under Danny was when Yoshiko sat astride him with her red dress bundled up over her thighs and her legs wrapped round his waist. Her abandoned panties mushroomed like the fruitbody of destroying angel at the root of the tree.

Better not think too much about that.

"I didn't want to disturb you," said Ethna, still swinging.

Danny held the rope. "Come in. I've been waiting for you."

Ethna was uneasy. The room still gravid with the ghostly presence of Liselotte. She was angry with Father Francis for just being there. And for the fact that he had noticed her quick furtive glance at the clocks on the mantelpiece and the sudden flush on her cheeks.

He could go and take a running jump at himself as far as she was concerned.

"I believe you've met Father Francis," said Danny. "Why don't you sit down?"

Ethna remained standing.

"Sorry to interrupt," she said once again, "but I need a camper. Can you help me get one?"

Calmly Danny poured her a cup of tea.

"A caravan? I see. A two-wheeler? Four wheels? Up on blocks? With or without an indoor toilet? And will that be a long-term or a short-term lease, Miss Ethna?"

"It has to have everything. It's for me and the twins."

"You're off your head!" said Danny.

"OK, I'll go to Tom." Ethna turned on her heel.

"Hold on!" said Danny. "Did they throw you out?"

Father Francis stood up. "I think I'll be on my way."

"I wish I was dead," Ethna whispered.

"Jesus!" Danny grabbed her by her shoulders and pressed her into a chair. "You can always stay here if you want to."

To stay at Danny's. In the best little whorehouse in the West of Ireland. To lie in the bed where Liselotte lay. To touch the piano keys that Yoshiko touched. To covet the hugs that Clare loved.

"No thank you," said Ethna.

"Do you really have nowhere to go?" Father Francis was concerned.

"I suppose there's always the home for fallen women," said Ethna uncertainly. "What's it called? The Magdalene Laundry?"

"Not anymore. If there's anything I can do . . . ," said Father Francis helplessly.

"You can't."

"Well, I could always . . ." Father Francis made an embarrassed gesture. He hadn't the courage to say, "I could always say a prayer."

"You pity me, but you despise me, don't you?"

Danny was startled by Ethna's continental brazenness. His

memory of her was of a pious schoolgirl in a blue Sunday frock. "What on earth has come over you, Ethna?" he asked.

"I'm fucked. So I've been thinking a lot. Sorry, Father."

"Maybe you see yourself too much as a victim? Or martyr?" suggested Danny.

"A victim? It's beyond that! It has nothing to do with me feeling a victim or not. It's the people here who expect me to be one! That's the only way for me to pay for my sins. There's no other role for me. Isn't that right, Father?"

"Sorry to be nosy, but why did you come back?" asked Father Francis.

"Because I lacked imagination," said Ethna with vicious pleasure.

"So you're going to live in a camper on a headland on an island off another island on the edge of Europe," mused Danny. "What do you think, Father? Maybe we have a new kind of saint here? The Blessed Ethna of Uggala, Hermit and Mother of Twins?"

"We'll need her to perform one or two miracles first." Father Francis grinned.

Ethna wanted to call them a pair of bastards and leave. But she also wanted the camper. Even more than being pissed off or wanting a camper she wanted to cry. But she could hardly cry in front of a stranger like Father Francis. So she swooped on him like a tern on a smelt.

"Very well, Father. What would you do in my place?"

"Me?"

"Yes. You're pregnant, destitute, nobody will give you a job, and worse, the only people that love you hate you!"

Father Francis watched Ethna's finger stray up and down the cracks and fissures on the table. The finger had a will of its own as it traced the stains and vicissitudes of Danny's life engraved in the wood.

He had no answer to Ethna's question.

"What would you do?" Ethna turned to Danny.

"Me? I'd stay with Danny Ruane if I was you. I'd offer to cook him the odd dinner and teach him Italian in exchange for bed and board."

Ethna nodded and gazed defiantly at Father Francis.

"I don't really know," the priest said apologetically. "I suppose I would pray."

"Of course you would!" said Ethna. "You know when I stopped praying? It was Christmas of 'eighty-five. In the Vatican in fact. I was walking round the inside of the cupola of Saint Peter's looking down on these tiny . . . minute specks of people below me in the aisles. And it suddenly dawned on me that this was what the Church means. Power. Vanity. It was obscene. There was no way I could relate this pomp to Christ in Palestine. I simply couldn't. And then when I climbed down there were these men in dresses. The monsignori with purple piping on their soutanes, and purple socks and . . . How could anybody ever imagine this bombast having anything to do with the Gospel?"

"So you think Luther was right after all?" asked Father Francis.

"No. I don't think any of these men were right. And I won't pray to the God to whom they prayed either."

Ethna's prisoner-of-war pallor and gauntness and her hungry eyes perplexed Danny. She was no longer the teenage girl who'd helped him to assemble the cloudbuster. He was excited by her cynicism and the tormented vehemence with which she spoke.

"Is there anything you believe in?" asked Father Francis.

Ethna cradled her chin in her hand and thought hard.

While she was thinking, Thresheen and myself gave her a good kick. But Ethna only put her hand on her belly and ignored us. She kept up an island tradition by answering one question with another.

"What do you have faith in?"

"In my vocation."

"What if you fell in love?"

"I would still be a priest." A broad, warm smile lit Father Francis's face. It eased the carved inhuman perfection of his features and made him mischievous and approachable.

Ethna smiled back before she knew what she was doing. His was one of those rare smiles that entices a smile from others as if striking an atavistic cord from childhood. Involuntarily, almost in a panic, Ethna wondered what it would be like to make love to Father Francis. And then, looking over at Danny, to both of them. She gazed at the two men with such hot impure eyes that they were suddenly abashed. And she, abashed by their bashfulness, dropped her eyes in turn.

"I'll get you a camper," muttered Danny. "You can preach your heresies to the choughs on the cliffs below."

Nervously, Father Francis gulped his fifth cup of tea. His unease was due less to the whirlwind of pheromones in the kitchen air and more to Ethna's brutal clarity. He was a man who preferred to live with hazy doubts rather than endure the pain of strong certainties. Six foot down, in his quiet grave, he could hear the body snatchers getting to work above him with spade and crowbar, determined to prize him out and expose him to merciless light. He remembered Father Kyne telling him before he set out for Uggala: Lucky you. Now that you're off to an arsehole of a parish, you'll have peace and quiet to the end of your days. No hures and no hustle.

But from what Father Francis had seen on his first day, Uggala was worse than any inner-city parish. There was a man with what? Five lovers? An unmarried girl with a belly as big as a haystack. And a devil in possession of the Parochial House. What worse was to come?

Biafra O'Dee was to come.

The Daimon of Father Francis

🐌 Biafra O'Dee's delicate worn face, bleached out by decades of self-abuse, gave Father Francis a start when it loomed above the geranium pot in the window.

Even though it was summer, Biafra wore a shrunken overcoat, a scarf woven tightly around his scrawny neck, and a peaked cloth cap. He stood in the doorway and batted his eyelids apologetically.

"Sorry sorry, I didn't know you had company," he said in a plaintive voice. "I'll come back another time. No. . . . Wait. . . . Do you have any junk food by any chance? Something like chips or ginger biscuits . . ."

"Biafra, this is Father Francis," said Danny, pouring him a cup of tea. "And of course you remember Ethna."

"Oh oh oh, nice to meet you, Father," said Biafra and gave Father Francis a cold limp hand. Then he glanced at Ethna, and his face grew long with amazement.

"Ethna! Oh, Ethna Ethna Ethna!"

He began to pant like a thirsty lapdog. "I thought you were dead!"

"I'm not far off, Biafra. How's life treating you?"

"Terrible! Complete full-blown anemia! Not a red corpuscle left in my corpse. It's absolutely dreadful! I can't eat anything but junk food. The worst kind of trash and refuse."

Biafra always berated himself in an imperious tone that refused to tolerate any contradiction. Father Francis had the impression that it was less self-critique than an indignant accusation directed at some malign force in the universe.

"I've been wretched for weeks," Biafra ranted. "But what do you expect if you eat nothing but sausages, biscuits, and tinned rice pudding? What can anybody expect for God's sake?"

He settled himself in a corner and dipped a ginger biscuit into his tea. He timed the dunk precisely so that the biscuit was soaked but didn't disintegrate.

"You have an original name," said Father Francis lamely.

Biafra squawked.

"It's my bony looks. It was the famine in Eastern Nigeria that the lads in the post office stuck on me. I like it. A bit of euphony. It's a damn sight better than Phoncy, short for Alphonsus."

"I'm glad you've dropped in, Biafra," said Danny. "We have a decision to make."

Biafra held out his dripping biscuit and panted again.

"Make a decision, any decision now! Anything that you start on today will be a roaring success." He glanced at his watch. "You have one hour and fifteen minutes before Saturn savages Venus."

Not for the first time Father Francis caught a glimpse of the old pagan gods reemerging on Uggala. Was it not his duty to protest? To say something in the name of the One Holy Catholic and Apostolic Church?

He said nothing.

The Daimon of Biafra O'Dee

෴ Biafra O'Dee was the man who explained to Father Francis that the day he arrived on Uggala coincided with a Timesurge. Timesurges are much rarer than two moons in a month. They happen once in thirty years or so to normal people (geniuses of course are something else). On such days life accelerates to an all-time high. You might, for example, win the lottery in the morning, meet the president at noon, be promoted at 3:00 P.M., and get laid by Barbra Streisand or Robert De Niro before nightfall. For thirty years you've waited and waited for something to happen. And all of a sudden, zap, you are in the middle of a Timesurge. There's a torrent of astonishing events and people coming your way.

But be warned! The next day you could be run over by a double-decker bus in O'Connell Street or choke to death on a wishbone.

Why it happens like that God only knows. Or maybe he doesn't?

What for Father Francis was a Timesurge for Biafra was just another normal day with all his stars teetotally fucked up. According to Biafra himself, his stars were to remain in this abject condition for the next six years. So the less he did the better.

On the second of June he got up as usual around noon and thereby missed the arrival of the mailboat. Every day during the summer season he promised himself to go down to the quay and cast a lascivious eye over the female tourists. He was getting tired, as he put it to himself, of the ride less ridden. But once again he had failed. So, muttering and cursing to himself, he heated a pot of linseed oil to body temperature, donned a pair of thick yellow rubber gloves, and began to rub the oil into his gaunt frame. That done he consumed two spoons of Amrit Kalash made of seventy-four herbs from the Himalayas and drank a pint of warm water mixed with ginger. Only then was he ready for his breakfast of fried bread, Roscrea sausages, and white pudding. He spent the rest of the day writing a song entitled "No Hole No Holiness" and devising a horoscope for Charlie Haughey.

Once in Bewley's in Grafton Street he met, not at all by chance, an Indian sage who explained to him the difference between Oriental and Western astrology. The Western variety was pure crap, the swami said. The kinds of horoscopes you find in women's magazines and in the Sunday *Times* with warnings like "On Monday Pluto forces issues so you have little choice but to take action" — these were an obscenity. Predicting the future had nothing at all to do with mushy in-

stincts, intuitions, or clairvoyance. It was an exact mathematical science, and there were computer programs available
if Biafra was interested.

After some months of intense study and vast expenditure,
Biafra had his first success. He foretold, to the hour, the break-
down of a temporary IRA cease-fire. Nothing could stop him
from then on.

His mind was in incessant turmoil, processing vast quanti-
ties of data and translating the results into elaborate graphs.
Every day he went to work in his own stellar stock market,
which soared or crashed according to galactic trends. He could
work only in fifteen-minute spurts because he tired easily
despite the linseed oil and the Amrit Kalash, and he had
to piss frequently on account of all the ginger and water he
drank. The vegetation within a hundred yards of his cottage
had cankered and turned yellow as a result.

Biafra was essentially a city man. But when his mother
died and left him a house on the island, he lacked the energy
to return to Dublin after the funeral. Besides, he felt comfortable on Uggala because almost everybody there was on
disability benefit and he didn't stand out as a wastrel. The
only obvious disadvantages were the annual seven months'
period of sexual abstinence and no Bewley's to mull over a
coffee in the long afternoons. Biafra compensated by visiting
Danny and quizzing him on his various exploits. Many of
these sessions of erotic revelations and lies ended up with Biafra insulting Danny: Who do you think you are anyway?
Golden Balls?

Older women were particularly fond of him because he
took the time to talk to them, each one resembling by the
mere fact of age and illness his sainted mother. Not to mention the fact that he was a regular churchgoer and carried a
first-class relic of Padre Pio on the inside of his lapel, which
he flashed on appropriate occasions.

Men pitied him and made snide remarks about his feebleness and the trousers at half-mast. But their spite was premature and would finally turn to bitter envy. Biafra knew with utter certainty that behind his own fusterings and disabilities lurked a genius that would be revealed to everybody in 1995. Uggala was essential to his renewal, and so Biafra clung to the island like a limpet to a piece of rotten timber.

The Daimon of Thresheen

Thresheen was enthralled by Biafra O'Dee's addiction to the planets and stars. "Just look at his tricks," she said. "He's trying to outwit Saturn and Pluto!"

I was skeptical. I thought he was surrendering his freedom to the Astrological Empire.

Though we both adhered to the Daimonic view that life is a personal search to recover the forgotten destiny of the soul, Thresheen was drawn to the wheels-within-wheels of Biafra's determinism. Her little half-formed heart went out to the oppressed and the downtrodden overwhelmed by powerful systems. Had she been born slightly earlier, she would have been a Bolshevik or a terrorist with the Sendero Luminoso. The world in which the great causes were either dead or about to be unmasked as mere facades for power and greed weakened even further her desire to join the humans. When I tried to argue with her, she bristled like a sea urchin and spread her cloudy gray venom to Mother.

The Daimon of Concepta

Once Colm O'Keefe discovered that his only daughter was living in a camper down by the shore like any common tinker, he fell into a Fomorian rage. It was one thing for that streel of human misery to leave home at sixteen and head off for Rome or I don't know where. At least he could spread the word that she was studying art or continental languages. But it was another thing entirely to shit on her own doorstep.

He tried to persuade Ethna to give up this tomfoolery and come home. But she stuck to her guns: she wouldn't return until her mother made peace with her.

Concepta was in a bind. She couldn't accept her prodigal daughter. But she couldn't accept the scandal of her camper delinquency either. She felt totally outplayed by Ethna. Before this she had garnered sympathy for herself for having a wild and heedless child. Now she was the monster who denied roof and shelter to her own flesh and blood. But the mere thought of relenting filled her with dread. Just as she had learned to derive strength from her blighted hopes with regard to Colm, so for the past seven years, she had fed herself on rancor for Ethna. She became attached to her disillusionments. She told herself over and over again the same anguished story: she had been wronged by Colm, she had been wronged by her daughter, humiliated by everybody. Her torment made her impervious to any other story. How could she abandon just like that the grievances that had kept her going for twenty years and still be Concepta?

The Daimon of Ethna

When Ethna moved to Rinneroon, to the little humpbacked camper on the shore, she was at first repelled by its dwarfishness. Like a homunculus, it had all its inner organs intact and to scale. There was a Formica-topped miniature table, a bench, a camping gas stove, a bunk bed laid along the back, and a pygmy washstand in the corner.

It humiliated her. She had to bow her head and to breathe in a vague semen-smell of bleach when she entered. She sprayed the air with her eau de cologne and brightened the table with a vase of brilliant blue cornflowers. If you sat at the table and focused on nothing else but the cornflowers, then the camper seemed habitable enough. So Ethna developed an art of looking only at what was pleasing: the flowers on the table, Danny's scarlet-and-black Japanese drape over the bed, and the seascape outside the window. She blocked out everything else.

The camper nestled against the flank of a drumlin that slumped into the sea. It was knee-deep in bracken, and there was a scraggy hawthorn hedge to one side visited by dainty squadrons of goldfinches and long-tailed tits. When Ethna moved in, the snow of the late hawthorn blossoms had begun to crumble. She withdrew into herself like a hermit crab into an empty whelk shell.

The Daimon of Danny Ruane

🐚 "Withdrawals aren't so bad," said Danny. "Incubation time. You know, Christ in the desert, Coleman MacDuagh on the Burren, Mad Max in the outback . . ."

He sat opposite Ethna at the Formica-topped table and looked around with what she must have known was forced enthusiasm. "You've made quite a job of this kip."

He didn't know how to console Ethna. He sensed that she had arrived at the X-ray stage of unhappiness, where she could see through layers of spurious flesh to the bare wretched bones and ligaments of things.

"Mad Max?" Ethna grimaced. "What about Danny Ruane?"

"I'm afraid he's not in the same league."

"What are you doing on Uggala?" She looked at him with a penetrating gaze that would abide no evasion.

"I suppose it's a good place to write 'Creation.' Short titles are in these days."

"I know all that. But why in this dreary damp place?"

"Why not?"

Danny looked out the window, aware of his own duplicity. "Next time I must bring my binoculars. There's some fantastic bird life out there on the shore."

"Answer me!" She was a child demanding a story. She would blackmail him with her despair. "Why didn't you stay on in Oxford?"

The answer to that question was like a snarled fishing line. Danny felt like breaking it rather than going to all the trouble of disentangling the loops and knots.

"You don't need to tell the truth, the whole truth, and nothing but the truth. You can lie a bit." Ethna smiled wryly.

It seemed to Danny that it wasn't the first time he had sat opposite Ethna in just this situation, in a small room suffused by a dying sun with the drawn-out, astringent calls of swifts and sand martins in the air. Ethna's pleading look mingled with disdain seemed familiar too.

In the everyday world in which they crossed one another's paths, he would have broken the tangled line and given her a short answer. But in the archaic half-light in which they found themselves, he felt compelled to unravel the knots.

"OK, I was doing research in physics, dynamic systems and chaos if you must know. It's not for nothing that Hitler chose Oxford as his headquarters if he were to take England. You know — the devil's longing to be in Paradise. Only what Hitler didn't realize was that when the devil does get into Paradise it's worse for him than being in Hell. He can't breathe the rarefied air. The very grass rejects him.

"I felt a bit like that myself when I first saw the deer park in Magdalen. Acres of smooth lawn, ancient trees, and tame deer browsing by the Cherwell. Christ! What had I to do with all that? I hated Oxford for never being devastated or humiliated. For standing so haughty and unperturbed through seven centuries. How it separated itself so completely from the destruction visited on so many other places!"

"So did you go to England to hate it or to study?" asked Ethna.

"Good question. By the way, there's a plaque in the Bodleian to commemorate benefactors to the library from around the mid-1600s on. One of them was the landlord who despoiled Uggala. Ne * tantorum * beneficiorum * memoria * obsolescat. I saw how easily beauty and violence consort together.

"I had lodgings in Plantation Street. Plantation Street, for God's sake! For the locals the name was probably all about a grove of beech trees. For me it was the rape of Ulster and Munster. So many foul deeds stifled in the heavy fragrance of laurel blossom in patrician gardens."

"So you jacked it all up?" asked Ethna. He was getting too lyrically self-pitying for her taste.

Danny shook his head. "It was difficult. On the one hand I was doing the kind of research I couldn't do in Ireland. On the other hand I was haunted by intuitions for which there was no place at the University. And then I had what I call my 'American moment.'" Danny smiled. "Though it happened in Oxford, you could never call it an English moment. It was, well, ferociously unempirical. On a wet spring afternoon on a half-deserted Broad Street, I suddenly became aware of the pavement at my feet. It seemed to have liquefied and shed its stoniness. Below me there was another city, complete with pale ocher palaces, spires, and spreading trees. I knew of course that it was a reflection in the wet stone. Yet it was much more than that. It was Dante's 'Look down and see how great a universe I've put beneath thy feet.'

"I was filled with an extraordinary sense that the Oxford below and above, the cars and bicycles by the pavement, were all part of the same living unity. If only I could prove it, I mean prove it mathematically."

Danny paused as if to renew his purpose with the memory of that afternoon.

"Wasn't Oxford just the right place to do the job?"

"No. My ideas were too off-the-wall. Besides there was something else."

"A woman," said Ethna flatly.

"Lots of women." Danny grinned. "Smart women like nettles with a kind of pent-up stinginess in them. Well, it was a cause. I was collecting money for the IRA and the struggle in the North."

Ethna blanched.

Danny stood up and opened the door. "It's getting very close in here."

When he returned to the table he avoided Ethna's gaze.

"Yep. Our famous Freedom Struggle. Well, I was home on holidays and I went to Belfast to meet some contacts. We met in a drinking club. There was this guy being feted in a corner, a fat slob who hadn't washed or shaved for days. He had just come back from shooting two retired policemen. The thugs around couldn't buy enough drink for him. A local hero. It made me sick. A few days later a car bomb went off in the street. It literally lifted me off my feet. It's odd how these things work. At first I felt no connection between my own activities and the butchery. Like everybody else on the street, I was in shock. I thought: The bastards who did this should be strung up from the lampposts. Then, when I got home, it dawned on me. I was a part of the killing machine too."

Danny drummed his fingers on the tabletop.

"Some combination! Dreaming of the grand synthesis and supporting murder and mayhem. A bit like the Nazi desk killers. So that life ended in August 'seventy-eight."

"How ended?" Ethna's gray eyes, previously weary and indifferent, had come alive.

"I dropped everything for over a year. I walked round Oxford feeling as if a bottle of chlorine had been poured into my skull, bleaching and scouring every bud of thought and desire."

"Poor Danny," said Ethna.

"Poor Danny indeed. One day I was sitting in the Mitre with a fellow who had just come back from abroad. 'You're a lucky sod to be from Ireland,' he said enviously. 'Life is real there, like in Nicaragua. There's blood on the streets. People take issues seriously. Not like this torpid hole, where nobody gives a toss about anything except their pension rights.'"

"'Most people most places would give their right hand to live in your torpid hole,' I said. He looked at me as if a serious conversation wasn't possible with me anymore. But he was still in pursuit of reality. Had I noticed the gorgeous girl in the corner? She was an expensive whore. One could have her for a hundred pounds.

"The girl was poring over a sheaf of photocopies. I'd never seen anybody so absorbed in my life. So I went up to her and asked her what was so enthralling. She handed me a sheet with a translation of a poem by Rumi. You'd like the situation. I was in deep shit. The whore was all got up in tight leather. The Victorian-style translation of the Sufi master was atrocious. And yet from the moment I read the verse I felt an extraordinary consolation. Don't you want to hear it?"

Danny didn't wait for Ethna's reply.

Every form you see has its archetype in the placeless world;
If the form perished, no matter, since its original is ever-
    lasting.
Every fair shape you have seen, every deep saying you
    have heard,
Be not cast down that it perished; for that is not so.
Whereas the spring-head is undying, its branch gives
    water continually;
Since neither can cease why are you lamenting?

"It all sounds very Platonic," said Ethna dubiously.
"For God's sake, Ethna. Almost everything that's interesting is Platonic. The rest is mainly sociology."

"Do you tell me now?"

"Well, it became clear to me that the only way forward was back. Back to the springhead and to the well at the world's end."

Danny's face seemed younger, and his voice bubbled with excitement. He liked this part of his story.

"What I had to do was reverse the direction of the fairy tale so to speak. I was already living happily ever after in what Hardy called the 'city of light.' I had to retrace my steps back to the proverbial poor cottage in a forest or by a lonely seashore. I thought of Granny's old house on Uggala. It had everything. Rain, rock, silence, solitude. A place where I could grow my own thoughts in secret."

"Like marijuana?" suggested Ethna. "But why this dying island? I still don't get it."

"It's not dying. It changes all the time. Like your face. It's got ontological flexibility."

Danny plonked down the philosophical phrase in front of her on the table like an ungainly crab.

"Bullshit," said Ethna.

"OK. Maybe I feel it's the only place I can write my book. I don't need to pretend to be sane here. And I don't need to look for a job since there aren't any. I have all the time in the world to do what I want. And maybe I'm a hermit at heart?"

Ethna stared at him. With his red locks and huge frame, he looked like Bacchus painted by Caravaggio. It was hard to imagine him as a hermit.

"So. That's my story. I hope you find it uplifting. May I have a fresh cup of tea now?"

As Ethna put on the kettle, Danny was struck once again by the sense that they were two shipwrecked travelers from a different time and space.

"You know what? I wonder if what you say really happened," said Ethna. "I find it hard to believe that it's true. Your angelic whore and all."

"Even if it never happened it's true," said Danny.

Just like his feeling that he and Ethna had met a long long time ago.

The Daimon of Concepta

❧ There are many pathways that lead a pleasant, pretty young woman to the point when she becomes a total bitch. Her man, lingering over a pint of shandy, questions himself: Was she always like this and I didn't notice? Or did I drive her to it?

Concepta had followed a well-trodden Irish path to Tír-na-Meán Aoise, the Land of Middle Age. She had married O'Keefe at eighteen in a little chapel brimming with wide-eyed dog daisies. Her mother had filled every nook and cranny with the midsummer wildflower in one last attempt to bolster up her daughter's virginity. She suspected that Concepta had lost it four months previously in the backseat of Colm's VW after a dance in the Parish Hall.

The wedding photo shows a triumphant Concepta in a long white chiffon dress accompanied by a dazed bridegroom in a hired dinner jacket.

Colm had everything that a million Conceptas think they hanker after in a man. He was drop-dead gorgeous, self-confident, had a vicious tongue, and owned his own business. A photograph from the Canaries shows a lithe, dark-haired Concepta in a brimstone yellow bikini, obliviously happy, only half aware of Colm in his Honolulu shirt reading the sports section of *The Sun*.

It's difficult to pinpoint the exact time, place, or reason for Concepta's slide into lovelessness. It's a little like trying to find the causes for a cold: Is it the wind? Wet feet? Late nights? Contagion? Or is it all in one's head?

The more scrupulous Concepta was about being Colm's

wife — combating spiderwebs, hastening her orgasms, feign-
ing girlish naïveté — the more he seemed to withdraw from
her into a male world of his own. He was always going somewhere: to Cheltenham, Punchestown, or Tralee. He threw
away massive sums of money on dogs and horses, eager for an
erotic paroxysm of loss that was completely beyond Concepta's understanding. When she spoke to her mother about
her growing anxiety, she was assured that Colm was perfectly
normal. Sure wasn't it right and proper for a man to be interested in sports and horses? What did she expect? For the
male race, marriage was only a distraction at best. A distraction and little more. How many of them knew why they got
married at all? Very few, very few indeed. It was only years
down the road and maybe after a bout or two in the regional
hospital that some discovered why they had wives and children in the first place.

But by the time Ethna was born nothing seemed normal
anymore to Concepta. She was like one of those injured pigeons you sometimes see huddled on an open road. You can't
tell whether they have a broken wing or neck or leg. They just
huddle and breathe and wait. What to do with them? Lift
them? Nurse them? Break their necks to shorten their suffering? Leave them be for the neighborhood cats?

For a full six months Concepta felt like a stricken pigeon
on the side of the road. And Colm was the passerby who didn't
know what to do and drove on.

When spring came, she obeyed the seasonal call to get
up and get busy. She washed down the house, threw out the
accumulated rubbish of three generations, and carried Ethna
to see the first primroses and cowslips under the hedge.
She wanted to be kissed by Colm again, but now it was his
turn to be anxious and resigned. He no longer went to Cheltenham, Punchestown, or Tralee, and found his only release
in playing with Ethna. The more he hardened himself against
Concepta the more she hardened herself against him until

they were like a pair of iron tongs clanging dully against one another.

One day as they clashed again, Concepta overcame her fear and asked him, simply, What's the matter?

"Nothing," he said. "I'm bankrupt. I'll have to sell the place."

It wasn't a long conversation. But it made Concepta go down to the pub and frantically comb through countless accounts, bank statements, and the bailiff's notice of eviction. She spent the night adding and subtracting and writing misspelt letters to creditors to pleese delay their axions. The following morning she sat down her husband with a mug of hot sweet tea and presented her plan. We sell that bit of land for sites. We knock down the dividing wall of the pub to make more space and get in a few musicians at night. We get Nana to live with us and rent out her place in the summer. And you get an allowance of twenty pounds a week and not a red penny more.

If Colm had only known the quaking depth of fear and uncertainty that filled Concepta as she lay down the law to him, he would have demolished her with a brutal guffaw. But what he saw in front of him was a new, steely woman, with hard unyielding eyes and a clenched jaw.

"It's either that," she said, "or you go to work in England."

He was like a bull befuddled by a toreador. He hung his head and pawed the ground in helpless fury. He decided that overnight Concepta had turned into a bitch like her crabby ould mother before her. Black cat, black kitten. Why hadn't he seen it from the start? Once he made up his mind that his wife was a bitch, nothing would budge him, even though Concepta's salvage operation was only the first of two acts of open defiance in the whole of their married life.

Over the next few months Concepta concentrated on two things: feeding Ethna and putting O'Keefe & Sons back on its feet. She found in herself a disquieting talent for making money, a talent which Colm both needed and resented. It didn't require any schooling in economics or management. It came to her as naturally as weaving a web to a spider. She knew instinctively where to invest, when to move, when to wait, who to approach, and how best to chat them up.

Had Concepta O'Keefe accepted her aunty May's offer to move to Los Angeles and taken up a job in a cat food factory, she would have advanced from assistant floor manager to executive secretary to financial director within three years. Within five years she would have bought up five other companies, moved to computers, and invested her surplus millions in the Star Wars trilogy. She would have crashed three marriages and acquired a stalker. As the Emerald Tycoon she would have been in constant demand for interviews by the business section of *The Irish Times* and for RTE programs on how to be an entrepreneur. Readers of celebrity journals would have grown familiar with her low décolletage, silver fox furs, auburn hair, and surgically classical profile.

Had she followed her Daimon and stepped into this glittering alternative reality, she would have been a glorious success — but just as loveless as in the gray mist of Uggala.

The Daimon of Ethna

❧ By July the fortunes of the O'Keefes had become Uggala's favorite soap. Will Concepta do the decent thing and take back her hure of a daughter? Will Ethna stick it out or traipse back home with her tail between her legs? Will Colm's blood pressure go through the roof? And what was it like to be up the pole in a camper on a windy shore?

After a visit to Dr. Greelish on the mainland and a large intake of Istin, Colm calmed down and decided to give Ethna a job in the bar. He belonged to the tribe of men who are vicious by nature but become kind under duress. He even added the odd tenner to Ethna's weekly pay packet.

Thresheen and I were silent most of the time. We had almost stopped moving. We felt the weight of Ethna's burden as she trudged home in the evening with bags of groceries cutting the palms of her hands. We smarted under the lash of the briers and bracken on the path to the camper. And our hearts went out to her as she cooked up her solitary supper on the camping stove while trying to ignore the geriatric mumblings of the sea. She would watch the waste of the evening and masochistically, for the umpteenth time, go through her own broken autobiography. Once she had a future. Now she was goalless and aimless. Once she languished on a vine-robed terrace under the polished azure sky of Cercina. Now she endured the weeping wind muttering unfinished sentences and hurting itself against the windowpanes. Where could she possibly go from here?

Late in the evening, when everything was enveloped in darkness and only the foxes were prowling through the bracken, she sat at the aluminum table and called out for Danny. She repeated his name over and over again in her head. She wanted him to come and say something, make a gesture, just be with her.

Danny was deaf to her sorcery. But he called all the same. When he hunched his huge frame into the camper, she felt relieved and soothed for a few moments. But then she was unable to talk to him. She was ugly, ungainly, and fat as a seal. She could hardly utter a sentence because she feared that it would be as clumsy and lumpy as herself.

Danny was solicitous and brotherly. He brought her flasks of mouth-wrying nettle and wormwood tea, which she drank dutifully. But never to the bottom. She always kept a few bitter drops for later.

"Why do you bother with me?"

Danny ignored the dark half-moons under her eyes and the

grimace of self-absorbed grief on her lips. "Because I'm an old idiot. Because I like the dauntlessness of your soul."

"I don't have a soul."

Her eyes were scalding.

Danny dropped his head for a moment. Ethna knew with an inner groan that there was a bit of Sufi wisdom on the way.

There was.

"You know what Rumi said?"

He raised his head again and spoke in quotation marks with ornate capitals opening every beat.

"You have a duty to perform. Do anything else, do any number of things, occupy your time fully, and yet, if you do not do this task all your time will have been wasted."

"So what's my duty?"

"Isn't it pretty obvious? What are you going to call the lads?"

Ethna shrugged. "The twins."

"That's not very imaginative, Ethna. I once knew a French woman who called her dog Le Chien."

"What are you telling me?"

"Why don't we give the babies names? You can change them later if you find they don't fit."

"What's the point?"

"That way you're not just Ethna anymore. You're Ethna and, let me see. . . . What about Therese shortened to Thresheen after your grandmother? She was a decent ould skin. And Finn as in Finn McCool? We could do with a warrior on the island!"

"Thresheen and Finn!"

For the first time our mother imagined us as two real live human beings with their own identities.

"Finn and Thresheen," she repeated intently and chewed on an invisible poppy seed.

Danny had seen that preoccupied chewing motion many times before, but for the first time it registered on him. It was a throwback maybe to her grandmother or great-grandmother.

It was a gesture that countless generations of women in Ethna's line had repeated all the way back to Babylon. Danny wondered if Gilgamesh had noted that poppy seed chewing when he returned to his preoccupied concubine in Erech.

The Daimon of Biafra O'Dee

🐦 By the time August came around Biafra O'Dee realized that he hadn't had a decent shag in two years. He was hunched on a springless sofa in front of the television when an ad for yogurt brought Myriam tumbling back to him. Like the springy girl on the yogurt trampoline, Myriam had the stretchiness of a cat and the transparent skin of a Capricorn. He hadn't actually shagged her. He'd almost shagged her. My God, it was three and a half years since he'd had a shag, and he was probably lying to himself about that too.

Biafra was back to his almost world.

He had almost foretold to the day the date of Charlie Haughey's return to power. He had almost convinced Gerry Adams to take up TM (he still savored the day Gerry met him in Grafton Street, his hands outstretched to him as if he were parting the Red Sea). He had almost got a respectable job as a math teacher, but he blew it at the end of the interview by saying he was a Unionist. He had almost got a deal with a record company to produce his songs when some fat-arsed executive said they sounded too much like Bob Dylan crossed with a maimed loon. He had almost bought himself a car with the bit of American money from his aunt in Peabody, but he'd backed off at the last minute. He just knew he couldn't take the stress of driving.

Where was Auntie Madeleine's money now? Gone to swamis in India to pay for yagias. The yagias were a sort of spiritual chemotherapy to improve his chances of avoiding whatever disasters lay around the corners of time. If it wasn't for the yagias and maybe Alice's prayers, he would be in a county home by now being sexually abused by octogenarians.

His love chart was the same as that of W. B. Yeats. No wonder he was all fucked up and hadn't had a ride in five years.

Was it five years?

Drenched in his own desolation, Biafra switched off the television to save electricity. He wanted a woman. This evening. Now. There must be somebody who was dying for it coming over on the evening boat. Maybe an American country and western singer? Or an ex-nun trying to sort herself out?

Of course, of course, why hadn't he thought of it before?

The excitement drove him to throw back his shoulders and stick out his scrawny chest. He studied his gaunt intellectual profile in the stained mirror and decided that there was still a touch of Edwardian refinement and class about him. He took off his skimpy overcoat and donned the tweed jacket that Danny had given him when he lost interest in tweed. Then singing under his breath "The sun went down on Galway Bay/ But the daughter went down on me," he headed for the quay.

Halfway there he stopped, dumbfounded by his own lack of forward planning. He quarreled energetically with himself before he turned, much to his own disgust, back to Danny's.

Golden Balls Ruane had everything: sex on tap from foreign females, no ould lip from the wife or kids, oceans of time to write his bad prose. Even his despair was more respectable and sublime than Biafra's. When Danny was down, he read the Sufi masters. When Biafra was down, he read old copies of *Playboy* and ate junk food. But just now Biafra needed Danny.

He stood in the door panting and mumbling excuses.

"Biafra, for Jesus' sake, would you come to the point?"

How could he come to the point faced with this Greek fucking god with his locks newly washed and his highfalutin multipocketed waistcoat straining over his muscular torso? Biafra could feel the hatred for all that was healthy and normal rising in him.

"I was thinking of going down to meet the boat . . ."

"Good, good," said the Greek god like a feckin woodpecker.

"Maybe I could nail a few chicks or something? I haven't had a ride for seven months, you know."

"I'd go with you myself but I promised I'd call on Ethna."

Biafra sighed with relief and hesitated.

"Would you by any chance loan me a few spare condoms?"

Danny looked at him in disbelief. It was the first time that Biafra had broached the subject.

"I washed out my last half dozen or so. They're hanging to dry on the clothesline."

Biafra's face darkened.

"It's no joking matter, you big ugly galoot."

"What about coitus reservatus?" Danny asked. "Have you tried that?"

Biafra panted indignantly.

"After donkey's years of disengagement he wants me to have an almost shag! You have no idea, you have no idea what it's like to rot away on your own in front of the tits on a feckin television screen!"

Biafra turned on his heels and marched towards the quay. Coitus reservatus! He cursed Danny for his lack of sensitivity. But Danny's suggestion had opened up a range of alternative practices with which he could entertain himself until he lost the need to approach the women coming off the ferry. They could only spoil the unbridled orgy going on in his head.

The Daimon of Ethna

✒ Apart from Danny Ruane, Ethna didn't have many visitors to her plywood hermitage. Father Francis called twice, but fortunately for all of us, Ethna wasn't in. Once on her return from work she found a punnet of strawberries dangling from the doorknob. There was a postcard of poppy red Tuscan hills in spring and a calligraphed "Good wishes from Francis."

Ethna grabbed the strawberries and devoured them ravenously before stepping into the camper. She hardly glanced at the card.

Next time there was a Dunnes Stores shopping bag bulging with an old Walkman and tape of Vivaldi's music. The enclosed card showed the same rolling Tuscan hills, this time in autumn. Ethna was irritated by the perfect handwriting: it was ornamental and futile as Francis's own beauty.

One camper-and-pub day was much the same as another camper-and-pub day. Except for the odd visit to Alice to wash her clothes, Ethna's days were as like one another as the beads of an old rosary worn by piety and anguish.

Until one day she noticed Father Francis's Walkman where she had abandoned it on the fridge top. She turned it over in her hands uncertainly, put on the earphones, and switched it on. She went to the window, her head awash with music. Stately harmonies swept back and forth like a receding and returning wave. The wave gathered a sheen of light and silver before losing itself in her soul.

Our womb-world was transformed. For the previous few weeks it had been pokey and tasted of juniper berries. Now it had the brisk airiness of a sea breeze.

Ethna put her hands on her belly and smiled at the melody breaking on the shores of herself. She was pregnant with us. But the camper was pregnant too. It was a womb in which she was gestating. She would give birth not just to Thresheen and me but to herself as well.

From that evening she began to see things differently. Or rather she began to see things. She noticed for the first time the convolvulus that had entwined itself round the hawser that stretched across the camper. And the hunched plover scooting like clockwork toys among the stones. And the fiddle tops of the bracken, which smelled of almond when she crushed them.

She discovered a secretive, unfinished landscape that, unlike the ostentatious perfection of Tuscany, required completion by her imagination. It offered her clues to a totality that she tried to divine in her sketch pad.

After work she headed for Cnocnashee or Mahoney's Stack to sketch over and over again the amputated tower or the eroded face of the stone cliff. But that was only the beginning. She spent hours sitting with a ruined cottage or a field gone to thistles and docks until she found what they wished to become. There was a tired low bank that wanted to expire and disappear off the face of the earth, a wall that longed to be three feet higher, a derelict pier that dreamed of being a promenade crooking a protective arm around a marina. Ethna trembled with joy as she coaxed them forward into their new realizations. Sometimes she laughed and talked to her sketches like a madwoman.

Her drawings became more and more extravagant. If you looked close you could discern bits and pieces of the here and now — Danny's Thinking Place, O'Keefe's pub, the Parish Hall. But they were all transposed into the future where the native Fomorian crudity of the island melded with a four hundred years' delayed Renaissance and the high-tech materials of the twenty-first century. Under Ethna's transparent colonnades, you could walk from O'Keefe's pub to St. Mahoney's Church without once getting wet or being pummeled by the wind. And the church itself, instead of turning its back to the sea, had embraced the congregation of the waves and the plovery shore.

The odd tourist bent over Ethna's shoulder, curious as to what she was at, shook his head, and asked incredulously: Is that Uggala?

It was too much trouble to explain to every Tom, Dick, and Harry that it was Uggala's dream of itself.

The Daimon of Danny Ruane

↻ The Vivaldi sea that had transfixed Ethna with its stately swell held the promise of a spell of fine weather on Uggala. Before he went to bed, Danny greased the underside of his sailboard and inspected the seams and zips of his wet suit in ritual preparation for a day out on the bay.

He awoke with the sun on his face. He was determined to make this morning a work of art. He began by brewing the best Colombian coffee, hoarded since his last trip to Dublin, and drank it with hot milk and a pinch of chocolate. Since everything had to be slowed down and savored, he grated an apple into his oatmeal porridge and ate it with raw cane sugar and dollops of thick cream. Then, with a mug of coffee in his hand, he sat like a pasha on his rocking chair to relish the last delight of the morning, a phone call to Yoshiko.

This bright day it wouldn't matter if her world were to collide with his or her testiness baffle his serenity. He was as strong and merry as a mountain stream, he could dash and dazzle his way over any obstacle.

Yoshiko was nine hours ahead of him, nine hours of Tokyo smog, grinding rehearsals, and the conductor's arrogance.

"He's such a pig," she said in her singing voice. "Waving his spare dick in the air and being the Big Man. I hate him."

"Oho!" This was strong stuff coming from the gentle Yoshiko. "I think you've got this guy all wrong. I'm sure he just wants to make love to you."

"What?"

"Every man who looks at you wants to make love to you."

Yoshiko himmed and hawed in her evasive Japanese way.

"Why don't you just tell him to go to hell, or whatever your equivalent is?"

"Danny, this is Japan! Here I am a good obedient girl! You would not like me anymore if you saw me."

"You're in the wrong country then. You should be here with me today. I'd stretch you out on the red clover of my Thinking Place."

Danny knew that a touch of Christy Mahon went down well with foreign women.

"And then what?" There was a provocative chuckle in her voice.

"Then I'd lecture you on Aristotle's theory of fine arts."
"No!"

"Using your exquisite torso as an illustration. I'm afraid we'd have to have your clothes off."

"All of them?"

"We could leave the earrings on. . . . Look here, why don't you just drop everything and come over for the regatta in August?"

Again those Japanesy hims and haws.

"I'm getting myself into training for the Windsurfer race. I swear to Christ I'm going to beat the Bejesus out of Colm O'Keefe."

"I'll come in the autumn, when we play Stravinsky in London."

"It'll be stormy then."

"I'll come for you, not for the sea."

When he put down the phone Danny imagined himself and Yoshiko deliciously cocooned in a gingham duvet while a ravenous sea tore at the island. Ever so often Yoshiko's slight, amber body would slip from under the duvet and tiptoe to the bathroom. His mother's ghostly countenance, like the puff-cheeked god in the corner of a medieval map, would blow fire and brimstone across the sinful pillows.

When he opened the door Danny was momentarily

blinded by the brilliance of the sky and the sea and the fuch-
sias dripping blood on the wall. He loaded his homemade
buggy with his sailing gear, whistled for Sharik, and headed
for the beach at Oran's Well.

There were four black shags perched on rocks out in the
bay. Danny liked their Austro-Hungarian imperiousness as
they stood there dead still with their wings held out to dry,
their heads averted from the meanness beneath them.

There was somebody else watching them through a pair of
binoculars.

At first Danny didn't recognize the well-built man in the
white sweater and slacks against the glare.

"Hello Danny. I see you're taking the day off."

It was the first time he had seen Francis in casual clothes.
All the priestliness had evaporated from him. He was more
like a heartthrob in a B movie, *Ladykiller of Uggala Part Four*.

"I'd love to learn how to windsurf," said Father Francis.

"It's dead easy. If you want I can teach you, but you'll have
to get the wet suit first."

"A windsurfing priest? That would really give them something to talk about below in Balor's Bar. Don't the cormorants
look odd out on the rocks?"

"They're shags. Are you free for half an hour or so?"

Father Francis shrugged.

"Would you mind timing me just to see how long it takes
me to get the lighthouse and back? I forgot my watch."

As once before, Father Francis found himself meekly succumbing to Danny's unprefaced request. Danny treated him
as if he had known him, man and boy, for thirty years. Francis found this casual intimacy both off-putting and endearing.

"How long is it supposed to take?"

"Colm O'Keefe brags he can do it in half an hour. So it
should take me twenty to twenty-five minutes."

Danny attached the boom to the mast, unfurled the yellow

and blue sail, and drew the ropes taut. He performed these preliminary tasks with stagy meticulousness, aware of Father Francis's admiring eyes on him. To top the effect, he threw the taut rig casually into the tide. In his wet suit and harness he looked like an aquatic gladiator. Especially when he strode into the sea with the sailboard under one arm and the dagger board dangling from the other. Mannan Mac Lir beware!

Father Francis sat on the close-cropped grass and watched as Danny took off from a standing start. He breathed in the cockly sea breeze mingled with the faint ambrosia of thrift. Danny's sail tilted like a butterfly on the ocean. Was this what was meant by "Ye shall have life and have it more abundantly"?

Father Francis tried to project himself into the curved figure that leaned backward in the harness, his hands scarcely touching the boom, his feet expertly guiding the racing board. The exhilaration of smashing over the waves! The invigorating rivalry with O'Keefe! Could he be like that?

"Thirty-two minutes and fifty seconds," he announced with glee as Danny drove his Windsurfer up on the shore.

"Blast it! Are you sure you timed me from when I got up on the board?"

Father Francis nodded. "Do you really need to beat O'Keefe?"

"Of course! That's the whole point. On this island at this time it's the only thing worth doing. How else does one become part of Uggala's story?"

Father Francis was puzzled. Could Danny really be so vain?

On the instant Danny caught the meaning of his silence.

"Look, it's like this. You're a priest. No matter what you do, good, bad, or indifferent, you're guaranteed a place in the island's memory. You can be what you like, a scoundrel, a thug, a busybody, a saint. Come what may, somebody in fifty years' time will date an important event in their life with 'It was when Father Francis, the good-looking one, was curate on the island.' The likes of me have a harder time getting into the record."

"Isn't it a bit like being a sub on the losing all-Ireland minor hurling team? Who cares?" Father Francis couldn't keep the derision out of his voice.

"I have a more cosmopolitan project on the boil," said Danny modestly.

He winked at Father Francis and waded back into the tide to rescue his foundering sail. Father Francis followed him to the sea's edge.

"So what's the big project if I may ask?"

"I'll tell you some other time."

Danny piled his sailing gear on the shore above the tidemark and took a flask out of his duffel bag.

"What about a quick shot of poitin?"

They sat on the shore in silence like the dark and fair protagonists of legend, drinking poitin and watching the sunlight kiss the waves.

"So how do you find Uggala?" asked Danny smugly. He knew the island couldn't fail on a day like this.

"It's so small and . . . well, comprehensible. You could hold it in the palm of your hand. Yet I can't help feeling there's something mysterious about it. Something just beyond one's reach."

Danny was suddenly alert.

"Maybe more mysterious than you think. You know who captures best the mood of places like this? Bad poets. Fin de siècle mystics, the likes of George Russell and Eva Gore-Booth. They write out of a waking sleep, I think. All incantatory verse and smudgy meanings. But they move you beyond the formal understanding. I think they got closest to what you sense."

"Things beyond the twilight vale?" said Father Francis mockingly.

"Something like that. Presences."

"Do you believe in such?"

"That's an odd class of question from a man who practices a religion with a whole menagerie of angels and devils and saints. But I suppose you'll say that's different from fairies?"

"Well, isn't it?"

"Not at all. Your lot drove the nature spirits out of the woods and hills in the name of a transcendent God."

"So what are you saying then?"

"It was hardly necessary. And they're still here."

"The fairies? You don't mean to tell me that you —"

"I saw them," said Danny curtly.

"Come on. You're too intelligent for that."

Danny looked at Father Francis with provocative mischief in his eyes.

A translucent blue dragonfly blundered past. Father Francis shook his head and laughed in disbelief. Below them on the rocks the shag family had unpegged their wings and begun to croak contentedly at the sun. They would recollect August 1, 1988, as one of the best drying days in the recent history of the shag population of Uggala.

The Daimons of Nature

✦ Just as the best way to look at the stars is to lie on the ground in an open field, far from the lights and smog of the city, so the best way to sense the inhabiting intelligences of a place is to settle quietly in a secluded spot and wait till they manifest. They rarely do. They are indifferent to whether people see or believe in them. They have no feelings and experience no conflict between desire and duty. Yet they hold the blueprint of things from a bluebell to a wave and mold matter to its appropriate form. Long long ago, when humans felt themselves to be weak and vulnerable they gave them names — nymphs, dyads, devas, salamanders — and worshiped them as the intermediaries between the human and the divine. Today, when the distance between man and his gods has been diminished or canceled, no such paltry messengers are required. Again, they couldn't care less. They remain in the placeless world as seed memories of what perishes and may grow again.

When Danny promised Yoshiko that he would show her the nature spirits, he had nothing more in mind than getting out of the pub and seducing her on the romantic, well-worn ramparts of the Danes' Fort. Where others resorted to Carlsberg Specials to secure a woman for the night, Danny knew on the spot that the Japanese girl in the red woolen dress required more imaginative handling.

He felt her eyes on him while he played out a musical duel with O'Keefe. It was a Friday night in June, and Balor's Bar was jammed to the gills with tourists. On such evenings someone was sure to provoke Danny and Colm into displaying their rivalry on the fiddle and spoons.

Danny was on the spoons. Colm on the bow. It was enough for Colm to see Danny casting pseudo-shy glances at the Japanese girl to know what the cur was up to. So he stepped up the pace and varied the melodic line to a hectic hi-diddly-hi-diddle-diddly-di-dee. Danny followed him valiantly on the spoons, clacking them by turns on his thighs, elbow, and on Biafra's bony shoulder. The Japanese girl laughed. Colm grimaced. Enough of this pussyfooting. Let's hear it for Paganini. He thrummed on the strings with the bow and soared to the rafters. Yahoo!

The drinkers gasped. The spoons flew out of Danny's hands. Fair play to you, Colm! Agus go maeara tú slan!

Danny was drowning his defeat in a pint of Guinness when he heard a soft cooing English. "Excuse me. Could I ask you something?"

The Japanese girl stood above him with a glass of water in her hand.

"Ask me anything you like."

"How do you do it — I mean the spoons?"

"The fairies taught me. Won't you sit down?"

"Seriously, I'd like to know. I'm a musician."

"Then you should go to the fairy fort some night and pick up a few new tunes for yourself."

Yoshiko hesitated for a moment and then decided to go with Danny's mood. "You think they'll teach me?"

"Well, if I'm around you stand a fair chance."

"You must be very important to them!"

"Not at all. I'm what you might call a simple druid."

"You do magic?"

"It goes with the territory."

"Can you show me?"

"This very night if you're up to it."

Already on the way to the Danes' Fort, Danny was beginning to backpedal. "I don't know if the night is right for it," he said, looking at the overcast sky. "And it's not just the night, it's the time of the year. They're at their best in early spring."

"You promised," said Yoshiko. "You said you'd do it."

"I think maybe I had one drink too many. It's best not to touch alcohol when you want to see them."

Danny walked ahead of Yoshiko to keep the briers from catching at her dress. He was so nervous that he hardly registered the fragrant hollows of meadowsweet and honeysuckle through which they moved. Fairies, my arse! He was making a complete fool of himself.

"How many times have you actually seen them?"

"Oh, many times down the years."

Danny was lying. It was his grandfather who had seen them. Dear Granddad, he beseeched the old man in his head, please let them appear tonight. Do it for me, your grateful grandson Danny.

"Is this all?" said Yoshiko when she saw the dark bank of the Fort. "I thought there would be a castle."

She wasn't bothering to be skittish or ironic anymore.

"Nature spirits have nothing to do with castles. You're thinking of ghosts."

"What do they look like then?"

"It depends. Balls of light. But it's better not to be too definite about their shape in advance."

"So what do we do now?"

"We sit and wait."

They sat on the exposed root of a stunted ash tree that stooped over the ring fort. Danny sensed Yoshiko's stiffness and unease. She was reproaching herself for the silly way she was flirting with a stranger. She covered her misgivings with a cough and the strained casualness of "Aren't you going to say any magical incantations?"

Danny shook his head. "It's up to them. We just have to be patient."

He had made up his mind. He wouldn't touch Yoshiko. He would be chivalrous and restrained. No fairies, no seduction.

To pass the time he told her about his encounters with the Otherworld. How he and John O'Flaherty had been astonished one night by a great ball of light traversing the bog below. And even though the wind was in their direction and there was no sound, O'Flaherty claimed the next day that it was a helicopter. Or how he and Tom O'Reilly saw a myriad of flickering lights sweeping in great whorls across Uggala Hill. Of course Tom said it was fireflies, even though there aren't any fireflies in Ireland.

"Fireflies! Helicopters!" exclaimed Danny in his grandfather's contemptuous voice. "People see what they want to see, even if it goes against all common sense."

The stories fired Danny up. It didn't matter anymore that it was Danny's grandfather who had seen the apparitions. Just now he was at one with the old man and could speak in his person.

"The truth of the matter is that people see these things all the time. But they can't make a mental shift from the ordinary and everyday to acknowledge something new. So they put them down to what they think is normal. Kids playing with matches. Tourists with camping gas and suchlike nonsense."

Yoshiko had begun to relax. She was back to her playful mood again. Should he make his move?

"Maybe I saw them too? Once when I was walking down in —"

She drew in her breath sharply and grabbed Danny's arm. "Look!"

Two lights low to the ground and shifting erratically moved slowly up the path they had come.

"It's them!"

Danny could hardly contain himself. He felt a surge of gratitude to his grandfather.

They jumped to their feet, holding hands tightly in innocent excitement.

"How's the yella belly, Danny?"

O'Keefe's two sidekicks, the Skipper and Johnny Mack, emerged from the darkness walking their bicycles.

"Did you get 'em off her yet?"

Yoshiko's hand slipped out of Danny's.

Peasants. Stupid fucking peasants.

"I'd like to go back." Her voice was edgy and childish.

Danny was desolate. Why had he resorted to the idiocy of rural life to charm Yoshiko? Why hadn't he simply told her how lovely she was and how much he desired her?

In the scrub the fairies were surely pissing themselves with laughter at his humiliation.

Yoshiko marched blindly forward, careless of the trailing briers and the clumps of stinging nettles.

"Please forgive me," said Danny when he caught up with her. "I'm an idiot to have brought you here."

"I'm the idiot to have come with you."

There'd be no winning her back after this. He'd see her to the door of her B & B as quickly as possible and leave it at that.

"What I forgot to say is that I'm a very bad, underdeveloped druid."

No response.

"I'm so out of practice that instead of conjuring fairies I bring on two sexist racist small farmers."

Still no response.

"The truth is . . . The truth is that the moment I saw you I thought of elves and angels and all kinds of corny magic. You bewitched me!"

Yoshiko stopped and looked at him with an enigmatic half smile on her lips. "So now it's my fault?"

"Yes, definitely! You have the magic and not me."

She was confused now. Or was she just playing a game?

"It's OK," she said. "Let's hit the road."

"Hit the road? Where did you get that phrase?"

"I studied in New York for five years. Is it very American?"

They walked in a charged silence towards the lights of the village. Somebody was following them. Something was happening behind their backs. There was no sound, only a hardly perceptible turbulence in the air. Yoshiko slowed down and glanced quickly at Danny. Was she aware of it too?

They walked on, not daring to look back, wary of another disenchantment, good or bad. Yoshiko was breathing deeply. Danny's mouth was dry. Whatever it was behind them seemed to slacken, as if inviting them to turn round.

Their shared obstinacy shattered like a windshield. Yoshiko looked back first. Danny heard her sibylline cry of wonder. He knew what she had seen before he turned.

"It's beautiful!" she exclaimed.

Twenty feet from where they stood, globes of scintillating light danced among the dense branches of a holy tree.

Danny had been waiting for this moment for decades. He had imagined how it would transform everything, how he would be a changed man in a changed cosmos. He had hankered for it the way an adolescent hankers for his first sexual encounter, as something that would enable him to give birth to a new self.

And now here they were, the nature spirits, the devas, the shining ones, call them what you will, whirling to their hearts' content, and it didn't make a damn bit of difference to anything. Danny was stunned at how normal the whole thing was. It was as if he had half-seen them every evening when locking up the hens for the night.

But Yoshiko was enchanted, her whole being made porous and pliant by the experience. She leaned against Danny in a soft, trusting complicity.

There was no going back to the B & B after this. They had to think it through, talk it through, make love it through, until the last boat left the following day.

The Daimon of Father Francis

Father Francis stood at the altar rails to get as close as possible to his congregation without frightening them while he preached on love. There in the front row was Holy Paddy, all on his own, stinking and praying steadily. Two rows behind, a well-scrubbed Colm O'Keefe sat beside Concepta, who wore a pious grieving face over a gray two-piece suit. Tom and Alice were on the other side of the isle, Tom so lost in erotic reveries that he would wake up only to cross himself demonstratively at the Ite missa est. Alice was a great nodder, and Father Francis derived enormous encouragement from her unquestioning approval of his every last word. Biafra O'Dee, looking like Max von Sydow in a Bergman film, cracked his knuckles and blinked his eyes, his face set in a grimace of skeptical concentration.

Father Francis talked with force and conviction, and people listened with grateful attention. But he was uneasy. Behind his vigorous cadence there was a small voice that told him their mutual understanding was that of badgers in solid agreement on what it took to fly.

The Daimon of Danny Ruane

ᔕ Danny Ruane didn't go to Sunday Mass anymore. When he had first come to Uggala, he went out of a sense of loyalty to the people around him. Whatever was important to them had to be important to him. And what could be more important than being present when the bread and wine became the Body and Blood of Christ?

Already on his first appearance in church the people smelled out the falsity of his attempt to go native. They were like beaten children cowed before the terrifying all-seeing eye of God. But Danny sat upright in his long black coat and blue scarf, relaxed and curious, like a man who was more than ready to take on the Almighty. They knew he wasn't like them. The things they feared hardly bothered him. And they saw that the things they prayed for — fine weather, the conversion of China, the island's dead, the Pope's intentions — only brought an amused half smile to his lips.

In the pub, in the fields, out in the boats, allowances were made for Danny and his extravagances passed over. But not in church. God saw into everybody's heart, and the people just knew that He couldn't have liked what He saw in Danny's: impurity, rebellion, and vanity. He never went to Communion and made a point of not reciting the Creed with them. You just knew that he didn't believe in the One Holy Catholic and Apostolic Church and One God for the remission of sins.

Nothing was ever said to him, but one day it dawned on Danny that his presence at Mass was merely tolerated. So when he stopped going everybody was relieved. At last they could revert to treating the Lord in the image and likeness of a Fianna Fáil TD without any Blueshirt intruding on their obsequious intimacies.

While Father Francis was botching his sermon on love, Danny was cycling to meet the twelve o'clock ferry. *The Morning Star* was churning the water in the harbor as it maneuvered awkwardly to the quay wall. Danny dismounted in his usual balletic fashion and inspected the new arrivals. The season of abstinence had long passed, and still his ritual of surveying the women tourists hadn't led to any close encounters, physical or mental. Usually, by this time of year, Danny would be in the throes of a romance and driving Uggala up the walls. Maybe he was losing his touch?

Most of the people onboard the ferry were nondescript windsurfers. There was the usual gang of incestuous French teenagers in red shirts and a few decaffeinated Dublin families. Danny scanned them hastily, with the impatience of a schoolgirl reading a romance and skipping everything but the love scenes. He waited until the last passenger had disembarked and was about to close the book on them when he spotted a slender figure with long dark hair and a thoughtful face emerging from the ranks of the windsurfers.

She wasn't one of them, that was for sure. She stopped to tuck her white T-shirt into her jeans and to tie her hair back with a rubber band. Then she opened her travel bag and took out a map.

It was time to move in and offer his assistance.

Act I: The setup was firmly in place.

Act II: They wander companionably over the cliff tops with panoramic view of the ocean. To dispel any suspicion that

he's just a local gigolo, he explains that he is a writer on retreat.

Act III: They are having dinner together. She marvels at
the number of books on his shelves. Where does he get the
time et cetera. He expounds on, let's see, androgyny in
Japanese culture.

Danny watched the girl orient her map to the territory and
decide on a direction. Involuntarily he straightened as her
eyes fell on him briefly. But he didn't move when she heaved
her bag on her shoulder and headed off towards the hotel. He
just stood and stared.

At this moment of his life she embodied no call or no
summons. Neither Act I, II, or III held any allure anymore.
His morning visit to the quay — what was it but a habit and
a playing up to others' and his own expectations of himself?
Look, Golden Balls is at it again!

He mounted his bike and with a growing sense of relief
and excitement pedaled back home to his "Creation."

The Daimon of Father Francis

ϲᴥ Mrs. O'Halloran was in the sacristy laboriously count-
ing the collection. It was swollen to three times normal by
the influx of August visitors. And as usual she was preoccupied by the sewage system on the island. How could it possibly cope with all these extra people? "Nature calls people
even on holidays," she said, as if it were a great revelation.

Father Francis was too preoccupied with worries about his
sermon to care about replying. His worrying was interrupted
by Ethna, who filled the door and, as usual, dispensed with
preliminaries.

"I liked your sermon, Father. Bits of it anyway."

"I didn't know you were a churchgoer." Father Francis's face colored brick red. Which bits, he wondered. Jesus' words to the woman taken in adultery?

"I just came to hear what you had to say."

"What do you mean bits, Miss Ethna O'Keefe?" said Mrs. O'Halloran. "It was as good a sermon in its entirety as you're likely to hear anywhere."

She wasn't going to let this young strap with her shameless bump get away with it. Just imagine her coming round to the sacristy and talking to the priest in her condition.

"Why don't you have breakfast with me," said Father Francis, "and we can talk about the bits you didn't like. There's nothing to beat Mrs. O Halloran's Sunday breakfasts. The full fry: smoked rashers, black pudding, sausages, eggs, and toast. Isn't that right, Mrs. O'Halloran?"

Pleased and indignant at the same time, Mrs. O'Halloran shoved the monstrance into the cupboard for altar linen.

Ethna's stomach heaved when Father Francis paraded before her a plate of hairy rashers, carbonized sausages, and greasy black pudding.

"Thank you ever so much," she said to Mrs. O'Halloran as she folded her hands on the table. "I'll just have toast and tea please."

"Are you OK?" asked Father Francis. "You look a little pale."

"I'll be fine. It's the last two months and the twins have been acting up."

Mrs. O'Halloran backed out of the kitchen with a don't-contaminate-me-with-all-that-stuff look on her face.

"So?"

"I liked what you had to say about love needing constant care and cultivation. That's true enough. But you didn't have much to say about what most of us actually experience. Love rejected. Or denied."

She spoke slowly and carefully, trying not to shadow her words with her own disappointments and failures.

"I tried to speak about love as it is offered to us in the Gospels. It's something to strive towards." He was getting defensive.

"I thought that as a priest your job was to explain to us the morass we're actually stuck in. And then to tell us how to get out of it."

Father Francis smiled his radiant Archangel Gabriel smile. "Do you mean I should tell everybody how deeply unhappy they are?"

Ethna blew her fringe off her forehead. "Have you seen how the magpies go after pigeons' eggs? How they delight in smashing and breaking everything? It's like what happens here. Love is destroyed before it's even hatched."

Father Francis shifted uneasily in his chair. "What right do I have to unmask to others their own misery? Maybe lovelessness, like war, is the normal state of affairs?"

"But aren't you deceiving them?"

Father Francis looked at her white-as-snowdrop face and toyed with the sausage on his plate. The pupils in his eyes were huge. Did he need glasses?

Ethna smiled. "Unless we assume that the whole business of religion is to delude people rather than to search for the truth."

"No. The business of religion is to save souls."

"Even if you have to burn the bodies at the stake?"

Ethna immediately regretted the crudity of her remark. Her embarrassment was relieved by Mrs. O'Halloran, who bustled in with a fresh pot of tea and a question: "Will you be wanting dessert?"

"But it's breakfast, Mrs. O'Halloran. Surely dessert is for after dinner?" Father Francis tried to filter the mockery out of his voice.

"Good God, how could I be so confused? It must be the pressure. Don't you find it very close?"

Red-faced, Mrs. O'Halloran retreated to the scullery.

Father Francis looked questioningly at Ethna. "Mrs. O'Halloran is in the early stages of dementia. Do you think it would help her or make her any happier if I pointed it out to her?"

"I don't know," confessed Ethna. "Maybe some of us should know the worst and some of us shouldn't? The question is how to decide."

"You're getting adept at unsettling me."

"Can I unsettle you a bit more?"

Father Francis nodded.

"I don't mean to be too nosy, but have you had any personal experience of love refused or scorned? Because if you haven't it's difficult to imagine what it's like."

Father Francis looked out the window. A distraught sun struggled through trailing veils of gray smoky cloud.

"I see. So what you're telling me is that I should stop sermonizing on love altogether. Maybe you're right. Maybe I should stick to Faith and Hope?"

"I'm sorry. I shouldn't have come here. I feel like some sort of Cassandra with a message I can't express."

"Try."

"I sense you have the ability to shake all of us out of our torpor. But you're too . . . nice."

Ethna struggled to lift her heavy bumblebee body out of the chair. "I must be on my way."

"I think you misjudge me," said Father Francis.

"Or you misjudge yourself." Ethna smiled.

Father Francis took her by the arm and helped her to the door. It pained him to see her weighed down by the burden of me and Thresheen.

"Poor man," said Thresheen. "He doesn't know what's in store for him."

"He still has a choice," I said. "But I see him haunted by a woman."

"I see him haunted by two women," said Thresheen gleefully.

The Daimon of Ethna

❧ Monday, August 20, was a fly-in-marmalade day for Ethna. She woke up wanting to go back to sleep for years and years. When she stood up the camper could no longer contain her. She kept on bumping into things.

She dragged herself to work in the pub in a bovine stupor. Once there, as always, she found the simple jobs allotted to her therapeutic: washing and drying dishes, making toast, mixing salad, and preparing the soup of the day, which always came down to the same chicken and noodle. When Ethna was at work, her mother kept to herself in the main building. Ethna felt like an evil spirit in a haunted house, a demon whose path it would be fatal to cross. She fantasized about her head rotating on her shoulders and her bare fangs drooling green gounge should Concepta enter the pub kitchen. She never did.

In the afternoon Colm popped in to see how she was getting along. He took one look at her, sat her on the tractor, and drove her directly to the camper.

"I'm bringing the doctor over first thing in the morning, and I'll drop in later to see how you're managing."

Ethna hardly registered what he said. She opened all the windows, lay down heavily on the bunk bed, and began to gulp in the salty sea breeze. But the semeny smell of the caravan tainted everything. She could hear the *peet peet* of the phillibin guarding her young on the shore. She had to get out.

She sat on her favorite rock with a drawing pad held in front of her, watching the Jacob's ladders as they shifted about over the surface of the sea. For half an hour she felt empty and happy. The long margin of her sketch pad filled with a lanky heron loitering by a pool. At the top she drew a roseate tern catapulting itself into the tide. And between them she began to sketch the face of a child. I think it was me, suspended between the still watchful heron and the frantic hyperactive gull.

"What about me?" asked Thresheen.

Just as Ethna began to outline another face, she was distracted by a familiar moan.

"Jesus, that sea wind is playing hell with me sinuses," said Biafra.

"I thought the sea was supposed to be good for the sinuses. All that iodine."

Biafra panted and folded his long emaciated body like a deck chair down on the grassy verge of the shore.

"Nothing is good for me. Not even the fucking walk. At least you're doing something, drawing something, going somewhere. You'll be famous. I've been walking round this bleeding island masturbating my brain for the last two hours, and all that comes out is snot."

"I'm just sketching, there's nothing special about that."

"Sketching is good. It shows class. It's respectability. Why can't I finish anything? I've been working on my rock opera for the last six years, and I'm still pissing against the wind. I've sent it to Lloyd Webber and Patrick Mason, and did they answer? Did they fuck!"

"Maybe you should try America?"

"Yeah, maybe I should. You know what I think? My opera is located between the eighth and the tenth pint of Guinness. At the eighth pint a man is sentimental and slobbery. By the tenth pint he's violent and would tear your head off for sixpence. The problem with the Brits is that they can't tolerate anything beyond the fourth pint."

"Maybe we should both go to America."

Ethna tried to stand up.

A searing pain raked through her body. She almost lost her balance. She dropped her sketch pad and put her hands to her belly, breathing heavily.

"Biafra!"

She felt another dart of pain.

Biafra looked at her with incomprehension and blinked his eyes. "You're not well?" he asked confused.

"I need a doctor. I'm getting contractions."

"Oh Jesus! Why did I ever come here? . . . Hang on, hang on. Where's the phone? No phone. I'll go to Danny. Just hang on, OK?"

Ethna slid down from the rock and burrowed into the sand. Pain was everywhere. She no longer knew if it was inside her or if it came flooding in with every red wave of the sea.

The Daimon of Danny Ruane

Father Francis read the paragraph from "Creation" a second time. It went:

> There are numerous theories of the origins of life from primary physical states, but none of them satisfactorily explains life's sheer persistence in the face of the physical law of increasing chaos. The mistake of the theoreticians lies in ignoring the nonphysical origin of physical entities — an origin expressed mathematically by the pseudopleromatic matrices we have discussed earlier. True enough, possessors of these matrices cannot avail themselves of their creative possibilities unless some spark of consciousness elucidates their sky once upon some milliards of years. The way back to the source of the All is infinitely more strenuous than the way away from it, although there is a guide to it, which humanity from immemorial times had signposted with symbols of remembrance.

Father Francis wondered what he should say. He said: "Interesting."

Danny jumped in. "The difficulty, you see, is that I have to move between archaic and futuristic paradigms. Between the Etruscans and Bohr."

"Do you think people will grasp it?"

"It's not for the present," Danny said. "It's for the future. The whole thing's about a Hidden Order for which there's no language — yet. I'm using reason and mathematics for what has been sort of intuited in poetry."

"Can't you leave it to poetry?"

"The poets have difficulties proving that the entire Creation can be deduced from a system of sixteen manifestations of the Primal Mystery."

Father Francis struggled to follow what the sixteen manifestations of the Primal Mystery might be or what you eat it with. He couldn't picture the Pleroma, the subjective passive Divine One from which Danny argued all cosmologies start. However hard he tried, the comparison of the Primal Subject and the Nothingness to a grammatical subject and the predicate of an utterance that is the One eluded him entirely.

"I suppose you think I'm off my rocker," said Danny jovially. "But it's basically very simple. You just need to grasp the dialectical matrix of the sixteen components. As a matter of fact they actually feature in the secret teachings of some advanced religions."

He grabbed a pen and jotted an equation on the page in front of them.

"It can be summed up in the following way: with

$$P = \sum_{n}^{16} p_n E_n \quad \text{with} \quad p_n = \pm\,(1/4)f E_n g$$

"And the original state must be equal to the sum of the pentadic states, which leads to

$$\left(\sum_{n=0}^{5} p_{mn}E_{mn}f - p_{16}E_{16}f \right)_k = 0$$

$$n = 0$$

$$n \neq M$$

Danny talked as if he were windsurfing before a steady breeze, a picture of poise, confidence, and self-delight. Father Francis couldn't help thinking, Here's a man who's been granted an eternal childhood and who feels he has inherited the earth.

"Let's take the origins of the heavenly bodies." As Danny was about to draw another intimidating diagram, Biafra O'Dee burst open the door and clung to the table in a state of semicollapse.

"Ethna! That woman will be the death of me."

"What's she done to you this time?" asked Danny.

"She's fainting or giving birth or something below on the strand. You'd better call in a doctor."

Danny and Father Francis ran to the strand, dragging the buggy for the Windsurfer behind them. Father Francis was relieved that he didn't have to pursue the question of the origins of the heavenly bodies. He was grateful for the lovely comprehensibility of the old story of Genesis I and the Garden of Eden. And it was wonderful too that there were aspects of Genesis as Such, like the one they were heading towards, that ultimately couldn't be reduced to mathematical equations.

The Daimon of Thresheen

❧ I had no answer to Thresheen's argument against being born. What's the use of living in order to die? Of going through the whole rigmarole only once again to return to a state of pure possibility? Why take a roundabout way when we could remain happy as Larry this side of time?

"Cowardly custard," I said bitterly. "You've come this far, why not go the whole way?"

"I didn't want you to be lonely."

"So: you're like a dog that goes a bit of the road with everybody. Let's get born!"

I was full of the fear and excitement of crossing the River of Forgetfulness. But stronger than both was despair at the thought of Thresheen staying on in that plenitude from which I was about to tear myself.

"I'm not ready."

"Nobody's ever ready. Come with me!"

But Thresheen turned her face away and gave no sign of recognition. The waves of the River, yellow and topped with foam like a mountain torrent, beat round my ears as I slipped away from her.

"Thresheen! Don't leave me!" I cried and gasped for memory.

I was in the river, but her voice was in my head. "I won't leave you."

"Thresheen!"

"You'll remember. Let go!"

The Daimon of Concepta

❧ I cried night, noon, and morn for the first three weeks of my existence on earth. Ethna was too exhausted and too aggrieved to assuage me, so I was held, rocked, and patted by Danny and Alice. We were all camping at Danny's house. Danny himself on a bunk bed in the outhouse, Alice in the spare room, and me and Ethna in the big bedroom looking out over the indifferent sea.

For Danny it was a glorious time. He had three generations under his roof with nothing to do but look after a baby and quote Rumi on life and death. While Mother and I cried our eyes out, Alice nodded and said, "There, there. That's good for you. Get it all out!" As far as she was concerned, one twin born alive was a fair percentage.

Thresheen's body was buried in Uggala graveyard as unobtrusively as possible. Father Francis officiated and blessed the tiny white coffin in Danny's arms. The only other people to answer the decade of the rosary over the grave were Colm O'Keefe, Biafra O'Dee, Tom, and Alice. Concepta refused to come. She didn't want to know anything about socially unacceptable forms of birth, life, or death. For her at this moment her daughter did not exist, and hence her granddaughter never died. She was very clear and logical about it in her sealed-up, tight-lipped way. She spent the day of the burial filing bills and going through her collection of recipes culled from Saturday's pages of the *Irish Independent*.

The Daimon of Father Francis

❧ The phantom of the girl accosted Father Francis as he bent over to tie his shoelaces. All of a sudden, without any warning, she stood there. First her shiny black shoes, then her knee-length white socks with the zigzag pattern, then the green plaid of her skirt and her navy blue pullover. When he straightened up, her tearstained face was fuzzy, almost as if it were reflected in slowly moving water.

Father Francis took a deep breath and turned away. When he looked back, she was gone.

He was tired. He must have been even more tired than he imagined. He had spent the whole night speed-reading through Beckett's novels looking for a quotation to illustrate his sermon. Something about patience and time. It was there somewhere.

He had no illusions about his congregation or their appetite for modern literature. But maybe there was a tourist who would return to London or Dublin with "Can you believe it? I heard this priest on Uggala quoting from *Malone Dies!*"

The following day he saw the girl again. He was reading his breviary on the shore, pacing back and forth along his favorite stretch of sand between the rocks, when Isabelle — was her name Isabelle? — came out of the sea towards him. He was startled not so much by the sight of her as by the fact that her clothes were dry. He closed his breviary and hurried away.

He headed straight for the Parochial House and made himself a cup of Earl Grey tea. He searched for a cigarette. He made an agreement with himself not to think about anything until he found one. The packet of Marlboros was in the bread bin.

He sat inhaling deeply and interrogating himself. Why was Isabelle appearing to him now? What had triggered it off? What could be the meaning of such hallucinations at this particular time? Not since the angels had climbed up and down the bed end had he experienced anything like this.

His attempts to answer these questions were interrupted by Mrs. O'Halloran, who called him for lunch.

"Will you be watching the big match on television, Father?"

She knew damn well he wouldn't , but it was part of her relentless campaign to turn him into a normal human being doing normal things. She was dumbfounded when he said, "Of course."

He went to bed early, determined to get a good night's sleep and put to rest whatever layer of his unconscious was acting up. He was afraid that Isabelle would break in on his dreams, but she didn't. She didn't put in an appearance until the following Sunday, when he was distributing Communion. She was kneeling demurely in front of him with her tongue out. His hand trembled as he withdrew the Eucharist. This time her face was as clear as those of the others along the altar rail — deep-set gray eyes, pale, tubercular skin, and her

dark blond hair gathered into a knot at the back. He noticed
how fresh and clean her tongue was. Odd for somebody who
was ten years in the grave.

After a moment of panic he made to offer her the Host. He
found himself staring at the black cavity of Holy Paddy, who
was panting for the Blessed Eucharist like a hungry dog for a
biscuit.

After Mass, Father Francis sat in the sacristy and tried to
pray, but Isabelle filled his mind. He had never thought much
about her, even when she took her own life. "Better forget the
whole thing," Father Buckley had advised. "It's a cut and
dried case. A neurotic schoolgirl with a crush on a priest? It's
an old story. There's nothing you could have done even if you
wanted to."

"Maybe I should have talked to her? Consoled her?"

"That would have provoked her even more. I know it's up-
setting you terribly, but it would happen one way or the other.
If not with you then with somebody else. She was the type.
Tuam, you know."

What was disconcerting was that it wasn't upsetting him at
all. The girl's suicide hadn't cost Francis a night's sleep. He
could draw a clean line between evil and misfortune. In this
case a misfortune had happened. An accident that couldn't
be helped. He was a celibate priest and she was an oversexed
teenager. He had nothing to reproach himself with.

So what was bringing her back?

Was it Ethna, with her talk of love rejected and scorned?
Or was it something inside him that had blundered out into
the daylight?

He tried to go about his daily routines as if nothing had
happened. But something had happened. Isabelle paced in
silence beside him on the shore or appeared in the mirror as
he shaved. This convinced him that she wasn't a ghost.
Ghosts don't reflect in mirrors.

Mrs. O'Halloran was the first to point out that he was letting himself go. She did so in her own insidious fashion. "Good God, I hardly recognized you with the stubble and the fag!" she exclaimed one morning as he slouched into the kitchen.

Danny, cycling down to the quay, reined in his bicycle when he saw Father Francis lurching across the road. "Francis! I'll be damned. What's happened to you?"

Father Francis gesticulated vaguely with his left hand.

"You look like something out of *Night of the Living Dead*."

"That's very close to the bone," said Francis with a cynical grin. There was a new, impenetrable aura about him.

"How's Ethna?" he asked. "And the baby?"

Danny took refuge in deliberate formality. "Mother and child are doing as well as can be expected under the circumstances."

He looked again into Father Francis's half-crazed eyes. "If it's God that's bugging you, I'm no good to you. But if it's something else . . ."

"I need to sort things out by myself, Danny. Thanks."

However meticulously Father Francis tried to sort things out, he always came back to the same questions. What did Isabelle want from him after all these years? An admission of guilt? Impossible. An exorcism? An expiation?

One night, as he talked to her and prayed for her and blessed her in delirious despair, Isabelle finally spoke to him. Her lips didn't move, but he heard her words in his head. She said, "I don't want your love. I want you to imagine my pain."

"How can I imagine your pain?"

He sat fully clothed on the edge of the bed, heedless of the ash of his cigarette falling on the covers.

Many times he called her to return and to explain it all to him. But this was the last time he saw her.

Isabelle didn't need to appear to him anymore. She was inside him, even when he spruced himself up, went on a vegetarian diet, and cut his hair to the approved clerical length.

The Daimon of Ethna

❧ Two weeks after my birth Ethna still hadn't settled. She was like a panicky thrush nesting in a garden patrolled by a tomcat. Inexplicably, she seemed to have abandoned her most precious desires and yearnings, and stepped into a realm of self-denial and defiance. She had always lusted after Danny, craved his attention, and prayed for his company. Now she and I were sleeping in his bed, eating from his table, and being looked after by him hand and foot. But one looked in vain for the soft beatific smiles that light up the faces of women whose dreams have come true. Torment, not love, was Ethna's element.

One day she would be packing up her things, stuffing me into the baby basket, and faltering off to God only knows where. Another day she would be overwhelmed with gratitude, grabbing Danny's hand melodramatically and thanking him with tears in her eyes. Most days she was recalcitrant and dazed by her own confusion. At times she resembled her father, who could spend months on end shielding himself from the threat of his wife's affection. Ethna didn't need Danny's charity. He thought he was God's gift to women, but fuck that! She wasn't going to be beholden to him or use her son as an excuse for handouts!

Almost immediately after my birth she recovered her long-limbed anorexic figure. But in her own mind she was still bloated and so hated to catch sight of herself in the mirror. She dug out her old crumpled Florentine dresses, ironed them ruthlessly, and wore them heedless of how little they matched with anything on Uggala. She was like a butterfly indifferent to its own gorgeous wings. And she never noticed the stealthy fascinated glances cast in her direction.

Like a squeamish patient averting her head from the prick of a needle, she avoided looking at the clocks on the mantelpiece. In her dreams she turned their faces to the wall.

Danny bore it all with lackadaisical fortitude. "Not to worry, Finn," he reassured me while dabbing my raw bottom with Johnson's baby powder. "It takes a bit of time for the old hormones to settle down. And when they do, God help the lot of us."

Danny knew all about hormones from a stack of books on child care he had bought on his last trip to Dublin.

When I was born he dropped all his other pursuits — his Big Book, the bees, windsurfing, and his enmity with Colm O'Keefe. Once or twice he even forgot to call Yoshiko, Clare, and Liselotte, and attend to their various disappointments.

Instinctively, as if knowing where the steady axis of our world lay, I clung to Danny and bawled my head off every time Ethna took me up in her arms. The more I clung to Danny, the more he hugged and caressed me. Ethna, spinning in an emotional whirligig, was at first glad, then hurt, then furious.

"You're overdoing it like you overdo everything," she protested.

"But the books say you can't give a baby enough attention, and the first three months are crucial." And Danny offered to read her a chapter on childhood and the growth of love.

"Look," she said in a trembling voice. "You behave as if you were his father. You're giving him a false sense of security. What's going to happen when you're no longer around?"

"I'll be around. Finn and me belong to the same tribe. We hunted dinosaurs together in the Pleistocene. We went to the same brothels in the seventeenth century. And we hung from the same gibbets in St. Petersburg. Isn't that right, Finn?"

And he went out to hang up my nappies on the blue binder-cord line that stretched from the gable end to the turf shed. He made a point of greeting cheerfully anybody who happened to be passing.

"There's nothing like nappies to put Hegel in perspective," he announced to Tom.

"Men doing the washing is all the rage in America," he assured Mrs. O'Halloran. "It's the coming thing in this part of the world too."

"Get a whiff of that," he said, poking a whiter than white nappy into Biafra O'Dee's sagging gob. "You can't beat Biological Surf."

The passersby all went on to the pub to dissect the current episode in the O'Keefes' saga. What exactly was going on between Ethna and Danny? After all, Danny was behaving very strangely. Perhaps he was the real father of Ethna's brat? Will O'Keefe take a shotgun to him one of the days? Oh lawsie me!

What was going on between Danny and Ethna was as shifting as the weather over Uggala. For Ethna it was merely the exchange of one kind of pain for another. Once over the fatigue of childbirth and the spasms of grief for Thresheen, she plunged back into her old Daimonic anxiety and fear of mediocrity. She called it her one-bar-heater syndrome: a dire vision of her middle-aged self huddled over a cheap electric fire in a shabby room. She could smell the acrid sparkles of dust burning on the glowing bar and see stripes of gaudy paper peeling down the walls.

Every time she and Danny had an agreeable conversation or a normal friendly afternoon together, the one-bar-heater syndrome switched itself on to taunt her. She would stand up abruptly, hardly bothering to finish a sentence, and go for one of her walks.

A week before the regatta, she returned to work in the pub kitchen. "I can't live here forever," she explained to Danny. "I've got to make some money and then I'm off."

"Oh yeah? And what are you going to do?"

"Neither Finn nor I is going to end up in Uggala," she said with determination. "If I stay here I'll die."

While Ethna was a temporary dogsbody in the pub kitchen, Danny changed my nappies and sang me country and western songs he made up himself about my old Uggala home. Ethna would dash in to feed me and announce something bizarre like: "The world is about drinking, Finn. There are ten men drinking black porter in the bar. The earth is drinking up the rain. Danny Ruane is drinking his fifth cup of tea, and you, mavourneen, are drinking me."

Whenever Danny tried to interrupt her blather and strike up a normal conversation, she shied away. And so something remained unsaid between them.

Many things were unsaid. One of them was hinted at by Biafra O'Dee when he revealed out of pure flippancy that Golden balls was shipping his whores in for the regatta.

"Great," said Ethna. "The more baby-sitters we have here the better."

And she went home with the intention of packing up her things and catching the last boat to the mainland. But when she pushed in the door, she saw Danny fast asleep in his armchair with his mouth open and a book on his knee. I was in my cradle, quietly contemplating the spiders on the ceiling. She tiptoed over to Danny and looked at him with a cold departing eye. He snored softly. There was something tame and worn out about him. She fast-forwarded him to see how he would look in twenty years' time. She would be forty-three, he would be fifty-eight. His mouth would be slack. There would be deep lines down his long face and squashy bags under his eyes. His red locks would have turned to salt and pepper.

She felt relieved.

Softly she lifted me up and carried me into the bedroom to feed me. While I suckled, Ethna composed her farewell speech. It would be nicely poised between gratitude and venom.

When she returned to the living room, Danny was fully awake and as annoyingly testicular as ever. He looked appraisingly at her in the way he had never looked before. It threw her. She forgot the first paragraph of her farewell speech.

"I emptied out your camper and found this."

He took her portfolio from behind his chair. "Why didn't you show them to me?"

"Because they're no good. Just fantasies. Give them back."

"Hold on! They're not exactly works of art. But there is something else here. Something very important, which you must pursue."

She could feel her heart fluttering like a wren in her chest.

"Oh yeah? What is it?"

"It's a vision. You need to clarify it a bit more, that's all."

"And then what?" asked Ethna bitterly. "Have an exhibition in the Parochial Hall opened by Father Francis with lots of plonk and little bits of things on toast?"

"Don't be silly. You're not exactly a graphic artist. You're an architect. And a bloody good architect at that."

Ethna felt a current of warm light running through her body.

"How do you know?" she stammered, all her defenses down.

"I have an eye for shapes and volumes. You've imagined Uggala in twenty years' time. Why not make it happen?"

"Go away," she said, delighted.

"I mean it. You can transform this place."

"But I can only draw."

"That's a good start."

"I'm not sure."

"You are sure. Otherwise you'd never have drawn these."

Ethna sat on the floor and put her hands together. "So what do I do now?"

"I have a house rented out in Dublin. It's yours for the asking from January until you qualify. There's only one condition. That you visit me every month with Finn."

"But what would I live on?"

"I'm sure you can persuade your father to look after that."

"Why are you doing this?"

"Because I'm an ould eejit."

Suddenly her farewell speech, the regatta, the girls, flew out the window.

Ethna stood up, bent over Danny, and kissed him on the forehead.

"Blast! I always wanted to be an architect. How is it that I didn't know it?"

"There's a lot you don't know," said Danny. "I mean there's a lot you desire that hasn't reached you yet."

Ethna flushed. These were mere teasing words. Why then did they feel like a caress?

The Daimon of Sharik

Like all dogs, Sharik was part of a group soul. The Daimon of dogs (unlike, say, that of cats) is the practice of devotion. So much is this the case that in some languages there is a telling phrase, "as unhappy as a masterless dog."

The name Sharik came from a film Danny saw while on holiday in Warsaw. The film was about four brave infantrymen and their supersmart dog, Sharik, fighting against Hitler. Being a sheepdog, Sharik had a special talent for affection and companionship, to which he selflessly subordinated the traditional canine pursuits of hiding bones, biting at his own fleas, or even smelling other dogs' piss.

One of the most important tasks in Sharik's life was to back up Danny's praise of himself by barking vigorously, wagging his tail, and thrusting his head forward. As soon as Danny remarked, "Well, Sharik, I'm a fucking genius," he performed on cue.

His second task was to assist Danny in the seduction of young women. He knew that when there was a woman in the house he had to be twice as intelligent, intuitive, and inventive. His display of these virtues invariably increased the admiration of young women for his master. It was exhausting, but fortunately, in Danny's case, romance was a seasonal occupation and rarely went much beyond September.

Sharik's third and most important task was to assist Danny in the composition of his Big Book. As Danny worked alone on stormy nights, he read aloud completed sections to Sharik that usually ended with a desperate This is all bullshit, Sharik. Then Sharik would crawl under the table until summoned once more to listen to the amended version of the same passage and further abuse.

The summer of 1988 was a particularly memorable period in Sharik's life. There had never been so many people in Danny's cottage, and he had never experienced such appreciative company. He blossomed and surpassed himself in giving the paw, casting sagacious glances, carrying slippers, even pushing open the door. Such rich aromas of goulash and bigos filled the house that he was in a constant state of happy delirium.

Then came the crash. Sharik's three major tasks went by the board. Worst of all, he had a rival in the house. For the first time in his life he felt redundant and spent most of the day with his long head stretched out on his front paws contemplating the view from the porch.

Then fate took another turn. Ethna noticed his misery and began to pet him. Sharik was always sure of a tug on the ear or a biscuit when Ethna passed. So he took to accompanying her back and forth to the pub. Once again his life was full of meaning.

But this bliss lasted only a few weeks. The change came about after a long night's conversation between Danny and Ethna. Once they had begun talking, they couldn't stop. They talked and talked as if trying to make up for the years, decades, and millennia they had been apart. They became so absorbed in one another that they didn't need anybody else, man, child, or beast. Sharik skulked from one corner of the kitchen to the other, completely at a loss. Where was he to invest his abundant affections? Occasionally he passed by my crib and looked in with distrust and hurt in his eyes.

One afternoon when Danny and Ethna went to the garden to see how the bees were getting along, I began to whimper. Reluctantly, Sharik came over, sniffed at my blanket disdainfully, and backed away. He padded towards the door, stopped, and turned back to my cradle. Finally, he sighed and plonked himself down beside me.

He stayed with me for years, watching over me with a puzzled frown on his noble head. That is why my earliest childhood recollection is not my mother's face but the tilted head of Sharik, grinning and carning at me.

The Daimon of Danny Ruane

🌒 It took Danny the length of one summer to wake up to the fact that Ethna had grown on him. Imperceptibly they had branched into one another like hawthorns in the same hedge and couldn't be disentangled without the undoing of both. For Danny this mutual entwinement was so natural that it was unnatural. All his previous relationships with women had begun with cataclysmic eruptions of lust and fascination. And, as he did with his other addictions, from field mushrooms to Wilhelm Reich to Hungarian cuisine, he pursued his romantic fantasies with the obsolete energy of Sir Lancelot breaking his balls in search of the Grail. He had taken as his private motto a mangled version of the lines Yeats addressed to the wild swans on Coole turlough: "Passion and conquest attend him still/ Wander where he will."

But this wasn't passion and it wasn't conquest. When he first came to Uggala, Ethna was a lanky precocious schoolgirl with freckles and dark brown plaits who shadowed his every movement round the island. He could still feel aggrieved when he thought back to his cloudbusting days and Ethna's calm dismissal of the whole crazy project. It was an engineering impossibility, she declared, though she was only fourteen.

"This is not about crude engineering but about subtle forces we know little about," he had protested.

"You mean abracadabra?" she asked scornfully.

When she returned to Uggala, the thing that struck him most was not so much that she was now a woman as the way in which her soul seemed to have aged and seasoned by centuries. She had become a sibyl in an exotic frock, elegant sandals, and an impossibly long plait.

On the evening Danny intuited her Daimon, she shed her old-soulfulness and became fourteen again. There was a new light in her gray eyes, and her voice rang with the rich thrill of arousal. The more she expounded her vision, the more luminous she seemed to Danny. He determined on the spot that he would shelter this entrancing flame come what may and see to it that it would not die down again into ashes and embers. The knowledge that he could do so excited him in turn.

But there were two things he had half-forgotten: that there was only a week left to the regatta and that there were three alarm clocks ticking like time bombs on the mantelpiece. One of them was ticking with careless alacrity the impending arrival of Clare.

But for now he was all caught up in Uggala time. He had begun to count the hours and minutes to the moment when Ethna's slight figure would appear on the ridge below the house. With her return, nothing else mattered. He would lose himself completely in a timeless juvenescence of watching her, talking to her, amusing her.

He was thrilled to see that Ethna too couldn't wait to get home. On the last stretch of road she would quicken her step and arrive flushed and breathless with a bunch of foxgloves or bishop's-caps in her hands. And then they would talk without listening.

There are two kinds of talking without listening. One is the sort of nonconversation polite grown-up sons have with their mothers. While the mother rambles on about the neighbors dying like flies, the latest murder, or the cost of electricity, the son thoughtlessly interjects Fancy that! and You're not serious! and Do you tell me now! and The buggers!

The other kind is the tensile conversation between about-to-be-lovers. Their words are like dainty caddis flies flitting hither and thither above the surface of a pond. The words don't matter. What matter are the shapeless feelings that blunder about like ponderous carp in the deeps and hollows.

A few days before the regatta there was an almighty storm, which cut Uggala off from the mainland. Danny was all in favor of such dramatic interludes because they returned the island to its primeval solitude and enabled him to get in touch with the night. When Ethna arrived home from work, he had the dinner ready and a bottle of his favorite Rioja open on the table. Scraps of flame from the newly lit fire wavered in the chimney. There was a delighted question in Ethna's eyes.

"I thought we should celebrate the storm and the third successive day of rain," said Danny.

"They say it's going to clear up for the regatta." Ethna smiled at his many-pocketed waistcoat and the new blue silk scarf round his neck. She took off her mackintosh before lifting me up in her arms. She held her cold cheek to my warm face but for a split second thought how Danny's cheek might feel.

"I met Father Francis today. He looks terrible," said Danny cheerfully.

"What's wrong with him?"

Her eyes were full of the festive table with the apple-shaped candle in the center.

Danny approached us and gently stroked my head. "I don't know. He looked haunted."

And you look gorgeous, he added in his head, and she heard it and blushed.

"Poor Francis. It must be the haunted house. What was the name of the last priest? You know the one I mean?"

"Father Skerrett. He of the cold spot. Why don't you sit in my warm spot and eat?"

As Danny sat at the table watching Ethna and me, he tried to imagine what it would be like to be on his own again. To fry a lamb chop for himself in the evening, sit down at the solitary table with the radio on and only Sharik for company. The thought appalled him. Then he began to wonder what would happen if one of the girls came over for the regatta. They would have to stay at a B & B somewhere on the island. But there would be no such place available. The island was already bursting at the seams with tourists. He became weak at the thought.

Once he entered on the road of self-torment, he couldn't stop himself. Perhaps Ethna thought he was too old for her. Maybe he was just a sugar daddy. He made himself so miserable that he couldn't eat.

"What's got into you all of a sudden?" asked Ethna.

"Something really awful."

"May I ask what it is?"

"You don't want to know. It's too dreadful for words."

"I want to know. Tell me."

"No. I just can't bring myself to ruin your dinner."

"Come on, Danny, out with it!"

"It's the end. I'm finished!"

"Danny!"

"If I tell you, you'll run screaming out of the house with the child in your arms."

"OK. OK. If it's that bad I'll finish my dinner first."

"You really want to know? You think you can bear to hear it?"

"Try me."

"Very well. You asked. I'm in love with you. Isn't it desperate?"

Danny's words stung Ethna. How many times had he said them before to other women? She gave him one of her surgical glances, as if trying to cut through the layers of his buffoonery and posturing.

"How do you know?"

"Jesus, Ethna, how do I know that I love you? I just know for Christ sake!"

It was only when Ethna heard the words for the second time that they reached her.

She panned her eye round the room to learn the scene by heart. She didn't want a single detail to escape her: the melting apple candle casting its shy light on the table, the rain pelting against the windows, Danny's blue eyes darting love and fear, a spider busy about a web above the dresser.

"Why do you think it's so horrible?" she asked in a low voice.

"Well, isn't it?"

"Why do you think you're done for?"

"Well, ain't I?"

"Please stop this."

"What am I supposed to say then?"

"I want to hear it for a third time."

There was dead silence in the room. Sharik and I, aware of the magnitude of the moment, held our breath. The clocks embarrassed us with their relentless ticking.

"I love you," said Danny.

The table lay between them. It would have broken the spell to have stood up and embraced. They were both resisting the stock scripts that told them what to do and that would botch and cheapen the expression of their affection.

They smiled at one another in wonderment. Just when I was about to cry for Ethna's breast, she reached her hand across the table to Danny. He took it in his hand and began to kiss it with devotion in an old-fashioned black-and-white movie way. But before the orchestra could reach an ecstatic climax, the scene changed to garish Technicolor.

"Oh my oh my," we heard an American voice exclaim. "Am I interrupting something special?"

We all swung round to the door. There, like a specter in her see-through plastic mac, stood a dripping Clare. She held a travel bag in either hand.

The Daimon of Father Francis

Father Francis stood in the bay window of his living room and watched the storm breaking over Uggala. Stunted bushes and scrawny hazel bent before the gale like Russian peasants before their czar. The telegraph wires were festooned with rags of seaweed blown from the strand.

He watched Holy Paddy walk backwards into the wind along the shore and thought sourly that, if the storm kept up for a few millennia, Holy Paddy and his tribe would have an evolutionary advantage over forward-facing folk.

When the spirit of Isabelle quit teasing him, he felt bereft. Not even his hallucinations could stick with him for long. He flinched every time he remembered her reproach. His inability to love anybody was inconsequential. It was even respectable and a safeguard in a priest. Agape and not Eros was his calling. But what really disturbed him was that he was a stranger to suffering. However much he knew about other people's pain, he himself felt none of it. Was he a Christian at all? Take up your cross and follow me! What cross, for Christ sake?

"God but you put the heart crossways in me," said Mrs. O'Halloran, "standing like that in the window."

"I didn't know you had such storms in August."

Father Francis was momentarily glad of her company.

"Sure fine weather isn't normal here, Father. It's storms that are normal."

"I see. No sign of the electricity coming back?"

"It should be back tomorrow. We're lucky there's a regatta. Otherwise we'd be waiting for a week."

"How often are we cut off like this?"

"Only four or five times a year. They're the times I like best. No bad news. Will you be wanting something to eat, or are you still on hunger strike? Everything in the house has gone stale on me. Do you want me to bake a farl of soda bread?"

"That'd be nice. I'll be back within the hour."

Father Francis was hardly out the door when he heard the wailing. It rose and fell on the wind. It was coming from the direction of the church. The sound galvanized him. He circled the building until he found a tall woman bundled up against one of the buttresses. She was crying inconsolably.

"May I help you?"

"No, Father."

He recognized Concepta O'Keefe. She was dressed in an old-fashioned green dress with an incongruous handbag over her shoulder. She was soaking wet.

"May I ask what you're doing here?"

"I'm crying to God, Father."

"Perhaps you should go inside? You'd be in shelter at least."

"No, Father. God won't listen to me inside."

"Oh, I'm sure He will."

"I have to cry to Him from the outside."

Concepta leaned her head on the buttress and began to wail again. He felt redundant and walked away.

He should talk to Ethna. Did she have any inkling of her mother's distress?

No. Better be careful. Perhaps Concepta would feel he had betrayed her.

Why then did he find himself walking to Danny's house?

The Daimon of Concepta

☙ Concepta's gusts of grief in the rain were goaded by the memory of an evening exactly twenty-one years earlier. She was cleaning out the attic and came on a bundle of women's magazines. She could hardly believe the dates or the Nellie Hickey dresses that the models wore and that she too once wore. Puzzled, she searched around for the green dress she knew was there somewhere. She found it in a box with her mother's clothes and put it on in spite of the faint smell of rot and mothballs. It was then the day in Galway twenty-odd years ago hit her.

After a somber meeting with the bank manager, she had strayed into a newspaper shop in Quay Street. To take her mind off things she leafed through the women's magazines, only to discover that she was living in the previous century. A women's destiny was not to be a good wife but to be a temptress and a slut with shaven legs and armpits. It was not enough just to be married: you had to have the right bust, bottom, and hips, wear silk jumpsuits, and serve fondue dinners that were contemptuous of cabbage, roast chicken, and Oxo.

At first Concepta glanced through the magazines with her mother's eyes. Like her mother, she reared up against English debauchery in the name of common decency and all that was high and holy. But then her eyes slid to her reflection in the shop window. She saw a sturdy woman in a nylon raincoat and head scarf with her hair coiled up in a bun. For a moment she tried to be Colm O'Keefe, wondering whether he wanted to kiss this portly apparition. She turned hot crimson in self-abasement.

Excited by her transgression, she bought five sinful magazines.

On her way back home she tore into the English debauchery like a desert traveler into a fata morgana. She drew red circles round the advice that would transform her:

- Re-shape Your Body: The at-home plan that works
- Think slim grocery list
- Small ways to get your way

- Bored in Bed? Thirty-five Secrets of Toe-Curling Sex
- Do Real Women Wear More Than Chanel No. 5 in Bed?

After three months of relentless dieting, exercising, controlling her temper, and rehearsing the twenty-five secrets of toe-curling sex, Concepta went back to Galway, had her hair cut and tinted mahogany, and bought herself a green rayon dress and a red bib for Ethna.

When she returned to Uggala, long-legged, fragrant, and kissable, she found her mother in her florid apron seated in the rocking chair with a pile of Concepta's ungodly magazines on her lap. Ethna was asleep in the cot. The room was filled with the asthmatic racketing of the electricity generator.

Her mother patted the magazines with an ancient blistered hand and swiveled her head like an indignant turtle.

"What have you done to yourself, you silly woman?" she asked. "What is it you've done to yourself this time?"

Concepta shrugged her shoulders, prepared for the worst. "Where's Colm?" she asked.

"Are you trying to be like these English hussies with their knickers up over their shoulders? Is that what it's come to in this house?"

"Get off my back!" shouted Concepta. Ethna woke up and began to bawl.

"I just want to know one thing. There's just one thing I want to know. What are you after?"

Concepta had one hand grenade that she had never dared lob at her mother.

"Love," she said. "I want love."

Her mother blanched as if Concepta had danced a cancan in front of her very eyes.

"These things," she said, jabbing the magazines with her index finger, "these things have nothing to do with love. Nothing at all. These things are all about lust."

Concepta would have given anything for Colm's lust.

"What do you know about love apart from what the priests told you?" she asked.

Her mother flung the filthy English magazines on the floor and rose out of the chair with a martyr's grandeur. She left the room in what she took to be dignified silence.

Concepta took up her baby, sat in the granny chair, and sang "Love me tender, love me do," rocking herself gently. She sat and rocked and waited for Colm to come home and embrace her. At three in the morning she fell asleep with Ethna still on her lap and a spreading urine stain on her new green dress.

Twenty-two years on, with her hair once again coiled in a bun and her body wrapped in her green dress, she was still waiting for Colm's embrace.

The Daimon of Father Francis

∾ The weathervane on the roof of Danny's cottage was veering north-northwest in the gusty wind. Father Francis made a mental note to remind himself to ask Danny where he had got it. He would like one for the roof of the church, but with a dove or dolphin rather than a chesty crowing cock.

He hesitated before lifting the heavy knocker. Perhaps the child was asleep? Better tap on the window.

It took Danny a long time to come the door. Then abruptly it was pushed open in Father Francis's face. As he stepped backwards, a young woman carrying two bags stumbled into his arms.

"Clare!" Danny's voice cried.

"Forgive me," said Father Francis, still holding her in his arms. Her warm light scent was like the rush of opium to his brain.

Clare was ready to strangle the first Irishman that crossed her path. "Oh, fuck!" she said.

But when she looked up at Father Francis's beautiful stricken face, she swallowed what was to follow.

Danny appeared in the porch.

"Hello, Francis! Clare, please be sensible. The boat is gone a long time ago and there's no place to stay on the island."

Clare ignored Danny and accosted Father Francis. "Do you have a place to stay? Just for one night. Please."

"Why don't we all go in and have a cup of tea?" beseeched Danny.

Father Francis gazed spellbound at Clare. She had sprung out of a picture book his mother read to him when he was a child. Her face in the rain ached with the gamin pluck of a Tinkerbell. He felt again the stirrings of boyish protectiveness. "I'd be more than happy to help out. There are lots of spare rooms in my place."

"Why, thank you so much. Are you sure I'm not intruding on your privacy?"

"You're a bit late for that," said Danny.

Father Francis shook his head and took Clare's bags.

"Hold on, hold on!" Danny was agitated and relieved in the same breath. "What about the tea?"

"No thanks," said Clare. "I need a shower. Can I have a shower?" she asked Father Francis.

"A bath if you wish."

"A shower's just fine. Good night now, Mr. Ruane, and please say bye-bye to your . . . your baby."

To the end of his days Father Francis will be unable to account for what happened the night of the storm. He won't be able to say whether it was Clare who followed him or whether it was he who trudged after Clare to their common destiny. He knows that they walked in silence to the Parochial House and that he tried to keep a little behind her in order to breathe in the soma of her scent. He knows that she maneuvered on the path so that she could dart quick sidelong glances at him which she disowned on the instant.

He knows that he prepared her strong coffee with a dash of Jameson while she was taking her shower. The last thing he will remember is that his own will and the will of God were at variance.

For the first time in centuries the Parochial House was shocked to shelter a young woman dressed only in a silk kimono, her long wet hair smelling of chamomile shampoo. Up to this it had known only sour celibate men and sexless housekeepers in stained aprons and rubber boots. Father Francis could sense the walls holding their breath as she passed from one panicky room to another. She strode around with a cup of coffee in one hand and a candle in the other, looking with faint amusement at the photographs of massed clergy.

She said nothing. Her silence confused and excited Francis. He was afraid to ask anything. He simply wanted to watch and relish her candlelit presence in the cold sclerotic house. Had he been sufficiently deluded to think in terms of energy he would have explained her presence as a new invigorating charge: fresh yin driving out stale treacly yang.

"So you know Danny Ruane?" she asked finally, settling one riotous haunch on a table.

Father Francis nodded.

"When did he father the child?" she asked directly.

"I don't know that he did. Ethna the girl came back to us pregnant from Italy."

"I guess I just wasn't quite prepared for a family scene. . . . By the way, I'm the clock marked Chicago."

"I'm sorry. Are you terribly disappointed?"

"Not really. Do you have a cigarette?"

Father Francis broke open the packet of Marlboros he kept in reserve.

"I shouldn't have dropped in on Danny just like that. If he had dropped in on my place three weeks ago he'd have found me — well . . . ." She laughed musically.

She looked at the priest with candid eyes that said through the smoke: I want you. He felt scorched by her lustful gaze and stood up awkwardly.

"You must be very tired. I hope you'll be comfortable in your room."

She gave him another lost gamin smile. The rebuff had glanced off her.

"Why don't you go on up to your bed?" she said. "I'll hang on here and have another cigarette if you don't mind."

Father Francis slept for an hour and woke up with a start. He should have been dreaming of caverns or low hills or Isabelle or the ghost of Father Skerrett. Anything that would have alerted him to what was about to happen. But his sleep was dreamless as far as he could tell, as if all his early warning systems had been shut down. He tried his reading lamp to see if the electricity was back, but no, it was still dead. So he lit a candle, propped himself up on the pillows, and tried to pray himself back to sleep.

The wind wailed and moaned in the fireplace, under the door, through the keyhole. He could hear its soughing in the telegraph wires outside the house, and he wondered about Concepta and her frightful openness to the wrath of God as she prayed in the lashing rain.

When he opened his eyes, Clare stood at the foot of the bed. She was wearing loose white silk pajamas, and her blond hair hung round her shoulders. The candle in her hand enhanced the pixie vulnerability of her face.

"It's a spooky night," she said with an exaggerated shiver of her shoulders that shook her breasts. "I just can't sleep."

"Would you like me to make you a cup of . . . cocoa?"

His heart was pounding, and he sounded absurd to himself.

"Don't be silly," said Clare, putting her candle on the bedside table. "Just give me a hug."

Before Father Francis could propose a mug of Ovaltine, Clare was beside him under the duvet. Her scent was a merciful toxin that paralyzed his will. He felt her long exploratory fingers on his chest.

"It's OK," she said assuaging his tension. "It's OK."

When she began to kiss him, he made one last attempt to assert his apartness, but she put her index finger on his lips and hushed him.

"You're a virgin," she whispered, "aren't you?"

"Christ!" said Francis. "I'm a priest."

"And I'm a Southern Baptist. Let's be ecumenical together, OK?"

II
ROAD OF TRIALS

Yes you have permission
Go back to the dream
Your heart sounds with emptiness
Without love
Go back to the dream.
Its tenderness and sadness
Is all that counts
Go back to the dream.
I've equipped you with longing
With the sun of love
You don't have that longing.

Go back to the dream.

— Jelaluddin Rumi

The Daimon of Uggala

෴ When the helicopter made its first pass over the island, people looked up and wondered who was sick. But then Biafra O'Dee pointed out that it wasn't an Air Corps job this time. More likely it was some mad gobshite of a photographer from the *National Geographic* doing a shoot to be called "The Western Ramparts" or some such crap. He and Tom O'Reilly stood gaping at the Thing outside O'Keefe's pub.

The helicopter clattered up and down the island, relishing the white panic of the sheep and the clumsy scrumming of Sean and Seamus's suck calves. To everybody's surprise it ignored the GAA pitch and landed on the road near Balor's Lounge.

There men emerged, crouching low and holding their briefcases across their chests in postures picked up from old TV footage of the Vietnam War.

"I recognize the cunt in the snazzy suit," said Biafra O'Dee. "It's that minister for I don't know what. Rob Roberts must be up to something really mega this time."

Biafra had a nose for Fianna Fáil types. There were two beasts in them, the bullock and the serpent. One sort bore down on you with his tail in the air and a fatuous smirk on his beefy muzzle. The other slid through the long grass, sleek and lethal, pretending not to see you but noting everything down to your Finna Gael tan leather brogues. Ideology had become biology in the Republican Party.

"It's the minister for western affairs," said Tom.

Colm in his best pin-striped suit greeted the visitors with a cupla focal, but when he noticed the glazed look in the minister's eyes he quickly switched to English. He made an inviting gesture towards Balor's Bar, but the men refused. The minister wanted to go directly to the field where the Heritage Centre was to be built.

Rob Roberts was gesticulating expansively, an imperious finger stabbing the horizon.

Biafra O'Dee stroked his chin. "It's beginning to happen. The New World Order arrives on Uggala!"

"That's all we need now," said Tom.

"Rob Roberts is going to deflower the island. I saw it from the start."

"More of your astrological bilge."

"Only a communist dimwit like you would fail to recognize the man and the moment," said Biafra. "You're about to see how the whim of one individual can change the whole history of a community."

"Pull the other one."

The Daimon of Rob Roberts

∾ Rob Roberts had come to Ireland at a time when the country was preparing its own funeral. The place had no future, the newspapers said. Economists, columnists, and historians gleefully dissected the Hibernian corpse that stretched out under perpetually leaking skies. The more hair-raising the condition, the more scintillating the conclusions. Those who couldn't afford to seek solace in offshore accounts in the Cayman Islands or in Marxist analysis at Oxford turned to moving statues of the Virgin Mary. The rain beat down every day, wetter and more malevolent than ever before.

The public were pestered by the Taoiseach to tighten their

belts and by earnest literature professors to rethink, rewrite, and reread everything. These were exorbitant demands: most people felt that they had enough to do to get from one end of the day to another with the help of Valium.

When Rob Roberts first spotted the wistful green pastures of Limerick and Clare from the port window of the Boeing 747, his gut feeling told him that *The Irish Times* in his print-blackened hands had got the story all wrong. The country of his forefathers seven thousand feet below was not moribund. It was waiting for him this October 1985 with all its riches. There was history, for example. And what a history at that! You had pagans, Christians, martyrs, heroes, battles, six hundred years of oppression, and best of all, white people who had the advantage of suffering in English. Heaney was right. Irish history was layered like turf. Except that it wasn't turf. It was fucking veins of liquid gold. If only one tilted the landscape at the right angle, it would come oozing out — guggle, guggle, guggle.

There were obstacles, such as the evident disdain for the mundane. No public clock in Dublin told the same hour. No bus followed any schedule. There wasn't any schedule. You could describe this as some kind of low Irish poltroonery. Rob chose to describe it as a longing for the Transcendent and to turn it to profit. He found the half-speak, half-style of Fianna Fáil perfectly suited to his purposes. After the bland literalness of America, the nods, winks, unfinished sentences, and eloquent silences of the F and Fers were piquant and exciting. As long, of course, as you were Sound on the National Question, ha ha ha.

Within three years Rob Roberts had mastered the threefold arts of noncommunicating communication, of acting illegally within the law, and of striking lucrative deals with the insubstantial solid men who ran the country.

It was time to move on Uggala.

My Daimon

🐦 "If I hit your circle with a pebble, you have to run and run as fast as you can," said Thresheen. "Then you must draw another circle round yourself before I count to five."

"Why?" I asked.

"Because if you're inside the circle you're safe. Everything outside the circle is dangerous."

"But why?"

"Because because. It's called safe circles, Silly Billy."

We were on Clydagh Strand, playing a game invented by Thresheen. The idea was to run like mad while she counted to five and draw a circle before you were hit by a pebble. It was great fun, but like all Thresheen's games it had very strange, complicated rules. I never knew who won or even how to win. But still and all I ran around the beach drawing circles and shouting, "I win! I win!"

"You're cheating again," said Thresheen. "That's not how you do it!"

"I'm just quicker than you!"

Sharik sat and barked. I wondered if he could see Other-wheres. Pigs could see the wind, so maybe he could see the place where Thresheen lived.

Danny cut across the beach towards me, lifted me up, and swung me in his arms. "Enough for today, Finn. We have to meet your mammy at the Quay."

He looked at the scattered circles on the sand. "Who were you playing with?" he asked offhandedly.

"Sarah Jane," I lied.

"But I thought you preferred Michael John Patrick."

"He's in jail today."

"What did he do this time?"

"He stole MacGowan's ass and rode it over the cliff."

I didn't have to think about these answers. They came to

me automatically, like the responses to the Litany. They were prompted by Thresheen. All I had to do was to think of her and there she was. I would first feel a warm glow in my chest, and then she would stand in front of me like a real person in military fatigues with an Indian feather stuck in her cropped brown hair. On special occasions she dressed as a ballerina, and she would refuse to climb trees with me because the green lichens stained her tutu. We had an agreement that never but never would I reveal her presence to anybody.

We arrived at the quay just as *The Morning Star* was docking. As usual Ethna and Danny ran towards one another and hugged and kissed forever and ever. I was deeply embarrassed, and so was Sharik. Then Ethna threw herself on me and the dog, and half-strangled us with caresses. But even that wasn't the end. On the way home she and Danny stopped in gateways and started the hugging business all over again.

Ethna came back to the island once a month for a long weekend. It was her last year of study in Dublin and the peak of her romance with Danny. While I squirmed with shame for the two of them, Thresheen relished their rustproof passion.

"Don't be such a prig," she said.

"But why do they have to paw one another all over?"

"They're reconnecting. They're like a plug and a socket, you see? Danny's got lots of pins set at all sorts of weird angles. It's not every socket he can plug himself into. Ethna is the only one that fits him to a T."

Thresheen loved to explain things to me, though I didn't always get the point of her comparisons.

I learned there were two reasons for everything.

Like: "Don't go to the Spanish Stone," Ethna warned me. "You'll fall into a bog hole on the way and we'll never find you again."

"Don't go to the Spanish Stone," said Thresheen. "The place is chock-full of unhappy dead men."

At last Danny and Ethna stopped clinging to one another and we walked home normally, with me riding piggy-back on Danny's shoulders.

"How's it going up there, Finn?" Ethna asked.

Danny answered for me. "He spent all day playing with . . . what's her name again, Finn?"

"Sarah Jane," I said reluctantly. In the happy plenitude of their presence, Sarah Jane seemed very foggy all of a sudden.

"The other one, Patrick John Michael, is in jail, you know," continued Danny. "He went too far. They caught him snaring puffins or something. Am I right, Finn?"

Danny enjoyed distorting my pretend world, and I was helpless to put it right.

"It's not true," I said. "You change things."

I bashed him on the head.

"Isn't he living too much in a fantasy world?" asked Ethna.

"He's not even five," said Danny. "What do you expect? And there are no other children to play with."

"There will be children," I said involuntarily. "Lots of them."

"What children?" Ethna was apprehensive.

"There will be lots and lots of children. And their parents too. They'll be coming in buses to Gortnanein."

"I'll be damned. To my Thinking Place! How do you know?" Danny was all ears.

"I just know."

"Are you planning something, Danny?" asked Ethna.

"Jesus no! I want to be left alone there."

They were so taken aback that I knew I had made a mistake.

"You've been talking to the fairies again, Finn."

Every time Ethna came home the house was the same — but it was completely different. Her comments and astonishments gave me new pairs of eyes and ears. All of a sudden I would notice that the swallows were flying with their young, or that the lupines had gone to seed, or that the rose in the porch smelled of vanilla. Danny's kitchen was the same old kitchen, but with Ethna around it throbbed with festive expectation like at Christmas.

Ethna looked around, and we looked around with her. When she exhaled a long sigh of content, we knew our own importance in the universe. And then the moment I loved best, when she asked us to close our eyes and she rummaged and rummaged in her bag for our presents and said things like Oh, maybe I left it at the station! Or Gosh, the man sitting opposite me must have stolen it!

My heart would stop beating for a moment.

No. Here it is!

And my heart was off again. Then, oh and ah, we sat down to Bewley's horseshoe buns and strawberry jam.

Danny always prepared the first dinner in advance and ostentatiously displayed all the dishes at once so that he could extort the maximum praise from Ethna. He was worse than Sharik. The more we extolled him the more puffed up he became as he flicked a flamboyant dishcloth from one shoulder to the other.

"How are things?" the ritual questions began. "How's Biafra O'Dee?"

"Wanking away as usual."

"And our beautiful Francis?"

"Pulling the divil by the tail. Literally. He's very tormented."

Ethna nodded triumphantly. "It was all so predictable. Remember when we sat here and I asked him what he would do if he fell in love?"

"No! Did you ask him that?"

"Come on, Danny. You must remember the evening when I dropped in and we talked about God!"

"God? Did we talk about God?"

Ethna leaned towards me. "You see, Finn! He remembers nothing. Soon he won't even know our names."

Then I made my second slip.

"It was the time of the three clocks!" I said eagerly. "Over there, above the fire."

Their jaws dropped.

"How could you . . . ? You weren't born yet!" cried Ethna.

I understood I had said too much and I withdrew into myself.

"How do you know there were three clocks there?" asked Danny.

I shrugged my shoulders. I was as puzzled as he was.

"What else do you know?"

"Nothing."

Danny and Ethna held a silent council with their eyes.

"Well, he's our little Dalai Lama," Danny tried to joke.

"I'm Finn Patrick O'Keefe," I protested.

Ethna chewed her poppy seed. Danny stroked the lobe of his left ear. Our eyes were drawn to the mantelpiece, where once the clocks stood.

"Look here, Finn . . ." Ethna began, but gave up in midsentence and plucked Danny by the sleeve. "Why don't we phone Father Francis? I haven't spoken to him for ages."

Father Francis was the expert on all problems pertaining to the preternatural.

The Daimon of Father Francis

 Every time Father Francis was on the phone to Ethna, he had the urge to frame a once-and-for-all statement of the changes Clare had wrought in him. But the statement eluded him. He had no language in which to speak about her. He tried his damnedest not to surrender to mushy raptures like I'm saturated with her, or She flows through me, or All the songs on the radio are about us, do you know what I mean?

Ethna always knew what he meant. She helped him to finish his sentences, told him what he felt and what he was going to do next.

"You say you can't give up Clare. And you can't give up your priesthood either. Fine. There's an obvious way out."

"What is it?"

"Join the Church of Ireland. Retrain as a minister. Get yourself a nice middle-class parish in Dublin. You're already a Protestant whether you like it or not. We all are."

However logical or reasonable this advice was, Father Francis's soul balked at it. Once again he cross-examined himself. Was it because he couldn't part with the comforting polytheism of Catholic belief: the Virgin, angels, and saints? No. Was it because of atavistic ideas of Irishness, Cromwell, and so on? No again, but that was closer. Catholicism had grown inside his chest like the alien body in science-fiction films. It had hollowed him out from the inside. It was a monster but it was his monster, fed not only with his own viscera but with the blood of generations of his ancestors. Plucking out the creature would undo him and leave him soulless and exiled from himself.

At the same time, how could he preach a gospel of love without ever knowing what love was? It was only now, just at the very moment he was finished as a priest, that he was ready to be a priest.

When he woke up beside Clare after the night of the big storm, she had glanced at him with a little smile on her lips.

"So what are you thinking about?" she asked.

"I know what I should be thinking."

He wanted to tell her that he was doing in his thirties what he should have been doing in his teens, that he felt like crying, that he wanted to caress her breasts all day long, that he would love and hate to give everything to her without leaving anything for God. That her skin was as silky soft as a cyclamen petal.

Instead he said, glancing with panic at the alarm clock, "Jesus! Mrs. O'Halloran will be here in ten minutes. You've got to go, I'm afraid."

And calm as you please, as if it was her daily routine, Clare packed up her things and left without breakfast and with hardly a word.

It was just the right thing to do. Usually she would have made a scene, or hung on to bargain, unwilling to pick up the broken bits and pieces of her life again. This time her Daimon told her to shut up and go. And she did so with an ease that surprised her. She left Francis to sink to the bottom of the sea.

He spent the following three days underwater in mute, muddy depths, with ferocious pressure beating on him from all sides. He began to fantasize about Clare, and the more he fantasized about her the more he longed for her. And the more he longed for her the more he fantasized. His mind was like a Dalí landscape where delirious torsos writhed on burning sands of paranoia. Towards the end of the week, he went to Danny and asked for Clare's number in Austin.

"She wanted me to send her something," he mumbled and blushed.

"So — she's made an impression!" said Ethna.

"She just wants something on Meister Eckhart."

"Clare? Meister Eckhart?" exclaimed Danny.

But Father Francis was already calling Clare in his head and apologizing for the abrupt way he'd asked her to leave that morning. God, he hadn't even offered her a cup of tea!

"May I speak to Clare Elder?"

"This is she."

That *she* of hers was jam-packed with estrogen. It was the sexiest word he had ever heard. She was a she that was self-consciously a she. Maybe Irish women hid their sheness from him because he was a priest?

Lies, he discovered, came very easily to him.

"I'll be in Austin next month for an interfaith conference. Maybe we could meet up?"

"Sure. You're welcome to stay a night in my place. No breakfast though."

He knew immediately from the mixture of playfulness and relief in her voice that she welcomed his call. It was odd to hear her addressing him as Francis rather than Father Francis. He felt it defrocked and re-penised him.

He stayed with Clare, how long did he stay with her? Together they entered the ephemeral, self-contained realm of lovers, where all the world collapses into a little room and one runs short of milk and matches and washing powder.

God who sees everything was merciful. He coughed discreetly when Clare taught Father Francis the orbicular caress of her buttocks that stirred in her delicious ripples of serenity. He raised his bushy eyebrows to the seventh heaven when Father Francis kissed Clare on the dimples of her knees and recited "I'll love you till the ocean / is folded and hung up to dry, / and the seven stars go squawking / like geese about the sky."

"Why don't you stay?" asked Clare as she trailed a hungry finger down her lover's face. "Why won't you stay forever and ever amen?"

"I can't. I need to be where God is."

"Well, isn't He supposed to be everywhere?"

"I thought so until now. But the God of Austin is senile and superfluous and living out his last days on a fat pension."

"How do you know? We haven't even gone out."

Father Francis palped the air with his hand. "I've stopped praying. And I don't feel fearful or sinful anymore."

"But that's great!"

He thought of Concepta crying to the Almighty in the rain

and the wind. Now he understood her. God, like the nature spirits before Him, had retreated to the waste places of the world.

The Daimon of Clare

❧ Masturbation is rarely the basis of one's destiny. In the case of Clare, however, it played a defining role. Her extraordinary charm lay in the way her beauty was alloyed with guilt — guilt for the death of her aunt Lisbeth. Only Danny knew the secret, whispered to him in a moist postcoital reverie while he stroked her pupcia.

Clare was exhausted by being fifteen years of age. She spent hours coping with an overwhelming lust for her own body. So compelling were her wants that she mastered the art of having an orgasm while talking to her mother at the kitchen table. Only her eyes rolled back in her head as she climaxed.

"Stop rolling your eyes!" her mother would berate her. "There's no need to be ironic all the time."

That Thanksgiving the house was full of family and Clare had to share her room with Aunt Lisbeth. Aunt Lisbeth took over her pretty single bed, in which she had so often stretched and tossed to the limits of human endurance. Clare slept on the couch, resolved to banish all fantasies for twelve hours and to maintain the virginal facade that Aunt Lisbeth chose to cherish in her niece against all reason.

"Good night, Auntie," Clare said in her most unchipped enamel voice.

"Good night, dear sweet Clare," said Aunt Lisbeth.

Those were the last coherent words she spoke on earth.

It took Clare ages to get to sleep because her aunt's heavy breathing filled the room like a bellows. Before dawn Clare awoke with a howl of want in her underbelly. She couldn't hold out any longer. She just had to give in. She was standing naked in the snow tied to a birch tree. The cold night wind was lurid between her thighs. There was a fox advancing towards her. She could see his tiny precise prints in the snow. Oh God oh God.

At that very moment Aunt Lisbeth uttered a low distressed moan. But tied to the birch tree as she was, with the fox beginning to lick her toes, Clare was in no position to pay much attention to anything but the red rollicking randy beast.

Aunt Lisbeth groaned alarmingly and muttered something desperate about Jes-us. But fear only tightened the laces of Clare's lust.

"Naughty boy," she whispered frantically to the fox, who was now standing on his hind legs. "Naughty, naughty boy!"

"Aaaaagh" went Aunt Lisbeth, as Clare finally dissolved before the soft probing of the fox's tongue.

After that there was a snoreless silence in the room. For a long time Clare was too afraid to get up and see what was the matter. When she finally tiptoed to the bed and saw Aunt Lisbeth's wide-open astonished eyes, she was paralyzed with fear. She had killed poor chaste Aunt Lisbeth with the sheer lewd force of her lust.

Ever since that night, she had a definite sense that she was meant for damnation and then before her final punishment odd things would happen to her. For once you provoke a concurrence between comforting yourself and the death of your favorite aunt, you trigger a chain reaction of Fortean events that persists to the end of your days.

Only Clare would find, on two separate occasions, letters in bottles along the New England coast. One contained a curse in pidgin English sent from Fuerteventura: "Fuk you who me find!" The other had been thrown overboard from a ferry and commanded: "Be wild and dangerous!"

This Clare took to heart as her motto in life. She designed a heraldic shield for herself with a tower, a book, a flying saucer, and an oyster shell in the four quadrants. And beneath it an uncurling scroll which read: Es savius et pericolosum.

Only Clare would come to Uggala to research her master's thesis on the sexual mores of an island community and trip over Danny of the Golden Balls. Only Clare would deflower a Catholic priest in the name of ecumenical relations. In her world the remote was familiar and the improbable possible.

"Stay on Uggala?" she had said to Danny all of seven years ago. "I'd rather die."

And now she was thinking of settling down on the island, Whore of Babylon as she was, and having Father Francis's babies.

My Daimon

᠆ Sometimes in my secret play with Thresheen, I became so absorbed that I was no longer clear which world I inhabited. The boundaries were paper thin, time was elastic, and the voices that spoke to me rang in my head with lilting cadences long after I settled down to the table for tea in Danny's kitchen. I could see the alarm on Ethna's face when she caught me talking to the thin air or inadvertently blurting out things I couldn't possibly have known. Once she sat me in the rocking chair and crouched down beside me.

"We have to have a talk," she said and rocked the chair gently. "You hear and see things the rest of us don't, don't you?"

I shrugged my shoulders.

"Are you just daydreaming do you think?" she said hopefully.

"No."

"So tell me what you do."

Even though Thresheen had forbidden me to tell anybody, I found it hard to imagine that Ethna didn't have a secret door into Otherwheres herself. Besides, I didn't have the words to describe It.

"I'm worried about you, Finn. I don't want you to be special."

"Why not?"

"Because I'm afraid you'll be unhappy. I want you to be average."

"But I want to be special!"

Ethna looked at me, surprised.

"I don't want to be average," I said defiantly. But I felt fear. If Ethna was so concerned, that could only mean that there was some mysterious force out there waiting to take its revenge on me.

"I don't do anything wrong," I said.

"No. But you know too much about the past and the future. You've got these, well, powers. Blast it, why can't you be a bit stupid and play with dinosaurs?"

"I hate dinosaurs."

"OK. You're free to be what you want, of course. But just the same I'd like you to know how I feel about it. Let's leave it for now."

As I climbed the stairs back to the attic, I felt a tremor of exaltation and unease. A sword had touched my shoulder, and I had risen a proud knight of Otherwheres. But at the same time I wanted Ethna to rescue me from my mysterious powers, to take me back to the kitchen, put the small apron around my waist, and ask me to beat the eggs for a sponge cake.

"Knight of Otherwheres me granny," said Thresheen, who appeared in a blue brocaded dress and a cockeyed sequined headband for the occasion. "Look here. It's up to you to be as happy or unhappy as you wish about coming and going to Otherwheres. It's your decision, brother! You can always tell me to buzz off any time out of time you want to."

"Let's play," I said heroically.

"Good boy," said Thresheen. "It's better than beating eggs any day."

The Daimon of Danny Ruane

🐦 On the night Father Francis recited Auden and kissed the dimples on Clare's knees, Danny staged his first rebellion against Ethna.

We were finishing our tea when Ethna slid a sly question to me across the table with a piece of sponge cake.

"What do you say to Christmas in Dublin, Finn? We could go to see the puppets in Brown Thomas's and then have horseshoe buns in Bewley's." Ethna smiled at me encouragingly, trying not to look at Danny.

On the face of it, it was a simple banal suggestion. But, as it turned out, it was like a shout in a valley that brings down an avalanche.

"Why Dublin? This is our home! Besides, I had planned out a whole chapter, the most difficult one in the book," said Danny.

"Can't you just as well write it in Dublin?"

"No. At Christmas in Dublin you do what the herd does. Shopping and eating and watching television. There's no way out of it."

"And on Uggala you slip into a coma."

In her tight green jumper (who had bought it for her?) Ethna looked more alluring than ever. But this evening Danny resented the slope of her breasts and the rich luster of her hair.

"Look, Ethna, are you trying to tell me something?"

"Like what?"

"Are you tired of Uggala or are you tired of me?"

"What a really silly question!"

"Well, which is it?"

"OK, Danny. You have your book. But I have my projects too, you know."

"But you always prepared for your exams here!"

"It's not just exams. It's other things. Better if I'm in Dublin."

He had seen it coming for months. It was almost a relief now that the moment had arrived.

"Do as you wish. I'm not going anywhere."

The vehemence of his refusal had little or nothing to do with Ethna's reluctance to stay on Uggala over Christmas. It was more that a bulwark between them had begun to crack. Up until the spring of her final year in college, Danny had managed to keep Ethna's life in Dublin sealed away in a separate compartment of his mind. It had nothing to do with him, the salt sea flowed between Uggala and Leeson Street, and he never made any attempt to imagine what she was doing or with whom. Ethna sustained the apartheid of their two worlds: when she did mention her other life, it was always to amuse us with horror stories of the love lives of her friends or the more bizarre events in college. It was not a life we needed to take seriously.

But then the phone had started to ring. A medley of alien voices demanded to speak to her or left messages or kept her on the line for ages. They conjured a different Ethna to the one Danny was used to: brisk, flirtatious, possessed.

Did he know her at all?

Perhaps their long-weekend intimacies were an elaborate cover-up? The assured voice of Professor Bollocks, as Danny called him, seemed to suggest a closeness and a control over Ethna that made Danny bristle. Were they shagging one another in the cellar of the Architecture School? And the dismissive arrogance of this fucker Fennel, whoever he was, told Danny that he and Ethna were having a good laugh at Uggala and its resident sage. Soon, whoever rang, man or woman indiscriminately, was shagging Ethna either in the cellar of the Architecture School or the George Moore Room of the Shelbourne or in an art nouveau villa in Dalkey.

Danny knew that these were all foul fantasies. And yet

once he opened the door to them, he couldn't drive them away. They swarmed around him for days on end and sapped his energy. But at the same time they provided him with one of the most perverse and addictive of pleasures: the acrid taste of victimhood leavened with self-righteousness.

The cyanide blue of Danny's delirium spread to me. A single word swelled out of the poisonous pool. Though Ethna's eyes were mildly bemused, I wasn't going to be taken in by her.

"I know what you want to do," I blurted out. "You want to go to Barcelona!"

"What?" Ethna gasped. "What do you know about Barcelona?"

We were all stunned — Ethna by my revealing her secret, Danny by the welling up of fear within him, I by what I had just let slip. But I had to protect us.

"How on earth do you know about Barcelona?" She was both startled and afraid of me.

"Why didn't you tell me you were going to Spain?" Danny broke in.

"I'm not going to Spain. There's just a suggestion that I should go for a job interview. I haven't even booked the ticket, for God's sake."

"And when is this interview?" Danny asked icily.

"January fifth. Look, I need a job. I'm almost finished with my studies."

"Of course. But in Barcelona?"

"It's probably the most exciting place to be architecturally right now."

"I see."

"Danny, we can't stay forever on the island. You might just as well bury yourself alive."

"I'm staying here," he said stubbornly.

"Very well. You'll be here. I'll be there. After all, you like long-distance romances. You can call me every Monday, eight o'clock my time."

They were moving very close to the danger zone where things once said can never be retracted. The next few sentences might plant a poison that the passing of time would never dilute.

"I'm going for a walk." Danny tugged on his raincoat.

"I'm going with you," I said.

That's how we punished Ethna. Let her feel how it would be like on her own. Let her stew in front of her one-bar-heater fire for a while.

The Daimon of Rob Roberts

🐚 "Never piss in your own wet suit," repeated Rob Roberts to all and sundry. Nobody quite knew what this injunction was supposed to mean at a deeper level. But he pronounced it with a learned wag of his finger and a mocking smile on his lips as if it contained all the wisdom in the world. Like Mickey Rourke in *Barfly* muttering enigmatically, "You've gotta roll the potato," to show what a shrewd Irish lad he was.

Even though Rob Roberts was a bit of a mystery on Uggala, people were proud and protective of him because he was their American millionaire and his grandmother was a Curtis from Clydagh. One summer he had appeared from nowhere on a kingfisher blue yacht and anchored for days at the back end of the island. He lived aboard and came ashore only for supplies and a quick pint in Balor's Bar. People called him Captain because he sported a baseball cap with oak leaves braided on the visor. The folklore about him was that his tanned Spanish good looks were four hundred years old and came from a Catalonian noblewoman who had been smuggled aboard one of the doomed ships of the Armada that had foundered somewhere off the coast. Women went warm-wombed at the sight of his tall muscular body and the naughty schoolboyish grin that said, I've got you but I'll keep you until later.

Never piss in your own wet suit indeed. What could he mean?

His resolute walk proclaimed that here was a man who knew where he was going and how to get there. When you asked him what he was up to and why he spent the summer diving off Clancy's Rocks, he scratched his beard and answered, half-apologetically, that he was studying the life cycle of the sea urchin. The sea urchin was an extraordinary creature: Did you know that there were over seven hundred species of the little buggers and they could excavate hiding places for themselves in solid steel?

He said he was an honorary fellow of the Marine Institute in Boston and tapped a florid badge of intertwined ropes and hieroglyphs on his sleeve. He spoke in a soothing voice with an American twang and exuded an air of superhuman ease and freedom.

On the rare occasions when he dropped into the pub, he bought a round for everybody and told jokes that were old in Boston but new to Uggala. He disarmed the most vicious calumniators. Even the Skipper, who never had a good word to say about anybody, clapped him on the back and shouted: Yer a gas man, Captain, that's what y'are. The scroungers shook their heads in wonderment that a man of his talents and wealth should waste his time on Uggala even if his grandmother was a Curtis from Clydagh. And that he should still be diving and snorkeling around the feckin place after what happened to poor Rory O'Reilly.

Poor Rory. The name was half-sunk in Rob Roberts's memory. When it drifted up to the surface, it aroused a mixture of anger and grief in him. He should have seen straightaway that the boy's eager, goofy innocence would only foul things up. At the same time, what could he have done? Rory had already been diving before he arrived on Uggala. Given his persistence and the amount of free time he had on his hands, he was bound to stumble on something. It was either team up with him or else.

Rory's pimpled face broke into a quick responsive smile when Rob proposed that they dive together in search of hatpin urchins off Clancy's Rocks.

"Smashing," said the boy. Tom and Alice were visiting relatives in Clifton, so there would be nobody to harass him about perpetually wasting his time fooling around in the sea.

Clancy's Rocks rose blunt and ominous out of a maelstrom of raging currents. The island lobstermen avoided them at all costs, and they could be approached only at the slackest of slack tides. But Rob Roberts, who had explored the seabed square by square on the windward side of the island, was not going to stop now. He knew that what he was looking for just had to be there. Sea urchins!

"If we look for a penny and find a pearl, we won't toss it away," he said jovially to Rory as he rowed him out in the punt that morning. "And we won't tell anybody either, OK?"

They'd been diving for scarcely half an hour when Rory swam towards him with an iron cannonball in his hand. He beckoned Rob to follow.

There had been many occasions when Rob had pictured this moment to himself. That picture did not include Rory. So when he approached the gray corpse of the long ballast pile that seemed to slip between two and three dimensions and was barely distinguishable from the seabed, he completely ignored the boy. This was his treasure. That ship was his destiny. Rory was nothing more than an insignificant accidental appurtenance.

Rob Roberts stopped breathing. Was it the *Sant Nicolas Prodanelli*? Or the *San Juan de Fernando de Hora*? He prayed that it was the *San Juan*. She was the fastest ship of the Great Armada and had been wrecked off the coast of Ireland sometime in August 1588. Never accounted for. Until now that is.

As he floated delightedly over the strewn seabed, Rob Roberts was already editing the moment for his biography. The opening would go: Not everybody's life reaches its climax at the bottom of the Atlantic Ocean suspended over the four-hundred-year-old wreck of a Spanish galleon. In the cold current, my hand reached out to touch a quartz bottle with a silver stopper that remembered the scent of orange blossom in sunny Andalusia.

Maybe he should get a ghostwriter after all? He picked something — a lead ingot? — from the rubble on the sea-floor and kicked himself to the surface.

"Nobody is to know about this," he said as they removed their gear aboard the punt.

"You're not going to report it?"

Rob shook his head.

"You're not going to tell the Guards?"

Rob was lethally calm.

"No," he said curtly. "I've spent four years of my life searching for this ship. I know everything that's to be known about her. I know her contents from the smallest cannon to the name of the cook. And you want me to call in the goddam Garda subaqua team! It's like asking a champion tennis player to team up with a rank amateur. Give me what you have there."

"It's only a rock," said the boy contemptuously. "You might as well throw it back."

Rob didn't mean what the boy held in his hand. He meant the figurine he had secreted in the folds of his wet suit.

"Look, I'll pay whatever it takes. And arrange a place for you in an American college. What about it?" Rob smiled encouragingly.

"I'll think about it," Rory said ponderously. He was enjoying having the upper hand.

"Fine," said Rob. "Have it your own way."

His voice was friendly and accommodating. That was the voice of one Rob. But there was another Rob, who raved and raged against the greedy blockhead sitting knee to knee opposite him.

The sea was level as a sheet of steel. "Weigh anchor and let's get out of here."

"So what are you going to do now?" asked Rory.

Rob saw what he was going to do in a flash of intuition.

"I need to get some hydraulic equipment, so I'll be away for a few days. We can settle things when I get back."

Rob hung around for the next slack tide. He returned to the wreck at dawn and strung a fine mesh fouling net between the ballast and an outlier of Clancy's Rocks. The currents would ensure that anybody who approached the *San Juan* would be caught like an eel in a trap.

Two days later he cut the thief loose from the netting. There was a jam jar of silver coins in his scrim bag. The body tumbled gently out to sea over waving acres of dirty brown wrack.

When Rob Roberts returned to the island in the company of the minister for western affairs with his vision of Uggala Rediviva, he wondered what he actually felt about the incident. It was like being in a film. No. It was like passing through a storm in one's head and emerging into calm on the other side. Sweet beneficent calm. Everything was going to be all right in the end. Whatever happened was meant to happen. He had been through hell. He had suffered. From now on he would be a better person. He would do great things for the island.

The Daimon of Ethna

 "Ah, the Queen of Uggala! Back to civilization in Dublin, are we?"

Larry Lydon was manic behind the bar. He winked craftily at Ethna as he pulled pints for his lunchtime customers.

"Before I can give you a drop to drink you have to sign the Book of Jubilations."

"What's to celebrate?"

"The death of the Soviet Union. I'm not selling a drink to anyone unless they sign."

He pushed an old ledger across to her.

Larry beamed. He had found another way to rile the tight-arsed socialists and radicals who treated his pub as a refuge for the gratefully aggrieved.

The page in front of Ethna was scrawled over with names, most of them in Irish to hide the signatory's identity.

"The intelligentsia struggled with their conscience, and the intelligentsia won." Larry cackled. "The usual G and T?"

The familiar stink of stale beer, cigarettes, and testosterone hit Ethna and made her recoil.

"Is there anybody with you?" asked Larry.

"I've an hour to kill before a meeting at three," she lied.

She had given herself an hour to decide whether she would head for Heuston Station and return to Uggala or book a flight to Barcelona.

She had left the island astounded by Danny's thickheadedness. He didn't need her, good bad, or indifferent. She was just a vignette in his life, a weekend recreation easily replaced by some wide-eyed, narrow-hipped creature with a foreign accent. What was the connection between her and Danny anyway? Worse, what was the connection between her and her son? How did Finn know her most secret plans? How could a completely ridiculous insemination by a git of a Frenchman produce a magus like him? Anyway, by now he was more Danny's son than anything else, ganging up with him against her and backing up his every yea and nay.

There was a bearded fellow leaning against the bar and watching her like a hawk. She knew the type. He would have extraordinary intuitive powers but be perfectly hopeless at everything else. Even the stained Crombie coat bundled round his middle was par for the course. It had come from the Vincent de Paul.

Like a ghoul he had locked on to her melancholy and was feeding off it. Even when she looked away she could sense his greedy-for-sorrow eyes on her. She resented the oppressiveness of his empathy, which pronounced that he and she were members of the same lost tribe and that there was nothing for them to do but get plastered.

She wasn't mistaken about the powers of his intuition. Just as she had made up her mind to leave, he shambled over to the bar and spoke to her without preface.

"What would you say to this? Pay attention now. In five minutes' time I could follow you outside and cut your throat. Just like that. Now think of the consequences. The kind of effect your death would have on your parents. Your brothers and sisters or on your children if you have any. In five minutes flat I could cause a mountain of sorrow that would last for decades. Now tell me this and tell me no more. Is there a single thing in the world I could do in the next five minutes that would raise a similar mountain of joy and happiness? There isn't. There just isn't. So you see, the world is weighed towards evil and grief. Sláinte!"

He passed on to the men's without waiting for her reaction, gleeful that he had planted another mind mine.

"Is that big galoot bothering you, Ethna?" asked Larry.

She shook her head and glanced out the window. It was beginning to snow. Ethna had always loved snow and thought of it as a good omen. As she tightened her scarf round her neck, she couldn't shake off the image of a quivering cut throat, like the throat of a fish. Suppose that sadist inside did follow her. How many circles and ripples of grief would her death cause? Was life merely a struggle to enlarge the circle of mourners when one was no more?

The Daimon of Tom O'Reilly

🙋 As the snow disappointed itself into sleet over Baggot Street, Tom O'Reilly stood forlorn in front of a newly decorated Christmas tree with a bloodcurdling idea in his head. There were two connected universes, he thought. One consisted of stars and planets and galaxies. The other was the world of projects, dreams, and aspirations begotten in the human brain. Some dreams densified and took on tangible shape, like the comets and the suns. Others remained incomplete and diffuse. They were like cloudy interstellar dust or cosmic debris — broken relationships, unfinished poems, unopened factories, rejected songs, abandoned revolutions, shelved policies, piers that, however much they ached, never became bridges.

He shivered at the thought of all the energy expended on these unfinished creations. Were they pure loss, he wondered. Or was there as yet some undiscovered ratio in the universe that demanded that for every success there be a thousand failures? Was his life part of the galactic litter?

Winter swooped on Uggala, and the island slipped into a dreamless void. Tom took long walks on the sea cliffs, muttering to himself, What am I to do what am I to do? There was a nameless depth in him that wanted to mean something. He felt like a tree that hasn't hummed its melody.

"All you have to do is to pray to God for guidance," said Alice, ignoring as always the fact that Tom was an atheist — that is, until he understood that he himself was God. "Or try Saint Anthony."

"What's he good for?"

"He finds things."

Tom shook his head.

"What am I supposed to say to him? Dear Saint Anthony, please find for me the meaning of life?"

Alice was skeptical. It seemed a lot to ask for all at once. People usually prayed for lost rings or watches or passports or suchlike.

"Ah, so he's only a small-time operator?" jeered Tom. "A heavenly pawnbroker."

Alice compressed her lips, went to the bedroom, kneeled in front of the Flaming Heart, and prayed: O holy Saint Anthony, comforter of the afflicted, we beseech you come to our Tom's aid and help him to recover the meaning of his life if it is God's holy will.

She added the petition to the trimmings of her rosary for a week without any improvement in Tom's corrosive melancholy. In the end she became annoyed.

"Why do you need this meaning? If you only believed in God you'd have all the meaning you want."

It was the one thing about Alice that made Tom see red. For her everything — health, their pension, Tom's love — was a gift from God, like a box of double-centered chocolates or Jameson seven-year-old whiskey at Christmas. For him things had to be fought for and searched out and there were no divine interventions.

The savage storms that tore through Uggala over Advent put a stop to Tom's rambles. He was boxed up at home with Alice and the *Eighteenth Brumaire of Louis Napoleon*. Alice got so fed up with him under her feet that at the first sign of a break in the weather she presented him with his blackthorn stick and said, "Why don't you go and talk to Father Francis?"

Father Francis was surely the last man on the island to lead Tom into a glorious future of peace, equality, brotherhood, and meaning on earth — but he was better than Marx.

There wasn't a soul to be seen on Tom's journey across the sinking gray Atlantis that was Uggala. Only the odd snipe broke like a heart attack from the tussocks at his feet. My God, Tom called out to himself, have mercy on me. I beseech thee show me the way!

A tall figure emerged from behind one of Sean and Seamus's platonically perfect haystacks. The Captain!

"Just the man I wanted," said Rob Roberts, giving Tom a Gary Cooper cool, breezy smile.

Tom stopped. His heart and thoughts were racing like rabbits. Something important was about to happen.

"Isn't it horrible weather we've been having?" he said, half in fear, half in delight, trying to relish the moment just a bit longer.

"I was wondering," said Rob Roberts slowly, "would you be interested in being a custodian of the Heritage Centre? I need somebody with a bit of knowledge about the place, youknowwhatImean."

Tom staggered, hardly able to speak with excitement. "Well, to be honest, the Heritage Centre has been on my mind since you've mentioned it first time. I'd be delighted to be of any use, if it's not too much trouble."

"Good man."

The Captain's face was radiant and dollar-eyed as he took a map out of his breast pocket and spread it on the cliff behind the haystack. "Now, with regard to the planning, I'd need your advice on a few details."

And so they bent down and drew and redrew the map of Uggala like Stalin and Churchill at Yalta, shifting places and people round as if they were no more than green markers. And so caught up were they in their own exalted omnipotence that they forgot of the tumultuous world behind the haystack: vengeful wind, thundering skies, and the ocean assaulting the shore. They were already inhabiting a golden future, where half the world wanted to live on Uggala and parade in shorts along their promenade.

When long after midnight Tom returned home, his face was luminous with the light of newfound meaning. The slouch and slack of pointlessness had left his body, and he gave Alice a brisk hug in the bed before frying himself three eggs and a handful of rashers.

"You see," said Alice, "Saint Anthony works after all! Now I'll have to start badgering him about your cholesterol."

The Daimon of Danny Ruane

❧ "We're the right pair of eejits," said Danny.

We were shivering in the stern of *The Morning Star*, looking back at Uggala as it stood clear and self-contained against a surprised December sky. It was the first time I had seen the island like that, not mixed up with me anymore. It was remote and whole as the pearly blue earth viewed from outer space.

"If the mountain won't come to Mohammed, Mohammed must go to the mountain," said Danny cheerfully.

I nodded mechanically to keep him at bay and go on with my own reveries. I was puzzled. On the island the pale lilac contours of the mainland to the east had filled me with longing for the romantic life that surely must be lived there. Now that I was on the sea and Uggala was on the horizon, it in turn had donned the blue veils and lilacs of allure.

"Poor Finn," said Thresheen. "Fooled by horizons."

She stood beside me wearing a blue and white sailor suit and a pillbox with a red pom-pom.

"I don't think it's a good idea to spend our time in Uggala wondering what Ethna's up to in Dublin," said Danny. He was trying to convince himself that he was doing the right thing.

"Besides, you should see a bit of the world."

I nodded again. I wanted to be back on Uggala.

Danny gazed off into the distance with a determined look on his brow, like a knight setting off in pursuit of a dragon or the elixir of life.

"Come wid me, me hearty," Thresheen put on a sailor boy voice. "There's a flock of razorbills to port."

I hated it when she did accents, but I was glad she was around.

"I want to watch the ducks," I said to Danny and followed her over to the other side.

"We're going to Dublin to see what Ethna's doing," I blurted out.

"I know. Danny's very rattled. But she's leaving Dublin."

"Where's she off to?"

Thresheen took a big silver timepiece out of her pocket and consulted it ostentatiously. "Right now Ethna is standing like Lot's wife at St. Stephen's Green trying to decide whether she wants to take a taxi to Heuston Station or stay in Dublin. It's snowing."

"Are we going to meet her?" I asked eagerly.

"I'd only be able to tell you that if the future were carved in stone. But it isn't. It's ever-shifting and it's shaped by thoughts and desires. Change your desire, change your future." Then, trying to recover her old salt personality, she added: "That's how it is, young fella me lad."

"I want her to come back to Uggala," I said nervously.

"There you go again! How do you know it wouldn't be the greatest disaster in the world for her to come back?"

"But she must!" I begged.

Thresheen sighed. "You can't force your will on anybody else. All the same, there's no doubt that your and Danny's strong desire to see her deflects the contours of her thoughts a little. It increases the probability that all of you will meet at Galway railway station."

"But I want to know now! Will we?"

"Who are you talking to, Finn?" Danny stood behind me.

"Nobody."

He sat on a bench and put me on his knee.

"When I was your age I talked a great deal to myself. And

to stones and shoes and trees. Tell me, Finn: Do they talk back to you?"

"Sometimes."

"You see, I can't remember anymore." He was probing again. I tried to wriggle out of his grip, but he held me like a vise.

"Once upon a time there was a young poet named Shelley at Oxford. He became convinced that people have a life elsewhere before they're born into this one. So one day on Magdalen Bridge he grabbed a child out of its mother's arms, shook it again and again, and implored: Tell me! What do you remember? What do you remember? Just now I feel a little bit like that with you. Except I'd like to know who you're talking to."

My locked-up face told him I wasn't going to say anything. He released me.

Thresheen stood on the bowspit and gave me the thumbs-up. I ran towards her. I was agitated.

"Let's play pirates."

"I don't want to play. I want to know what's happening to Ethna."

She spat over the rail through a gap in her front teeth.

"All right. She's looking out for a seat on the train. She's still coming home to you and Danny if you really must know."

"Are we going to meet up with her?"

"Now this is interesting. Who would have thought that a small thing like a train being overcrowded and forcing one to find a seat in first class could change the course of a whole life?"

"But how?"

"Because there's a man sitting in first class who wants to offer Ethna a job. He's waving to her already."

I looked back at Danny. He was reading a fat book and poking at his nose. The sky was a deep ignorant blue.

"Should I say something to Danny?"

"Over my dead body. Besides, this is only one probability, one Now. There's another Now in which Ethna is in a Dublin pub feeling sorry for herself. And just when she's about to leave Dublin, the same man, the one in the first class, bumps into her and offers her a job. That's how it works, you see."

I could see, sort of.

Thresheen nodded sagely. "But that's not all. There's a third and a fourth Ethna that never board a train or visit a pub."

As always when I was in touch with Otherwheres, my trepidation about events in this world gave way to excitement at the abundance and mystery of things.

"There's nothing but Now," said Thresheen, stealing my thoughts. "You know that as well as I do. The thrilling bit is the ways in which one Now competes with another Now. Adios!"

As I returned to Danny, I wondered what he would do if Ethna met up with the first-class man. Would he leave Uggala for good and maybe go to Japan to Yoshiko? Or perhaps to Liselotte? Or maybe he would just stay on the island and die? I brought myself to tears when I thought of this dying Danny. I put my head in his lap and saw him thin and unshaven as Holy Paddy with his ash plant beside him on the bed. He was telling me to feed the bees after he was gone.

"Why are you sniveling, Finn?" asked Danny.

How could I tell him I was crying over one of his probable corpses?

The Daimon of Ethna

✎ "May I ask you if you're going to cross the street or stand here forever?"

Ethna turned to find Rob Roberts standing behind her wrapped in an elegant steel blue woolen coat and looking at her with a mixture of contemplation and appetite.

"Rob!"

"I thought you'd be on Uggala by now. Christmas is coming and the geese are getting fat."

"I'm trying to make up my mind whether to go or not."

She regretted her frankness immediately. It sounded too much like a come-on.

"Well, shall we start from crossing the street first?"

She followed him uncertainly, wading her way through her own torpor and Dublin slosh.

"You've been on my mind a lot lately," Rob Roberts went on. "Can I persuade you to consider something? An offer."

She offered her honor, he honored her offer, and all night long he was on her and off her, Ethna thought scabrously.

"Well, what's the offer?" she asked.

"I want you to design a model village for Uggala."

"You can't be serious."

"I'm very serious. The island has terrific potential, and we're going to need lots more accommodation."

Who's this we? wondered Ethna.

"Look, I've only finished my studies."

"Don't worry, I've seen your portfolio, and I like your extravagant touch. I want an imaginative project, not some makie-uppie Mother Machree sort of village for idiots." His voice darkened. "It's all very hush hush at the moment."

"But I hate Uggala."

"All the better. You won't go soft round the edges. Besides, you can work out of our offices in Galway."

He moved closer to her so that he brushed against her leg. To her surprise she liked the smell of his aftershave and the rough texture of his tweed jacket.

"You know I call you the Advent Lady."

"Advent?"

"Are you a Christian at all? The time of waiting and soul-searching before something happens."

"Nobody's ever described me like that."

"So how do they describe you?"

Ethna remembered what Danny had once said: "You're full of frightened light."

She shrugged her shoulders and said, "Ah well."

"I know Uggala is not for you. You should meet more people. Not for your sake. For theirs. If this project takes off, I'm sure I can fix you up with an exciting firm in New York. I know at least three top architects there."

"Of course you do," said Ethna.

"Which is it then: will you go for it or not?"

She was being seduced. There was a promise on the horizon. The very process intrigued her, especially the way in which Rob addressed her as if she was totally unattached — no man, no child, no commitments. She felt the thrill of being created anew and dislodged from her old tired self, rejuvenated.

"Am I supposed to sign something first?" she asked archly.

"Oh God, no. That's Larry Lydon's style. Just the usual contracts."

He looked at her musingly. "There's something I'd like to show you if you have the afternoon off."

It was unlike her to say yes. It was unlike her to be attracted to a man she hardly knew, even if he did have a face like a pewter plate full of Roman virtues. She eased herself into the seat of Rob Roberts's Porsche because she was driven by curiosity. It was the same ancient curiosity that enticed Eve in the Garden of Eden. She wanted to know how wicked she could be in her compulsion to punish Danny.

As Rob drove she was silent and self-contained round her desire. He tried to surf the tension between them with his talk about a place in America called Rosetto. People in Rosetto were happy and content up to their eighties. It had nothing to do with eating yogurt. The mystery of Rosetto is that most people there are happily in love and sexually fulfilled.

Ethna ahemmed dismissively.

Rob stopped in midsentence, as if guessing her thoughts.

"I'm talking rubbish, ain't I? I must sound vulgar."

Ethna waved her hand in absolution.

"Here we are," said Rob as he turned the car into an avenue lined by stricken elms. "That's Castle Miriam."

The castle was a renovated Georgian house, its walls thickly veined with leafless Virginia creeper. There was the faint ghost of an early December moon suspended above the chimney stack.

"Did you have the builders install the moon?" asked Ethna, stepping into the cobbled yard.

"Along with the Jacuzzi and the central heating, yes."

They ascended the short flight of steps to the main door.

"How long have you been living here?"

"I haven't."

Rob flung open the door with an exasperated look on his face. The entrance hall was dominated by a splendid wooden staircase covered with a red carpet. On both sides, step after step, arranged with Prussian precision, stood an array of stuffed birds — herons, pelicans, storks, hawks, shags.

"So you're a collector of castles and birds," said Ethna in wonderment.

"Not exactly. The birds were meant for Anne, my ex-fiancée. She's an ornithologist. I bought the castle for her and did it up to please her."

"So — did it please her?"

Rob sat down on an ornate armchair with somebody else's coat of arms carved on the back. He looked deflated.

"I had a medieval banquet prepared for our engagement. She never turned up. She just fucked off without ever saying why — like in those pop songs. So I was left with . . . this fantasy. And now I don't know what to do with it."

The birds stared vacantly down at them like a row of stunned lackeys. Despite herself, Ethna felt sorry for him. She checked herself. Powerful man shows vulnerability. A well-rehearsed ploy.

"Would you like something to drink?"

Ethna shook her head and sat on the stairs between a
lanky stork and something that looked like a deranged black
turkey with red wattles. Nice company to be wicked in, she
thought, and laughed.

"Do I amuse you?" asked Rob with a reproachful air.

She covered her mouth with her hand and laughed even
harder.

Suddenly he was standing below her.

"That's what the place needs," he said. "The exorcism of
laughter."

He took her laughing face in his hands and covered it with
kisses.

So that's how she's going to betray Danny. Ethna thought
about herself in the third person while Rob put his arms
around her. That's how she's going to do it.

"Hold on a sec," she said and restrained his eager hands. "I
don't think it's the right time or place."

"I'm sorry. I didn't mean to . . ."

"Could you drive me to Heuston Station?" she asked.

She wasn't going to make love on a staircase among dead
birds with a man who wanted to exorcise his despair with her
despair. It was too much like driving out one nail with another.

The Daimon of Clare

🖎 It took Father Francis several months to find the right
names for Clare's breasts. At first they'd seemed haughty and
Episcopalian, and he had called them Elizabeth and Margaret after the Queen and her younger sister. Merely to touch
their proud pink nubs was a delicious violation of British sov-
ereignty and territorial integrity. Cupping or cuddling them
was out of the question. Nor dared he surreptitiously creep
up upon them in, for example, a cinema. Elizabeth and Margaret were firmly ensconced in an immaculate white brassiere

that opened down the front. Their formal entrances and exits took place only under conditions of the tightest security. They were icy and majestic and didn't like to be sucked.

Over time, as they grew more familiar and homely and lost their sectarian reticence, Father Francis took to calling them Kitty and Kate. Kitty and Kate were a pair of tits that had the likings and leanings of scullery maids. They loved to be hot and sweaty and crushed against his chest or groped by his prowling hands. They tumbled out of polka-dot bras or the top of a bikini when Clare ran short of fresh underwear.

"What are they but lumps of lard anyway?" she said in a deconstructive moment.

Then he understood he had gone too far in demythologizing Elizabeth and Margaret. He could live with neither lumps of fat nor regal ice maidens. He had to find some middle register of names that would evoke breasts as a fine fusion of flesh and flame.

He was trying out Emma and Emily for size on the plane from London to Dublin.

"I don't really mind meeting in foreign cities," said Clare, "but I draw the line at eating gluey pizzas in cheap restaurants for the rest of my life."

Father Francis didn't want to hear. He was glancing at her unassuming bosom. Emma and Emily were sisterly, refined, and had a good pedigree in romantic fiction.

"If we live on the island, we'll have to move from the Parish House," Clare went on. "Where do you propose we go?"

Father Francis hadn't thought of it. To be perfectly frank, he hadn't really expected that Clare would banish herself to Uggala with him. He leaned over and kissed her lightly, partly in gratitude for her selflessness, partly to avoid answering her questions.

Emma and Emily were maybe a bit too Anglo-Saxon, but you can't have everything, as he was learning very fast.

"You'll have to tell everybody," Clare said, straightening her blouse. "I'm not going to move in as your housekeeper."

"Everybody will know," he replied, kissing her ever more passionately.

"I wonder if they'll burn us out," she mused.

It occurred to Francis that Clare's personal romance was largely an eighteenth-century New England affair. Men with torches strode in silhouette across a ragged skyline. Fork lightning lit up the ravaged facade of an old manse. A wild scream broke on the midnight air as a livid *A* was branded on the sinner's breasts.

O Kitty and Kate!

No.

Emma and Emily it was for sure.

The Daimon of Uggala

✺ If in the winter of 1992 you walked the bohereens of Uggala, you saw things that were sure of what they were. A stone wall was a stone wall and not a historic relic. Clumps of hazel were clumps of hazel and not microzones of biological diversity. The Well Field was the Well Field and not Area 7A. Alice O'Reilly was Alice O'Reilly, a kindhearted ailing woman and not a vacillating petit bourgeois. Concepta O'Keefe was Concepta O'Keefe, an unhappy harridan and not an eco-fascist.

The first premonition of something about to happen reached people in church. There were unspoken tidings on Father Francis's lips, and the aisle was restless with conspiratorial whispering.

The anxiety spread to the fields and the bogs. Sean and Seamus made the rounds of their fifty acres with an apprehensiveness they hadn't felt before, checking and rechecking their cattle and the sturdiness of their walls.

The seas round the island were unusually calm and sly, slipping in and out of inlets without the usual bustle and brawl. There were footprints on Silver Strand that only Thresheen could see.

Then in April a thunderbolt struck and broke Uggala in two like an old alder tree.

The Daimon of Father Francis

❧ Father Francis dropped the first thunderbolt at Mass.

"My dear friends. I feel as nervous and unsure of myself as the priest in the story of the Sacred Heart missionary and the lion."

He was taken aback by the strength and firmness of his own voice. Maybe he should have said a Holy Ghost Father? Sacred Heart it was now. Alice will be offended for her brother in Bulawayo.

"One day Father Brendan was confronted by a lion while crossing the savanna. The savage beast hadn't eaten for days and was slavering at the mouth. What could the unfortunate unarmed missionary do but pray aloud? 'Please God,' he exclaimed. 'May this lion be a Christian lion!' And with that the lion knelt down on the path in front of him, put his front paws together, and began to pray. 'Are you really a Christian lion?' Father Brendan asked, amazed. 'Indeed I am,' said the lion. 'I always pray before meals.'"

Father Francis had written "pause here," but he forgot about it.

"Well, this morning I'm the missionary and you're the lion. And when I tell you what I have to tell, you can either tear lumps out of me or be generous, compassionate creatures and help me with my task. The fact of the matter is that I want to marry a woman whom I love . . ."

"I fuckin knew it," whispered the Skipper to Colm. "That fellow has been after his hole ever since he came here."

Whose hole? wondered Colm.

"At the same time, I feel unable to abandon my priesthood, and I do not wish to leave the island. That's it. I place myself in the hands of Providence and in your hands. I ask you to pray for me as I now pray for you."

Father Francis had thought that his announcement would be the difficult bit and that the remainder of the Mass would be plain sailing. It was the opposite. He could hardly find his way around the altar so heavy was the burden of Uggala on his shoulders. He tried not to look at his congregation directly as he performed the act of Consecration and raised the Host in the sight of all.

What a cock-up, thought Colm O'Keefe. He was embarrassed for the whole race of men. It was all very well beginning with a cod story about a missionary and a lion. But to use the altar to display your dirty linen in public was going far too far. Was the sacrament valid at all?

Alice couldn't stop batting her eyes and swallowing. She had always thought of Father Francis as a living incarnation of beauty and purity, in spite of all the rumors about him and her own harlequin dreams. She was too dumbfounded to pray.

Biafra O'Dee had spent the morning debating with himself whether to go to Mass or not, so bad was the aspect of Pluto over Neptune. Fuck it, he should have stayed on in bed. At the same time, he wouldn't have missed the scandal for the world.

Holy Paddy — muttering prayers that failed to banish the images of naked, disemboweled children — hadn't the faintest notion of what the priest had said.

"Who is the hussy?" wondered Mrs. O'Halloran and searched through her gapped memory. She hadn't noticed anybody about the house apart from herself and Ethna. Could it be . . . ? Her neck shook with indignation at the thought like that of a self-righteous turkey.

Concepta O'Keefe struggled to decide whether Father Francis was disgusting or romantic. The thought of the priest's long white fingers distributing Holy Communion and then fondling the secret places of a woman's body both appalled and excited her.

There are two ways in which an island like Uggala makes up its mind about matters that affect its destiny. One is by scratching away at the sore spot till it bleeds. The other is by pretending that the sore isn't there and letting matters fester away quietly to themselves under the scab. The second works by rumor and innuendo, which remain in suspension like thin drizzle that never thickens to rain.

After a few days of confusion, people found to their astonishment that there were actually some good reasons to wait and do nothing. Summer was coming, Father Francis and his sermons were already a bit of a tourist attraction, and surely a whiff of scandal wouldn't harm the trade. Besides, didn't the priest say he wanted to settle on Uggala and stay sober and sane, unlike all his recent predecessors? Vocations were falling precipitously in the dioceses and, who knew, they might never get another priest.

In the end it was the women who nudged things to an inconclusive conclusion. Like generations of their ancestors back to the Neolithic, they felt a compelling urge to forgive a handsome, guilt-ridden transgressor.

The Daimon of Danny Ruane

❧ When Danny and I bumped into Ethna at Heuston Station, he announced that Murphy's law required to be complemented by Ruane's remonstration. If things could go fine, they absolutely would. We were reunited before Christmas, Ethna didn't want to go to Barcelona any longer, and she had just found a job in Galway. You couldn't ask for much more than that.

"All happy endings have a leak in them somewhere," said Thresheen. She was trying to prepare me for what followed.

Ethna spent the first three weeks of every month working out of her office in Galway, and there was a needle in the air prior to her departure from the island. During their week together on Uggala, she and Danny meshed their separate selves into one another. They wore the same lumpy Aran sweaters and blue jeans, and both smelled of Danny's lemony aftershave. But on the Mondays of her travels, Ethna uncoupled herself from him in a charcoal gray suit, high heels, and Yves St. Laurent perfume. As soon as she put on her makeup and city clothes, she became compact and driven, meticulous and impatient. Even the hug she gave Danny on the quay was an executive hug. Don't crush my blouse, don't smear my lipstick.

That March morning when she had completed her separation from him with eyeliner and amber tights, she said, "I've been wondering: perhaps you could take a computer course? Or maybe look for a lectureship in philosophy or physics somewhere?"

"What are you talking about?" Danny knew exactly what she was talking about. There had been hints and nudges in that direction for some time now.

"We could move to Dublin if we had a double income."

"You know I can't go anywhere before I finish my book."

"You've been at it for twenty years, for God's sake! How many more do you need?"

"As many as it takes," said Danny defiantly.

"What if you're just deluding yourself?"

"I'm not."

"How do you know? Has anybody read it? Have you ever thought that you might have wasted twenty years?"

"If it's not recognized this century, then it will make it in the next," said Danny with conviction.

"Preferably when we're all dead I suppose," said Ethna icily and flung her dark plait over her shoulder.

For the next two hours, as he pored over his chapter "The Great Religions as Splinters of a Single Mystery," Danny tried to ignore what Ethna had said. But as the day went on, a bitter cloudy resentment began to diffuse itself through him. She was trying to push him out of his natural path, to twist him into another shape. Computers! She wanted to drive Niagara through a sieve. He had seen too many of his friends end up succumbing to their wives' plans for them. They had lost their own purpose, however bizarre it was, and very quickly became flaccid and sour like old cucumbers.

"We won't allow it," he said to Sharik, who looked up at him with understanding senile eyes.

He had been here many times before. As so often the resentment began to settle at the bottom of his being, and the thought of the loss of Ethna became unbearable. She was his maddening peace, his perfidious truth-teller, his metaphysical daughter. She needed a larger world than the one he could offer her, and there were many wide boys who would like to escort her over the hills and far away.

What to do?

"Creation" was still years from completion. The only thing he had to hand was his collection of ruminations, as he jokingly called them. He opened the folder and leafed through it despondently. But as he read one of the brief pieces, his antennae picked up. Maybe there was something there after all?

He started again. He read the ruminations first as Danny Ruane, then as Concepta O'Keefe, then as Alice O'Reilly. He even tried reading them as Colm, muttering bollocks! at the more soggy bits. They were about loss, hope, disappointment, happiness, being creative, being somebody and being nobody.

It takes talent, he decided, to write cheap philosophy.

By the time the tentacles of the ash tree in the back garden were breaking into leaf, the book was finished. The typescript had an archaic look to it, imparted by the yellowed paper and his old Olivetti typewriter.

"It will seem to the publisher like a missive from the Dark Ages," said Father Francis.

"It is from the Dark Ages," said Danny.

"So what's the title?"

"'Ruminations from the End of the World.' I want you to hear the 'Rumi' in 'Ruminations.'"

"'Rumi' sounds fine, but what is it?"

"*Who* is it, Francis. A Sufi poet who said in the thirteenth century what I'm trying to prove in 1992. The guy lived in the bloodiest period of Persian history, during the Mongol invasion, but he sounds like he was born yesterday. Listen to this:

> Our desert has no bound,
> Our hearts and souls have no rest,
> World in world has taken Form's image;
> Which of these images is ours?

"So. What do you make of it?"

"Rumi-nations," repeated Father Francis slowly. "Who knows, perhaps you'll become the Walt Disney of metaphysics."

Danny spat on the manuscript for good luck, posted it to an American publisher, and forgot all about it.

The Daimon of Thresheen

🐦 In the beginning I took Thresheen for granted. I brought her in like I might switch on a lamp or the radio, never wondering where the light or the music came from or where they were when they were turned off. But when I was five Ethna sent me for lessons to Alice, and I had less and less time to slide into Otherwheres. Alice read me stories from the Gospels, taught me about the seasons, and showed me the continents on the globe. Thresheen's visitations grew erratic, and when she vanished she left me puzzled and confused. I became fearful that she might be the devil, and I prayed to my Guardian Angel to protect me from her. I glanced furtively at her shoes to check if her feet were really feet and not cloven hooves.

"Silly boy!" She chuckled, slinging a pink boa over her shoulder. "Next thing you'll be giving me horns and a forked tail. I really don't fancy them, so please restrain yourself."

"So where's Hell then?"

"In Alice's poor head."

"Why do you dress different every time I see you?"

"I don't dress. You dress me."

"Me?"

"Of course. Not that I object. Most of the time I like being an Indian or a ballerina."

Was she having me on?

"Take a look at the illustrations in those Cassell's Books of Knowledge you've been stuck in for the last while. You've only got as far as K. God only knows what I'll be wearing when you get to Z. I might appear as a Zulu warrior!"

"Where is Otherwheres? I can't find it on the globe."

"So I don't exist then, is that it?" And she left in a huff.

I couldn't wait to get back to Danny's old encyclopedia. I loved its dignified musty smell and the feel of the paper, especially the greenish full-page illustrations. I opened it on "Ballerina," and there was Thresheen's tutu. Even the gauzy fairy wings sticking out from the shoulders were the same. And her pink boa was stolen from a picture of "Butterfly, Madame."

The Daimon of Father Francis

Father Francis didn't make a conscious decision to ignore letters from the Archbishop or notices from the Diocesan Office. He read the first two or three with weary indifference and then stopped opening them altogether. They were the debris of his previous existence. They lay around the hallway of the Parochial House in little piles and gradually became invisible to him. He felt despondent every time Mrs. O'Halloran remarked, "There's this letter here. It's been lying around for ages. Why don't you . . ."

He was reading the Russian poets and their gospel of suffering. He transcribed long quotations from Mandelstam, Tsvetayeva, and Akhmatova, and learned them by heart. At last he had found the sages he was searching for all his life. They awakened an answering power within him and brought his self to a new and belated birth. It was ironic that they should all be in their cold graves thousands of miles away and that their fathomless pain reached him only in translation.

Now when he visited the sick and dying on Uggala, his ministry was suffused with a new, all-accepting Russian compassion. The tawdry pictures of the Sacred Heart and Saint Patrick treading snakes which had once repelled him now glowed with simple peasant holiness. Worn rosary beads strung from a nail or tangled in the spears of an iron bedstead spoke of patient devotion rather than thoughtless habit. His Masses acquired a new intensity, especially at the Blessing. Where previously the congregation had begun to shed piety and shuffle their feet before the Last Prayers, they now bowed their heads devoutly and wished that his healing hands and gravely spoken benediction would hover above them forever.

Clare was due to move to Uggala in August, so Father Francis enlisted Danny's help to paint the drawing room and bedroom a welcoming primrose yellow. They were sitting in the kitchen having a cup of tea when the phone rang. It was part of Father Francis's self-protective strategy to have the answering machine on permanently and only to lift the receiver if it was one of his parishioners in trouble. This time it was the Bishop's secretary, who spoke in a low pedagogical voice, as if addressing a delinquent child. After the usual complaints about not receiving answers to letters or phone calls, he announced that Father Francis had a week to vacate the Parochial House. A new curate was on his way to the island.

"That's it," said Father Francis, looking around. "At least we don't have to paint the kitchen."

"What are you going to do?"

"Read more Akhmatova. She faced much worse problems."

"But where will you stay?"

"I can always rent Tom's brother's cottage for a song. All I need now is somewhere to say Mass."

Danny was surprised by the mixture of exaltation and practicality in Father Francis. Here he was faced with a momentous change and yet he was as acquiescent and defiant as a Russian boyar.

"We'd better keep the remainder of the paint for your new place."

"Yep," said Father Francis, "and charge it to the diocese."

"You'll survive," Danny grinned.

A week later the Monsignor arrived. By accident on purpose, two Guards traveled in the same boat and hung around a bit until he was safely installed in the half-painted Parochial House. He was a gaunt man in his early seventies, intimidatingly suntanned and clerical. Tom dubbed him the Exorcist on sight. It was he who brought the gossip to Father Francis.

"Did you know that the Exorcist spent most of his life as a volunteer on the missions in Brazil? He put all his energy into making minced meat out of priests and nuns who strayed into liberation theology!"

"Why isn't he a bishop then?"

"Well, sure enough a grateful hierarchy was about to nominate him. But the poor hure got a heart attack and had to return home a red-socked Monsignor."

Father Francis looked luminous and purged, as if he had recently endured a spiritual enema. Where before the smoky glass of his diffidence and impassiveness had obscured his spirit, now that the glass was clean, the leaping flame within was clear for all to see. He felt the ecstasy of a man who has momentarily resolved the contradictions of his life but has yet to face the dreary consequences. He was so buoyed up that he even felt able to go to Monsignor Herbert's Mass on Sunday.

People gasped when they saw him sitting in a pew dressed in a pullover and jeans. The cheek of him! But then isn't he obliged to go to Mass on Sunday like the rest of us? Still, you'd think he'd do the decent thing and let the kerfuffle quieten down a bit. On the other hand, it was great gas to see the clergy trip one another up. And so on.

The congregation waited keenly for the Exorcist's sermon. It was all about humility. Humility before God, before the Church, before the Bishop. People seemed to have forgotten the promise of the Holy Spirit to be with His Church to the end of time. Life was short. Too short to spend on willful rebellion and in following one's own fads and fancies. We all of us need guidance . . .

The Exorcist went on like a Black & Decker, going *dr-rrrrrrrrr*, drilling away at the same hole all the time.

Father Francis glanced around to gauge the reaction of the congregation. Were they just sitting there as always and taking with equanimity whatever was thrown at them from the altar?

No. Alice wasn't nodding in her usual schoolgirlish way. Biafra was yawning like a seal. Mrs. O'Halloran turned back several times to look with meaningful eyes at Father Francis: What's the poor man talking about at all at all?

For a moment he was filled with glee. He had won the day. The Consecration brought him to his senses. Behind the Monsignor's self-assured platitudes there were two thousand years of sedating repetition and divinely sanctioned threat. Wasn't he the fool to think that his own outlandish sermons on love could shake people loose from their millennial bondage? Perhaps poets could do it, but not priests.

The Elevation plunged him even deeper into remorse. He had abused the sacred mystery. He had come to Mass to size up the opposition, not to partake in the Body and Blood of Christ.

Nobody looked at him directly, yet he itched all over from the furtive glances of the congregation as they went up to the altar rails. Would he receive? What would the Monsignor do if he approached God's table?

To everybody's secret disappointment, Father Francis remained in his seat like the public sinner he was. He held his head in his hands and was the picture of penitence. By now he had given up all attention to the Mass and his own scruples. He was back in the Belgrave Hotel with Clare, kissing her arched neck and softly sliding the strap of her bra over the round of her tanned shoulder.

The Daimon of Clare

🌹 The sun blazed from a cloudless sky as Clare and Father Francis strolled up from the harbor. It was the same eager sun that had shone on her first visit to Uggala.

She had stopped to take a photo of the hill rising behind the village when she saw a man in a long coat and a blue scarf freewheeling his bike down the narrow road towards her. Afterward he would claim that it was the sheer Colgate radiance of her smile that caused him to fall over the handlebars.

He lay there motionless in the dusty road with the wheels of his upturned bicycle going *tick-tick-tick* and the contents of his satchel scattered along the stone wall. Lots of colored pens, a notebook, a Penguin edition of the Upanishads, and several letters addressed to women.

When she bent over him in a panic, he opened one eye and asked why did the chicken cross the road? Not exactly original or what she expected from an Irish-speaking peasant, but it showed he was still alive.

"You're smiling," remarked Father Francis.

"I was just thinking of the day I first arrived here. It was a day like this."

Only the man was different. There were a million men available in Austin, and yet she had fallen in love twice on an island with no more than two hundred people altogether. God, already she had slept with 1 percent of the male population!

Danny disentangled himself from the bike and rubbed the dust from his trousers.

"They told me y'all spoke Gaelic here!" she said.

"Was it the skipper of the trawler who told you that?"

Clare nodded.

"The old bollocks. Maybe you're on the wrong island?"

Danny looked at her with unabashed desire. She straightened her shoulders.

"No, that's great! I thought I would need a translator for my interviews and now —"

"Are you a journalist?"

"Oh no. I study anthropology. I'm here to do some fieldwork."

He bent to check the chain of his bicycle. With his big

head of flaming locks and his flamboyant blue scarf he reminded her of Cuchullain, not that she had the remotest idea what Cuchullain looked like.

"Is it kinship systems or land tenure you're interested in?"

She hesitated. Perhaps he was an anthropologist too?

"Actually it's the sexual economy of the island."

He grinned.

"You mean who's shagging who and how? You've definitely come to the wrong place. Sex is even rarer than Gaelic round here. Let's go for a drink."

The bohereen she was walking on now with Francis, the speckled stone walls and the arthritic blackthorns bent away from the wind, seemed so much less real than the memory of that encounter with Danny.

She had woken up with a massive hangover on that first morning, wary of the insouciant man bending over her.

"Where are we?" she mumbled.

"Uggala," he explained. "I'm Danny Ruane. We shagged most of the night. Would you like the full fry or tea and toast?"

Clare was fascinated by the ease with which Danny moved from one persona to another. One moment he was a lover, the next a companionable philosopher, the next a father. She by comparison was stuck in her own skin, still trying ways of escape that left her feeling awkward and embarrassed. It was her first field trip as an anthropologist, and she had even equipped herself with a pair of squarish glasses to add authority to her questions.

Ethna had been her first victim. She was only fifteen and bristling with shy willfulness.

"Do you intend to stay a virgin till you're married?"

Ethna was sipping Coke through a straw.

"I hadn't thought about it." She shrugged.

"Do you fantasize about men?"

"You mean in the bath?" Ethna seemed suddenly eager.

"Exactly."

"I have to go now and dry the dishes."

"What do you mean by position?" O'Keefe looked at Clare with a mixture of repulsion and lust.

Why was it that everybody on the island answered one question with another?

Tom was repairing a net on the quay wall.

"How do you spell it?"

"F-e-l-l-at-i-o."

"Ah, that yoke! We haven't had it on the island since the old people died."

"Really?"

"No. These days we go in for cornflakes."

"God, I was such an idiot," said Clare half to herself.

Francis stopped. "You're not with me at all."

"I was just thinking about the time I interviewed people here about their sex lives."

"Did you ever publish anything on it?" he asked apprehensively. If she had, it was sure to find its way back to the island. Such things always did.

"I wrote it up OK. But all the journals turned it down. They said it lacked scholarly rigor."

"Thanks be to God."

"But . . . I thought I should write a novel based on my experience."

"Look, half the West of Ireland is writing a novel about sex or death. Promise me one thing. Wait until I'm three days in the grave before you write anything about this place."

"Are you sure? I thought it would be my first project!"

"Why don't you write poetry instead? At least nobody here reads the stuff."

"Well, I'm keeping a journal."

Father Francis knew all about the journal. Once when she was out he had peeped into it. The entries were mostly about the ebb and flow of her sexual feelings for him. He was astonished to discover that she felt he desired her more than she desired him. Later he wondered if she had wanted him to find out. It gave him a new insight into women's deviousness.

"Oh, definitely. The journal is a great idea."

They stood in front of the ramshackle cottage of Michael O'Reilly, which was to be their new home. It was ludicrously camp and romantic in the sunshine, with Alice's blood red geraniums craning to the light in the windows. Clare wanted to kiss Father Francis, but she knew his diffidence about public acts of affection. So she held his hand.

"I wonder where we will all be this time next year," she mused.

This time next year she will no longer feel any connection to the wild girl from Austin. Only occasionally will she stop to think of her first summer on the island and the way Danny said, "We shagged most of the night."

Of course it wasn't true. It was merely a manner of speaking. Gross.

The Daimon of Father Francis

✍ Danny paid for the advertisement in the *Connacht Tribune*: "Mass for People on the Edge, Michael O'Reilly's Cottage, Old Town, Uggala, every Sunday 11:00 A.M."

Father Francis fretted over the title, but Danny explained that the edge could be any edge: psychological, social, theological, financial. Besides, wasn't Uggala itself an edge place?

At ten to eleven Father Francis lit candles in the windows of Michael O'Reilly's cottage to welcome the edgemen and the edgewomen. Danny and Ethna and me were sitting on one of the benches Danny had knocked together. We were twice as nervous as our pastor and couldn't take our eyes off the door to see who, if anybody, was going to show up.

The altar was a low coffee table with an iron cross and a chalice and paten of glazed pottery Father Francis had bought at the Saturday market in Galway. Clare's tiny loaf of bread lay on a starched linen handkerchief that had once belonged to Danny's mother. I recognized our Waterford crystal sugar bowl as well, with a sprig of rosemary in it.

Father Francis lit charcoal in an old frying pan and sprinkled it with frankincense. The kitchen filled with the resinous scent of ancient prayers and benedictions. Still nobody arrived.

"We'll give it another five minutes," he said and circled the room with the smoking pan. Just when he returned to the altar, the door opened and in came Tom. He sniffed the fragrant air, and as he made his way towards the rocking chair he began to intone the Asperge me domini. Father Francis joined in and did another round of the room.

"The pair of them must have been practicing on the quiet," Danny whispered to Ethna.

Ethna was uneasy. Here we were, the only four agnostics on the island, waiting impatiently for the true believers to arrive and begin a renewal of Christianity on Uggala.

The door creaked faintly. Mrs. O'Halloran hesitated on the threshold with a to-enter-or-not-to-enter look on her face until pushed in by Biafra O'Dee. They were followed by three older women, who took their places silently along the wall. Father Francis recalled seeing them occasionally at Mass, the most anonymous of the anonymous. Why had he never got their names?

The last to arrive was Concepta O'Keefe. She was dignified and self-contained and never as much as glanced at her daughter.

"Jesus!" whispered Ethna.

"We're really on the edge now," said Danny.

The Mass began. It was simple and short. Everybody sat throughout with the exception of Concepta, who stood and knelt at the appropriate places as if she were in a cathedral and not in Michael O'Reilly's kitchen. Father Francis's sermon was on waiting. We are all in our different ways waiting for somebody or something, he said. We get tired of the waiting and our deepest wish is for it to be over. So we rush out of it into false closures or premature arrivals. But maybe the true meaning of our lives is in the waiting itself? We celebrate many faces of Christ — the Son of God, the Lord of Mercy, the Cosmic Christ, the Prince of Peace. What will we call this Christ that waits with us on the way? Christ the Loiterer, have mercy on us. Christ the Dawdler, pray for us.

He hadn't written down his sermon. Over the previous few days he had simply kept the theme in his mind and let it draw to itself the appropriate words and metaphors. He had always wanted his sermons to be more a thinking aloud than a formal presentation of God's truth. Now, in Michael O'Reilly's kitchen, with nine souls to speak to, it was at last possible. He could pause to think or to look for the right word, to correct himself, to quote Akhmatova, to ask questions and not fret for answers.

The sermon took no more than ten minutes. Yet he could tell from the absorbed faces of his little congregation that everybody was waiting for more. Maybe he should have gone on for longer?

At the Prayer of the Faithful he invited everybody to ask God aloud for their intentions. The nervous silence was broken by Biafra O'Dee.

"I've written this song. It's a sort of country and western called 'Make Me or Break Me.' I sent it to Van Morrison last week. I just want him to play it. Lord hear us."

"Lord graciously hear us," we said, surprised at ourselves.

"Well, while we're at it, we might as well pray for the success of President Yeltsin," said Tom gruffly. "Lord hear us."

"Lord graciously hear us."

"I'd like to pray for the poor people in Afghanistan," said one of the three fates against the wall. "That they may have food and peace, Lord hear us."

"Lord graciously hear us."

I wanted to pray for Ethna and Danny to be happy together on Uggala, but I was too timid to say it aloud.

When it came to offering one another the sign of peace, there were so few of us that nobody could escape shaking hands. I liked going around greeting everybody with "Peace be with you": it made me feel important.

"Peace be with you," said Ethna to Concepta, reaching out an uncertain hand.

Concepta touched it without looking at her daughter.

"And with you too," she murmured.

It was the first time in ten years that their hands had touched. Danny practically broke the bones of Concepta's fingers as he bellowed his "Peace be with you" at her. She winced and then blushed.

Holy Communion was given under both species, with Tom awkwardly distributing the fragments of Clare's loaf and Father Francis holding the chalice. At this stage everybody was in a state of mild elation. When Father Francis rose to bless us, we didn't bow our heads as the liturgy required but raised them to bathe in the amber light that streamed from his open hands.

Concepta was the first to depart, briskly gathering her bag and umbrella and averting her gaze from everybody. She left a pile of coins on her seat. The three sisters were about to follow her when Father Francis approached them and shook their hands. The eldest was dressed in black like a Mediterranean widow. The other two wore heavy green gabardine overcoats.

"Thank you for coming," he said. "I'm sorry we haven't met before."

The eldest spoke for them all. "Oh, sure you're a busy man, Father."

"It was brave of you to join us," he stammered.

She gave him a toothless grin. "We wouldn't miss your blessing for all the tea in China."

"I'm happy to hear it."

Father Francis was about to reach out and lay his hand in blessing on each of them in turn, but he restrained himself.

"Why don't you join us for a cup of tea?"

"No no no. We have to be on our way."

The elder took a five-pound note out of her purse and pressed it into the priest's hand.

"That's not necessary."

"We must contribute to the support of our pastor."

The echo of the catechism quelled his scruple.

"We'll see you next week then?"

Biafra O'Dee jabbed his finger in Father Francis's chest. "The point you made about waiting: that was super-seminal! It hit me right between the eyes. I've been waiting for bleeding thirty years to hear why I was waiting."

Ethna came up to Father Francis and kissed him on the cheek.

Danny said, "You're going to give the Monsignor a good run for his money."

Mrs. O'Halloran made tea for everybody and warmed up the apple tart she had brought with her. Biafra O'Dee spat out the first mouthful. "You forgot to put sugar in it," he said accusingly.

"Go sugar it yourself, you mad bastard," she replied unperturbed.

Biafra winced and turned to the rest of us. "It's very good we started ten minutes late. Exactly at eleven-ten Venus entered Jupiter. You couldn't do better than that for timing. That's why I was late myself."

"You're a pagan," said Mrs. O'Halloran solemnly. "With a devil in you as big as a house. Speaking of the devil, I was quite taken aback to see Concepta O'Keefe here. I wonder what she's up to."

The Daimon of Concepta

Concepta's unexpected appearance at Father Francis's Mass was her second attempt to heal herself of herself. The first one was when she tried to win back Colm's affection by reinventing herself as a woman. When that failed, her soul went into hiding for years on end and she blanked out anything that would lessen the dividend of disappointment in her life. On the odd occasion when Danny attempted to reach out to her by bringing news of Ethna's latest success or my precociousness, she would stiffen up inside and ask about his new microwave or how the bees were doing. And so he would go on talking about Ethna and she about bees until he lost heart and gave up.

She woke up in the mornings feeling dirty and tired, as if she had been snorkeling in bog holes all night. She never remembered her dreams. Her days, spent among the kegs of beer in the cellar or the steaming pots in the dark kitchen, were only a little less subterranean. She cherished a secret, shameful hope that a third world war would break out soon and release her from all her meaningless chores.

It was the smoking ruins of a pub caught on the late night news that detonated the dam that held back her dreams. So many bombs had gone off, so many people had been killed and tortured that she hardly registered them except to shake her head and ask: Have they nothing better to do with themselves in the North? Why this particular bomb had opened a glass-strewn doorway to her dreams she couldn't tell.

Men in black balaclavas flagged her down on lonely roads.

She called to Colm for help, but he was out somewhere walking greyhounds. She called to Ethna, but Ethna threw a stone at her. Sometimes Concepta was one of the hooded men herself, smashing kneecaps in stinking alleyways.

Her dreams were contorted with gagged faces and maimed bodies, and she never knew which side she was on. It was a relief to wake up to the reassuring sound of rain and the indignant screech of vagrant gulls over Uggala. But the barbarities of the night stayed with her, replaying themselves over and over until she wanted to scream.

However big the scream in her, she couldn't bring herself to tell anybody on Uggala. She suspected it wasn't the North that visited her nightly. It was a vision of Hell. She was being made to suffer for the sins of her husband and daughter; her own trivial transgressions hardly deserved such torment.

When she finally confessed her dread to an Augustinian friar in Galway, he said, "Look here, my good woman, this has nothing to do with religion. You need a psychiatrist."

It was the final blow. It was Colm's relatives who were forever in and out of the madhouse, not hers. When she sat in a Quay Street café in Galway to mull things over, she couldn't resist seeking out secret sharers of her desperation. Could it be that the cheerful man in a three-piece suit was only pretending to be sane? Was this grim young woman in the corner on the verge of suicide?

With a sharpened appetite for aberration, she examined the notices pinned to the wall. What an extraordinary number of weird things people got up to! Silk painting. African drumming. Levitation. A blue poster caught her eye. It was for a dream workshop. "A dream not understood is like an unopened letter. Dreams are the royal road to self-understanding, healing, and creativity. Learn to unravel their meanings with the aid of an internationally renowned therapist."

A dream workshop. It sounded so much more respectable than going to a psychiatrist. And better still, it was being held in a country house in Clare where there was a library and a sauna.

Abbey Park was everything that Concepta had hoped for in a house. It reminded her of illustrations in an old copy of *Winnie-the-Pooh* that had fed her dreams as a child. She loved the sash windows in her bedroom that looked out over the Burren Hills and the attention to detail revealed in the basket of rose petals in the bathroom. It was just the sort of house to which she felt she belonged. Dream workshop, or no dream workshop she was going to have the time of her life.

She squeezed into her best salmon pink dress flecked with tiny white flowers. She felt it gave her a note of distinction as she ambled down the staircase to the drawing room ten minutes late for the first session.

There were eight women and one man sitting in chairs around a vase of flowers when she entered. They all wore jeans and sweaters, and some were barefoot. The International Therapist beckoned Concepta to take a seat. She was a small wiry woman swathed in a rainbow of silk scarves.

"Why don't you close your eyes for a few minutes and attune to the group?" she said to Concepta. "Go on, Penny."

Penny spoke in a working-class English accent, which Concepta thought very common and which led her to mistrust everything the girl said. She was glad she had her eyes closed.

"There was this tree y'know. I'm not good on trees so I dunno what kind of tree it was. Anyways it had a heavy top and the wind blew it over and there were these small roots stickin outa it. It left a big hole in the ground. It was like scary y'know. So I woke up Joe, and he said I'd been bleeding dreaming about his dick again. We laughed, but I couldn't get that fallen tree outa my head for ages. It was really real like."

"Wonderful!" said the International Therapist. "This is what we call a Big Dream. But we don't have to agree entirely with

Joe's interpretation. A tree with a large canopy and thin roots — what does that remind anybody of apart from a penis? No? Nobody has any connections?"

"A mushroom," someone said.

The Therapist leapt in.

"A mushroom cloud! It's the atom bomb, isn't it? The cloud over Hiroshima! So now we have a penis and a nuclear explosion. Is there anything else there?"

"Yggdrasil, the Nordic tree of life and the worm nibbling away at the roots?" said a male voice.

The Therapist drew in her breath sharply. "Oh, my God! This is too perfect! We have a penis, a nuclear bomb, and a tree of life. So what's Penny's dream telling us then? What do these things have in common?" They're all male, right? And the male parts are top-heavy! They're going to topple over because they're not grounded properly. Our Penny is a caterer in her waking life and a prophetess in her dreams!"

Penny demurred.

"I think maybe Joe was right. He can't get it up much these days."

The others laughed.

"What do you think, Brian?" asked the Therapist.

"Why do we have to focus on the tree? Perhaps we should look at the hole in the ground instead?"

Concepta felt embarrassed for all of them as they went on and on wrangling about holes and mushrooms. It was just as well that she had her eyes closed.

"Is there anything the matter, Concepta?" asked the Therapist.

"No. Yes. I'm just feeling a little faint."

Faint was better than weak. It was like her dress. It was out of tune with the group but in tune with the house.

"Why don't you go to the library and lie down on the couch?" suggested the Therapist.

Concepta was relieved.

Library was a big name for a small room with a few book-shelves and an ornate mullioned window facing south. There was a five-foot-high cactus plant standing in a corner. Concepta had an instinctive repugnance for such desiccated un-giving things.

She sat with her back to the plant and flicked through old copies of *One Earth* magazine. But she couldn't distract herself. Why had she left the dream workshop? Was it because she found it silly? Or was it because she feared that when her turn came her dreams would reveal too much about her?

A sudden thought seared through her mind. She had just done what her mother had done twenty years ago. She had left a room upset and offended by talk of sex. And that surely said more about her than her dreams ever would. Her salmon pink dress burned her body. What in God's name had become of her? What had become of her?

It was then that she heard the groan. At first she thought it came from her stomach. But no, it was on the other side of the room. She looked around. Nothing. She wondered if she should cut short her stay in Abbey Park and return to Uggala.

There was another groan. This time it was accompanied by a dry snapping sound, as of knuckles being cracked. When she turned round she saw the cactus, slowly and painfully, keeling over. It collapsed, it seemed to her, with calculated deliberateness until it lay on the floor, the stump propped on the edge of the pot, pointing a few puny obscene roots at her.

Concepta was electrified. It wasn't an accident. It couldn't just be an accident. The universe, or God, or whoever was in charge of things had thought enough of her to send her a message! She was both frightened and exalted.

She rushed out of the library and returned to the drawing room.

"Are you all right, Concepta?"

"The cactus in the library has just exposed itself to me. . . . Like you were saying about the tree."

"What do you mean?"

Everybody rushed to the library, where sure enough the self-destructive cactus lay defeated in a spill of fresh soil.

"It happened while I was sitting on the sofa. I heard it before I saw it."

The workshop people crowded around her. She had to go over and over again exactly how it happened. They looked at her with awe. It wasn't an accident. There are no accidents in a world of victims.

The Therapist addressed her. "You are a very special person with great powers. Come, group! Let's all try to attune ourselves to Concepta."

For the remainder of the weekend Concepta felt like a live magnet from whom the others drew their power. Some of the disheveled women even went so far as to put on long dresses in emulation of her style. Her dreams were given the most careful attention as examples of an extraordinary receptivity to the anguish of pathogenic places. The Therapist said that however much people in the South of Ireland might wish to pretend the North didn't exist, the Troubles were beginning to seep through to sensitives like Concepta. Only imagine what they were doing to the dreamlife of southern babies! It had to be stopped.

Nobody but Thresheen and me knew about Concepta's escapade and elevation in Abbey Park. She straightened up inside and outside. She no longer saw herself through the eyes of the drunken bowsies in Balor's Lounge. She needed only to invoke the excited crowd around her in the library and the reverence in their eyes.

It was the new image of herself, as a special, compassionate person, that drove Concepta to side with Father Francis. There was only one thing that occasionally disquieted her. Hard as she tried, she found she couldn't remember her dreams anymore. She felt abandoned, like a pious visionary to whom the Blessed Virgin no longer appears with dire warnings in a dripping grotto.

The Daimon of Colm O'Keefe

❧ Colm O'Keefe would no more think of examining his dreams than he would of examining his stool. For him dreams were the muck of the mind, to be evacuated and forgotten about on the spot. As a good materialist Catholic, he was certainly fearful of God, but he felt uneasy about the soul, its origins, purposes, and exact dwelling place. The only moment when he penetrated through visible forms to the pattern of things was when he fell in love with tall slender Signe and pursued her as far as Oslo airport. This was his midlife crisis insofar as he was capable of having one.

Midlife crises are much misunderstood. They are cheapened into hormonal blizzards from which a middle-class, middle-aged man or woman emerges with a new partner, massive debts, and vengeful children. But these upheavals are often last attempts to get in touch with one's Daimon and find the right path in life. A man turns back towards his secret origins, stripping his life of trinkets and trumpetry, abandoning security in the hope of finding faith and vision. If he persists, he may undergo a purifying renewal, something like a personal version of the Reformation in the Christian Church. The clear light, undistorted by riotous panes of stained glass, streams through the high windows again.

A decade or so on, there follows a second crisis, much less publicized or talked about. It happens to men and sometimes to women who have failed to find their destiny but who no longer have any energy left to pursue it. They accept things as they are: a spouse they dislike, a job they are indifferent to, a lump they have no intention of showing to the doctor. They no longer take risks or shock their acquaintances with a new hairstyle or allegiance or turn of phrase. One knows what they'll say, what they'll do, what they're going to wear to a wedding. And yet, predictable as they are, they are frantically

playing the last game to be somebody and to mean something. Vision has perished, but power and control are still
within reach. And so baroque grandeur and regalia become
all important. This is their Counter-Reformation.

Colm O'Keefe was a Counter-Reformation man. His mission in life, he discovered, was to defend Uggala's tradition
and identity. When a bout of enthusiasm and eloquence took
hold of him, he would declare his intention to hand over the
island to the next generation just as he himself had found it.
It didn't seem to matter that there was no new generation to
receive the sacred trust. The Uggala of his boyhood glowed
imperishable inside him: an island of larks' nests, stories of
revenants, and fat basking whales seen from cliff tops. The
people were all close relatives, full of admiration for his skill
with the fiddle, his prowess with snares, and his prospects as
the coming man.

As long as his fantasy went unchallenged, Colm was the
great good man of Uggala, though pestered, as he thought, by
a bitch of a wife. Even Danny's experiments with cloud-
busters and foreign women posed no real challenge to his su-
premacy. It was only when Ruane and his gang began to
meddle with the Heritage Centre that Colm became virulent
and hyperactive. Rob Roberts had appointed him as his rep-
resentative on the Steering Committee of the Atlantic Fringe
Project, and it was his bounden duty to hold the line against
subversion. He printed a newsletter and discovered a new
talent in himself for satire and slander directed against
Danny and his ecofreaks.

The more threatened he felt the more he excelled himself
and the more besotted by power he became. Shafting the opposition, plotting the next move, and pulling the rug from under the likes of Danny Ruane: there was nothing to beat it!
Nothing could equal the sensation of having the fate of others in his hands. And so Colm sparkled and sizzled all
through his Counter-Reformation crisis.

"It's the first time in a long time I've seen you happy," Biafra O'Dee remarked to him after Mass on Sunday. "You must be getting a kick out of throwing the shit in the fan."

"I won't let fuckers like Ruane mess with the future of the island."

"You care as much about the island's welfare as I care about last year's snow," said Biafra. "All you're after is Rob Roberts's money."

But Biafra was wrong. As a Counter-Reformation man, Colm wanted only power and glory, a lion's mane and a peacock's tail. Only then would he be ready for the fulfillment of a stroke and for peacefully joining his forefathers in Uggala Old Cemetery.

The Daimon of Rob Roberts

❧ A mere three months after Father Francis renounced his vow of chastity, Rob Roberts let loose another thunderbolt over Uggala.

"I've got news for you, folks," he told a public meeting called by the Development Committee. "We're gonna move this island from the nineteenth to the twenty-first century in three years flat."

Normally the islanders would find this sort of talk offensive and tell the perpetrator to go and fuck off with himself. But the minister was there, there was lots of technology lying around on the table, and Rob Roberts was an American, so what could you do?

He was profligate in his invention of Uggala. Ideas sprang out of his head like showy nasturtiums. He projected them on two screens, one for slides, the other for overheads.

"Here's an architect's model of the Heritage Centre. It will house the museum of the Armada, with a fully reconstructed admiral's cabin. There'll be rooms to display artifacts such as cannons, medallions, maps" — he changed the slide — "and priceless objects like this piss-pot from Seville. There'll be a graphic history of the great fleet and the invasion plans. Think about it! A hundred and thirty ships on the high seas, twenty of them galleons, 30,000 men, a cargo of 110,000 quintals of biscuits, 1,000 quintals of salt fish, 11,000 barrels of wine, 1,233,000 pounds of gunshot, 6,000 grenades, and 11,000 pikes. Only in Spain could such a scheme be hatched. Even if they lost they won."

"Yeah, just like the Irish soccer team," Danny sneered, but Tom hushed him.

"In these days of European integration and so-called multiculturalism, Uggala's welcoming of the distressed Spaniards was, to employ an overused word, exemplary. It will be seen as such by the Spanish Ministry of Foreign Affairs if approached in the right way. The Heritage Centre is only the beginning. The islands of the West should link themselves together to provide a sequence of different but related experiences of the Atlantic Fringes of Europe."

The audience murmured their approval. Why hadn't they thought of that themselves? They liked the sound of Atlantic Fringes of Europe. It was a hell of a sight better than the West of bloody Ireland.

"Where is the value added in this?" Rob went on.

"It lies in each island specializing in the area it is best at. Inisheer should foreground Irish and W. B. Synge. Clare Island, film locations, and what do-you-call-him's movies. Uggala's thing is clearly the Armada, two of whose ships sank off the island. Don't you see it?"

Rob's spotless Aran sweater, stone-washed jeans and High-Tech Silver Shadow runners were just the right combination of tradition and modernity. His soft voice with its Boston inflections warmed the hearts of those who saw in him a son of Uggala's diaspora made good, a man who had returned to his roots to replenish them. They listened entranced by the audacity of his vision. He had thought of everything, from establishing a breeding colony of kestrels and quails on the bog to a glass-bottomed submarine to bring visitors on expeditions to the graveyard of the Armada.

The audience drew in their breath as he showed a sequence of slides of a similar operation off Crete. Of course the Heritage Centre would draw tourists like flies. So it would be necessary to develop a new village, best round the core of the empty cottages in Clydagh.

Rob flashed another quick sequence on the screen. There was Tom's grandfather's cottage, in all its degradation and squalor. There it was again, delighted with itself, all blinding whitewashed walls, manicured thatched roof, and blood red geraniums tumbling out of window boxes.

Tom swallowed hard. Rob knew he had them by the balls. It was just what he expected. He was walking on water.

"What do you say?"

"Two questions." Danny stood and half-turned to embrace the audience. "Who's going to pay for all this? And where do you propose to build this Heritage Centre of yours?"

Rob knew that if there was any possibility of trouble, it would come from that loser Danny Ruane. He was ready for him.

"Part of the money comes from the EU, part of it is government funding already agreed on, part of it my own contribution to kick-start the venture. And the idea is to locate the centre at Gortnanein. It's the highest point on the west side of the island, with a wonderful prospect."

"No way," said Danny curtly.

Everybody turned to him.

"You'll destroy the only place where there are Scots pines left on the island. There are gentians and orchids in the fields around, not to speak of other unique species of arctic-alpine flora."

People looked at one another. For the first time they heard that there was such a thing as a flora on Gortnanein.

Danny laughed contemptuously. "And you want to build it on the hill? Can't you see it will be an eyesore? It'll draw attention to itself and change the whole character of the land. It'll be a monstrosity."

"There are ways of blending buildings into the landscape," said Rob quietly.

"In this case there isn't. You have to think of sewage disposal, tarmackading acres for a parking lot — my God, the fields are full of larks. I simply can't believe that you're serious."

"I'm serious about a new, more prosperous life for the island, where there will be work for everybody all the year round."

People nodded. Colm O'Keefe was quick to catch the popular mood. "Larks and blue flowers, Ruane? Give us a break!"

"It's an outrage," said Danny. "I'd like you to know that as of now I'll do everything to oppose it."

Rob's inner voice raged against Danny and said terrible things to him. His outer voice was measured and accommodating. "There's no need to go head to head on this one. We can find a compromise."

Like fuck we can.

The Daimon of Ethna

🖎 In all the years that Ethna had been a student in Dublin, the journey home to Uggala was a long reverie over the promise that was Danny. As she lost herself in the rhythm of the train, she lingered over endless restorative chats at the breakfast table, evenings spent pondering her projects and drawings, and best of all, the weight of his body in the Barnaclugga embrace. She had never imagined that one day she would consume the same journey in giving herself good reasons for betraying Danny. They weren't married, so it wasn't exactly adultery. Besides, what was there to be said against adultery? It was the natural state of affairs in the animal kingdom. In the human its prohibition was the invention of patriarchy to keep women down. In all the myth and literature she knew, virtuous women were bores. It was the adulteresses that shone. Besides, as she had learned from Armand, adultery did not necessarily preclude love for one's spouse (love: whatever that means, as Prince Charles said).

And yet for all her attempts to program herself to be free and easy, she shrunk and withdrew the moment Rob Roberts reached out to touch her. I'm a real prig, she thought. A dull, boring, fucked-up prig.

Yet her shrinking only inflamed the air between them. Rob relished her hesitant, virginal lust for him.

"How 's the Advent Lady today?" he would sing out as he breezed through the office to call a client, make a deal, plan a takeover, screw somebody. Everybody was his but Ethna. She clung to her uncertainty with the fervor of a drowning woman clinging to a lifeboat.

Later that spring she was so exhausted clinging to the boat that she decided the only way out was to drown or strike for land. She preferred to be a seductress rather than be seduced. That way she had a measure of control.

After a reception for Arts Week, when they shared a taxi to the Town Hall Theatre for a late-night premiere, she leaned over and kissed him.

"Do we really need to go to this play?" he asked, delighted and astonished.

Ethna tapped the taxi driver on the shoulder.

"We've changed up our mind," she said. "Can you take us to the Great Southern Hotel?"

She knew she hadn't changed up her mind. She'd switched it off.

The Daimon of Father Francis

At the height of the tourist season in August, Father Francis's congregation had grown to thirty and sometimes even hit the forty mark. The kitchen was too small to hold everybody, so they moved to the shed behind the house. A few days later an article appeared in *Hot Press*. It was entitled "Back to the Stable: The Edgemen of Uggala":

We are in an outhouse still pungent with the smell of old hay and limestone. There is the occasional flurry of swallows as the birds enter and leave their nests in the rafters. What's going on beneath doesn't seem to bother them. A crowd of some fifty people with their heads bowed respond to the Kyrie as Father Francis leads them in a Latin Mass. In his simple Franciscan habit, he looks like a cross between Mel Gibson and Padraic Pearse. His sermon is peppered with quotations from Beckett and Brodsky.

Until recently curate of the island, he has been ousted by your regular Monsignor from Hell, an Exorcist-like figure who refers all queries to the Archbishop's Office. A couple of miles from the stable where Father Francis is chanting the Salve Regina, the Monsignor is berating his much diminished flock for reading English Sunday newspapers. And you thought it was safe to go to Mass again in rural Ireland!

Father Francis lives on the dole and is believed to be married to a feisty American blond. But he refuses to abandon his priesthood and insists on carrying on business as usual in the stable. If you plan on island-hopping in the West this summer, don't fail to drop in for 11:00 A.M. Mass at Michael O'Reilly's place. Father Francis's blessing alone is worth a session of shiatsu.

Dozens of copies of the *Hot Press* piece were posted back to Uggala by gleeful relations of the islanders. Put that in your collective pipe and smoke it! Uggala was always good for a laugh if you didn't live there.

By the end of September those who despised Father Francis for reneging on his vows were complaining that you couldn't turn on the radio without having to listen to that feckin friar explaining his so-called vocation.

On the first Sunday in October, the Monsignor had a go at Father Francis from the altar. He was tired; so many of his confreres, so many of the faithful, were tired of breakaway clergy seeking cheap publicity by criticizing the Church. If they must leave, could they not leave with dignity and in silence? Why seek to scandalize the People of God? He would say this much; it was sheer vanity, vanitas vanitatum, nothing less. Those who chose to sit through a sacrilegious Mass celebrated by a renegade priest, a Mass read without the say-so of Bishop or Pope, were not only endangering their mortal souls but bringing the island to perdition as well.

At this point Biafra O'Dee, who was covering all his spiritual options by attending both Masses, could no longer hold himself back.

"Ah bollocks!" he said out loud in the clear hearing of the horrified congregation and walked out. The Monsignor pointed with his surpliced arm. "That's how it all begins," he declared, and he broke out in an uncontrollable fit of coughing.

Biafra O'Dee's exit put it up to everybody in the congregation. Were they to stick with this dry shell of a man at the altar, a man who spoke the language of their grandparents and thus keep the odds of salvation in their favor? Or did they dare to be à la carte Catholics, though they had no clear idea what à la carte meant.

In the conversations in the pub after Mass, people had the illusion of making a momentous choice. But in fact the decision had been made long before, as far back as their toilet training. A week after the Monsignor's sermon, Michael O'Reilly's stable was nearly empty and Father Francis moved his Mass back to the kitchen.

But those who looked on the Monsignor and saw only a figure of impregnable authority underestimated how vulnerable and shaken by the conflict the old man was. The season of storms and blackouts hadn't even arrived on Uggala when one day the clatter of an Air Corps helicopter landing on the football pitch alerted everybody. The Monsignor was carried from the Parochial House on a stretcher with a medical orderly holding a drip over his head.

When Mrs. O'Halloran called the Diocesan Office she was told there was no replacement priest available. Perhaps the people should gather in church on Sundays and say a round of the rosary?

The people knew better than that. Next Sunday they clustered six deep round Michael O'Reilly's cottage. When Father Francis appeared in his Franciscan habit, they had an exhilarating sense of being back in the good old Penal Days, when priests were hunted and the Mass was treason.

The Daimon of Danny Ruane

෴ At first Danny had been intrigued by Rob Roberts. Rob had definite opinions on everything from the best propulsion system for fishery protection vessels to the debilitating effect of literature on the Irish economy. Between Irish poetry and the Church, he asserted, the nation had been blackmailed into beggary and sitting around on your arse. Look at our bloody fiction — nothing but misery, madness, and failure. If you fed the stuff to pigs there wouldn't be a slice of bacon in the country. He casually dropped the names of Harvard professors and Far Eastern archbishops with whom he had engaged in various ventures and controversies.

In the cabin of his yacht there were photographs of him with J. F. Kennedy, the Great Leader of North Korea, and Fidel Castro. The peacock in Danny envied Rob's wonderful hand-printed silk ties, acquired, according to Rob himself, in Java. But the hawk in him watched the Captain for the slightest slip.

When Rob Roberts announced his plans to build the Heritage Centre on Gortnanein, the sense of outrage in Danny struggled with triumph.

"That Roberts is a real bastard," he announced to Ethna. "He's going to desecrate the island."

She didn't even bother to look up from her drawing board. "You're just jealous," she said.

"I don't believe the fellow has done half the things he says he's done."

"I like him," said Ethna. "He's a doer."

"Are you saying it because you're on his payroll or what?"

Ethna gave Danny a studied look. "Some people make things happen, some wait for them to happen, and others wonder what has happened."

That was enough to shut Danny up. It sounded too much like one of his own glib aphorisms.

He ruffled my hair. Then he scratched Sharik behind the ear. Then he put a kettle on for a cup of tea. I knew he was still hammering away at Rob Roberts in his head. He returned to the attack when he had set the table.

"The whole thing stinks to high heavens. Even the stuff about the Armada doesn't ring true."

"Come on, Danny. One grasshopper recognizes another," said Ethna.

"So you think I'm a fraud too?"

"That's what the *Irish Theological Quarterly* said."

They kept their voices down, but their gibes were splinters off their mutual disillusionment. They were not speaking about Rob Roberts at all. Danny was wounded, not so much by Ethna's siding with Roberts as by her cold disregard for what he once described to her, floridly, as his isle of soul-making. Of course she abhorred Uggala. But she also knew that for him it was a place of reenchantment. She knew about the special blackthorn bush where generations of mistle thrushes had hatched their young and to whom he had given names and stories — Lars and Linda, Dave and Therese, Pat and Sharon. She knew where the chanterelles flared in October under the Scots pines. He had shown her the secret path that skirted the Danes' Fort and that led into a hollow where one's limbs seemed to feel lighter. OK, she might not care for these things. But she surely knew what the loss of them meant to him.

Ethna was in no mood to appreciate tokens of a Hidden Order. So he turned to the historical record. "This hullabaloo about the Armada. . . . There isn't a titter of factual evidence that the sailors were ever rescued. Hold on! Finn, you said that you don't like going near Leach na Spanaigh."

The Spanish Stone. The very name made me shiver.

"Why don't you like the place, Finn?" Danny knew he wasn't appealing to facts anymore but to intangibles.

"Because of all the blood."

I wanted to divert Danny and Ethna from the undeclared war between them.

"Stop frightening the child," said Ethna.

"The child is frightening me. What happened there, Finn?"

"They were all killed."

"Who was killed?"

"The men from the ships."

"And then?"

"Stop it, Danny," said Ethna. "We've agreed not to do this."

She could feel the hysteria building in my body. I couldn't stop now.

"They were thrown into a hole," I shouted. "They're under the Spanish Stone."

I was shaking. Ethna took me in her arms.

"Do you really have to upset him? Just because you're so full of begrudgery and spite."

"Sorry for pressing you like that, old chap." Danny struggled into his raincoat. "I have to get at the truth."

"Yeah," said Ethna derisively. "The truth of four hundred years ago from a five-year-old child."

Danny made a beeline for Tom's house. He was full of an excited sense of his own mission. It was hard for him to know which was the more important, to get at the terrible truth about the Spaniards or to nail Rob Roberts.

Well, it wasn't that hard.

My Daimon

⟿ I had to wait until I went to France to find an image for the way I saw the sailors of the Armada and many things besides. In a bar off the Rue Mouffetard, an old man poured a drop of water into his Pernod, and the liqueur churned to a milky whiteness. In just this way the air thickened round certain places, and through the pearly opalescence I could glimpse Otherwheres.

Thresheen explained that what precipitated sudden cloudings of the air and the breath of coldness that accompanied them was the amassment of memory. A place was not just a casual container of things; it remembered all that happened to it, good or bad, it held the past in a perpetual Now. I was blessed and cursed with an ability to see the spots where the wells of memory overflowed. Sometimes the denizens of Otherwheres passed through me, and I seemed to stretch like an accordion, growing tall or short with them. I was always amazed that nobody noticed my change of size. Sometimes a stone or a mound seemed like an open wound and filled me with dread. So that when Danny and Tom collected spades from the backyard and headed over the bogs towards Leach na Spanaigh, I followed them to see if I could master my fears. I kept after them though Danny asked me several times to have sense and go home.

"It won't do the lad any harm," said Tom. "What's there but a few old bones if anything?"

They dug for a good hour before they reached the first skeleton. They both took off their hats. As they stood opposite one another, it began to happen. Through the vaporous light I could see exhausted men struggle from the sea. I closed my eyes. When I opened them again, I was among dunes that were higher than today's. A rabble of screaming islanders waving axes and knives dashed towards the shipwrecked sailors. Once more I closed my eyes in terror. When I opened them again I was on a blood-blackened shore among mutilated bodies. The islanders stabbed and hacked in a stone-blind fury. I heard strangled prayers and cries for mercy above the pitiless crashing of the waves. I fell into a pit of darkness. When I came to, my head was on Danny's shoulder.

"It's all right, Finn," he said. "You shouldn't have come here."

There was a nest of yellow bones in the shallow pit they had dug.

"That young fellow of yours must be lacking in iron," said Tom. "Alice used to conk out like that if she didn't get enough iron."

When I looked back at the sea, the tide was red and heavy with lolling corpses. "I want to go home," I said, turning my head away.

Danny hoisted me on his shoulders.

"Maybe you'd tidy things up a bit and fill in the grave?" he said to Tom. "We'll deal with all this later."

How comforting it was to be carried home along the Long Mile of the bog road, where the stonechats played peekaboo in the furze bushes. What a relief it was to move through a humble landscape that remembered only brisk windy days when men footed turf or drank cans of buttermilk and smoked Woodbines in the lee of heeled-up carts. In that moment I was grateful for the mortal world, in which there were bones and graves and an end to everything.

The Daimon of Rob Roberts

Many women claimed that when Rob Roberts entered a room the air tightened and the temperature changed. You might despise the ground he walked on and take it for granted that he was a right shit, but once he strode in you found yourself gratefully surrendering to his spell. All his wrongdoings seemed only to add to his magnetism. If he lied, then his lies were in the service of a greater truth that you hadn't yet properly grasped. If he stole, then it was more a matter of liberating something from a wrongful constraint. If he was an adulterer many times over, then that was but the tribute the weak paid to the strong. As the man said: Better murder an infant in its cradle than nurse an unacted desire!

Once he approached you and introduced himself humbly as Rob — though of course you knew already that he was Rob — you involuntarily suspended your resistance to him. It wasn't that he was witty or even affable. It was more the sense of an intense, coiled-up energy, which he was charitable enough not to unleash in your face.

Biafra O'Dee, who had been in rebellious awe of Danny of the Golden Balls for years, shifted his allegiance to the greater god Rob. "The fucker is practically indestructible," he declared. "Even if they get him, they won't get him. He's got the luckiest array of stars of any man I've ever met apart from Charlie Haughey."

The Daimon of Father Francis

෴ Father Francis knew that there were many good haters on Uggala, but he never counted Danny among them. He thought that the worst enmities were over when the Parish Council asked him to return to live in the vacant Parochial House. That way he would be more easily contactable for sick calls. Yet the evening when Danny rushed into his parlor with only a perfunctory knock on the door, he was breathless with rage against Rob Roberts.

"The bones have disappeared from Leach na Spanaigh!" he shouted. "I'm sure Roberts and his cronies had a hand in it. The bastard wants to stop the forensic tests going ahead."

"You can't know that, Danny. Sit down."

"This guy is able for just about anything!"

"You're paranoid."

"I know. And that's why I want you to intervene."

"How am I supposed to do that?"

"You're a force on the island. People respect you. At this stage everybody is so beguiled by that fucker that they won't listen to me."

"You overestimate my authority," Father Francis said.

It wasn't what he meant. What he meant was: You overestimate my willingness to act.

Danny sat down at last. "This guy Rob Roberts is evil. Isn't it your job as a priest to fight evil?"

Father Francis felt a momentary flicker of annoyance: Don't you tell me what my duties as a priest are. But he said nothing.

For the next two hours Danny hammered away at the moral question, the ecological question, the historical question. He drank a pot of tea, ate all the apple cake, and in the intensity of his self-propelled indignation never noticed that Father Francis wasn't paying the slightest attention to what he was saying. For while Danny went on and on, Father Francis was sitting deep inside himself and thinking about the ineluctable irony of life. Danny clearly regarded him as a fellow rebel and dissident. But that wasn't him at all. His transgressions in the past — marrying Clare, saying Mass in defiance of the Bishop — were deeply against his nature, and he'd had to violate himself to go through with them. Clare was the only one who twigged it.

"You're a conventional man, Francis, aren't you?" she said one night, kissing him between the eyebrows. "You want to be left in peace to immerse yourself in your own 'I am for and even against.' You're a rebel that hates rebellion."

Clare was right. All his life Father Francis had longed to go back to the bliss of his childhood, when the angels congregated on the bed end and he no longer had to struggle for anything. He had thought that once he resolved the conflict between carnal love and his priesthood he would be able to quietly marvel at the world again — be up with the dawn chorus, sink himself in a book of poetry in order to have something to say to his congregation, sit with Clare by the fire and talk about what they had read in *The Irish Times* while glancing dreamingly at the taunting V between her thighs.

And here was Danny trying to blackmail him into a new struggle, for which he had no appetite whatsoever.

"What do you want me to do?" he asked in a weak voice.

"Have you been listening at all? I think you should tell the truth," Danny said. "The truth that the islanders slaughtered and tortured the Spaniards. The Heritage Centre is a piece of bogus history and a moral offense!"

"But how do we know that?"

"All the folklore that has been so conveniently forgotten speaks of a great massacre. I've checked it out in old proceedings of the Royal Irish Academy. Then there's the rifled grave. And besides, Finn saw the slaughter. You know he can see things."

Father Francis shrugged his shoulders. "Folklore. A clairvoyant child."

"For God's sake, Francis. The Church makes saints on a lot less evidence. Will you speak out?"

Father Francis felt two hands hanging a heavy, unwieldy albatross round his neck and centering it meticulously on his chest. He had never expected that Danny would be the one to do it.

The Daimon of Clare

❧ "We've got to do it," said Clare, disentangling herself from Father Francis's embrace and reaching for the packet of Marlboros she kept on the bedside table. "If the slaughter of the Armada marines took place on the island, the Heritage Centre will be a sick joke."

Not for the first time Clare was getting at him, needling him mere seconds after they had made love and she had reached orgasm. He had thought women were supposed to bathe in the squelchy afterglow of sex. But Clare turned argumentative on the instant and invariably smoked a cigarette, like the melancholy postcoital girls in the pretentious French movies that she'd been addicted to as a teenager.

"Oh Christ." He sighed. His little stabilization was coming to an end. Life was a series of pleasant green uplands that gave way to ravines and unholy precipices.

"But it's a lost cause, Clare. It's unnecessary to turn people against us."

"What if it is? Somebody has to do what's right. If you want I can do some leafleting."

"God, no!"

Standing up for lost and impossible causes came easily to Clare, as if it were encoded in her American genes. Doing the right thing was demanded by high-noon sheriffs, batmen, and *Washington Post* journalists. Ah, damn the lot of them.

"Well?" asked Clare imperiously and blew philosophical circles of smoke down the length of the bed.

"If I do anything I'll do it for you and not for Danny or Uggala or Humanity As We Know It."

Clare turned to him with a nicotine mouth and rewarded him with another erection.

My Daimon

When I came to *I* for *totem* in Cassell's Books of Knowledge, it dawned on me that the corncrake was the totem bird of my tribe. Ever since Danny had first told me about the harsh *crex crex* coming from the hayfields at twilight, I couldn't get the corncrake out of my head. It was one of the rarest of birds now and hadn't been heard for over twenty-five years. When Danny was a boy on holidays in Uggala, he couldn't get to sleep at night, so loud and persistent was the crexing from the callows. In the mornings, when he followed the faint trails of the birds through the long grass, they teased him, calling now here, now there, always behind or in front of him. But he never actually saw one or found a nest.

Danny had a weakness for migrant birds the way he had a weakness for foreign women. He had no interest in resident species, like blackbirds or seagulls or crows, though he made an exception for goldfinches. All his enthusiasms when he was a boy went into studying the habits of swallows and swifts and snow buntings. But the real samurai of the migrants were the corncrakes. After their brief summer in Uggala, they flew thousands of miles to the Horn of Africa. They had to brave the guns of manic Sicilian hunters and nets strung out along the Nile Delta. Roast corncrakes were a delicacy in Cairo, and you could have them for breakfast wrapped in banana leaves and flavored with turmeric. The few that survived Egypt took the long flight down the flank of Africa, past Madagascar, only to be menaced yet again by snares set in the barbs of juniper scrub by bushmen.

I cried when I imagined this journey. Such dangers, such hazards they had to endure! I would have given anything to bring them back safely to Carrowtreila, the quarterland of the corncrake.

Danny took a comb from the dresser and rasped a bit of stick across the teeth. "That's exactly what they sound like."

The same evening I stole out to his Thinking Place with the comb and stick, determined to raise an answering call. Surely there must be one corncrake left that nobody knew about, that had crossed in safety over the Nile Delta and Sicily and France? Only I knew of his existence. Only I could provoke him into combative song.

I imagined Danny, Sean and Seamus, Tom and Alice cocking their ears in astonishment as they heard the lost bird's call. I saw them running into the fields like children: The corncrakes are back! The corncrakes are back!

Suddenly I heard it, a low rasping call. I swung round trembling with expectation.

"Fooled you that time," said Thresheen. She was dressed like Robin Hood, all in floppy green cotton. I was sick with disappointment.

"Aren't you pleased to see me? I'm a lot rarer than any corncrake."

"Go away."

"Sorry, Finn. That was silly of me. Look, the corncrake hasn't disappeared at all. No species ever does."

"You're trying to make up to me."

"Seriously. Nothing is ever wiped out in nature. It just moves on to Otherwheres."

"Do you mean it can come back again?"

"Just wait and see."

I'm still waiting. The voice on my answering machine says: This is Finn Patrick O'Keefe. Please leave your message after the call of the corncrake. *Crex crex.*

The Daimon of Father Francis

Before he opened the meeting, Father Francis was seized by panic. He took deep breaths and tried to follow Clare's advice: "Just talk to the women. Don't even look at O'Keefe and company." Which only drove him to glance nervously at the brawny loudmouthed knot of men at the back.

Danny was sitting in a corner like a cat licking his own tail. He probably had a thunderous speech prepared, which he would deliver as if it were extempore.

The hall was packed even though the rain was coming down in buckets. Clare had rearranged the seating into a half circle to create an intimate, trusting space. But as soon as people began to drift in, they broke up the new arrangement and returned to the familiar factious rows.

"I've asked us to come together this evening," Father Francis began, "to reflect on the dramatic changes that are being planned for Uggala."

"What's to reflect on? Isn't it all decided?" A contrary voice was raised at the back. Everybody craned round to see who had interrupted the priest before he had scarcely begun.

"Even the best projects are improved by discussion and teasing out the implications for ourselves." Father Francis was determined not to be riled. "Let's look at it this way. There are two Uggalas. One of them seems to be dying and apparently has no future. But it's been a home of sorts for all of us and certainly for you and your ancestors. There's another Uggala coming into being, with a Heritage Centre and improved communications and all the rest of it. There'll be a great deal more money on the island, that's for sure. As you all know well, I could hardly be described as an old-fashioned priest who's against change . . ."

People smiled for the first time. Maybe this was the tack to take? Be a bit more personal.

"I'd like to see a stronger and more adventurous Uggala. But I ask myself occasionally if we are going about it in the best way. Uggala Mark One didn't have any past or history in the big-world meaning of the word. Of course people have lived here for thousands of years, but they lived ordinary lives far from the main events. Uggala Two has suddenly acquired a history and a place in the world. The new Heritage Centre will proclaim this history, if not from the rooftops then at least from the heights of Ard na nÉin. The question is, What is this history about and does it matter for us? I'm asking this because as it turns out there are two versions of the story. And one of them says it never happened or happened in a shockingly different way. Let's say the people of Uggala didn't in fact save the seamen from the Armada. On the contrary, let's say they massacred them as they came ashore. Would we still want to go ahead with a Heritage Centre? Or should we not try to face up to what our heritage really is?"

"What would you know about it?" asked the same venomous voice from the back.

"We don't know for sure," said Father Francis. "What we do know is that somebody has done away with the skeletons that were found near the beach."

A red-beet-faced Skipper was on his feet now. "Are you accusing somebody?"

"I'm not accusing anybody. This isn't a court of law. It's a discussion. The skeletons bore the marks of terrible violence. And before the proper forensic examination could be conducted, they were spirited away. That's just a fact, I'm afraid."

The people's eyes were fastened to his face. They were arming themselves against him.

Mrs. O'Halloran shifted uneasily in her chair and stood up with great effort.

"My grandfather always said that terrible things were done at Leach na Spanaigh. I thought it was the English. The kind of thing we learned at school."

A few people around her nodded, as if to say, Right Enough. We heard the same thing from the old people — but so what? Sean and Seamus were nodding too.

"So what do you want us to do?" Colm O'Keefe asked in a querulous voice. "Do you want us to give up the Heritage Centre because maybe a few Spaniards were knocked about four hundred years ago?"

"I want us to ask ourselves if the future prosperity of the island is to be based on a piece of bogus history."

"What does it matter?" said O'Keefe. "It's only a museum."

"I don't think so," said Father Francis. "I think a museum represents Uggala's identity."

He was losing them. *Identity* was too big a word, and it frightened them. Their faces said: We have enough problems without having identity shoved down our throats.

"Hold on a minute," interjected Biafra O'Dee. "Just hold on a minute. I'm a musician and not a scholar. But I know enough about history to know that everybody lies about it. Did you know that William Tell never existed? I read about it in the *Reader's Digest*. The Swiss made him up as a national hero. Same with us and Cuchullain!"

The audience brightened up. Biafra was setting things to rights. A pity the mad bastard had to drag in Cuchullain by the heels.

Alice raised a schoolgirlish hand. "Forgive me, Father, but you're a stranger here no more than myself after forty years. We don't understand the island people. If it's their past, surely it's their future as well? I don't think anybody has the right to tell them what's good for them. We can only pray it turns out well for everybody."

People were strengthening their links with one another with nods and glances. Father Francis had an overwhelming desire to flee. He wanted to delete everything he had said, all the questions he had raised, and to pretend the meeting never happened. He was no longer faced with Tom or Alice or Seamus or Biafra O'Dee but with a hydra-headed, alien body with one relentless conviction. He might have been able to talk to Alice and Biafra, even O'Keefe, individually, and explain the nuances of his thoughts about memory and truth, morality and identity. But confronted with this multiheaded reproach, he felt weak in the stomach. Previously when he defied Uggala he was fighting for something concrete: a woman, his vocation, a roof over his head. Now he felt the amorality of his fight for morality.

Danny had been waving his hand for ages. Now he was on his feet, ready for a salvage operation. Just when Father Francis was about to call him to speak, his sense of impotence vanished and was replaced by belligerence. No way was he going to let Danny be the cavalry riding to a last-minute rescue.

"Very well," he said. "I see you have no real problem with Rob Roberts's plans for the island. But I have a problem."

He was thinking of Laurence van der Post in the Jap prisoner of war camp. How he turned the tables on his tormentors by hitting a cultural weak spot.

"I have a problem with the dead. If people were murdered here on Uggala, their restless souls will haunt whatever enterprise sets out to exploit them."

A frostbitten silence filled the room. That was the way to get them, by the funerary tabula and fabula, he thought with malevolent glee. He had always prided himself on never resorting to fire and brimstone as a way of cowering his congregation. And now he was shoving the dead in their faces as much as to say: How do you like that?

The front of solidarity they had mounted against him began to crumble. He was again addressing individuals: Alice, Tom, Colm, Biafra, each one uneasy and vulnerable to the predations of the dead.

"Just because something has slipped into the past doesn't mean that it ceases to be," Father Francis said quietly. "That's why we can't erase an ugly event and change it round at will. OK, if you're an atheist that might make sense. But if you're a Christian you're always accountable to the dead and ultimately to conscience."

They were waiting for him to go on and terrify them even more, but he stopped there.

"That's all," he said curtly. "Are there any questions?"

Danny grinned and raised his left thumb.

The Daimon of Uggala

ꙮ For the next few weeks the islanders could speak of little other than Father Francis's warning. What had been straightforward and obvious before had now been mixed up with the dead.

"Watch out for the zombies crossing Cranberry Bog," joked Biafra O'Dee. "They're coming to get ye!"

The more the islanders argued with one another, the more they discovered who they were. Those who were for the Heritage Centre found themselves to be tolerant, progressive, and as Tom told them, left liberal. Those against considered themselves ecologically aware, Christian in the true sense, and the moral conscience of Uggala. Tom called them, regretfully, ecofascists.

Biafra O'Dee was in his element. "We're going through the Third Battle of Moytura here, folks," he said. "Bright boys — Milesians — to the left, backward Fomorians to the right."

"You've a point there," said Tom, taken by the mythic analogy. "God but doesn't history repeat itself! When did you say the Second Battle of Moytura was?"

"Oh, about 2500 B.C.," said Biafra sardonically. "Nothing much has changed in the interim. If I was Seamus Heaney I'd write a poem about it. Something like 'North,' only called 'West.'"

Tom knew there was something askew about the comparison with the Battle of Moytura, but he liked the idea of mobilizing the mythic potential of the old native struggle between the forces of light and darkness.

And so neighbor turned against neighbor, and families were split down the middle. Danny and Father Francis and Clare were on one side, Ethna, Tom, and Biafra on the other. While Colm O'Keefe led the pro campaign, Concepta, to everybody's amazement, declared herself against the project and took every opportunity on her walks to tear down pro–Heritage Centre posters. Was it just spite against her husband, people wondered, or had she a conscience for all her bitchiness?

Alice vacillated, as Tom knew she would. It was the permanent instability of the petit bourgeois, who could turn progressive or reactionary at the drop of a hat. She feared for the island's innocence and quietly nodded her agreement with those who spoke of the dangers of venereal disease and late-night cider parties in the graveyard.

Sean was strongly against and would have nothing whatsoever to do with a shower of young cunts and jackeens coming to Uggala on field trips. Let them try and cross his land! He had joyful visions of giving them a good root up the arse if they as much as tumbled a stone from the top of one of his walls.

Seamus didn't dare disagree. But he fantasized about taking the clothes off an easy woman from the city. He had struck a mental bargain with God that it wasn't a mortal sin so long as he didn't go any further than taking her bra off and didn't touch himself. Again and again a woman he had pieced together from mannequins in the shop windows in Galway was left stripped to the waist and shivering with the cold in the cart shed.

Mrs. O'Halloran lamented the bickering and backbiting that split the island. She longed for the good old days, when she didn't need to remember who was who and who was for what.

Tom said that the split was all to the good and long overdue. We had reached a political moment in our existence. Whatever we said was political and whatever we didn't say was political too. When we were walking on the Silver Strand, we were taking political steps on charged ground. Everything on Uggala was political from now on — the bog, the Danes' Fort, the church, the decision to have or not to have a pint of Guinness. Even the contemptuous sun that so rarely put in an appearance over the island had lost its insolent natural candor. Just ask yourself who's behind global warming.

The Daimonlessness of Sean and Seamus

❧ Tom thought Sean and Seamus would leap at the chance of selling off a few acres for the Heritage Centre, but Colm O'Keefe said, No, not a snowball's chance in hell. You might as well try to remove one of their fingers as take a biteen of land from them.

Thresheen had a different explanation. The Daimonic world is composed of seekers who find their calling and of anguished souls who fail in the quest. But, as always, there is a third group, made up of those who are indifferent to the search, men and women who are dropped into existence like erratics disgorged by a retreating glacier. They are left behind on hillsides or grassy plains, and there they remain, like the granite boulders near Silver Strand, lashed by the wind and the rain and sometimes consoled by the sun.

Sean and Seamus were two such erratics. They seemed to

have always been in the landscape, bent under forkfuls of fodder or carrying buckets of nuts to starving calves. From first light to last they tended their cattle and land, spreading dung in spring and keeping the ditches open in winter. They never stopped to ask themselves what's the point or where it all leads to. Or why they hadn't married and settled down like everybody else. The point was simply to get up at seven, rekindle the fire and boil up the porridge, catch the weather forecast on the radio and not bother listening to the news. Clinton my arse. Nothing will ever change in America. And then they went on to milk the cows and turn out the calves and drive the yearlings down the bohereen to the mountain. The only world that Sean and Seamus cared about was the world of their ancestors, and they followed its rhythms to the letter. They walked the land in the morning like their father and grandfather, one after the other, never together, and never exchanging a word except to hurl a vehement "Cunt!" at grasping briers or loose stones in the walls. Hail rain or shine, winter or summer, they wore the same ashen clothes, changing only for Sunday Mass and funerals.

Colm O'Keefe assured anybody who cared to listen that they were millionaires. They had made their money on cattle when cattle were worth the money and had come in for two legacies from granduncles in America. But even if they were millionaires, it wouldn't occur to them to paint their house or to put shades on the bare bulbs in the parlor.

As parents blossom when their children are praised at school, so Sean and Seamus glowed when somebody, preferably a stranger, remarked on how green and clean were their fields compared to the weedy, unkempt gardens of their neighbors. It never occurred to them then when they died their fields would go back to heather and rushes, and all their slavery be for nothing. In the meantime the hiss of a scythe slicing through a sward was the sweetest sound they knew.

As erratics, Sean and Seamus had never embarked on the

search for their Daimon. They were not even aware that they existed. They were just there, and any change in the landscape around them was a threat to their existence. So they opposed all change, just as the stones do.

"Come with me, I'll show you something," said Thresheen.

I followed her to the brothers' cottage, and she led me round the back, where the laurel bushes crushed against the wall. We peeped through the window into a bedroom lit by a tiny naked bulb. The brothers were climbing into the same iron bed. Seamus took the head, Sean the foot.

"They slept like that when they were boys, and they don't know any different now," whispered Thresheen. "They'll sleep like that, head to toe, in the grave. God love them."

The Daimon of Danny Ruane

❧ When Ethna began to spend more and more weekends away on courses and seminars, a worm of pain bored deep into Danny's chest. He had sworn to himself that if ever she wanted to leave him, he would simply let go and put no obstacles in her path. He had always felt contempt for the emotional and verbal agonies of about-to-split couples; the spilling of entrails on kitchen tables, rehashings of old wrongs, the fumbling with crooked fingers in one another's wounds. He had rehearsed the situation in his mind. You want to leave? Fine. I'll get your suitcases down from the loft. There's a boat at 3:30. The imagined scene gave him pleasurable pain.

He knew she was betraying him by the remote look in her eyes, a forgotten phone call, an unexplained absence, a heavy investment in new underwear. She didn't say anything, and he didn't probe. It was Biafra O'Dee who brought the Good News. One afternoon he dropped in to beg a loan of Patrick Kavanagh's *The Great Hunger*.

"I'm writing this song," he said. "It's really a heavily disguised allegory of premature ejaculation. I've the impression there's a lot of that kind of stuff in PK."

"Where would you get an impression like that?" asked Danny.

"We wankers have an ear for one another."

"An ear?"

"While we're on the subject. You know of course that Rob Roberts is shagging your woman? I saw them together in Dublin."

"How do you know he's shagging her?" asked Danny, swift elvers of pain dashing through his bloodstream.

Biafra gave him a pitying look.

"You're in the Dáil Bar, right? Tucked away in a nice quiet corner casting a horoscope for the Labour Party at a hundred pounds a go. Next thing you see RR and his moll being feted by a bunch of Fianna Fáil arseholes. When the bell rings for the division, the Fianna Fáilers feck off. RR has his hands all over the woman, and she's saying, Later, Rob, later. That's enough for me."

Nothing cheered Biafra like an opportunity to have a go at Danny, the man who had it all: a regular ride, a nice house, published books, brains, a multipocketed waistcoat of the kind worn by war correspondents. By stabbing at Danny now and then, Biafra felt he was merely righting an injustice in the world.

Danny gave him *The Great Hunger* without a word.

Biafra was suddenly abject. "Look. It's not as bad as being a homosexual Jew with AIDS in Algeria."

"Fuck off," said Danny.

He opened "Creation" and read the last paragraph with dead eyes:

Man is, therefore, unable to grasp the nature of the entire Creation. Only three-fourths of it are within his reach. He tries to grasp the remaining fourth, but he does it with only three functions at his disposal. So he does not get further than $3+ (1 + 1/4 + (1/4)^2 + \ldots)$

This time Danny didn't get any further either. In the course of his work he had got used to the pendulum swing from elated vanity to desolating humility. Yet he never lost the sense that every page he wrote was more important than the petty turbulences of domestic life. But this time he felt that Ethna's slippers thrown carelessly beside the dresser had more meaning than the seven hundred pages of his magnum opus. Its conceited formulae, its paleontology, psychology, and quantum physics were more banal than a turd in a toilet bowl.

For a good hour he doodled skeletal figures on the margin of his manuscript. They clamored up from the graveyard of his heart. He would have to do something. The sea was the penalty and the cure. It was the elemental antagonist, whose sheer physicality would haul him out of himself. Or kill him.

He performed the last domestic rites: washed the floor, fed the querulous hens, and put a bowl of fresh water in front of the sclerotic Sharik.

The sea was belligerent and flung insolent waves at the shore. Danny pushed his Windsurfer beyond the breaking crests and made a standing start, the full balloon of the sail pulling him up on the board. With his harness hitched to the boom, he stretched back and went on a long reach out into the bay.

The shifting winds from the land and the changing currents forced him to concentrate, to Be Here Now. The waves grew choppy, opened gulfs and piled up hillocks before him. A sudden gust wrestled the sail out of his hands and flung him in a giddy arch into the running tide. He struggled to reattach the foot of the mast and to haul the wallowing sail out of the waves, but it loosened again and again and flipped him over on his back. Climbing up on the board, attaching the sail, raising the sail, and facing into the pounding of the sea exhausted him to the point of indifference. When he was no longer able to retrieve his mast, he lay flat out on the board and faced it into the wind.

So that's what the end is like, he thought. He had a cartoon image of himself lying stretched out on the Windsurfer in the heaving sea. Above him the Pleroma stretched itself like a ragged Blakean divinity full of its own conceit. The Pleroma pointed a finger at him and said: "I'll save you if you renounce your heresies."

Danny didn't even consider the offer. No, he said. If I survive I'll keep at it.

"You poor prune," said the Pleroma. "Are you trying to kill yourself?"

Colm O'Keefe leaned over the side of his motorboat. He had the broken wing of Danny's lost sail already tied to the stern.

Before Danny could reply, he was grabbed by the harness and pulled into the boat.

Colm grinned at him. "Biggles to the rescue, Algy! By Jove, you've really hit the drink. Poor show."

That was not how it should be.

It was Colm who was Flight Lieutenant Algy Montgomery. Danny was Captain James Bigglesworth, D.S.O., D.F.C.

My Daimon

➣ I had just returned from Alice's, where we had been going over the first theorems of Euclid, when Colm O'Keefe and the Skipper helped Danny to the door. He was still in his wet suit. He looked defeated and sunken in on himself. His rescuers were only too happy to make things worse by telling me to look after the shipwrecked sailor and to boil one of them chicken for strong soup. They wrestled the Windsurfer off the tractor, and Danny didn't protest when the Skipper knocked a dent in the board as he stashed it awkwardly against the pebble-dashed wall.

I was afraid to say anything because I was heart-stricken by Danny's beaten look. And I knew what he was thinking: I'm an old softy. A martyr of the worst kind. I should have kicked that woman out on her arse months ago.

"You're not going to throw Mummy out," I said in a timid voice.

He looked at me wearily. "Don't you start."

Danny drank hot whiskeys all afternoon. When he was drunk enough to have recovered a sense of balance, he climbed up to me in the attic and sat on the floor.

"You see things, Finn," he said. "Do you see Ethna staying on here?"

"I don't know," I said, confounded by the multitude of probable Ethnas.

There was only one man on the island who could answer the question: Biafra O'Dee.

The Daimons of Biafra O'Dee and Danny Ruane

➣ Biafra O'Dee believed that every man should plant a sturdy ash tree in front of his house so that when the time came he would have a bough from which to hang himself. The morning Danny called for advice, Biafra was in a dangling mood and didn't want to hear about Ethna or Rob Roberts or any such tripe and onions.

"This is a non-problem, Golden Balls," he said with contempt, mixing his ginger and hot water at the sink.

"What would a real problem look like?" Danny searched around for a chair, but there were books and clothes everywhere. So he sat on the floor.

"I'll tell you what a real fucking problem is." Biafra pointed to the skeletal ash tree just visible through the grimy window.

"What's the point of going on with life if you're not Seamus Heaney? Or Van Morrison at the very least?" He shook his finger. "That's a real existential question for you! Do you top yourself? Or do you just go on creeping and crawling through the mud of mediocrity day after day without even the *Galway Advertiser* noticing your puny existence?"

Danny was thrown by the vehemence of Biafra's despair. "Jesus, Biafra, the *Galway Advertiser*?"

Biafra turned on Danny savagely. "You understand nothing! Never have, never will. When did you last have a ride? Three days ago? Four days ago? You have simply no idea what it's like to be mediocre and rideless. A ride!" Biafra snaffled contemptuously. "Not even a trot for me."

"But you said yourself you're going to take off!"

"I'll be three days swinging from the bough of that ash tree and the flies eating out the gunk from my eyeballs before I take off. Now what do you want?"

"I want you to do my chart."

"I don't fucking believe this. Golden Balls wants a chart! You must be really up the creek. I can't take the responsibility anymore. I'm into rap and reggae now. And I still don't know why I'm wasting my time. If I was Seamus Heaney it would be different."

"But you're Biafra O'Dee, the one and only, the god-given, the craziest lonesomest corncrake west of the Shannon," Danny said affectionately. "I'm in the pits and I need your genius. I'll give you thirty quid."

Biafra batted his eyelashes.

"Fifty."

"Thirty-five."

"You're some cunt. OK, date, place, and hour of birth."

Biafra's tone was pissed off and professional. He took out

his calculator and sank into a squeaky armchair on top of a pile of old unwashed shirts.

Danny had a sudden compulsion to lie about his date of birth, but that would be a waste of time and thirty-five pounds. The whole thing was ridiculous enough already.

Biafra punched the digits of Danny's destiny into his calculator. When he raised his head, he looked shocked.

"What?" asked Danny. "Am I supposed to be dead or something?"

"You lucky fucker! You've got Saturn exalted in the tenth house of public career. Just like Yeats. Hang on! Venus is also exalted in the tenth. Lots of rides there too."

"What's it supposed to mean?"

"It means public acclaim and lashings of sex on the side, you gobshite!" roared Biafra in a paroxysm of jealousy.

"Sex with whom?"

"How the fuck would I know? I'm not a clairvoyant. I'm a mathematician."

"So where's this public acclaim? I don't see much sign of it around."

"Hang on, hang on." Biafra fiddled again with his calculator. "Give it three to four years."

"Four years!"

"Your sun is in Leo. I don't believe it! His sun is in fucking Leo!"

"Is that good or bad?"

"Virgo rising in the west, Leo in the east, and he's asking me if it's good or bad! Jesus Christ, if I had this chart I'd be president of the United Fucking States of America by now. Why are you such a lazy son of a bitch?"

"But what's going to happen?"

"The sun in Leo never goes retrograde. It's only in fall for four measly weeks of the year. Did I say fifty pounds?"

"What about Ethna?"

"Your ruler of the fifth house is dodgy."

"Does it mean she's going to leave me?"

Biafra derived exquisite pleasure from Danny's anxiety. "How would I know?"

"That's what I thought I was paying forty pounds for."

"Forty-five and rising. Now look, the ruler of your seventh house of marriage is strong, OK? So don't be pestering me for Christ sake. But . . ."

"But?"

"But there is a problem."

"She's going to leave?"

"Ethna's mother," said Biafra with relish. "The mother is destroying everything. She's like Saturn or Mars eating away at whatever house the poor bitch aspects."

Danny was dogged. "Let's get back to Ethna. Will she or won't she stay on Uggala?"

"Do you have the exact date and time of her birth?"

"No."

"Of course not! I told you I wasn't a reader of crystal balls. Speaking of balls, you have Venus exalted in the tenth house!"

Biafra began to pant like a thirsty dog. "Why you and not me? Why do I get the gristle and bone and you get the filet mignon? Where's the justice in that?" He had almost brought himself to tears.

Danny knew that were he to mention Seamus Heaney or Paul Muldoon at this point, Biafra would scour the island for a rope with which to hang himself.

"Look, Biafra, I don't care what your stars say. I know you're going to make it and Loreena McKennitt will sing your songs."

"You do?"

"Yep. And Polygram will beg you on bended knees for a contract."

"Do you think so? How do you know?" Biafra's voice was tremulous with hope.

"I just know. I feel it in my bones. I'm never wrong about these things."

"If I could only get my stuff to America," moaned Biafra.

"You'll get your stuff to America," said Danny with thumping conviction.

"But my moon's in Rahoo. Steeped in it like a leaf in acid! Do you fucking know what that means?"

As Danny trudged home along the purgatorial bohereens, where even the stones groaned and shivered in the wind, he laid into himself mercilessly. How could he stoop so low as to hand over good money for Biafra's farrago of nonsense? It was worse than paying for sex.

Now that he was reassured that his stars had all the right alignments and conjunctions, he was a rationalist once more, full of disdain for Biafra O'Dee's lunatic ravings.

The Daimon of Ethna

From the moment Ethna decided to seduce Rob Roberts rather than be seduced, she dictated the course of their romance. It was exhilarating because for the first time she was with a man over whom she had power. She had power over him because she didn't love him. She relished his savoir faire and his easy entrance into many worlds. As with Armand, so with Rob she was the princess young and fair beyond compare. But she was blissfully certain that her life wasn't dependent on him. She would feel no stinging grief were she to lose him or any of the luxuries that came in his train. She discovered that she quickly got tired of eating in expensive restaurants and longed for homemade soups and the reassuring ritual of cooking together. She hated the anonymity of hotel rooms and the disquiet of new beds, however crisp the linen and plumped up the pillows. Caviar and champagne made her nauseous. She was seasick on yachts. The more she detested these things, the more power accrued to her. It was as if she were taking revenge on Armand by being difficult with Rob Roberts, who was at his wit's end how to please her.

It was when Rob was fishing for sea trout in Ballynahinch and she had nothing to do but count the ripples on an expanse of twilit water that the sense of power lost its allure for her. As Rob shouted ups-a-daisy to a fish thrashing on the end of his broken rod, she felt the vacuous pain of homelessness. The glowing water and the gloom of evening frightened her.

"I'd like to go back now," she said like a small girl.

"Just give me ten minutes or so and we'll walk back to the hotel."

"I don't mean the hotel. I mean Uggala."

There was no home for her on Uggala, and well she knew it. What she meant was Danny. She wanted to go back to Danny. It had come to her with the force of a bitter revelation. The only place she properly inhabited was Danny. It had never struck her before that one person could be a home to another. It wasn't his body or his words she yearned for. It was the sum of all their moments together, a sense of being at peace in a familiar, protected place.

"I must be getting old," she said to Rob as he gathered up his fishing gear.

"You'll get over it," he said lightheartedly. "What weight would you say the fish is? Five pounds?"

Ethna didn't go to the hotel. She took off her shoes and dipped her feet in the cold pebbly stream. A gibbous moon lay on its back above Ballynahinch Castle. Waiting for a ride, as Biafra would say. What did she think she was doing?

As a young girl she had been filled with despair because she couldn't imagine her future. Now she was filled with despair because the future came to her in a rush.

The rain was falling on Danny's grave and the graves of her

children. Her own mouth was full of clay. There were strangers moving into Danny's cottage. A man in her bedroom lay daydreaming over a blank page. The gibbous moon drifted into his reverie and with it a wet woman. She strolled by a twilit stream thinking of death. The water rose and swamped the page and left his mind dark.

My Daimon

🐚 If Ethna had ever taken the trouble to check how I slept, if she'd smoothed down my pillow, studied the calm pink blossom of sleep on my face, stroked my cheek, she would have seen what she had always feared. A clinical case. I didn't sleep like a log, like an angel, like a mouse under a broom. I didn't sleep at all. It was only at night that I opened myself up without fear that somebody would spot my gambols in Otherwheres and start asking silly questions. I laughed my head off talking to King Macius II, I quarreled with my dead sister, I sobbed over Holy Paddy, I composed rhythmical spells. I was a corncrake with a body of wind, I was an eye that sees everything through phosphor, I was somebody else's dream.

This July night I wasn't in my bed. I mean I was, but at the same time I was sitting on Danny's roof staring at the Aquila constellation, which would be discovered in fifteen years by a Lithuanian astronaut from Novogrodek. Fully awake, I sat on my bed wondering where I was, here, in or on the roof? And who was I, Finn O'Keefe or a citizen of the Aquila constellation? Though normally I was slow to take action, this time I jumped onto my feet and ran to the garden. I had to check where I really was and what I was doing.

The Aladdin moon hanging over the house illuminated the ladder which leaned against the wall under the half-collapsed chimney. I climbed up to the moonlight, trembling with curiosity. I was talking to Thresheen, I was sure; I would recognize my voice at the end of the world. When I climbed the last step, the ladder swayed under me.

"What a nincompoop you are!" said Thresheen.

She sat on the edge of the chimney dressed in black overalls and top hat, a spiral chimney broom hanging flamboyantly from her shoulder.

"Whom did you talk to?"

"To you, silly boy. I was answering your questions."

"And what did you say?"

"Why do I have to repeat everything one hundred thousand times? If you want to find out who you are, open Danny's 'Ruminations' on page twenty-two."

"I want to know now."

"How did it go?"

> You are a script of God's letter
> A mirror reflecting His face
> This universe is not outside you
> Look into yourself
> Everything you desire
> Is already you.

"Now mind the ladder, dear!"

It was only then that I felt I stood on a slippery ground and the ladder under me was tilting dangerously.

Mummy!

The Daimon of Ethna

❧ Why is it that Ethna woke up that night and — without rhyme or reason — found herself in the garden flooded by the immobile Assyrian, Egyptian, and Roman moon? As I have said, it wasn't her custom to check on me. When she suffered from insomnia she would get up, sit at her drawing board, and chew an invisible poppy seed until the papery void in front of her would give birth to an impatient fetus of a facade or a portal or an edifice that she would then caress with her crayon until the bleary-eyed dawn.

That night she didn't sit down and didn't look into the papery void. She put on her dressing gown and circled restlessly round the living room like a trapped moth. She felt an urge to escape, the same urge which twelve years ago made her run away from her mute mother buttoned up with ten zippers. If she had stayed one more day on Uggala, she'd be like Concepta, a frightened, Fomorian, fundamentalist, dark presence. She gasped for light and life like a caged bird in springtime banging the bright bars. Somewhere else there was a city of real presence, of real trees and voices and friendship and love. One more day on Uggala and . . . She checked herself. Better not to think about it, better take nitrazepam.

She approached the cupboard and opened a drawer stuffed with medicines for 340 diseases except death. When I was climbing the ladder to find out whether I was sitting on the roof, Ethna's hand halted. Nitrazepam was one more escape. Perhaps Uggala was her Bethlehem? After all, wasn't her destiny to give birth to half an alien, half an angel — half a schizophrenic? Maybe that was all there was to her life?

The very thought filled her with dread. How on earth was she to relearn the humility of Maria, Magdalene, Brigit, Columba, Agnes, Rita, Teresa, Lucia? All those meek souls who knew their place and showed respect? And yet and yet — how could she be a stepmother of her own child, straight from a Grimms' fairy tale: ruthless, selfish, perfidious, unfeeling? She could explain her lack of motherly instincts in a dozen of overripe interpretations — Freudian, Frommian, Kleinian, Lacanian — but the fact remained. For her, biological laws were one more oppressor, one more limitation to her freedom. She reeled in a nauseous mist, so odious she seemed to herself. No, she won't take the sleeping pill, or any lozenges or concoctions that would wet or warm her humors. She will torment herself just a bit more — why not, a vivisection under the Aladdin moon might shake her up.

She put a shawl round her shoulders and went out on the porch. She swayed on her feet and looked at the moon blowing into its horn in alarm. Beneath the trees, foxgloves and wood anemones looked up with tearful metamorphic eyes. Not so long ago, when they were still intoxicated with one another's names, Danny would come after her and they would love themselves dizzy in the moon's honey. Oh, see me hold me love me because we are sinking to the bottom of the night! But Danny no longer ran after her, gaped at the moon, quoted Rumi, and made her climb down from the tenth floor of her misery to the ground floor of his lust for her. If he did she wouldn't have betrayed him. Or would she?

Basta.

She stopped swaying on her feet and stood petrified, as if being touched by flaming steel. An icy wind blew across her heart. It blew from something she saw with a second pair of eyes. She saw her son clinging to a ladder which was sliding down on the other side of the cottage. He was sliding with it, talking to the moon, to the stars, to a black wing of the cloud. A horror that wasn't hers exploded in her like a warhead, tearing her out of herself. In the microsecond of that horror, her whole life, all her anguish, all wounds and bruises became what they really were: a line of dots in parentheses. I saw her hands reaching out for me, I saw her soul jumping out like a cork from a champagne bottle. I was a precious little angel, Mummy's sunshine, honey bun, shhh, let's not start crying, sugar.

For a moment I bathed in the foam of her tenderness, which until then I had seen only in American movies where Mary Lou hugged her only son crying, "Are you all right? Are you all right?"

When Ethna hugged me I regretted that I didn't break my legs or hands. I wanted to fall a hundred times from the ladder right into Ethna's arms, even if I were never to find out whether I was in the bedroom or up on the roof asking Thresheen existential questions.

The Daimon of Uggala

🐦 Uggala had managed to escape the ministrations of four Celtic Revivals. Ossian had never set foot there, Young Ireland didn't know it existed, Lady Gregory had never sat by the turf fires collecting its visions and beliefs, and Declan Kiberd hadn't got round to analyzing its postcolonial psychoses. For centuries the island had lain off the west coast, inert, unassuming, and unsung. Nobody ever dreamt that it might have a destiny beyond mere survival. It was a place where nothing happened very slowly, as a mainland poet put it. There were no aboriginal Irish speakers. There was no warm face-to-face community to rhapsodize about. Nobody gave a tinker's curse about nature. It was a dreadful kip, but it was great all the same.

The greatness of Uggala could be seen only by comparison with other places. There was nothing like a good bloodcurdling disaster elsewhere in the world to make you realize how lucky you were to live on Uggala and what a Noah's ark it was: a foot-and-mouth outbreak in England, plane crashes in India, or coups d'états in Guatemala, for example. In moments of absentminded reflection the locals would lean back in their chairs and say contentedly: We have a good life here after all. Look at Calcutta and all that Mother Teresa has to put up with! Or think of the Congo with the niggers at one another's throats. Or again, what about Siberia and being thrown out of your plank bed at five o'clock in the morning and the temperature minus forty?

People culled horror stories from the radio and newspapers and stored them against wet summers and the same salty cuts of bacon every day.

And then, in the summer of 1994, the islanders ceased comparing Uggala to the Congo and began to mold it anew with their minds. Uggala no longer simply was: it wanted to be. It wanted to be rich and then it wanted to be even richer. It wanted to be spiritual and then even more spiritual. It wanted to be popular and ever more popular. It wanted to be the center to the point where it elbowed Lisdoonvarna off the tourist map completely. Once the energy of all these wants was strong enough and the lacks were simply ignored, everything changed. The ferry came on time, there were no more blackouts, even the weather improved. Biafra O'Dee crowed to the young worshipful women who surrounded him in Balor's Bar. "Now we've got heritage and respectability. We're no longer a bunch of pastless and rideless wankers. We shafted six ships of the Armada, didn't we, Skipper? The energies here are getting so frisky I'm half-afraid to think of anything in case it happens. Yesterday I thought of group sex, and look what's arrived today. Yippee!"

The Daimon of Ethna

◕ A month had passed since Ethna had left Rob Roberts. But still she hadn't managed to come home to Danny. She was so odious to herself, so broken on the wheel of her self-recriminations that every available word or gesture of reconciliation seemed shameless or obscene. It would be simply idiotic to say in the middle of washing the dishes or cooking together: Danny, I love you. I'm sorry, please forgive me. What if he just went on stirring the tortellini?

In films and novels people returned to one another in the rain. The rain made them bedraggled and hence more authentic; it washed out sins, mistakes, and all the bad things that good people do to one another. There was plenty of rain on Uggala and no lack of opportunity to run towards Danny in a clingy wet dress with wisps of hair streaking her face. But she knew life wasn't like that. Not even a fervent rereading of *Doctor Zhivago* showed her a way forward.

For Ethna returning to Danny was as delicate and intricate an operation as landing on the moon. It required extraordinary emotional navigation: one wrong move and she would tumble for good into the icy blankness of space.

They moved warily around one another in the house, cautious and formal as two mayflies on the taut surface of a lake. Danny's behavior was impeccable to the point of cruelty. He wasn't playing at being hurt, he wasn't vengeful; rather he acted out of a center of frightening self-sufficiency. He was restrained, pleasant, and lethal all at once. There was no landing place on him.

He seemed to have constructed an invisible glass wall around himself so that even in bed together their bodies never touched. She knew about the way in which couples in their sleep go through a balletic sequence of adjustments in response to one another's movements. But she was sure that it wasn't happening anymore between Danny and herself. The great unconscious reciprocity between the moon and the tides, flowers and the sun and lovers in their slumber had broken down between them.

Ethna felt she had regressed to the days when she had first moved to Danny's cottage and was there on his sufferance. Probably the decent thing now would be to get up and go. But she knew that Danny would never come after her. If she left that would be the end of everything.

As she bowed over her drawing board, she felt oppressed by the aching presence of her mother and grandmother. There was a whole lineage of disturbed, unloved wives and consorts stretching back to the great unloved ur-consort herself. She had passed her misery on to her daughter, who in turn had passed it on to her daughter, and so on until it reached Ethna.

She stayed up late for nights on end to finish her commission. Danny never looked over her shoulder to see how the design was coming along or made her an encouraging malty of Ovaltine. On the night she drew the last strut, she was so exhausted that even her fears were faint. Danny was fast asleep, facing her side of the bed as if subconsciously waiting for her. She slipped in beside him and fitted herself to his body. In the secret language of their early lovemaking, it was the first move to attain the Barnaclugga position. She was prepared for him to move over and away into cold indifference. Instead he opened himself and seemed to nestle her inside him. He was her shell, her carapace, her armor against the terrors of herself. Never before and never again did she lie in such naked intimacy with a man.

"Wrong!" said Thresheen. "She lay with Rob Roberts like that before the battle of Grunwald in 1410."

"Oh, shut up," I said, "and let them get on with it."

III

DEPARTURE

You've been an ascete, I've turned you into a singer
You've been mute, I created a bard
Your name was not known in the world
Not a word about you, no sign
Until I, bringing you to the path
Made you into a discoverer of secrets

You've lived here just a few moments
And yet you've befriended life so much that
I can't talk about death anymore
You're on your way home
But your donkey fell asleep
In the middle of the road.

— Jelaluddin Rumi

The Daimon of Danny Ruane

It was Ethna who took the phone call. She was in the middle of frying sausages, and by the time she finished talking they were carbonized. It wasn't often that she used expletives, but this time she said to me: "I don't fucking believe it! Danny's being offered big bucks for a book. And it isn't 'Creation.'"

"It's his 'Ruminations,'" I said, unable to conceal my selective omniscience. "It's going to be a best-seller."

Ethna sat down, chewed her poppy seed, and blew the fringe off her forehead.

"The fellow on the phone said Danny is the voice of the new millennium. And I said, That's a likely story. Have I spoiled everything, do you think?"

Ethna was appalled by the way the book had suddenly materialized as if by magic. She kept thinking of an Irish word for mushroom she had picked up at school: fas-aon-oiche, the growth of one night.

When Danny came in with a lobster squirming in his hand and began to undo his old oilskins with the other, we said nothing. We just gawked at him. So this was the voice of the new millennium: a burly man in rubber boots whose red locks were beginning to turn gray. For a disconcerting moment Ethna saw what I saw: the adulatory crowds at readings and lectures that would restore his youth and magnetism.

"What are the two of you staring at?" he asked. "Is somebody dead or something?"

"A publisher has just called from New York. He was raving about something called 'Ruminations.'"

"How much?" asked Danny.

"More than they're worth."

"Good," he said. "Even if it took them two years to read it. So I don't need to take computer classes anymore." He sniffed the air. "I see you've been trying to burn the house down again. Why don't we have this lad for dinner?"

He flung the creaky lobster on the table.

Seven years ago he had seemed to Ethna the most romantic man in the world, more romantic even than the schoolmaster in *Ryan's Daughter*. Then when he had started growing shiitake mushrooms in a woodpile, she had decided he was going slightly mad. Two years ago she was betraying him because he was basically a wastrel. Now he had come full circle and was going to be romantic again, and American sophomores would swoon as he explained in his deep voice how hugely important this or that was.

The Daimon of Ethna

✒ I watched my mother bent over the drawing board, chewing her poppy seed and staring at the impudent blankness of Uggala that refused to make itself visible. First I saw her on the outside, as she plotted Uggala against her very being, beautiful beyond belief at this passing moment, at this passing moment that never passed. Then I saw her on the inside, infused with Uggala's poisons, pinioned by ghosts and animosities, by huge grudges and small gain. She wanted to punish, punish, punish. To put the stone back into Uggala's gaping mouth.

"We need to take the lout by the snout, Finn," she said to me, blushing, aware that she was watched and disembodied. I knew she really wanted me out of the room and allowed me to stay only because she didn't want to make me feel rejected.

Unlike the fire stations, schools, chapels which she had always delivered briskly, pouncing on the page, her tongue following her labor, her combat with Uggala was a perfect three days' long eternity, a long nosebleed surprised at itself.

I watched as she opened Seamus Heaney's *North* to get herself going, if only on angry resistance. See what we have here: quagmire, swampland, and morasses. Slime kingdoms, domains of the cold-blooded. Lovely. The landscape fossilized in stone, wall patternings and melting graves holding hatreds. Pap for the dispossessed indeed.

I watched as she leafed impatiently through her old rapturous drawings from the camper time: Gothic spires, Elizabethan canopies, Norman towers, ivy-clad doorways. Today they seemed kitsch, schlock, clichés. Angrily she sliced the board with cylinders, rectangles, wedges, steps, vertical stripes and disks, semicurves, diaphanous voids. Nope!

She tore the page from the drawing board and cast it on the floor.

What about Danny's Rumi-nescent village? She sketched a few semicircular forms recalling the tombs of saints, a mandala in the center, spaces as places of meditation, et cetera, slash, slash. "Rumi my arse. This isn't Uggala, this isn't me, this isn't anything," she said aloud.

"Sorry, Finn."

I swallowed hard. I never got tired watching her work. I was in love with the wrinkles of fury on her forehead, her losing and finding the way, her heedless cursing and biting the nails, her shining chestnut plait beating the air like a fierce cobra. Watching Ethna drawing was like reading a fairy tale where nobody knows what the princess will do next. She knew I was in love with her, that I was her knight errant ready for the seven mountains and the seven hills and the seven seas, wanting to wait on her, wanting to die for her, relishing the moment when she picked up the crayon and froze in mid-gesture, mid-breath, trying to keep the cold from her mind.

"Do you know this tale, Finn?" she said. "It goes like this:

> There was a dark dark wood
> And in the dark dark wood
> There was a dark dark house
> And in the dark dark house
> There was a dark dark room
> And in the dark dark room
> There was a dark dark coffin
> And in the dark dark coffin
> There was a dark dark . . .

"Treasure?" I asked quickly.

She smiled, touched, and surprised.

"You're like Danny."

She added a skylight on top of a primitive hut to ensure a half sunburst. Then she drew something between an obelisk and a pyramid, a kind of a moon station crossed with a miners' camp. I didn't like it.

"I can see them savaging me for reviving romantic rural ideas from the past," she said, guessing my thoughts.

She tore the page off the board, folded it with a painful pleasure, and dropped it into the rubbish bin.

"I can't do it," she said.

As Biafra O'Dee put it in his "No Hole No Holiness," she was deep at the bottom of her misery, sparkless and harmless to boot, bewildered like a pearl oyster, without hand or foot.

The Daimon of Biafra O'Dee

🢒 Biafra O'Dee crouched over a timid turf fire and stroked the back of a flame. As a child he had often stroked flames in the same way to find out what it was like for lost souls in

Hell. They had to endure for all eternity what he couldn't endure for a second.

Crouching in front of the fire invariably brought back the grievances of his childhood. There was a simple line drawing on the cover of his first exercise book. It showed a boy with a blue cap and a red haversack on his back striding on a turning globe. The boy was him. Going nowhere in the short trousers his mother forced him to wear in the summer so that the sun could get at his spindly rheumatic legs. He should have stood up to her and said no. He could still feel the hungry eyes of the Christian Brother on him as he asked him to come up to the blackboard again and again. Hungry eyes and hairy wet hands. But for Biafra's mother priests neither kissed nor pissed, and if they touched you it was with a sole intention to bless or anoint.

"I should have stood up to her!" Biafra said aloud. He looked around to see if anybody was listening and then wondered why he had done so. There was nobody within half a mile of him.

He took his hand out of the fire, appalled at its age.

"I'm going mad like my father and my grandfather before me," he said to the ever more rapacious flames. "Mad mad mad," he whispered, shaking his head. It was different for them. They slipped into madness as easily as into their pajamas. But he had not only to go mad but also to know he was going mad. He was like a man half-buried in sand and forced to watch the incoming tide that would drown him.

He thought of the quarter pound of streaky rashers in the fridge. His mouth filled with their juicy palatal pink taste. He could see them curling and crisping on the iron pan. He went to the fridge and unwrapped the soggy bundle that Alice had sent over to him. He held it in his hand and trembled. Christ, he thought, is there anything more pathetic than an anorexic bugger shivering in a hand-me-down jersey the color of shite and salivating over a measly quarter pound of somebody else's bacon? His eyes filled with tears.

He put the package back with a gesture of snarling contempt that was redolent of his dead mother on Great Friday. He banged the fridge door just as she would have done and shambled over to a rickety armchair. Tenderly he cupped his brow in his left hand and closed his eyes. His father had sat like that night after night at the kitchen table when the tea things were cleared away.

Biafra felt he was only partially inhabiting his own skull. Half of him had moved over to some other mind that required that he repeat ancestral gestures.

"Oh fuck!" he hissed aloud.

What would it be like to have a wife? Not some kind of skinny nymphette in white bobby socks and tight cotton knickers, but the real thing with a little bit of a belly and maybe even varicose veins. A woman who would make blackberry jam in August and surprise him the odd morning with her apron full of field mushrooms. Ah! They'd fry the mushrooms in butter with the rashers! And then they would compare dreams from the night before and talk about all their pains and aches. It struck him for the first time that you could talk about your pains only to a woman like that, a woman who would beat carpets in the yard when the wind was right.

What would it be like to have brains like Danny Ruane? Not the yellow flabby feel-of-tripe thing that he was endowed with but an airy hall where the swallows of thought darted in and out. With a brain like that he could be as good as Bob Dylan any day.

What would it be like to have children? Two daughters, say. Pretty, chatty daddy's girls. None of that oedipal shit with sons, who basically want to castrate you or stuff your head down the toilet. Two girls in blue dresses with sashes out picking cowslips.

Why wasn't he meant to have any of these things? Why was it that every half-baked arsehole in the country had these things and not him? The lost souls in the fireplace howled and gnashed their teeth.

"Mr. O'Dee." A tentative voice reached him from the doorway. "Is it Mr. O'Dee? I'm sorry, I knocked a few times like, but nobody answered."

The man who stood in the door was immaculately dressed in a navy blue velvet suit and lemon silk shirt. His ponytail proclaimed he still remembered the 1960s. And his singing pedagogical intonation reminded Biafra of voices from Bergman films in the Irish Life Centre.

"I tried to ring you many times like, but the phone didn't answer," the man sang.

"It's cut off," said Biafra reproachfully. He was annoyed by the ponytail.

"My name is Gunnar Bjerklund. I'm from KLB Records in Sweden. I heard your demo tape and —"

"How did you get it?" asked Biafra filling up with paranoia.

"A friend of mine, Rob Roberts, sent it to me. You know him? I like your songs. 'Me and Seamus' I think is the best. And then 'No Hole No Holiness.' They are gems. Can you come to Stockholm and record them? We can maybe discuss the contract like?"

The rancorous unfulfillment of decades half-choked Biafra.

"Why didn't you come ten years ago?" he groaned. "It's no use your coming now. Christ, I can't even get it up."

"Get what up?"

"My dick, you fool! What's the point of going to Stockholm if I can't get my bloody dick up?"

"Ohohohoh," said Gunnar. "We can maybe fix that for you."

"Too late!" shouted Biafra. "Everything's too late. Can't you see that it's all over? I'm like some Marcello Masturbati put out to grass on this fucking island. You know what I say to myself in the mornings? That the Night come! That the Night come!"

"It's not the best way to start the day like," said Gunnar politely.

At that moment Biafra hated Gunnar with the hatred of Richard III for the uncrippled world. All his torments were because of Gunnar or the likes of him. His unrecorded songs, his destitution, the long lonely evenings on Uggala were all Gunnar's fault.

"Get out of my sight!" he panted.

"Why?" asked Gunnar mildly.

"Because I don't like your fucking ponytail, that's why."

"Oh, I'm so sorry," mumbled Gunnar and headed meekly for the door. "You're a very difficult man."

"Get a fucking haircut!" shouted Biafra after him.

When Gunnar Bjerklund departed, Biafra's first and last chance of fame and fortune departed with him. For a good hour he slumped in his armchair, stunned and dumbfounded by his own toxicity. He felt again the chronic almostness of his life in the arrhythmic pulse of his temples. He panted and mumbled curses to himself. The room lay two inches deep in a dark, viscous plasma that was leaking out of him. If he went on leaking like this maybe he would be spared the trouble of hanging himself or eating the dried death cup mushrooms he kept in a jam jar in the kitchen.

He didn't have the strength to stand up and find the jar. He would have to crawl through the sticky tar that coated the floor to get to it. Why was everything so difficult?

As he slid down on all fours, there was another knock on the door. Couldn't a man be left in peace to poison himself?

"Mr. O'Dee, are you there?"

Biafra sprang to his feet like a young goat.

"You see," said Gunnar turning around. "I got my hair cut. How do I look?"

"You shouldn't have done it," panted Biafra. "I'm sorry. My soul was sort of fluctuating when you called. Like Rasputin's."

"That's all right," said Gunnar jovially. "My head feels lighter."

"Who did the job?"

Gunnar smiled slyly.

"A beautiful woman with a long plait. A real gem. I have a special influence on women like. So when she told there was no hairdresser on the island, I asked her if she could do it for me. So we went to the hotel and she did. I liked it when you said I needed a fucking haircut. I'm Swedish like but I have a sense of humor."

Gunnar turned around again to display his normality. "Now," he said. "Can we talk business?"

That's how Ethna saved Biafra O'Dee's life and restored him to his Daimon.

The Daimon of Ethna

˷ "Don't try to make milk on the Milky Way," said Danny, standing in the door with a cup of tea in his hand. He had been watching me watching Ethna. He put a cup of tea on her sidetable. "Why don't you use what's already there?"

She hated him for knowing what was there and she hated what was there. She felt there was something pitiful and obscene about the gaping doorless entrances and eyeless windows of the cold, half-ruined cottages of Clydagh. She tried to imagine the place alive with the sound of honking geese and braying donkeys. She could vaguely remember the last two men who lived in the village and who hadn't spoken to one another for twenty years. When one died the other found the place intolerable, packed his bags, and went to the County Home.

Defiantly she thrust her hands in her pockets and began chewing again the invisible poppy seed. Why on earth did she ever think of resurrecting this godforsaken place? Why was she trying to design homes on an island which she knew would never be a home to her? She saw her drawings lining the mice's stomachs.

For a split second I felt her rage.

"What about Balor the monster?" I said.

"That's my magical boy."

She gave me a knowing look and snapped her finger. Then, almost immediately, she began to draw a tectonic structure, undulating, zoomorphic buildings, half-embedded in the hill of Clydagh, emerging from the ground like some primitive animals with their hooded eyes fixed on the approaching visitor. She was once focused and pedantic, once amused and boisterous, adding adventure to a rigid form. For a moment she was sketching in a mild elation touched with fear, the rain cackling maniacally in pipe and drain.

"Best if we start from scratch and build everything into the hill," she said. "That way you could at least achieve thermal coupling."

"What about the old cottages? I think people are still attached to them," said Danny.

"What do you mean attached? It's words and stories they're attached to! And the dead. I can't do anything with these houses! They're cold, loveless, sunless ratholes. Oh damn, Rob Roberts will have to find another architect!"

Defiantly she flung her plait over her shoulder, got up with a groan, and went to the kitchen. We followed her like anxious dogs. We felt that the fate of Uggala, the fate of all of us, depended on Ethna's next line or circle or curve.

Danny wanted to say something clever, something that would make her sparkle and smoke, but instead he approached her and gave her a hug. It was one of those fatherly hugs, designed to calm her down. They were standing in the middle of the kitchen, and as he glanced down at the back of her neck and slender shoulder blades beneath her thin blouse, he was struck by the contrast between her outer gracefulness and the turbulence within her. If only women could be aesthetic all the way through.

"You said something about the external as a manifestation of the internal. Maybe it's the other way round? Maybe your hatred for Uggala is just a writing large of your hatred for yourself?" he said.

"So now I'm supposed to fall in love with the place as a way of healing myself? You like everything to be aligned, don't you, Danny?"

He shrugged and tightened his embrace. "I'm just asking you to let go of your own contempt for the island. You create it so badly. Is it any wonder it creates you badly back? What can you expect from a place you hate but hatred in return?"

"Am I so bad?"

She didn't care if she was bad or not. She tried to prolong the moment of being a rebellious daughter locked in Danny's life-restoring hug.

"Yes. Even the apples won't ripen when you're around."

"Suppose I try to be nice to Uggala," she said, running her fingers through his hair. "Where would I start?"

"You could look again at your old Uggala sketches."

"I could," she said uncertainly.

She wasn't herself in Danny's arms. This is just the trouble with women, she thought savagely. But when she asked herself what was the trouble, she didn't know.

At this moment I loved them in fear like a needy child, and I loved them haughtily, from heights beyond life, from the future, looking down at all of us from the stars.

The Daimon of Clare

∾ In her fantasies about attaining happiness and fulfillment on a remote Irish island, Clare projected herself into various roles. There was coy and cozy Clare in a long cotton apron, who conjured up gourmet dishes that nobody on the island had ever dreamt of. The logical next step was to open a seafood restaurant and a summer school for chefs. She could see the startled eulogies in the national press.

There was bohemian artistic Clare, wrapped in a green silk kimono writing haikus and making etchings based on objects thrown up on the shore. Her first exhibition in New York would be called "Uggala Dreaming."

There was chick-flick Clare dressed all in black with a camcorder bag over her shoulder. She hopped from island to island along the west coast and was one of the leading visual anthropologists of the day.

Luxuriating in a plenitude of possibilities, Clare was in no hurry to get real. She spent her time lying in bed reading old copies of *Gnosis* and making love to Father Francis. She told herself: I'll do what I like until I get pissed off. And then I'll really do what I like. After all, there were those tribal societies where the men worked the bare minimum of two or three hours a day and spent the rest of the time gossiping with their friends, playing poker, and having sex. Which was closer to the human norm: sterile hours spent commuting in New York or London, or storytelling in the afternoons in New Guinea?

"I'll tell you what I'm going to be," she announced triumphantly one evening while sitting on Father Francis's lap. "I'm going to be a healer!"

"Oh," said Father Francis uncertainly.

"You could be a bit more supportive," said Clare, swinging her long legs.

"Well, how did you hit on the idea?"

"It hit me! You know how I have this special sensitivity to people?"

Right. Father Francis knew all about her special sensitivity to people.

"It was when I was reading the life of Dr. Bach, who is a true saint of our times."

Father Francis hadn't heard of Dr. Bach. Clare was delighted to instruct him on the main points.

Harley Street specialist. Gives up and goes to the country. Heal the person and not the disease. Induces various conditions in himself and then goes out to find the appropriate plant remedy. Very subtle. Not so much the plant as the dewdrop resting on the plant. Develops a system of thirty-eight healers for thirty-eight negative states of mind. Dies young and in poverty.

"Maybe not so much a saint as a shaman?" offered Father Francis.

"You're right!" said Clare. "I hadn't thought about him quite like that. So what do you think?"

"How are you going to go about it?"

"Just do it. Send for the books and the thirty-eight healers. Some of them, like crab apple, holly, and honeysuckle, already grow on Uggala. I could prepare the Mother Tinctures myself using the sun method."

"But there's no sun on Uggala, Clare."

"Don't be so pedantic."

"But how do you know you're a healer?"

"The call came straight off the page." Clare wavered. "A sort of inner knowing."

Father Francis didn't really appreciate such talk.

"Besides, we can all be what we choose to be, can't we?"

Had Clare declared her vocation some ten years earlier, Father Francis would have dismissed it with a guffaw. He knew the syndrome all too well: the creative anguish of well-heeled middle-class women like his mother with lots of time on their hands and no idea what to do with themselves. Then one day they're all taking courses in homeopathy or reflexology or aromatherapy to minister to similarly well-heeled, confused middle-class women who one day start taking courses in reiki or the Alexander technique or macrobiotics to minister to similarly well-heeled women who . . .

It was only as he came to reflect on it that it dawned on him that the contempt their enthusiasms roused in him was the contempt of the priest for the shaman. The women who became healers were deeply wounded themselves, and their woundedness pierced through to the very core of their identity. It was soul injuries they suffered from, and it was soul remedies they sought. The Foxrock shamans ran the risk of quackery and battiness just as his profession was susceptible to aridity and the tantrums of ritual queens. It was the difference between the poetry of Seamus Heaney and that of Paul Durcan. One crackled like well-starched altar linen and exuded the scent of incense. The other was a broken filament after a surge of ECT from the gods.

"I'm starting on Monday," said Clare.

She had it all planned out. First she surveyed Uggala to find the nooks and crannies where healing plants might thrive. She wrote to horticulturists and gardeners everywhere in Ireland and England, soliciting advice and bedding plants: mimulus, centaury, red chestnut, cerato, scleranthus, hornbeam, olive, mustard, agrimony. All over Uggala tiny plots appeared marked out by stone circles like children's gardens, where Clare ritually planted her medicinal shrubs and flowers. Sean and Seamus stumbled on three of them, secretly nested in an out-of-the way corner of the Well Field. What was the cunt up to now? they wondered and wrecked them on the spot. They could hardly know that with the wreckage went the cure for dread, lovelessness, and feelings of isolation.

Clare was undeterred. She had well-established plantations of wild oats, impatiens, and chicory, and a greenhouse where she grew olive and vine. Her plant symphony was complete. She fantasized about a tall man in a prickly tweed jacket and open-necked shirt, a bit like Wittgenstein, who wandered over the island at dawn. It was Dr. Bach, M.D. He alone knew that she had reenchanted Uggala.

"So what's the next move?" asked Father Francis as Clare curled up on his lap for her statutory evening hug.

He wouldn't have risked the question unless he knew.

Clare shook her head dolefully. "I've got to discover a remedy of my own."

"Against what?"

"Irish clergymen."

Next morning she woke him at five o'clock with a tongue in his ear. She was like a child on holidays. "Come with me to see if the rockrose is in bloom on the cliffs!"

"Have mercy on me, Clare!"

"No. I'm happy and I want you to be happy with me. Come on."

She skipped ahead of him over the crags through the June dawnlight. Father Francis asked himself: What does a jubilant young woman leading a tired man at first light signify? He paid no attention to the angry choughs drifting above them like bits of burned paper.

"There it is!" she called to him exultantly. "The cure for terror and helplessness."

As she danced to the edge of the headland, he felt his throat contract. It was like a dream where he wanted to shout but couldn't. The collapse of the hollowed-out bluff beneath Clare hardly made a sound. And she was too startled to do more than raise her arms, as if in a gesture of surrender.

When he crept on his belly to the edge, the blood from her crushed skull glistened like a red silk scarf on the dry scree below.

The Daimon of Father Francis

❧ Sorrows always come in threes, an island sean fochal says. Father Francis had hardly buried Clare when a notice of eviction arrived and with it a frigid letter from the Archbishop. A new priest had finally been appointed to minister to the people of Uggala, in spite of the shortage of clergy in the dioceses. Father Francis read the letter with as much interest as if it were the weather forecast for Ulan Bator.

He was trying to find a language to talk to himself about the loss of Clare. If he failed to find the right words, she would drift away from him beyond any hope of recall. There would be a gap in himself which he would never be able to cross over. Thomas Hardy had passed down the same haunted lane. Faltering forward, Leaves around me falling, Wind oozing thin through the thorn from norward, And the woman calling.

But that wasn't right. Those were words for a more somber woebegone woman. Clare was a happy trickster. He could hear her saying: Come on, Francis. Can't you find something beginning with "There was a young lady from Austin" and rhyming with "exhaustin"?

How stoically she had borne the harassments of the past year! Ever since he had spoken out against the Heritage Centre their life together had lost its pastoral innocence: its amiable transitions from breakfast to long walks on the cliffs to planning what to have for dinner. There were ominous hints, obstructions, threats even. Sometimes it was a seemingly casual remark of the Skipper's: I hear there are big changes in store for the parish. Or it was the Social Welfare inquiring into Father Francis's entitlement to the dole. Or an unexpected difficulty with Clare's residence permit. The Parochial House was broken into twice. Clare's underwear was taken from the clothesline and spread along the church wall. And yet nothing could suppress her childlike excitement about her self-appointed task to cure the island. All the odd vexations, she said, were merely signs of a healing crisis.

Danny read the notice of eviction with an eye for the letter behind the letter.

"You don't need to be paranoid to think somebody's after you," he said.

"Who's the somebody?" asked Father Francis.

"I'll give you three guesses. Rob Roberts. Rob Roberts. Or Rob Roberts. He's not a Knight of Columbanus for nothing. The Knights are the Ku Klux Klan of the West. I'd say he's pulling every string he can lay hold of to get rid of you."

Danny took a fat package out of his coat pocket. "This is the Brown Paper Bag." He grinned. "The quintessential cultural symbol of our time. I want you to have it."

Father Francis didn't need to open the package to know what it contained.

"I can't. You're mad."

"I got you into all this. Besides, it's only ten percent of what I got for the German translation of 'Ruminations.' Tithes for the support of my pastor you might say."

"No!"

"Well then, I'll put it on the plate next Sunday. Knowing you, you'll declare it to the tax man and I'll be in the shit along with you."

Danny flipped the package in the air. "It's a lot easier with politicians. You just leave it on the hall stand and say nothing. But I'm too vain for that I'm afraid."

Ostentatiously he put the package on the table. "If you need anything else let me know."

Father Francis didn't have a safe. So he put the package in the icebox of the fridge.

The following Sunday at the end of his sermon he announced that he was leaving the island. Uggala needed a break from him, and maybe he needed a break too. People seemed to expect his departure. They looked at him with passive compassion. Already they thought of him in the past tense, along with Father Herbert and Father Skerrett.

In the evening he sat at his desk, still trying to find words to name his grief. He tested the bare lines:

Death is deaf and hears no wailing,
Or it would weep with bloodied heart —
The grim reaper's heartless; if he
Had a heart, he'd weep stony tears

For a keen moment Rumi's sorrow melted with his own. But then — where was the Resurrection and the life to come?

A knock on the door roused him from his brooding. It was Mary, Rita, and Madeleine, the three sisters. They stood on the doorstep, jostling one another uneasily.

"Come in, come in. Would you like a cup of tea?"

Rita thrust a frayed brown envelope into his hand. "We just wanted to show our appreciation," she said.

They didn't need to seek for the right words. The right words were the well-worn but kindly clichés to hand. "We'll be thinking and praying for you, Father."

They turned on their heels and left before he had the time even to say thank you.

Half an hour later Tom arrived, blustering about no hard feelings and his own half atheism. It was only when he left after a series of inconclusive farewells that Father Francis found a brown envelope skillfully stuck in the corner of the mirror. How had Tom managed it? And when?

They came in drips and drabs all week, muttering their farewells and compliments and stuffing brown envelopes into his pockets or leaving them discreetly on the hall table.

Towards the end of the week, when he returned from a sick call, he found Mrs. O'Halloran at the kitchen table going through piles of banknotes and torn envelopes. Danny's massive contribution was the centerpiece. She looked up at him with stern eyes. "It's a big mistake to be keeping over fifteen thousand pounds in the fridge. Especially after two break-ins."

Father Francis had to sit down with the shock.

"It's simply not nice," she went on. "You should show more respect for the people's hard-earned money."

It was news to Father Francis that anybody in Uggala had worked hard for their money. But he let it pass.

The Daimon of Ethna

☙ "Two years more and that's it," said Ethna, staring out at the rain plastering the grass to the ground. "Two years more and we're out of here."

"And where would you be after going?" asked Danny in his best mock Anglo-Irish. The kitchen was piled with planks from which he was knocking together a new bookcase. Such improvements always brought on a bout of insecurity in Ethna.

"I need a city. And the sun. And trees."

"Didn't I invite you to come with me to San Diego?"

"As what? A groupie? No thanks! Do you think you'll finish that book of yours within two years?"

"Ethna, you know that I can't work under pressure."

"Weren't you an awful eejit to invite the pressure under your own roof then?"

A malignant doubt had begun to spread in her mind. In interviews Danny had taken to talking about the island as "my omphalos" and saying things the like of "On my rain-beaten island the morning is wiser than the evening."

Ethna squirmed. She had begun to read *Ruminations from the End of the World* but gave up after ten pages, aghast at the half-baked spiritual soufflé Danny had concocted from Sufi wisdom, Gaelic folklore, and Franklin Merrell-Wolff's *Philosophy of Consciousness Without an Object*. She looked in despair at the growing pile of letters from women around the world who had been "ravished" or "deeply moved" or in "larmes délicieuses" or "opened up" by the sheer energy of his island wisdom. The bastard has put back the women's movement by a generation, she thought.

What had become of Danny? True, he could joke about his newfound celebrity ("Fuck me pink, the Sage of Uggala strikes again!"). At the same time, he took himself very seriously.

"Isn't it mostly middle-aged women who lap up your stuff?" Ethna asked accusingly.

"The people who buy my books are people in crisis," replied Danny in his most dignified voice. "And most middle-aged women are in crisis. What's wrong with looking for some support? The middle-aged are human too you know."

Ethna felt a sense of helplessness. He was right of course. But still there was something fishy going on, and she couldn't put her finger on it.

All she ever dreamed of was to stroll with Danny through a learned city with its music, books, and cafés. She had wanted a proper office on a wide street with, say, poplar trees. Instead what had she got? A pokey hole in Galway and a bizarre eco-village on Uggala.

"I have a feeling you'll be off someday soon. Off to Barcelona or Palo Alto or Seattle."

He was indulging in one of his deadly, vegetable-calm moods.

"You'll surely fall for some bigwig architect or scientist." He hammered a nail hard on the head. "Or businessman."

He wanted to hurt her. The ghost of Rob Roberts was traipsing through the kitchen.

"Make sure he's rich enough to have a big estate and a proper wooden shack in the park," Danny went on relentlessly. "You can take me on as your gardener and I'll spend the few years left to me brewing tea and talking Italian to the thrushes."

It was a piece of pure projection, decided Ethna. It was Danny who was thinking of leaving her.

That was the time when a black frost was on my whole being and my heart in its bone belfry hang and was dumb. Oh how I wished they could free their selves from their selfness and see what I saw: two souls and two faces with just one soul, her and him.

The Daimon of Uggala

 Rob Roberts altered the destiny of Uggala guided by the potent, erroneous maxim time heals everything. You could get away with almost any scheme or stunt if you wised up to the fact that two or three years down the road naysayers would accept whatever had previously been unacceptable and put up with what had been unsupportable.

Despite the commotion and squabbles, he pushed ahead relentlessly with the Heritage Centre and the Eco-village. His flex-form was ubiquitous, serene, infinitely stretchable. The world would rather see hope than just hear its song, he repeated. That's why he had to smile reassuringly, to be full of cheer, with a friendly gleaming set of teeth. He knew that he needed only to imagine and encourage and fantasize and fiddle-faddle Uggala long enough and hard enough to see the day when the cowslip meadow below Danny's Thinking Place was tarmaced over and a landing strip inserted right beside the Danes' Fort — just as he had planned.

If before the islanders felt that Uggala wasn't so bad by comparison with the Congo, now they repeated Rob Roberts's mantra that it was sentenced to death if it stayed out on its own. The only way forward was to join the Atlantic Fringe Alliance. No man is an island, Rob Roberts said, and no island is an island either. Archipelagoes are the way forward for the next century.

The dead, who had being lying too near the surface of Uggala, gradually sank deeper into their long graves so that you hardly noticed they were there anymore. All-seeing Almighty God grew more shortsighted and lenient. Danny Ruane was so preoccupied with signing copies of his international best-seller here there and everywhere that the loss of his Thinking Place slipped down the hierarchy of his grievances. And the absence of permission for all the new projects was rectified by a metaphysical clause in the planning laws for the retention of existing structures.

Danny's Thinking Place, Sean and Seamus's Well Field, the Danes' Fort (Danes!), and the Straight Mile were mere atavisms. *Atavist* became the new term of abuse on Uggala, much worse than *Blueshirt* or *tinker*. *Striking* was the word used about the Heritage Centre, with its treated pine facade and frosted glass dome. It was nearing completion, and most of the exhibits were in place. Tom as curator gave intense, traumatic interviews about the importance of a cultural link with the long valued past in our turbulent times. His expositions were modeled on those of Michael D. Higgins, down to the last "Let's be very clear about this." Ethna's eco-village was praised for its "uncompromising megalithic in-your-face bluntness." But Biafra O'Dee — leather-jacketed, perched on a barstool, savoring the Timesurge — pronounced that it was so perfectly livable that it was found unlivable by the islanders.

Thresheen was sardonic about the new Uggala. "There's a fundamental flaw in all this craich about the healing powers of time," she said. "Time heals sweet damn all. Thoughts are independent of time, and if they keep returning to a wound the wound stays open. Fortunately for your man Roberts, the thoughts of the islanders are all diverted into new tasks and new enmities. But the mind of Uggala is like Clydagh Harbour congested with rocks. They're no threat at all when the tide is high. You can float above them and even be excited as you look down on the monsters. But watch out when the tide falls!"

The Daimon of Father Francis

∾ Her name was Virginia, she said. Virginia Malick from Ontario, Canada. She hoped she wasn't intruding on Father Francis's time. But there was something urgent she needed to discuss with him.

Her hands sliced the air as she spoke and seemed to have an anguished life all of their own. Father Francis had to make a conscious effort to keep his eyes from following their swift karate chops. Her loose checkered dress with its white lace collar had a touch of Laura Ashley primness and chastity.

Not an anthropologist or archaeologist, he decided.

"Sorry about the mess." He pointed awkwardly to a scatter of cardboard boxes and half-filled suitcases on the floor and table.

What on earth was he going to do with Clare's books on homeopathy? Should he bring them with him?

"The thing is I wanted to ask your permission to look through the parish records if I may."

A genealogist. Maybe a Mormon.

She caught his surmise and squashed it immediately. "I'm working on the Catholic Church's attitudes to fascism."

She spoke pedantically, but again her mobile hands belied her careful phrasing.

"On Uggala?"

She nodded.

Sell Clare's books off to Charlie Burns was the best bet. That way they would eventually get into the right hands.

"I'm interested in a particular priest. His name was Father Hackett. He served in this parish from 1945 to 1951."

Hackett? Didn't Hackett go gaga in the end?

"So what have you got on Father Hackett?"

Father Francis was leaving the island. He kept the conversation going out of politeness.

"Well, according to my findings there was a network of

priests who helped . . . how should I put this, certain Croatian refugees to escape mainland Europe after the war."

"You mean Croatian war criminals?"

"Ustasha." She nodded. "Father Hackett's name has cropped up several times."

"But he's long dead. Matter of fact he's buried beside the church below."

"Yes I know." She chopped the air. "But perhaps he left some documents or letters that would help me fill out the picture a bit better."

"I very much doubt it."

He was puzzled. Why this Virginia creature and why Father Hackett just at this point in his life? Why were their fates crossing his when he was about to disentangle himself from everything that had to do with Uggala?

"May I look?"

"As far as I've heard, your Father Hackett ended his days trying to brew beer from seaweed."

Should he check if she had approached the Archbishop for permission? No. That would be ridiculous coming from him.

"Could you tell me a bit more about your research?"

"We know Ustasha people passed through a seminary in Galway. Not to mention the fact that some of them may still be around the place."

War criminals here? She was a bit cuckoo.

"Isn't it a bit too late for all that?"

"Well perhaps but . . . it's about justice. I'm looking for somebody specific. You see, I was born in Ontario but my parents were Serbs. Both my grandfathers were murdered in the camp of Jasenovac in 1944. A neighbor who survived testified that a camp guard named Zdenek Bogdanovitch cut off their testicles and then cut their throats. Bogdanovitch held the record for the most testicles and throats cut over a period of three months in Jasenovac."

"I see," said Father Francis with his mouth dry as if he had tasted galvanized zinc plate. The recent press photograph of a Bosnian girl hanging in a field cut across Virginia's grainy World War II picture of victim Serbs.

Virginia Malick was conventional through and through — conventionally pretty, conventionally dressed, conventionally spoken. But there was something steely behind her Victorian facade. Perhaps she was as relentless as the hangman she was pursuing?

Father Francis wondered why he resisted. Was it just inertia? Was he being clerical? Or was it because, even as they spoke, her people were disemboweling Muslims and Croats?

Reluctantly he climbed to the attic and retrieved an old U.S. mailbag stuffed with letters and yellow newspaper cuttings. It was all that was left of three successive priests on the island. Sometime in the seventies Mrs. O'Halloran had bundled the bits and pieces of their lives into the bag and forgot all about it.

He handed it to Virginia and told her she could use the kitchen as her workroom. He was pretty sure she would find nothing.

That same evening while Virginia worked her way carefully through the mailbag, sorting the material into little bundles tied with rubber bands, Father Francis searched high up and low down through the tattered volumes in the small Presbytery library. He knew he had seen something somewhere when he had first moved into the house. At the time he had been more interested in the overprinted stamp on the envelope than in the letter within. Long after midnight, when Virginia had left for her B & B, he opened the torn C volume of the old *Encyclopaedia Britannica*. There it was, beside the entry for Croatia. It was a brief letter from a priest in Manchester recommending a certain Zdenek Bogdanovitch to Father Hackett's care.

Zdenek is a pious and God-fearing young man. He has worked shoulder to shoulder with our Irish labourers on the motorways and they regard him as one of their own. Force of circumstance, of which more later, makes it imperative that he find temporary refuge in a place where he is unlikely to be traced. I trust you will understand and make what provisions you can for this unfortunate soul. We will discuss the matter further when we meet in Cheltenham.

Father Francis read it again, dumbfounded. There was only one man living on Uggala who had worked in Manchester and who wasn't born on the island.

The Daimon of Holy Paddy

❦ Holy Paddy was walking backwards, he didn't know where. Maybe to the shore or to the house or to the church. It happened to him now and again. He wasn't thinking. Even when he prayed he didn't think anymore. He prayed with his heart and not with his head, and the invocations to the Sacred Heart followed the beat of his pulse.

He traipsed past the Skipper and Mrs. O'Halloran, who stuffed a round of black pudding in the pocket of his jacket with an urgent "Don't forget to say a prayer for me now when you're at it." He frightened Mrs. Byres and her two daughters, who hadn't got used to his ways yet.

"Zdenek!"

He thought the angels were summoning him, and he quickened his pace. A young woman stood in the middle of the road athwart his path. She had a flaming sword in her hand.

"Zdenek Bogdanovitch!" she repeated. "Do you remember Jasenovac?"

She addressed him in a language which he understood but

which wasn't his anymore. It wasn't his and it wasn't him. But it filled him with dread. Her eyes were bleeding. It was a long time since he had seen eyes bleed and breasts hang by a thread of skin. He bolted for the church door and blundered his way up to the altar rail.

He was safe in the house of God.

The Daimon of Father Francis

☙ Father Francis knew he should give some serious thought to Holy Paddy. He should but he couldn't. He wanted to be left alone with Clare and God. He had joined the multitudinous community of victims whose grief was not only ignored but had to compete with the grief of others. The past, history, the Virginia woman, a dead priest, other people's bestialities: what right did they have to encroach on the small plot of his love and sorrow? A voice deep inside him said: Every right and you damn well know it. Wasn't that the whole point of priestly celibacy? To have no commitment other than to the People of God?

And instead here he was sitting over Clare's open diary, tracing her big looping script with his finger as if the very shape of the letters contained the memory of what she had felt and thought or even what she had worn.

Often in the past he had peeked into her diary to discover those secret wishes and lusts she had not dared to voice to him directly. Clare knew, without a word ever being spoken, that he consulted her private jottings. So she used the diary to provoke or rouse or outrage him, leaving it on her dressing table when she left for the mainland for a few days and returning to be gratified by a new and daring tenderness. It was her discreet method of educating him without harassment and in a way that both of them could disown if anything went wrong. She was an emotional genius.

There was a recurring pattern of argument in her diary that he immediately recognized as being borrowed from *Robinson Crusoe*. When a choice confronted her, she would set up two columns on the page, one of pluses and one of minuses, and then do the tot to arrive at a decision. In the early pages of her first Uggala diary, she had debated with herself whether or not to tell Francis about dancing naked in titty bars.

−	+
disgust him	excite him
everybody has secrets	the Truth
mistake to tell too much to a man	understand me better
all over and done with	bye to guilt
think I'm used goods	better communication
not trust me anymore	
Minus wins.	

In this way she managed both to tell him and not to tell him about her nude dancing days.

Father Francis wondered if he could resolve his dilemma over Holy Paddy in the same way. Should he break his silence? On the plus side there was the question of justice and truth. There were the facts of history to be considered and facing up to the past. On the minus there was the duty of compassion, Holy Paddy's repentance, and a whole life spent amending for whatever he had done. There was the question whether or not he was the same person as the young man of fifty years ago. There was the futility of opening old wounds.

The minuses win, decided Father Francis without much conviction.

As in the old Icelandic sagas, there were two choices before him, both of them equally repellent. Father Francis ventured what the Vikings or Robinson Crusoe or Clare would never have considered. He knelt down and prayed earnestly for a third way out, i.e., for Divine Intervention.

The Daimon of Holy Paddy

🕊 Holy Paddy sat staring at the clock, watching the spasms of the minute hand as it shifted from now to now. Many's the evening he sat like that dozing off, only to be jerked awake as the clock struck the hour.

But not today.

Savage thoughts swooped on him like a pack of ravenous dogs. He tried to hide from them by skulking behind a shield of prayer. Hail Mary, full of grace, the Lord is with thee. Blessed art thou among . . .

The tubercular sun that shone through the grimy west window bred fitful shadows on the kitchen wall. They were the same shadows as those in the cellar in which . . . Holy Mary, Mother of God, Pray for us sinners . . . There was a high small window, which was always locked, and a naked lightbulb swinging from the ceiling. The bulb was the last thing their terrified eyes fastened on. Pray for us sinners, now and at the hour . . . now and at the hour . . .

Holy Paddy's eyes fell on the dead fireplace, the stained, mismatched table and chairs, the soot-smeared walls. It was his own soul made visible. It choked him.

He stumbled out of his chair onto the sticky floor. He didn't know what he was doing. Like then. He slouched over to the table and grabbed the bread knife. He would slit the throats of the ravenous shadows.

An hour later Father Francis pushed open the door and found him slumped in a pool of blood. His pulse was still beating and his breath rasped in his throat.

Father Francis bent over him and whispered an act of contrition in his ear. Then he sat by him in the chair, waiting and praying. It was two hours before Holy Paddy's heart stopped beating.

The Daimon of Ethna

🐦 The evening Holy Paddy's heart stopped beating Danny decided to propose to Ethna. She was standing on chairs in all the rooms in order to see where her new Samuel Palmer reproduction would fit best. He waited for her to hang it next to the dresser and then to take it down and hang it in the hallway. And then to look at it critically from a number of angles (does the light fall on it properly I wonder?), take it down once more, and install it on the mantelpiece. It wouldn't rest there either.

I could see that Ethna was a vexed tenant of this world. Her kind moved into a room and disturbed everything. She shifted the bed and turned the sofa, lifted the carpets, repainted the walls and, given half a chance, opened a skylight in the roof. The exterior shape, color, and light all had to reflect her inner shape, color, and light. Any dissonance caused her pain.

The Danny kind moved into a new room and looked around to see how best he could fit in with the minimum of disturbance to things as they were. He accepted the previous lodger's arrangement of the furniture and hardly registered the clash between the color of the carpets and the curtains.

"Tell us, Ethna," said Danny. "Are you ever happy?"

"What kind of question is that?"

"Seriously. Finn and I would like to know."

Ethna stood on a chair with the Palmer held to her chest. In her forget-me-not blue dress and long plait, which she stubbornly refused to cut, she looked vulnerable and con-

fused, like a schoolgirl at an examination. It struck me how
unfinished, almost prenatal her face was, especially around
the eyes and mouth. One minute she looked interesting-ugly,
the next interesting-beautiful. Maybe it was because she was
born two months premature? I wondered if her face would
ever be finished.

"Well, I'm happy with the two of you," she said uncertainly.

"I don't believe it," said Danny. "I'll tell you what you want."

"Not again please."

"You want beauty. And neither I nor Finn nor this house
nor the island is sufficiently aesthetic for you."

"So?"

"So," answered Danny. "Will you marry me?"

Ethna was caught on the hop, as he intended.

"After all these years together? What's the point?"

"That's a really romantic response! You never fail to subvert
the occasion, I'll say that much for you."

"Why now?"

"Maybe we're old enough to get married? Maybe we'll become less paranoid about you leaving me or me leaving you?
And maybe Finn could do with a legal father. What do you
say, Finn?"

"I'm easy," I said. I was.

"And afterwards we could go to some of your favorite cities
for a break. Salamanca or Siena."

"And then?"

"And then we'll follow our separate paths. Whoever said
that husbands and wives have to live in one another's hair?"

Ethna chewed on her poppy seed.

Like most things in most women's lives, Danny's proposal
had come too late. Once the consorting together of desire
and consummation is endlessly postponed, one loses the de-
lightful illusion that from now on things will change for the
better. Ethna knew now that every dream has its time. Seven
years ago she had looked surreptitiously at wedding dresses

in shop windows, her flesh in goose pimples as she tried them on in her mind. Now the mere thought of walking down an aisle in an outlandish outfit made her grimace. She had moved past that precious time when fulfillment follows hot on the heels of expectation. She knew that marriage would change nothing, and so her heart didn't beat any faster.

"OK," she in a flat voice. "Let's get married."

She hung the Samuel Palmer back beside the dresser. She loved the packed scene it portrayed, a harvest moon over a fruitful valley filled with pious folk on their way to Vespers. The church in the foreground had the nubbly contours and warm fawn tones of a forest mushroom. Crammed into the one frame was a mingled vision of two worlds, one which Ethna knew and one which she longed for but could never attain.

The Daimon of Danny Ruane

❧ Every weekend when I came home from school my job was to go through Danny's mail from the previous week. I stapled the envelopes and letters together, then sorted them under different headings: fan mail, begging letters, invitations, requests for interviews, letters of abuse. The most tiresome part of the work was replying to devotees who wanted to come and visit Uggala. They wrote that *Ruminations* had so changed their lives that they simply had to commune with an island which inspired so much insight and compassion. Not since the Master of Stravopolus or the Sage of Tvergastein had a remote and unknown place incited such pilgrim longing.

Danny instructed me to discourage the devotees as much as possible. So under his direction I wrote things like: "Dear Friend, I was greatly moved by your generous letter. Please accept my best thanks. However, before you think of visiting Uggala, I should perhaps warn you that the climate here is very inhospitable. Near continuous rain and violent winds make walking on the crumbling cliffs a hazardous enterprise (we had a dreadful fatality recently I'm afraid). Hotel and B & B accommodation are rather rudimentary. Connection to the mainland is haphazard at best and comes courtesy of Mannan mac Lir. I myself will be lecturing in the States/Australia/Canada/South Africa for the foreseeable future and will not be available for consultation. Beir bua — Danny Ruane."

This kind of letter, as I soon discovered, was a big mistake. Many of the recipients interpreted it as a challenge to their faith and a test of their commitment to the transformational journey. They came to Uggala precisely because of the rain and winds. Just as gales and isolation had prompted Danny's epiphanies, surely they would lead other earnest seekers to similar realizations.

And so I found that even the most obscure backwater can become shot through with significance, depending on the kind of story you tell and sell about it. For the pilgrims to Uggala, the rocky lanes were a magic labyrinth and the whiff of silage from Sean and Seamus's haggard distilled the very essence of old-time authenticity. Danny's *Ruminations* had ensouled them all.

But that wasn't the end of it. Many discovered that visiting Uggala was like visiting a library in search of a particular book and finding other, more fascinating titles on neighboring shelves. Ethna's eco-village, for example, or the half-constructed Heritage Center or Biafra O'Dee's sessions in Balor's Bar where he sang about his failures to get a ride. When his "No Hole No Holiness" became an underground classic, he badgered Danny to write a sequel to *Ruminations* in order to bring even more tourists to the spiritual orgasm that was Uggala. Danny said no; he had to get back to the unified view of reality.

But he didn't. He was constantly going somewhere or coming back from somewhere, and the adulation showered on him clung like a bad smell. He tried not to show it, but for the first few days after his homecomings he choreographed even his most casual activities as if they were destined for an international audience. "I have to go to the bathroom before I meditate," he would announce grandly to nobody in particular, meaning: Look, the acclaimed author and lecturer has to pee occasionally!

Ethna and I were nostalgic for the early stage of his fame, when he was so amazed at the success of *Ruminations* that he treated the whole thing as a joke.

I was the archivist of his dream. I saw that others could live it but he couldn't.

"Do you recall what Francis Bacon said about two kinds of search?" he asked me one sinking evening.

I waited for him to tell me.

"One is arduous and difficult in the beginning but leads out at last into an open country. The other, at first easy and free and pleasing, draws us to pathless and precipitous places."

He paused, whether for me or an invisible audience I couldn't tell.

"I've taken the second path, Finn. I've come to a precipice. I have to turn back."

My Daimon

As I grew older, Thresheen appeared less often to me. She dimmed to a wraith and then became no more than a voice in my head. But she had lost none of her tartness and continued to berate me with her "Silly boy!" and "When will you ever learn?" I missed her theatrical entrances and exits and her constant change of costume. One of the last times I saw her she was dressed for the Eurovision Song Contest in a shimmering gown of sequins. She had grown her hair long and blond and said she was representing Monaco.

I went to school in Galway and came home most week-ends. Unlike my mother, who had a phobia for the island and grimaced every time she saw it raise its tired corpse above the ocean, I loved Uggala and the amorphousness of Saturday af-ternoons there. At school I was forced into awkward shapes. At home I was the creator rather than the created. I rewrote the island geography and renamed places to my own satisfac-tion. I fused the bogs and bohereens of Uggala with Wuther-ing Heights, Thrushcross Grange, and Gimmerton ("You see," said Thresheen, "for all the crap about Irishness, your culture is basically English!").

At school I was nicknamed the Goolan and accused of shagging dolphins and being in cahoots with the devil. Once when the second-years were playing with a Ouija board at midnight, it spelled out a farewell "Say good-bye to my twin."

I kept my head down and said nothing.

The Daimon of Biafra O'Dee

❧ It was the first time in years that Danny and Ethna decided not to celebrate Biafra's birthday, which fell on February 1. They had established a tradition in the house of preparing a birthday dinner of sausages, eggs, bacon, white pudding, and fried bread followed by Ovaltine and ginger bis-cuits in deference to his refusal to eat anything more whole-some. But this time Ethna said she was tired of Biafra's moaning and groaning. Besides, now that he had lots of money he hadn't shown the slightest bit of generosity to anybody.

Danny protested mildly that Biafra was a martyr to his own ego. But Ethna was vehement. "Can't you see that he resents you more than ever and can't bring himself to speak a good word for you? He's even hinted to some of your admirers that you stole your best lines and ideas from him."

Danny was amused by Ethna's annoyance. He had never

expected anything but betrayal from Biafra O'Dee and wondered what the fuss was all about. While Ethna fumed he beckoned me into the back kitchen and gave me a honeycomb and a birthday card.

"Take this over to Biafra," he said, "and give him our best wishes."

"Do I really have to?"

"Please. He's a miserable poor hure at the best of times."

When I arrived at Biafra's house he was sitting in his old armchair watching television and munching vinegary chips from a paper bag.

"Happy birthday, Biafra." I presented him with the honey and the card.

His face fell. "What's that for? I don't eat that stuff."

"OK," I said and put the honeycomb back in the bag.

"You might as well leave it now that you brought it this far. Why is it that nobody will give me what I want? They all think that just because I made a few bucks in Sweden they can throw any old slops at me."

"But now that you are rich you can do whatever you want," I ventured.

Biafra panted. "Do what I want? Can't you see that I've become more vulnerable? That I have to put up with all kinds of shit I never had to put up with before?"

"Are you going to be on television?" I asked.

"No television!" he roared. "Don't you understand I have to keep my head down? Haven't you read any Greek plays? Anybody that sticks his neck out gets his head chopped off."

"Danny didn't."

Biafra was enraged. "Don't try to compare me with some smart-arsed New Age git. I'm going through a Saturn return."

"Well, I'll be off," I said.

"You're so fucking lucky, aren't you?" said Biafra. "You've got a nice house, respectable parents you wouldn't be ashamed to bring to the horse show, you're good-looking and have lots of great shagging ahead of you. And me? I was born with an oedipal limp. I might not any longer be the penniless derelict that the likes of Danny Ruane uses for comic relief. But I have to pay for everything."

By now Biafra was oblivious of who I was.

"I want to eat pussy and watch television at the same time. I want to ride in the cleft of a female buttock towards the absolute. But it has to be a beautiful, intelligent, soft female and not any old dog."

"I promised Ethna I'd be home in half an hour."

He looked at me appraisingly. "You're kind and good, aren't you? Too kind and too good! When people see the likes of me and you they see weakness. And they take advantage of us! The good people in *King Lear* all get the chop. Same in Dostoevsky."

"But not in Robert Louis Stevenson," I protested.

Biafra ignored me. "Get evil, Finn. Get evil before we all fucking die."

His mobile rang, and he grabbed it like a drowning man. "Who the fuck is this? . . . How did you know it was my birthday? . . . Don't talk to me about the astral level of anything! I want the ass-thrill level."

He turned his back on me and within five seconds had forgotten all about me. He jabbed his forefinger into the honeycomb and sucked it while he talked about his desire to be somebody else entirely.

The Daimon of Concepta

➥ Concepta fed Colm semolina with a teaspoon. She had sprinkled it with cinnamon and castor sugar just the way he liked it. She was very happy.

She had to make sure Colm didn't choke. His right side

was paralyzed, but his eyes were alive and full of devotion. They followed her every movement around the hospital room.

When she finished feeding him and had cleared up round his chin, she sat down beside him with the *Irish Independent* and read aloud the GAA news and the English racing results very slowly and distinctly. This was a new experience for her. Left to herself she would never have bought the *Independent* and certainly never have touched the sports pages. The names of the horses amazed her; she wondered how they had got them. Was First Light a foal born at dawn? Was Loman's Sally called after the owner's wife or daughter? And what did Avanti mean?

After Colm's stroke she set herself up in a B & B in Galway near the hospital. In the afternoons on her way home from visiting him, she passed a bookie shop and began to place small bets on English point-to-point races. Soon she had a grasp of the language and would explain to Colm that the going was rough or the ground too hard or that an each-way bet was a waste of time. She had no interest whatsoever in the jockeys, who seemed to her ignoble appendages to the horses. She looked forward to the day when the fillies would do it all for themselves and not require gaudy whip-wielding dwarfs astride them.

She made sure to be in Colm's room when the nurses woke him. She brushed his hair, fed him his porridge, and helped him as far as the bathroom. The ward sister was astounded at her cheerfulness and patience. "Sure there's nothing to beat a good marriage when all is said and done," she repeated. "The island people know how to look after their own."

Colm couldn't protest, even if he wanted to.

Concepta was at peace with the world. So much at peace that she hardly blinked when Ethna, Danny, and I burst into Colm's room one afternoon. We had just got back from a holiday in Tunisia.

"Why didn't you let me know?" Ethna confronted her accusingly though Danny had coached her to keep the cool. "We would have caught the first plane home."

"I didn't want to bother you," said Concepta calmly.

"But he's my father!"

Concepta might well have retorted: "So now you're discovering that much" or "It's a bit late in the day for daughterly feelings." Instead she said: "Don't worry, pet. He'll be all right."

Ethna gasped, astounded by her mother's mildness.

Concepta continued as if she were picking up a conversation from yesterday rather than fifteen years ago. "He had a baked apple for lunch. You know how much he likes the sugar caramelized on the skin."

"The doctor says he's paralyzed!"

"Only a bit. Isn't that right, Colm? Soon you'll be fit for Cheltenham. Five to four the field!"

Had Concepta gone gaga? Had the strain of fifteen years of silent warfare finally caught up with her?

She rambled on about how good the nurses were and how well Colm was coping with his little accident.

"Accident!" exclaimed Ethna. "He's had a stroke for God's sake."

"He's improving already, aren't you, Daddy? You can't keep a good man down," said Concepta.

So Colm was Daddy again.

"How was your holiday, Finn?" Concepta asked me. "Did you take to the Arabs?"

I too could scarcely believe the way things were going. I had always imagined that if Ethna and Concepta were ever to make up it would be a passionate encounter with heavenly music and lots of suspense as they held back from a tearful embrace until the very last moment. Mother! Ethna! Mother!

What happened in the hospital convinced me that just as there is a banality of evil there is a banality of crisis. If it is true that we are the authors of our own lives, then we have a talent for anticlimax. As Thresheen said, little things that we hardly notice, a stone in a shoe, a rusty nail, maim us for life and create havoc. Big things pass like steam off a boiling kettle.

The Daimon of Alice

 Alice's favorite poem was Joseph Mary Plunkett's "I see His face in every flower and in the sky the glory of His eyes." She had taught it to generations of Uggala schoolchildren, who with one or two exceptions, all thought it the greatest load of tripe they had ever heard. When she recited it to herself on spring mornings or in the stillness of an autumn evening, she felt a stab of pain. Unlike Joseph Mary Plunkett, she was incapable of seeing Christ in everything. She could perhaps glimpse Him in the rose tree crucified to the gable end of her cottage or in the passiflora plant she kept by the range.

Every time I came for lessons that last spring she would hold a flower in her trembling fingers and tell me over again how the stamens and anthers and the boss represented the nails, the hammer, and the crown of thorns used at Golgotha. She was satisfied when I nodded and acknowledged that the flower was truly extraordinary, just like the shroud of Turin you might say.

Though she never told anybody, the changes on the island drove her in on herself and rekindled the pains in her body. She no longer felt at home on a Uggala that had become a playground for city people and where topless bathing was the order of the day. Unlike Concepta, who carried Danny's book in her handbag and read it when she felt down, Alice was disturbed by *Ruminations*. To her mind it showed a lack of humility.

Her old certainties had allowed her to live with her various afflictions, and the humble, prayerful world around her accepted and honored her pain. But now that pleasure and happiness were at a premium, she could see no more meaning in colitis, sinusitis, asthma, aneurysm, or sciatica. It was merely a question of what she would choose to die of.

The last time I visited her she was lying fully clothed on her bed and praying to an icon of the Sacred Heart on the wall opposite.

"I think He's looking very angrily at me at times," she said and screwed up her eyes. "I hope He's not going to send me to Hell."

"There's no hell," I said.

"Don't tell me that!" she pleaded. "Don't say that!"

"For sure there isn't. And there's no devil either."

She looked at me with pity. "Is that the kind of thing they teach you in Galway? Poor lost soul."

I shook my head.

"There's a hell only if you believe in one. There's no hell and no heaven, only different Otherwheres."

"Don't confuse me now!" she cried. "I'm five minutes from my grave and you're turning everything upside down on me."

"I thought you'd be glad to know."

She turned away in dismay. She preferred to stick with the familiar horror of damnation than to face the unfamiliar prospect of postmortem homelessness.

When she died I asked Thresheen where she had gone.

"She's up to her oxters in a lake of molten lead and there's a hairy devil driving a pitchfork up her arse. But don't worry: she'll get over it. Soon she'll be sunbathing in the nip in Summerland with the best of them."

The Daimon of Thresheen

❧ When Thresheen said, "with a pitchfork up her arse" I began to suspect that the voice I was hearing was more mine than hers. She could be sarcastic but never coarse, and as

Danny pointed out, my language was getting cruder by the day.

It unsettled me to think that I was talking to myself rather than listening to the wisdom of my dead twin. Just when I needed her most she was abandoning me. For months on end I would have no sign of her presence in the daylight world, though she sometimes showed up, pensive and disquieting, in my dreams.

Soon after Ethna's reconciliation with her mother, Thresheen appeared to me vividly, wearing a white satin dress and a tulle veil.

"You've forgotten about me," I said, truculent with adolescent grievance.

"I haven't. I'm always around you."

"I called you many times and you never answered."

"You don't hear me anymore."

She pulled her veil across her face and peeked at me. With her pale face and big sad eyes, she looked just like Ethna in the black-and-white First Communion photograph.

"It's not me that's leaving you, it's you who are closing the doors on me, silly boy."

I felt a surge of anger.

"OK," I said. "I don't need you hanging around me. You're not real anyhow."

"There you are." She smiled sadly. "You are leaving me!"

When I woke up next morning I felt a festering soul ache, as if part of me had shelved away into nothingness.

The Daimon of Tom O'Reilly

❧ Like many men on the island, Tom didn't really know the contents of his own house. He knew the big things, of course, like the beds, the table, the chairs, the dresser, and so on. But ask him what pictures hung on the landing or what lay in the drawers of the spare bedroom and he wouldn't have a clue. Had he known, his own destiny and Uggala's would have taken a different course. As Thresheen said, our lot depends on small things.

After Alice's death he felt like leaving everything exactly as it was on the principle that it would last out his lifetime. At the same time he felt promptings — as if Alice were nagging him from the other side — to go through the house, throw out all the rubbish, and start over again.

He began with her room. He spent days sitting on the bed lingering over shoe boxes of old photographs, letters, and yellowed press cuttings. He was surprised to find how much stuff she had accumulated on the links between Marxism and Christianity. It was as if she was trying to arrive at her own homemade version of liberation theology. There was a photo of her with ponytail flying while she danced the twist in the Parish Hall. All the men in the background were now dead like her. Then there were the pictures of baby-faced priests in hayfields on their summer visits to the island. Once he had wanted to strangle them, but now he couldn't care less. They too had fallen from their perch.

If he felt a spirit of companionship and indulgent reproach in Alice's room, he was uneasy the minute he entered Rory's. From very early on something in him had hardened against his son: they belonged to different tribes. Tom had loved and respected his own father and expected no less from his son. But Rory was heedless, as if the very idea of having a father was repugnant to him. Tom felt cut off from the boy's life. To keep the peace between them, Alice had gone so far as to have two dinners in the evenings, one with her son and the other with her husband. After Rory's death, Tom felt less the grief of loss and more the grief of never having been able to know who Rory, the cuckoo in their nest, really was.

Now that he entered the room, it was as if a cold hand was pushed in his face. Alice had left everything just as it was, the

Elvis poster on the wall, the diving diplomas, the red plastic gramophone in the corner. If ever Tom felt like blessing himself before beginning a task it was now.

First he opened the wardrobe and packed Rory's clothes into a black plastic bag for the Vincent de Paul. The top drawer of the bedside chest was jammed shut, and he had to prize it open with a screwdriver. A diver's logbook and some old issues of the *National Geographic* tumbled out. Stuck in the back was a bronze figure covered in verdigris.

Where had he seen it before? He turned the bug-eyed angel over in his hand in puzzlement. How had it got there? Had Alice known about it? He flicked through the logbook. The last couple of entries referred, casually, to dives off beaches on the east side of the island. Then there was a dramatic capitalized D + RR @ 25.

D was for diving. 25 was at twenty-five feet. How comprehensively the boy had disobeyed him! And + RR meant . . . ? It could only mean with Rob Roberts. Tom felt faint. He knew now where he had seen the bronze angel before. It was in the Heritage Centre. There was a portable altar thing on exhibition with a crucifix and an angel on one side. This was the companion angel.

D + RR @ 25! So that was what Alice had been going on about when she asked him repeatedly in the days after Rory's body was found what this formula meant. At the time it had seemed one of her obsessive tics, and he had no context to make it intelligible. Now the meaning flared up at him like a strip of magnesium in a jar of oxygen.

Alice must have locked the angel away because she thought Rory had stolen it from somewhere. But she couldn't have known — none of them had known — that the boy was diving with Rob Roberts.

The angel linked Rory with the wreck. He must have been diving with Rob when he was drowned. Why hadn't Rob come forward? Why did he disappear that summer? And why

did he send them so much money out of the blue? At the
time it had seemed an endearing foible, a rich man trying to
buy his way into the island community.

Tom sat in the old deck chair in which Rory had listened
for hours to Elvis. There was only one answer to all these
questions: Rob Roberts had somehow been involved with
Rory's death. A lot of things made sense now: the man's exaggerated interest in Alice's and his well-being, Tom's own unease at Rob's so-called charisma, Danny's warnings. Though
Tom didn't believe in such things, the chubby green angel
seemed like a messenger from Alice.

He laughed grimly. Heritage! Some heritage this. How could
he have been so wrong about everything? There was a malicious irony in the situation. It wasn't the proverbial ghost of
the father or forefather that demanded vengeance. It was the
stricken voice of the unloved son. And you'll have it too, said
Tom aloud.

The Daimon of Ethna

↶ Ethna sat on the plane from London to Dublin and
composed a list of her New Year's resolutions. The first five
points ran

1. Be kind to Danny.
2. Be a better mother to Finn.
3. Be a better daughter to Concepta.
4. Accept Uggala as your home.
5. Don't let the prize for Clydagh go to your head.

She paused. For a moment she felt that the empty seat beside her was occupied by somebody, a roguish presence that
chortled at the Better Self she plotted.

"Good girlshia," said Thresheen. "Well done."

Ethna stared at the transparency that was her daughter and chewed her poppy seed in a Protestant concentration. Then she looked at the patches of sky, specks of sky, gusts and heaps of sky in the window and a tide of sunlight between them.

6.   Stop thinking you are a sum of your misfortunes.

This was difficult. Even the award for the Clydagh village — an earth-sheltered housing estate which she'd modeled on slumbering dragons biting into a slope — did little to quench the burning coal of doubt in her.

How different they were, she and Danny. He was sky-born and royal, his mind big with golden apples, his future hung with trophies. She was full of sickness that even death wouldn't cure. He was the treasure, she was the trap. For him everything was his forever, including a drop of water falling on his head from the Ganges or the Nile. For her life was a dream interpreted by death. She searched for despair as poets search for rhyme, the sick search for health, as prisoners their freedom and children their Friday. His soul was mixed with his body like water with wine. Her soul was a dark toxic sea. He was the guy who, when thrown into her sea, would come up with a golden fish in his mouth.

Many a times she felt a compulsion to ask him: How are we to live and so on and so on since we can't avoid the void? Once, in a phase of Fomorian contempt for herself, she wanted to be Danny. She wanted to go to him and ask after Rumi: You the only one tell me who I am. Tell me that I am You. She wanted to follow him like a thread follows a needle. Now she knew that everyone is sentenced to oneself like a flea to a dog's tail. One could try to polish the hard edges which hurt the others, but one could never remove the spiky glass within.

7.   Be more compassionate.

He he he, chuckled Thresheen. The next point will be about *love*.

Ethna crossed out point 7.

7.   Stop being cold as . . .

A swan's foot, if you ask me, said Thresheen. A bit of poetry wouldn't harm here.

Cold as . . . ?

Sometimes when Danny embraced her she felt as if a rose was flung into her soul and filled it with warm hue and scent. Why couldn't she embrace like that?

Let's move to love.

Did she really love Danny as he loved her, and if she did what was it all about? Her love wasn't ideal, blind, tragic, friendly, matrimonial. It was not an effect, emotion, sentiment. It wasn't a habit or a word. What was it?

Love is an eternal unselfish radiation, just as the sunness is an eternal unselfish radiation of sun, said Danny once. Or was it Rumi? Love makes dead bread into soul, love makes soul which is perishable eternal.

Ethna made up her mind. When she stepped out of the plane into Danny's arms, she would have blue skies in her eyes and sunflowers in her smile. She would be brand-new, hopeful, pliant, absorbed unconditionally in breathing in the fresh scent of the Atlantic wind dripping from his locks. Ignoring a stain on his trousers or a button missing from his coat or the weight he'd put on since the last time.

When she walked down the hall to passport control, she spotted a folded page lying on the carpet. Normally she would have passed by in a hurry, but as the prize-winning architect on a New Path she looked for signs. She lifted the piece of paper and read the message:

TO ETHNA: KEEP YOUR MIND IN HELL AND DESPAIR NOT.

It couldn't be. Such things don't happen outside Lord of

the Rings or Harry Potter. She read it again. TO ETHNA. She looked around. Was it a coincidence? Somebody's bad joke? A higher intervention? Was she hallucinating? She read it once more, folded it slowly, put it in her pocket, and walked on, followed by the guffawing Thresheen. The Dublin airport said: WELCOME TO IRELAND THE LAND OF HEALTHY PROFIT.

Behind the exit called Nothing to Declare there was Dublin with its eternal drizzle and sunny spells, with its withering Christmas decorations and prim Georgian houses, with Danny bathing in *The Irish Times,* a bunch of ritual fifty roses exploding on his lap. Soon she would be pressing her face to his new flamboyant tie and breathing the scent of lemon aftershave mixed with roses and telling him her story breathless, bashful, bewildered. Keep your mind in hell and despair not. What could it mean?

"Show it to me," said Danny.

She reached into her pocket, but she found nothing.

"I could have sworn . . ."

"I believe you."

"You don't."

"You must have seen it in a book or a newspaper."

"It was written on a scrap of paper. It was addressed to me."

Danny looked at her with a superior amusement which she hated.

"Of course it doesn't sound very much like Rumi," she said caustically.

"No. It sounds like you."

"You mean I've imagined it?"

He stopped and lifted her like a small girl, in front of everybody.

"You look lovely in this new red jacket — whether your mind is in hell or in heaven. I've never seen you in red."

As they were walking to the taxi, she kept rummaging through her pockets. What else could disappoint her? The cancerous city, shampoos with methylparaben, the amount of bacteria at St. Stephen's Green, Danny's nonchalant "Why don't we go to La Stampa and get plastered?"

Let your mind stay in hell! Was she forever doomed to her afflictions, working blindly towards a throat contracted in bewildered unfulfillment?

"Oh, if only what you beg for would come true," sang Thresheen, squeezed between them in the black Ford. "You would give for it half of your life! And later it comes true. Followed by bitterness and pity. So don't beg, mortals! You will be heard."

The Daimon of Rory

⤞ After Alice died Tom would sit for hours on the bed, breathing and staring at the floor. Life had been just a sum of breaths. With each breath which passed a part of life was lost and he was getting closer to Alice, thanks be to God.

Now it was different. There was hardly a day he didn't think about the sea-eaten corpse of his son, Rory, and the various ways in which he would point this corpse at Rob Roberts so that the bastard would choke on it.

Tom was possessed by Rob Roberts just like he had once been possessed by the class struggle, the enemies of the proletariat, and the hyenas of capitalism. Rob Roberts had a hand in Rory's death. He should be punished full stop. The sooner the better. One more day and he'll become a minister or a senator, maybe even the president of Ireland. One more minute and he'll become a model of a democrat and humanist.

"Over my dead body," repeated Tom aloud. Rory would turn in his grave if this son of a bitch was allowed to get away with it.

In the meantime Rory was neither in his grave nor turning. He was hovering above the landscape transformed by a magic stopping of the sun and planning his next incarnation. Now, when he saw the lining of the world, the other side beyond the bird, mountain, and the moonset, he could at last create himself anew in the bubbling energy of Otherwheres. This time round he'd like to come as a girl, her eyes violet, her hair blond touched with russet, with fair-haired young men, as handsome as she, in her retinue.

For a few months, which felt like eternity, Tom talked to Rory in his head, asked for advice, argued with him about the best way of doing it. A shot in the occiput, kneecapping, strangulation, knifing, or hanging seemed crude and unimaginative. It had to be something spectacular.

When the plan finally emerged from the very mud and mire of his veins, Tom felt the triumphant joy of an exterminating angel. He waited until he was sure that the last stragglers from the pubs were safely at home in their beds. About two o'clock he put on an old donkey jacket and a pair of galoshes over his shoes. Alice's woolen gloves stretched to bursting when he pulled them on.

This time round Rory would make his return somewhere in the Adriatic. He would leave the cloudy provinces behind. No. The Adriatic meant the shame of whispering to the confessional grille, behind which heavy breath and a hot ear. Better Australia or New Zealand.

Tom walked briskly to the Heritage Centre, his path crossed only by a lumbering badger. There was a light in the glass dome. Rob must be in residence in his penthouse. Good.

He let himself in through the back door with his own key. He collected a bundle of planks from a half-finished counter and tiptoed down the hall. The floors were being redone, and there were tins of varnish and thinner stocked along the wall. Rob Roberts had ordered twice what was necessary for the job. There was no honor among thieves. Tom opened three tins of varnish and arranged the planks around them. There were rags left by the painters, and they lit quickly. He tossed them into the open tins and hurried out, pulling the door after him.

Rory was swimming in the oceans of seething energy and pure radiance, where Mozart composed music which had been ready before he himself had been born in Salzburg.

Tom took his time going home. He was thinking of one of his favorite moments from Irish history. A petty prince burned down the cathedral on the Rock of Cashel. When he was called before the High King to explain his actions, he defended himself by saying that the reason he burned the cathedral was he thought the Archbishop was inside.

Rory somersaulted in proto-space, in the seventh heaven, where everything was the opposite of the word *was* and *is*.

The Daimon of Danny Ruane

❧ Danny was haunted by a sense that, however hard he had to labor at "Creation," it was somehow, somewhere, already complete, footnotes and all. There were days when he could capture thirty pages without a hitch, accurate to the last colon and comma. At other times he seemed to lose the wavelength altogether, and for weeks, even months on end, he wrote with an appalled sense that he was getting it down wrong.

Good or bad, however, he never lost the certainty that work on "Creation" was his life's task, even if others thought it was pure, unadulterated lunacy. The book was like a river in his mind, with long, restful, finger-trailing stretches, abrupt turbulent weirs, and lazy meanders where it seemed to back up on itself. It flowed into the sea through deltas and winding channels priested over by mysterious white egrets. They were the silent vigilant Watchers to whom he was responsible.

The Daimon of Tom O'Reilly

The Admiral's Cabin was the biggest hit with the school-children. They wrote things like "Smashing!" and "Better than Bunratty" in the visitors' book. The cabin enchanted them with its low arched ceiling, fretwork ornament, and secret compartments. They were allowed to touch things. No doubt the quill in the screwed-down inkpot would disappear by the end of the day, but there were plenty of wild goose feathers to replace it.

"Let's have a look at the map," said Tom. "It's a gift from the Spanish Embassy. Here we have the route of the Armada from Santander. The big battle with Drake took place here in the Channel. Now after the Spaniards were defeated, they tried to make for home by sailing round Ireland. It wasn't the wisest thing to do if you ask me. The *San Juan* went down just off Uggala in only twenty-five feet of water. The sailors thought there'd be a welcome for them on the island. You'd have thought the same, wouldn't you? Instead, what happened? The poor fellows were slaughtered by the natives. There you are. That's how it was."

Tom absorbed the shocked look on the children's faces.

"Why did they do it you might ask. Well, that's the sixty-four-thousand-dollar question."

He spun the ocher globe on the Admiral's desk. "My guess is that the people here were greedy, ignorant, and afraid of strangers. Though of course they called themselves Christians."

The children followed him in baffled silence into the next room.

"This is what we call the Gun Deck. This part of the Centre was badly damaged in a fire a while back. But the architect incorporated some of the charred timbers into the building. It sort of gives you an idea of what it must have been like aboard ship after a battle."

The children took the blackened timbers in their stride, but adults always wanted to know more about the attempt to burn down the Centre. That had become a legend within a legend.

"There're any number of stories about it," said Tom. "Who knows? Maybe it was just the result of a careless accident. Maybe it was the opposition on the island. There are lots of people around who never wanted the Heritage Centre in the first place. Or maybe it was the revenge of the dead Spaniards." He smiled.

Of course there would always be a smart aleck in the crowd to suggest that it was done for compensation.

"Compo is out of the question as a motive," Tom assured them tartly. "The owner himself fought the blaze like a demon with fire extinguishers. Bits of the wall there collapsed and fell on him. He's now back in the States, crippled for life, poor fellow. It looks like the Spaniards had their revenge after all."

Every evening Tom went through the visitors' book to see how he was doing. One entry in a child's hand leapt out at him: "The people of Uggala are a bunch of savages."

On impulse he added, "Amen to that."

The next day he tore out the page.

The Daimon of Ethna

❧ "It's not me that's giving up Uggala, it's Uggala that's giving me up," Ethna said to Father Francis.

They stood side by side on the deck of *The Morning Star* contemplating Uggala with dispassionate eyes. The island was sharp and distinct as a child's crayon drawing. And like a child's drawing, it bristled with suppressed rage: fanged inlets, lopsided houses clinging to a dark malevolent hill, the orange sun detonating in a corner.

Eight years ago they had stood together on the same mangled deck. Ethna was writing suicide notes in her head. Now she glanced down at the seething caldron to catch a glimpse of her Ophelia body streaming past.

All that was detaching itself from her. She was a free woman again, this time on a journey to a place where things would make sense again and she'd be able to wake up every morning and say, "This is what I want. That's where I belong. These are the people I love. That's who I am."

The neck-breaking fulfillment of her most unattainable wish still frightened and excited her. It had taken Danny four fate-changing minutes to find a way out of their conundrum. One wet evening he sat at the kitchen table chewing a sour apple and glancing through the manuscript of his "Creation." Ethna and I were putting photos into a family album at the other end of the table. The telephone rang. Don't answer it, Finn, Danny said. Answer it, I thought (or was it Thresheen?) and get it over with.

"There is some foundation or other from Baal that wants to come to see you." I repeated the message.

"Right," said Danny and sighed. "We're going to London."
"What?"

"That's what I've just said. We are leaving Uggala. Are you happy in yourself at last?"

It was so simple that it was ridiculous. Ethna burst out laughing. We all laughed and laughed.

"Let's be serious," she said, still levitating from the reeling impossibility of what had just been said.

"I can't spend the rest of my life being a sage of Uggala," said Danny. "Nope. It'll destroy me. What do you think, Finn?"

I wanted to say that it wouldn't. But when I looked at the two of them now — and imagined several different futures where their love would ripen and ferment, I nodded.

So. Ethna no longer had to wrestle with the Balor spirit of Uggala until one of them lay defeated. She meant the monster no harm.

"Uggala isn't giving either of us up," said Father Francis ruefully. "It couldn't care less."

"Come on, Francis, you know they all fell in love with you," said Danny. As usual, he sat on the bench immersed in a book, completely immune to seasickness, homesickness, soul sickness of any kind.

"Well, at least they've changed you, haven't they?" said Ethna.

"Not every irritant in the oyster becomes a pearl," Father Francis replied.

Ethna was taken aback by how calm and composed he seemed after all the misfortunes that had befallen him over the past year. He was no longer a Renaissance courtier with cruelly innocent eyes. Joe Boske might have painted his handsome sunburnt face and jammed an iridescent mackerel in his left ear: Man of the West.

Man of the West on his way to Brazil.

"Do you have to go so far?" she asked.

"A missionary friend offered me a parish in São Paulo. He's too old to cope on his own. It seemed just right."

Ethna was surprised at the tightness in her throat. Francis the missionary was like one of Danny's corncrakes, the last of a dying species heading off into hostile territory.

"I hope you'll be happy in your new office in London," Father Francis said. "But you, Finn, won't you miss Uggala?"

"Yes," I said. It was no use pretending.

Father Francis nodded. "There's just one thing I can't imagine."

"I know," said Danny. "The de-Uggalized me."

"You've always said that there's no Creation' without Uggala."

"We still don't know if we're doing the right thing," said Ethna with wonderful certainty. "There is only one thing we're not sure about. That is, I am not sure."

"Oh," said Danny, "I think I know what it is."

"I don't think you do," said Ethna curtly.

"Well, let me guess. You know, Newton's most famous work was his *Principia Mathematica*. But he thought it was one of his least important works. He said something like "All my life I had been a child playing on a beach while the great ocean of truth lay undiscovered before me." And everybody quoted it thinking how modest he was about his discoveries. But that wasn't Newton's point. His point was that his *Principia* was like playing on the beach while his *Comments on the Bible* were the real thing."

"That's not what I meant," said Ethna, blushing.

Damn, she shouldn't have thought what she thought.

"Ethna suspects 'Creation' is my *Comments on the Bible*," Danny said, totally unperturbed.

"One way or the other, it's a new life for all of us now, whether we delude ourselves or not." Father Francis smiled.

The Daimon of Danny, Ethna, Father Francis, and The Morning Star

 ℘ Ethna marveled at Father Francis's smile. She wanted him to smile more — to make it all more Hollywood, glamorous and sweet and painful and tearful to the point of vomit — when *The Morning Star* shuddered to a halt.

"What's going on?" she called up to the Skipper.

"The engine's conked out."

"We have a plane to catch. How long do you reckon we'll be idling around?"

The Skipper's look said: Why don't you get yourself a fucking helicopter?

Two hours later we were still adrift. Ethna paced the deck, trying to talk herself out of impatience and a resurgence of her grievances against Uggala.

Danny lay stretched on the bench and looked up at the

fleecy clouds. "I like this time out of time. Everything's so quiet and pure!"

Except me, thought Ethna. It was only then that it dawned on her.

"Finn, what are you up to?"

"What?"

"Damn, I should have known it. This whole trip is just a sham. Neither you nor Danny have any intention of going anywhere!"

"Are you accusing us of stopping the engine?" Danny grinned.

"I'm not accusing anybody. But I wouldn't be surprised if it was one of Finn's tricks."

"Come on, Finn," said Danny. "Perform some of your magic or she'll throw us overboard."

"I haven't done anything!"

"As far as I know, it's enough that you're half in doubt about something and strange and wonderful things begin to happen."

"What's going on?" asked Father Francis, bewildered by our exchange.

"Ethna has just formulated her own theory about the individual and the nature of mass events," said Danny. "In a sense I'm pleased to see that she's become a bit of a follower of Rumi in this regard."

"Which means?"

"Well, facts are very handy but a weak brew of reality," Danny began in a mock pedagogical fashion, which infuriated Ethna even more. "Facts immediately consign certain kinds of experiences as real and others as not. The psyche, however, is not so limited, as we know. It exists as a realm in which all possibilities exist. Natural occurrences such as the stopping of the boat on the Atlantic may rise from the psyche of men just as giant mountain ranges emerge from the physical planet."

"Could you cut your bullshit and do something!" shouted Ethna. "We've got to be in London before six P.M."

We could all see she was utterly desperate.

"At your service, ma'am," said Danny, taking off his jacket and rolling up the sleeves of his immaculate white Armani shirt. "Let's see if we can counteract the psychic nature of events."

While he and the Skipper fiddled and faddled with the entrails of the engine, I stood at the stern and called my dead sister. Come on, Thresheen, if you're out there somewhere! But however hard I strained my psychic lineaments, I heard only a gurgling, powerless void around me. Could it be that I really wanted the boat to stop and now I couldn't undo it? Thresheen always insisted that one could undo almost everything. I strained again, but the gurgling only got more moronic.

The Daimon of Ethna

☙ "Why don't you join me for a cup of tea?" said Father Francis.

Of course he would have a jumbo flask of Barry's tea. Of course he would have bulging sandwiches and half a carrot cake wrapped in silver paper. Of course he would have napkins. Mrs. O'Halloran would have seen to everything.

He smiled disarmingly. "I always bring twice as much as I need."

"I'm sorry for being so preoccupied," said Ethna humbly.

"Come on, Finn, have a Clare sandwich. Sliced egg on smoked salmon with wild watercress. She experimented a lot."

So it wasn't Mrs. O'Halloran.

"I regret now I never got to know Clare properly," said Ethna.

She and Clare had circled one another warily for years. Despite the fact that they lived on the same small island, they had made no direct effort to meet, as if fearing one would expose some hidden defect in the other.

"It's hard to think she's gone. You've coped really well."

Ethna itched to go beyond the formulaic phrases, to probe behind Francis's serene mask. Typical of me, she thought. Fill my belly first and then turn vicious.

"You never know how much you can cope with till it happens," said Father Francis. "Maybe it's a question of finding the right story to hold things together."

"You mean God and the afterlife and such?" Ethna tried to keep the scorn out of her voice.

"No. Not at all. In a way I envy Clare. That moment, a second before she fell, she was completely happy. She had no time to imagine death."

"But it was such a terrible waste," protested Ethna.

"We don't know. Maybe all her plans would have misfired. Maybe if the cliff hadn't collapsed she would have grown to be bitter and disillusioned. She died in a kind of plenitude, at a moment when she thought that everything was possible. I imagine her entering the Otherworld like a rocket, in a blaze of joy and energy. Not limping in like the rest of us."

"But you miss her." Ethna was determined to drag some sign of grief from him.

"You know the song 'Donal Og'? Where the girl laments the exile of her beloved?

You have taken the east from me;
You have taken the west from me.
You have taken what is before me and what is behind me;
You have taken the moon and you have taken the sun from
    me;
And my fear is great that you have taken God from me.

"Now that's what I'm supposed to feel. But for me it's not true. That's just a literary convention. Clare's death gave me the east and the west, the moon and the sun. God even."

Maybe that's what fulfillment means, Ethna thought. Not

so much getting on or doing what you want. Something deeper. The ability to be reborn, to jump over the corpses of your dead selves again and again. Begin afresh and unencumbered at any age, anywhere.

"It looks like we need a new engine altogether," said Danny, emerging from the Skipper's cabin. He looked like an Oliver or a Hardy after one of their famous accidents: face covered with sweat, shirt in black oily tatters, tie turned into a smoking knot of licorice.

"Look at you," said Ethna.

"What?"

She didn't know what. She felt like crying. Not over the dream of London. Over her own stupidity. She approached Danny, put her arms around him, and kissed the stain in the corner of his mouth.

"Mind your dress," he said, delighted and bewildered.

"Sorry, Finn." She looked at me guiltily. "You can relax. We'll get wherever we're meant to get, OK?"

She scanned the horizon eastward to see if there was any sign of the boat that had been summoned from the mainland. Nothing. When she turned back she was astounded. Uggala was creeping closer and closer, baring its black teeth. Was this the highest blessing Providence had in store for her? Perhaps the one-eyed Balor wasn't finished with her yet?

The Daimon of Uggala

☙ Many moons ago, when I began to cut the navel cord with Otherwheres and ask about the origins of things, Thresheen told me the following story:

Once upon a time a magnificent spaceship crash-landed on a black boggy island. The interstellar voyagers were taken captive and enslaved by the natives. Over the centuries they forgot who they were and where they had come from. Now and then, however, a shape of beauty or the play of light and shadow over the bog jolted them awake, and they remembered their lost home. Or again a soulful glance or playful gesture plucked at their heartstrings and they recognized for a split second a trapped comrade. In that fleeting instant they caught the gleam of Otherwheres.

I sit in a conservatory designed for me by my homesick mother. From here I can watch the comedy of clouds and their mock assaults and brief forays over the island. If Danny had a Thinking Place, I have a Dreaming Place. The moist skies feed the rainbows and my reveries.

I look around me at the primal forms of rock and water. They seem permanent by contrast with the fragile lives I have tried to chronicle. But I have learned from my sister not to be deceived by the seeming durability of stone and sea. They will perish like the clouds while the Daimons of those who dipped, however briefly, into this wintry island go on forever.